DEADLY EYES
(Now with two alternative endings, the second being the original, much darker ending)

"Michael Meyer has done it again, weaving a fascinating tale of murder and intrigue in the tropical paradise of St. Croix that will keep you turning the page to the very end." - Nick Russell, bestselling author of *BIG LAKE*

"This is an excellent example of good writing that will keep you guessing until the very end....If you have never read Michael Meyer, do yourself a favor and pick up this book or all of his books; you won't be disappointed." – D. Everetti, author of *PUNISHING A GOOD DEED*

"The ride is fast and furious and the outcome will leave you blindsided....I recommend Deadly Eyes to all readers for its fast paced action coupled with the mesmerizing and intense suspense." – Marilou George, *THE KINDLE BOOK REVIEW*

"As a mystery suspense novel this book was out of the ball park EXCELLENT!!! oodles of suspense...a dash of horror and a mystery right up to the end! Mystery suspense just doesn't get any better than this!" – Beth Cutwright, a top Amazon reviewer

DEADLY EYES

By Michael Meyer

ALSO BY MICHAEL MEYER

Covert Dreams
The Survival of Marvin Baines
The Famous Union

Chapter 1

The Caribbean sun was hot, but the gentle trade winds and cold Heineken made everything just perfect. The little island of St. Croix truly was paradise in the flesh.

"I've got a proposition for you."

Cuff looked up at the man's paunch. "You're talking to the wrong guy."

"It's not what you're thinking."

Cuff let his silence do his talking for him.

"One hundred bucks in it for you, for six hours of your time."

"A hundred fifty, and twenty to listen to what's on your mind. The twenty upfront."

The man sat down. "You're pretty cocky, aren't you?"

"If you say so."

The man turned to the bartender. "Two more beers over here, Roger." He shifted his weight on the hard chair and then returned to Cuff. He frowned. "I can't quite get a finger on it. You're either rash or stupid. What is it?"

"Depends on who you talk to."

The beers arrived. Roger replaced wet coasters with dry ones, carrying away the two empty bottles.

"What I'm proposing is—"

"Twenty bucks to listen."

The man set his Heineken down, spilling a bit of beer on his fresh coaster. "You really are, aren't you?"

Cuff tossed out a grin. "I really *are*."

"Stupid, I mean. Here I am about to get a hundred bucks into your pocket—"

"A hundred fifty."

The man took a swig of Heineken and leaned back. "You know, you really are acting stupid. What if I decide to just get up and walk away? No hundred bucks, right?"

"Hundred fifty."

"Jesus…"

Cuff ignored him. He went back to work on his own Heineken.

"Look," the man said, "I'm willing to negotiate, but you've got to be reasonable about this. You haven't even heard me out yet."

"I'm not," said Cuff.

"What's that?"

"Willing to negotiate. A hundred fifty or no go."

"That's it?"

"You got it."

The man frowned. "I should have listened to my wife." He polished off three quarters of his beer. "Okay, a hundred fifty." He exhaled loudly. "Here's what I'd like you to do."

"Twenty to listen."

The man began shaking his head. "I can't believe this." Then he relaxed. "Okay. What the hell? It's a deal."

"The twenty upfront."

"What am I getting myself into?"

"You took the words right out of my mouth," said Cuff.

The man stood up and dug in his back pocket for his wallet. He removed a twenty and handed it over.

Cuff studied the bill for several seconds, then stuck it in his shorts. "I'm all ears."

"Well that's a welcome change." The man sat down, adjusting himself on the beach chair. "It's like this. Someone's after me. They've been casing my place. What I'd like is for you to stake my house out tonight. I'm certain it's going to be hit." The man was enjoying this. He seemed pleased with his choice of words. It showed in his eyes, in the way he waved his bottle of beer in the air when he talked.

"Why me?

"You gonna hear me out, or not?"

"Why me?" Cuff said again.

The man exhaled loudly. He was a big guy in a small pair of shorts. His belly protruded with enormous pride, and his cheeks were puffy from having lived the good life for too many years. He was probably quite a bit younger than he looked.

"I'll tell you why. Because I'm pretty hard pressed at the moment. I know they're coming. And besides, you project a formidable presence."

And Cuff knew the guy was right on that account. Cuff's angular jaw, coupled with his athletic body, did indeed project muscular strength. His five-eleven frame added to the effect.

The big man waved his beer around again. He was animated, like a big rubber ball rolling down a meandering slope. Though obviously completely out of shape, with a body of a god—but too bad it was Buddha, he always liked to remind people—his mind still seemed as clear as gin, though his cheeks bore the reddish color of the pimento that was stuffed in the olive in that gin. Then he stopped moving his limbs every which way and stood still, huffing and puffing a bit in order to catch his breath. He looked directly at Cuff. "But mostly because of what I heard about you from Rosie."

Cuff acted as if he hadn't heard. He signaled to Roger for another beer.

"Hey, I want you with a clear head tonight."

Cuff stared at his drinking partner, but said nothing, forcing the man to finally back down and focus his eyes elsewhere. Cuff signaled again for a beer and finally got Roger's attention.

After the Heineken arrived, Cuff swallowed a third of it very quickly. "What'd you hear?"

"From Rosie?"

"Naw, Frank Sinatra."

The man sighed, loudly. He leaned back. "Plenty."

"Such as?"

The man finished off his Heineken before answering. "She seems to think quite a lot about you." He looked past Cuff, at the surf. The water here was so clear, and it felt like a heated bathtub year round. "She told me about the episode in town, the guy whose nose you broke. Said you're plenty handy with your fists and not afraid to use them."

"Only when they're called for. The man was trying to grab the woman's purse. What could I do?" He took a long swig of Heineken. "What else did Rosie say?"

"She told me about why you left the States."

Cuff took two rapid slugs of beer. "Rosie sure can talk. She's got a mouth on her about the size of Texas, and just about as discreet."

The man chuckled. "She's really in love with you, you know. Said she wished you'd get something going for yourself, find some steady employment. Get yourself back on track."

Cuff watched two sailboats on their way back to town from Buck Island, the home of Buck Island Reef National Monument, six miles from shore, home of popular underwater coral formations of every size and color imaginable, which drew tourists like a magnet. Both full and half-day trips could be arranged by catamaran, a glass bottom boat, or an island sloop. Many of the trips included beach parties along with nearly free-flowing Cruzan rum punch and tasty barbeque. It had to be getting on in the afternoon since a few boats were already starting to make their back home to the town of Christiansted for the evening. "And just what makes you think something's going down tonight?"

"I don't *think* it, I *know* it. I've seen them snooping around the past few days, casing my place out. Everything points to tonight." He looked away from the question mark on Cuff's brow. "By the way they've been acting. I'm certain tonight's the night."

"Why not go to the police?"

"I've been there. Four times."

"And?"

"They say they can't do a thing until a crime's been committed."

"The American way."

"What's that?"

"You got dogs?"

"One. And he's good. But he's getting on. He's nine, and that's pretty old for a big dog."

Cuff finished off his Heineken. "Just exactly what is it you want me to do?"

"Protect my place—from midnight to six in the morning. Scare 'em off for good. Make 'em prey on someone else, far from Betsy's Jewel." Tourists to the island were always charmed by the historically descriptive names given to the old St. Croix estates. Names like Betsy's Jewel, Judith's Fancy, Humbug, Upper Love, Lower Love, Hard Labor, Anna's Hope, Profit, and Whim among so many others, provided newcomers a glimpse into the island's rich history. In fact, in the late 1700's, the age of opulence on St. Croix, the little island was the richest sugar island in the entire Caribbean.

The names of the old estates showed opulence, fortune, misfortune, hope, despair, hard work, love, and intrigue. The island's history could be read in the names of its old estates. Their names had always intrigued Cuff, a man of letters.

"Your home's in Betsy's Jewel?"

"That's right. With a gorgeous view. Just magnificent. But it's isolated. It'd take Public Safety a good fifteen to twenty minutes to get there in an emergency, and that's in the best of circumstances."

"A hundred fifty, you say, from midnight to six?"

"That's correct."

"I'll need half upfront."

The man stood again, pulled out his wallet, and handed over three twenty-dollar bills, a ten, and a five. Then he looked around apprehensively, found nobody else paying him any attention, and he gingerly pulled out a gleaming new handgun, which was so sparkly clean that Cuff could almost see his own reflection in the handle.

"No guns," said Cuff. "Guns only mean trouble."

"That's what I'm expecting. Trouble. Here give it a try." He handed the gun towards Cuff, who wouldn't budge.

"No guns," I said.

The man looked quite put out. "Do you know what this is?" he asked. "This here is a Kimber Pro Covert II, one of the best of the very best."

Cuff tried to stare him down, but the man's eyes held steady. "I said no—"

But the man cut him off before the word *guns* could emerge from Cuff's tight lips. "Just hold this thing. Feel its power. It'll come in handy, believe me."

Cuff sighed, shook his head, muttered what sounded like *oh shit, what the hell.* And he finally relented. He fingered the gun, which was so lightweight that it surprised him. And it had such beautiful lines. How could such a deadly weapon feel so good to the touch and look so good to the eye? It was a real dichotomy to Cuff's way of thinking.

He quickly handed the deadly piece of artwork back to the man standing there before him. "No guns," I said, "and I mean it." He was well aware that the expression on his face depicted the meaning he meant.

The man stared back, steady stare to steady stare, until a seagull flying low broke the trance. "Can I count on you?" the big man in the short shorts finally asked.

"I'll be there," Cuff said.

"Good. I'll meet you at the entrance of the Gentle Winds Condos, and you can follow me up the hill to my home. It's hard to find."

"It's a deal. Hey, Roger, I need another beer over here!" And as Cuff waited for Roger to bring the beer over, he looked out into the lovely Caribbean, completely unaware of the eyes on him, the eyes that had been intently watching him from the moment he had sat down.

These were not naked eyes, for the distance between these eyes and the beach bar at Cathy's Fancy was too great for the naked eye to discern who was who. No, these eyes had planned meticulously. The eyes were glued to a pair of terribly expensive and unbelievably powerful Swarovski Optik binoculars. The balcony on which they now worked, taking in the scene before them, was the perfect place to see but not be seen. The powerful binoculars saw to that.

The distance, the palm trees, and the rays of the sun all helped. The position had been hand picked, after careful consideration. Every angle had been considered, and, one by one, they had all been discarded for one reason or another until this very spot, the perfect place to observe while not being observed, had been selected.

Yes, the eyes had seen it all. The eyes had seen precisely what they had hoped to see. They were like a master puppeteer. They planned, controlled, and observed, but from a safe distance. They did not miss a trick.

The eyes. The deadly eyes of St. Croix.

Chapter 2

Cuff drove into Christiansted, considered by many to be the most charming town in the West Indies, let alone the Virgin Islands, and the little island of St. Croix. The Danish influence was pervasive, the small town's colorful and elegant buildings proof of the long-ago prosperity from the island's large sugar plantations, where the magnificent Greathouses, mansions rivaling those anywhere else in the world, had once been filled with the finest china, silver, and furnishings that money could buy back then in the opulent 1790's. The flamboyant planters had ruled the roost, their plantations wealthy beyond belief, but their wealth had been built upon the backs of slaves. Though weathered with age, the beauty of the historical architecture was still clearly evident.

The downtown area of Christiansted, which houses many of the island's well-known landmarks, has been designated a National Historic District, and walking its streets was like walking back through time, where the Dutch, the English, the French, the Knights of Malta, and finally the Danes had controlled the island, which the United States finally bought in 1917 in order to keep the Virgin Islands out of German hands at the outbreak of World War I.

Cuff drove the length of King Street, found no parking spot, turned into the wharf parking lot, found no spot, and cut back onto Company Street but had to drive the several blocks to the public market before he could find a space for his four-year-old rusty Honda Civic. Christiansted was no St. Thomas, the shopping mall of the Caribbean, yet parking was also becoming a major problem here. Too many people were discovering American Paradise, as the logo reads on the growing number of license plates from the too many cars congesting the historical streets of the small island.

He thought about walking over to the King's Alley Café to see Rosie, but it was Happy Hour and the open-air bar would be packed. Rosie wouldn't have a lot of time to sit with him. She'd be working hard for her pay for the next couple of hours, the hectic atmosphere of the hour only serving to bring about stress. To Cuff's way of thinking, it just didn't seem to fit in with the reasoning behind having decided to move to the Virgin Islands in the first place, a paradise where people learned how to relax, or they moseyed on off to somewhere else.

"Take it easy, man," Crucians say. "Don't worry. It will get done." And maybe it would get done, but only in its own good time, and that is if it does get done at all. Life here on the island was lived in the slow lane. "No rush, no hurry, man. Take your time." Work, work, work was for the mainland. Relaxing, and enjoying life was not optional down here; it was a necessity. That's just the way life was supposed to be lived here on the island. Running from one job to another was so mainlandish, definitely not the recipe for happiness down here on St. Croix. But it was *her* life.

A few tourists were still on the streets, not yet settled upon where to eat that evening's dinner. Cuff walked at a leisurely pace, the only way in which to move around throughout the West Indies. As he passed the Carib Cellars, a taxi man asked him if he needed a taxi. A block down, another asked the same. Cuff had the same reply to both. He pointed to the writing on the front of his black T-shirt: *I'm not a tourist. I live here.*

Cuff crossed the street at the Chase Bank and joined the men standing around the first of the two food trucks in the square, drinking Old Milwaukee out of a can. Cuff, however, ordered a Carlsberg Elephant beer while he waited, and he exchanged small talk with the three or four men who recognized him. Then he ordered a second Elephant to take along with the fish and fungi dinner, with all the condiments, or provisions, as Crucians say.

He sat on a bench at the edge of the park, directly in front of the Reef Queen, the blue and white glass-bottom boat that made two trips daily to Buck Island, the country's only underwater National Park. The entire wharf area, filled with beauty in all directions, is now a National Historic Site under the jurisdiction of the U.S. Park Service. Fort Christiansvaern, just to the right of the bench on which he sat, had been built by the Danes back in 1749. History was resplendent nearly everywhere one looked on the island, and nowhere more so than here at the wharf, colorful boats tied to their moorings much like those of the earliest years of St. Croix's colorful past.

The lights from Protestant Cay, a small gem of an island only a stone's toss beyond where the Reef Queen was moored for the night, flickered across the water, tossed about by the ever-present trade winds.

The hot and spicy food was delicious, the view of the harbor was extraordinary, and the weather was close to being world's most perfect. This *was* paradise, just as the books said, and yet he was nearly broke.

But at least he'd gotten out of Dubuque. And in one piece. Things could have been much worse. Maybe the horror of it all would turn out to be a blessing in disguise. He sure hoped so!

The fish and fungi all gone, he looked for a trash can, could find none, so he ended up carrying his dirty plastic plate and empty Elephant bottle back to his car, and then driving it clear back to the Pink Fancy Hotel, where he still had a room for five more nights, paid in advance with the money he'd picked up the previous week by clearing debris from around the ramp area of the Virgin Islands Seaplane Shuttle, the downtown airline: only 20 minutes to St. Thomas, 20 minutes to St. John, 20 minutes to Tortola, and 40 minutes to San Juan, Puerto Rico. The Pink Fancy didn't quite live up to its name, but at least it was affordable.

And it *was* in paradise, after all.

#

Suzy, the young school teacher from Denver, on holiday by herself, sat alone in the tiny bar in the courtyard of the Pink Fancy Hotel. She had gotten in two days earlier, and Cuff had been practically the first "native" she had met. He had been sipping on his third Glenlivet straight-out-of-the-bottle, no ice, when she had followed her taxi man up the concrete steps and into the courtyard. Standing there by the pool, her taxi man burdened down with luggage containing who knew what—how much did a person need to bring to a place like St. Croix, where the sun always shone?—she had been a pretty sight.

Twelve minutes after checking in, Suzy had sat down with Cuff, the only other customer in the bar at the time. She ordered a planter's punch for her free welcome-to-the-Pink-Fancy-Hotel drink.

"I feel like I don't fit in here," she had said, smiling coquettishly, "this being the *Virgin* Islands."

"I've heard *that* before," Cuff said. First-time tourists ate the phrase up.

"I'll just bet you have." With that she demonstrated, for the first time, the most incessant and grating giggle Cuff had ever had the misfortune to hear.

The constant and terribly loud giggle (cackle?) was the beginning of the end. Cuff wanted out. Like yesterday. He could take no more of it...of her.

And now there she was again, waiting. Cuff tried to get by her unnoticed, but no such luck.

"Hey, Cuff, it's me!" Giggle, cackle, giggle.

Cuff turned, half smiled, and waved.

"You gonna join me, or what?"

"Or what," Cuff said.

Suzy giggled. Loudly. "How about a drink? I'm buying." She giggled again. "This time."

"Can't. Got to catch some winks. I've got to go to work tonight."

Suzy cackled. "Then I'll join *you.*"

The bartender didn't hear or see a thing, but he was smiling as he kept his eyes on the glasses he was washing.

"Sorry, Suzy." Yes, that's exactly what she was: Sorry Suzy! "I've got to work tonight, like I said. Midnight shift. Got to get some shut eye."

"Midnight, shit."

"That's just what I was thinking." Cuff waved once more, turned and went into his room, shutting the door on Suzy's little world.

Chapter 3

The wharf was jumping. People crowded around the two food trucks, and loud music blared from several directions. Cuff parked in front of the old Bolero Building, which now housed the Cruzan Elegance Restaurant, which was closed for the night.

He stood before the window of Nini of Scandinavia. He looked at the colorful Marimekko dresses from Finland and wondered how Rosie would look in the red and black one displayed there in the larger window. Maybe one of these days he'd surprise her. Maybe. She'd love it.

But then he began to think about what such a thing might mean, what it might lead to. But *did* it have to lead to something? Couldn't a gift be just a gift? For friendship's sake? On a special occasion?

Cuff wasn't sure. Not anymore. Not after Dubuque.

He went around the corner, crossed Company Street, and found her right where he thought he would, on a bar stool at the Charte House Hotel, where the most delicious rum punch on St. Croix sold for only five bucks a glass.

"I'm late," he said to the back of her head, her long black hair leisurely lounging well below her shoulders.

Rosie twirled around to have a look. "You can say that again."

"I'm late." Cuff sat down beside her and gave her a squeeze. "One more for the lady, Doug, and a Beck's for me."

"That's no lady, that's Rosie," Doug blurted out, his white teeth beaming for all to see.

Rosie showed the length of her tongue to Doug and turned back to Cuff. "Where you been?"

"Sleeping."

"With who?"

"Whom."

"Sorry, smartass professor."

"Ex."

"Sorry, smartass *ex*-professor."

"Cunning, if I say so myself."

"Not this again," said Rosie.

"Yes," said Cuff, his grin as wide as the table where they sat. "As a recipient of an M.A. in linguistics, and clever to boot, I guess you could say that I am a cunning linguist. Wouldn't you say, Rosie?"

She faked gagging, playing it to the hilt.

The drinks finally arrived, bringing the curtain down. Doug placed the rum punch in front of Cuff and the Beck's in front of Rosie.

"Hey," she said, "*I'm* the lady. The rum's for me." She switched drinks, and this time she feigned a finger in Doug's direction.

Doug laughed. "Sorry about that."

Rosie feigned a pout, and Doug, always the joker, laughed. Sometimes he just couldn't help himself.

"How long you been here?" Cuff finally got the chance to ask her.

"Too long. Two drinks. You stood me up. Again."

"I stood you up lying down? Is that what you're saying? Doesn't even make any sense."

He knew what was coming, but Rosie was quick.

She punched him on the arm, took a gulp of her rum punch, and winced. "You got anything but rum in this drink, Doug?"

"Barely."

"I thought not." She made another face, then turned back to Cuff. "And just to think that I can remember back in the States when I used to wonder if they'd put any *alcohol* in the drinks. Hell, the mix here costs so much more than alcohol. Unreal, isn't it? A rum and Coke with just a splash of the latter in order to keep the price down. Don't you just love tax-free ports?" She took another swig. "This sure ain't the States."

"That it's not. It's sure a far cry from Dubuque."

"Don't make me puke."

Cuff laughed. "Nice rhyme, Rosie."

"I know. And hearing that from an ex makes it even better."

"Did you say ass?"

"Whatever." She shrugged and turned her attention back to her Cruzan rum.

"Speaking of asses," Cuff said, "what's this you been spreading around town about me?"

"I don't know what you mean."

"The man from Betsy's Jewel."

"What man?"

"The guy with the paunch."

"What guy you talking about?"

"The guy who gave me seventy-five bucks—no, ninety-five bucks—today."

"Why'd he give you ninety-five bucks?"

"Because you told him about me."

She set her drink on the bar and stared at him. "What in the hell are you talking about, anyway?"

"He hired me on your word."

"On my word? But I wasn't even there!"

"And the weird thing about it, Rosie, I don't even know his name. I forgot to ask him his name. How's that for stupid?"

She studied her rum punch. "But he gave you ninety-five bucks?"

"Yeah."

"What for?"

"He wants me to watch his place for him."

"House sit?"

"No way. He hired me to just watch his house for him tonight from midnight to six in the morning."

"For ninety-give bucks?"

"And seventy-five more."

She picked up her drink, but then set it back down. "You know, Cuff, you really run up against some strange people."

He grinned. "I know. Like you, Rosie. So who is he?"

"Who's who?"

"Who we been talking about?"

"I haven't the foggiest."

"There's no reason to be coy about it."

She nearly spilled her drink. "Coy? Me!"

"He said you'd told him about Dubuque."

There was a long silence. The world seemed to stop. Everything came to a complete standstill as if they were in the middle of a DVD movie when the stop button on the remote control was suddenly pushed. The silence that had come between them pierced the night. Not a moan could be heard, not even a rustling of tree branches and leaves in the Caribbean breeze, where the sweet fragrances of the tropics teased one's nose much like the most enticing perfume with the ubiquitous hibiscus, bougainvillea, oleander and aloes. "He was just some guy who came in to eat. That's all. I've never seen him before...or again."

"So why'd you happen to tell him about me, and about Dubuque?"

"I don't know. It just happened. We started talking. Things were slow at work. It was nothing. Really. Just small talk. I'm sorry, Cuff. I really am. It just came out. We were talking about how we ended up here on the island, and it just seemed fit in so naturally."

"Naturally." Cuff thought about it.

"It was just one of those things," Rosie said. "Please don't be mad. I didn't mean anything by it."

"I see," he finally got out. But he really didn't. After all, Dubuque had reared its ugly head once again. It never seemed to go away, to be forgotten. He took a deep breath to steady his nerves, to calm himself so that words he didn't want to verbalize would stay unsaid. He knew full well that Rosie hadn't meant anything by it, but, still, the idea that she just didn't know what to keep to herself ate at him at times, but she was so damned cute, her smile an irresistible force that could immediately make up for any verbal indiscretion that might suddenly pop out of her mouth.

Then Cuff did something that just didn't come naturally to him. He checked his watch. The only reason he was wearing it at the moment, here in paradise, where time practically stood still, was because he had to be somewhere at a certain time tonight. He stood up and stretched. "*Ciao*, Rosie. I've got to go to work. Earn my keep."

"You're serious, aren't you?"

"I'm serious."

"You're not shitting me, are you?"

"I'm not shitting you, Rosie. It's on the level. Like I said. I've got work to do. In Betsy's Jewel."

Rosie's expression found a home somewhere between awe and surprise. "Well, good luck, whatever it is."

"That's what scares me, Rosie—the whatever it is." And his chiseled face was not smiling as he said it.

Chapter 4

The guy had stood him up! Of all the—

But that wasn't it. No. If he'd been stood up, then why had the man forked over the upfront money? No, *stood up* wasn't it. Wrong choice of words.

So what was it?

Ten to one now, and still no sign of the man. What was going on? The guy had seemed so insistent about the time and the place.

The Gentle Winds tennis court was dark, quiet, as was everything to all sides of him. How people could even think about playing tennis in all this humidity beat the hell out of Cuff. The car was getting cramped. How much longer should he wait?

Wait for what? The man wasn't coming. That was clear.

But what if? What if the man had been delayed somehow? The ninety-five bucks upfront demanded a longer wait.

Chirping in the distance. Crickets. And more crickets. The road deserted. Cuff alone.

He checked his watch, but couldn't see clearly, so he turned on the inside light. Thirteen minutes after one.

This was getting silly, waiting for a man who didn't come. And gradually it dawned on him. What if something had gone down?

Gone down? What was he doing, trying to sound like some kind of paperback detective? He was no such thing. He wasn't any private eye. What he was was a prof, and an ex at that.

But memories of Dubuque were the last thing he needed at the moment. He shoved them aside and glanced again at his watch, once again having to switch on the inside light.

One twenty-three.

Enough was enough. The man had said eleven-thirty. What had gone wrong?

Wrong? The word sounded so ominous.

Cuff had made a deal, and he had stuck to it. But the man hadn't shown. So what was next?

The ninety-five bucks provided the answer. It was a large sum of money in Cuff's book. He sighed, breathing deeply. Cuff would try to give the man real value for his money. How could he do otherwise? He'd given his word. And a man's word still meant something.

It did to Cuff.

\#

The North Shore Road here was right above the water, and it was as curvy as a snake slithering through tall grass. Cuff slowed to take the curves, constantly reminding himself to stay on the left side of the road, a carry-over from the days of the Danes. Even though he'd been on St. Croix for over half a year now, a little reminding didn't hurt. Better safe than sorry. After all, that's why he had had ventured off to the Caribbean in the first place, to feel safe from the sorry he was so valiantly attempting to leave behind in another world, back in Dubuque.

The lights of St. Thomas sparkled in the distance, forty miles away. If he squinted, Cuff could even make out cars along the St. Thomas shore. It was that close at night.

Cuff stopped, pulled to the side of the road, and took another look at his map. St. Croix was only 84 square miles of land, 23 miles long and 6 miles wide—from furthest extremity to furthest extremity. Though it was small, it felt big. There was a large flat area in the center of the island and numerous hills throughout, the highest point being Mount Eagle, an 1165-foot climb from the sea.

It was easy to get lost on St. Croix, at least for a short time. Eventually the road would lead to a view of the sea, and the newcomer would get his bearings by recognizing a familiar landmark. There wasn't really too far to go in any one direction, but most of the roads were windy, and unmarked, often not paved, especially in the more out-of-the-way places.

Cuff was sure that this was Canan Road. If he were right, then it would lead him in the general direction of Betsy's Jewel. The ninety-five bucks kept him going. There was no other way he would have fumbled around in the dark like this, looking for who knew what.

So he turned and followed the road.

Though a pin prick on the map of St. Croix, which, in turn, was but a pin prick on the map of the world, Betsy's Jewel was a considerably more expansive area than would meet the eye of the uninitiated. In the old Danish estate for the first time, Cuff had no idea where the home of the man in question was located.

But he kept on looking. For something. Anything. A clue, perhaps.

A clue? There he was, playing TV detective again.

But a few more bumps, and Cuff was ready to call it quits. At least for the night. He'd spent the greater part of his savings on the four-year-old car he was driving, and, though young, it was already showing severe signs of age. The constant salt air flowing in the trade winds on the island spelled pure havoc on cars. Rust was everywhere, fighting from both the inside out and outside in, no metal a match for the salt particles carried by mist and wind that served as a constant reminder that manmade materials were no match for Mother Nature. Fighting rust was a losing battle.

But the fight went on. All across St. Croix.

The roads in Betsy's Jewel were steep, and the rains had bored huge ruts in the dirt. His poor Honda Civic was holding its own, but, in the dark, it was taking a terrible beating.

Cuff pulled to a stop. This was it. He began the delicate turn back down the narrow road—back towards a good night's sleep in the Pink Fancy, where he'd be able to get by Suzy sight unseen this time of night…morning.

The shot missed the top of his car by inches. It had to be only inches, because the sound was so close.

Cuff wrestled with the steering wheel and dug his foot into the accelerator. Where the shot had been fired from, and who had fired it, he had no idea.

But whoever had fired the gun, the bullet had been meant for *him*. And Cuff did not like the feeling. Not one bit.

Chapter 5

It was not Halloween. The man standing in the headlights of Cuff's four-year-old rusty Honda Civic was wearing a black witchdoctor mask. And holding a gun. Pointed right at Cuff's windshield.

Cuff didn't have time to react. He floored the accelerator and raced the Honda towards the man in the road.

What happened next came as a blur, and lived that way in the future. Cuff was down the hill, around the bend and nearly back to North Shore Road before he realized what had occurred.

He slowed down, but kept going. He wasn't about to stop until he'd gotten back to the safety of the Pink Fancy Hotel. Having a gun fired at him was a first for Cuff, and he hoped a last. His adrenalin flowed like rum in a Cruzan bar.

But what *had* happened? A shot. A man with a gun. A race against time. For life.

But why? Robbery? For kicks?

Cuff had no idea. Had he merely been in the wrong place at the wrong time?

Or did the man and the gun and the mask have something to do with the seventy-five bucks upfront, seventy-five more to be paid later, twenty bucks to listen?

But why?

Who was the masked man? And how had he missed Cuff? At such a short range, Cuff had been a sitting duck. There was no way the shooter should have missed. But he *had* missed, thank God.

Cuff blinked his eyes quickly, shook his head, and tried to bring himself out of his bad dream.

But it wasn't a dream, and he wasn't watching a movie on television. It was real, just like the shot was that had been fired. At *him*.

Somebody had actually shot at him!

Cuff prided himself on being a sensitive individual, a caring person, a good man.

But now he was angry, fighting angry, like a Marine charging against the enemy, the American flag proudly right at his side, and he vowed to fight on to the bitter end, to unmask who was who and what was what, no matter what, no matter if, because somebody had fired a shot at him, an unforgivable thing in Cuff's book.

Nothing or no one would get in his way. Not now. Not this time. Not after the shot, a life altering event in his life. This was now a matter to be settled, a life and death one at that, and Cuff was determined like no other time in his life, and that included Dubuque.

The very last straw had been reached.

Chapter 6

"Cuff, is that you?"

"No, it's Peter Fonda." He sat down on the edge of her bed. She turned on the lamp and sat up. He had wanted to go back to his room at the Pink Fancy, but instead he'd come to Rosie's small Scotia apartment. "Who'd you expect, anyway?"

"You. But not at this hour of the morning. What time is it?"

"How many keys you give out, anyway?"

"Now that isn't fair."

"All's fair in love and war."

"War?"

"Yeah, war. Somebody tried to kill me."

"What!"

"At least he shot at me."

"Shot at you!"

"What are you doing, Rosie, taking dictation?"

"Who shot at you?"

"You got it."

"Got what?"

"The who. You got it right that time."

"My God, Cuff. Somebody tried to kill you and here you are being a professor again."

"I'm still an ex."

"Who gives a shit about who or whom?"

"I don't. Not anymore. But I'm trying to forget."

"What happened?"

"That's what's so funny. It's all a blur. A big fat blur. I've never had a gun pointed at me before. And the bastard *shot* at me."

"Why?"

"Because I was there, I guess."

"Where?"

"On my way up the hill to Betsy's Jewel. The guy who paid me to watch his place for him didn't show. I waited for almost an hour and a half, just like he said. At the Gentle Winds Condos. But he didn't show."

"So what were you doing up in Betsy's Jewel?"

"Looking for his house. He *did* pay me a lot upfront."

"Do you know just how big the Betsy's Jewel estate is?"

"How big?"

"How should I know?" She looked away, then back at him. "You really thought you could find his house up there in the dark?"

"I don't even know if I *got* to Betsy's Jewel."

"You could have gotten killed."

"If his aim had been better. How he missed, I'll never know. I was a sitting duck."

"So what are you gonna do about it?"

"Now that, Rosie, is the question." He spotted a small black bug slowly making its way across the floor. He stood up, grabbed two sections of the morning's newspaper and followed the bug, which tried to scurry away. But Cuff was having none of that. He patiently placed one section of newspaper in front of the small bug and pushed with the second section of paper, the sports page. When the little bug was settled in the middle of the section of paper in his right hand, Cuff walked to the front door, opened it, and gently slid the bug to the ground, where it promptly hurried to hide in the nearby oleander plant.

"Good luck, little buddy. Have a good life." Cuff shut the door and sat down again.

Rosie had been watching him in total fascination. "What was that all about?" she asked.

"Reincarnation."

"Reincarnation?"

"Yeah. I don't believe in it."

"That right?"

"Yeah. That little guy has only one life to live, and I ain't God." Cuff liked using *ain't* now that his professorial days were behind him.

Rosie studied his face. "You're sweet, you know that?"

"I try to be." He looked off into the distance, in deep thought, his mind now entirely on the man in the black witchdoctor mask and the gun that had been fired at him. "But somebody's gonna be made to pay for taking a shot at me," he said. "You can take that to the bank."

And that was that, nice guy or not. No if's about it since Cuff was not one to sit still and take such a thing, sweet as he may be. No way, Rosie.

Not he. Not Cuff.

Chapter 7

"How big was he?"

"Big."

"How big?"

"Really big."

"You're not helping much, you know."

"He looked huge with the gun in his hand."

"Taller than you?"

"Yes…maybe…no."

"I'm trying to help, Cuff."

"I know you are, Rosie."

"So, was he taller than you?"

"Couldn't tell. He was standing and I was sitting."

Rosie watched a mongoose and her three young ones cross the road, as Cuff began slowing down for rounding the curve at Salt River, which wasn't a river at all. There were no rivers on St. Croix. How the designation of river had come about was anybody's guess. But it had stuck.

The bay was filled with boats of various shapes and sizes, but the mongoose and her offspring could care less. They were on a mission. They were off to see something; maybe the foraging was a bit better across the way. The mongoose, native to India, had been brought to the Caribbean on the 1870's to control the huge rat problem, the scourge of the enormously profitable cane fields. Ferrets, fire ants and marine toads had not been the answer, but the mighty mongoose, deceptively frail looking but with razor like teeth, and who can move almost faster than the human eye can blink, had finally done the trick. Today, St. Croix and its two sister Virgin Islands have the highest density of mighty mongoose population on the planet. Back when the first nine of these seemingly meek creatures were introduced to this part of the world, who could have guessed at how their population growth on the small islands would be so explosive? They were cute, quick, but deadly to their prey. And they were everywhere. It seemed that they especially liked to cross roads, maybe to get a better look at what was on the opposite side, usually several little ones in toe, in a line, much like quail in a completely different landscape. The fierce little creatures were cute like quail too, though they had not one physical resemblance to the bird.

"What's the plural of mongoose, Prof?"

"Ex," Cuff said. "Three mongoose?"

"Probably."

"Mongeese."

"No way."

"Mongooses?"

"Doubt it."

They drove along in silence. They passed the entrance to the expansive Gentle Winds Condos complex. The tennis court, as always, was empty. Who had the energy to bang a little ball around in this humidity? The bar, beside the water, was undoubtedly full.

"I've got it," Cuff said, ending the silence that had come between them.

"How tall?"

"Mongoose dem," he said.

"What?"

"I heard a little girl a couple of weeks ago. She was pointing towards a mongoose family that was dashing across the road, and that's what she said. 'Mongoose dem.'"

"That's one way around it, I guess. Them mongoose. A good plural." She faced his profile, his own eyes on the windy road ahead. "What'd he look like?"

"A little like me…a little like you."

"Was he black?"

"Yes, he was black. Or white…maybe brown."

"Which?"

"Another good question, Rosie. I couldn't see. It was dark. Besides, he was wearing a mask and he was dressed in black. Everything black. Not a hint of skin showing."

"You didn't see his hands?"

"I saw his gun."

\#

"Yeah, this is it."

"You sure?"

"More sure than not sure."

Cuff pulled up and silenced his rusty four-year-old Honda Civic's engine. They got out.

She went up ahead, bent low to the ground, eyes covering a large radius with each step she took.

"What are you looking for?"

"A lead," she said.

"Who do you think you are, Rosie, Honey West?"

"*Mae* West."

"Honey. Probably too sweet for you, I would imagine."

"Probably." She had no idea what he was talking about. She kept moving, slowly. "You certain this is where he was standing?"

"I'd bet twenty bucks on it."

"You probably would, wouldn't you?"

"Yes." He had no idea what she hoped to find. What was there to find? At least they'd returned to the scene of the crime. It was only noon, so they had the whole day in which to locate the house of the man who had paid him seventy-five bucks upfront, plus twenty to listen. In Cuff's book, that was top priority. Find the man. Talk to him. Find out what was what.

He'd deal with the guy with the gun when he found him. It was a small island, and Cuff's eyes were alert. He'd find the man with the gun. You could chalk that much up as fact.

\#

One fifty-three p.m.

Rosie leaned forward, her nose within inches of the windshield. The car was moving slowly. The going was rough. The dirt road was like a gigantic peach pit.

"Poor dog. How many I've seen since I've been here. Running loose, nowhere to go, crazy drivers everywhere you look."

"I think not, Rosie." Cuff stopped the car and got out. She joined him. "I think we're there."

"Why?"

"He's got a collar. This dog belonged to someone."

"So?"

"And he wasn't hit by a car."

Rosie looked closer. "You're right."

"Shot through the head."

Rosie glanced at the dog, but quickly tore her eyes away. "Jesus…"

"What an ugly mess." Cuff steadied his breathing.

"Who'd do such a thing!"

"A guy who'd shoot at another for no damned reason."

"You think—?"

"Yeah, I think. I'd bet the store that is the man's dog—the guy who asked me to watch his house for him. The man who didn't show when he said he would. I'd wager big money on it. Come on, Rosie, let's find the house."

#

It was huge, with commanding views to both sides of the island. They stood on the front patio, where they could see the turquoise water of Salt River Bay, almost right upon the spot where, back on November 14, 1493, Columbus had tried to come ashore, his men beaten back though by fierce Carib warriors, whose arrows most likely were poisoned by the native Manchineel apple, one of the many native apples found on the island, but the only variety that is poisonous.

Cuff knocked again. He watched a sailboat glide towards open water as he waited. The sails were full, filled with the trade winds for which the Caribbean is so well known. The boat was tilted, and the scene reminded Cuff of pictures he had seen of President Kennedy off Hyannis Port, a world away from the balmy little island of St. Croix.

And as Cuff stood there at the door, the lovely Caribbean trade winds beginning to kick in all around him, the delicious fragrance of sweet smelling jasmine filling the air, there was also something else, something so far removed from the almost picture-perfect scene of paradise that it was too horrible to even contemplate. But there it was, evil incarnate, a diabolical evil that was so intense, so grotesque, that smothered everything all about it. There it was, the powerful pair of Swarovski Optik binoculars ensuring that the eyes had a front row seat to all the action. The eyes had known that he would appear sooner or later, and they had staked out the perfect position so as not to miss anything, and then they had waited patiently, for a couple of hours, just biding their time until they would be put to work, and put to work they were. They were like super glue on Cuff, the zoom feature bringing forth every nook and cranny of his chiseled features, highlighting even the bits of hair in his nostrils.

The power of the binoculars was extraordinary, and the eyes gloated. The wait had been well worth every second, and every hour. Not a flicker in the vegetation, from either the soft breeze or a flittering butterfly or roving bird, could distract the concentration the eyes possessed. Nothing could be seen, heard, or felt except what came to life through the powerful binoculars.

The eyes were out there, and they were focused. They did not miss a beat.

The eyes. The deadly eyes of St. Croix, unnoticed, but the very center of the little world it had created, the world of life and death.

But neither Cuff nor Rosie, growing impatient now by having to wait so long for the door to be opened for them, had the slightest inkling of their existence, the terrible eyes, let alone of their bulldogged persistence. But the eyes were out there, and nothing or no one could dissuade them from carrying out their life's mission.

#

Rosie banged on the door again, for the umpteenth time. "Nobody home."

"Maybe."

"What's that supposed to mean?"

"I'm not sure." Cuff started around the house. "You coming?"

Rosie stood in her tracks. "Where are you going?"

Cuff stopped. "Maybe he's around back. So are you coming or going, Rosie?"

Her eyes never wavered from his. "Both," she finally said.

Cuff didn't get it at first.

"I'm going to come with you," Rosie explained, and her teeth shone as white as the clouds starting to form on the horizon.

Cuff had to admit that she was clever. It was a good one, *going* and *coming*, seemingly opposites, now as one. As a guy who prided himself on his way with words, he felt a touch of envy that he himself hadn't come up with it. She was good, really good. Rosie was a real looker, and she was smart as hell, quick of both body and wit. What a combination. Cuff was so impressed that he high-fived her, and then, once again, and they continued their search of the yard.

The man wasn't anywhere to be seen. The large wooden deck they now found themselves on stood high above the south shore, five miles away. The large Hess Oil refinery was easily visible, dark smoke billowing into the blue Caribbean sky. The ugliness of the black belching smoke, fouling the otherwise beautifully blue sky, filling it with its unhealthy stench, was like the poisonous side of the ubiquitous oleander plant, found all over the tropical island, bearing its pretty cluster of deep pink and white blossoms, such a wondrous sight to see, yet deadly to the touch. Such was life on St. Croix, an idyllic island of savage contrasts.

Cuff noticed it first. Four louvers had been broken from a...bedroom?...window.

"Do you think it means—?"

"I'm not sure what it means. But it doesn't look good."

"I don't like it, Cuff."

"You're not alone there, Rosie."

Cuff banged on the back door, hollering out, "Anybody home?" For close to half a minute. Then he tried the knob.

It turned.

#

"Hello! Anybody home?" Cuff followed his voice throughout the house. Rosie was right behind. "Hello! Anybody home?"

The living room was large, airy, surrounded by louvered sliding-glass doors, each leading to a deck overlooking the opposite shore of the island. The furniture, for the most part, was rattan, the perfect choice for tropical living. A few original paintings hung on the walls, and a large built-in bookcase was overstuffed with paperbacks and a few hardcover originals, including several volumes on New England. It was midday, the West Indian sun was shining brightly, but several lights in the house were turned on.

The hallway was long, with two doors to the right and three to the left. The first, on the left, was a bathroom. Like the rest of the house, it was tiled and spacious, big enough in itself to house a small family.

They moved onward, their sandals snapping gently against the tile. They looked into the next room.

Rosie screamed and screamed, her voice abruptly shattering the quietude of the bright Caribbean afternoon.

The man was lying on his bed, his neck hanging grotesquely to one side, his mouth wide open, his chest covered with dried blood, a large knife grotesquely stuck in his chest, his reading glasses only half on. His stiff fingers clutched a paperback. The book was entitled *The Only Investment Guide You'll Ever Need,* dried blood staring out at them from the cover.

Chapter 8

"Stop screaming, Rosie. It won't do any good."

A dog barked somewhere in the distance.

"Let's get out of here, Cuff."

"We will. Wait." He went into the room, trying to keep his mind from the body, which was impossible, and groped about for a clue. Anything. He was certain that the man who had shot at him had also killed the man lying here on the bed. It just seemed to make sense. But what was the motive? Was there a connection, or had Cuff merely been where he shouldn't have been, at a time when he should have been elsewhere?

Nothing in the room seemed to be disturbed, except for the dead body. Nothing looked out of place.

Could robbery be ruled out, then?

And the man had obviously been surprised. Why else would he have been lying on his bed reading a book? He wouldn't have if he had been alarmed by, say, a noise. Had the man put that much trust in his aging watchdog?

Lying *on* his bed, not in it. And wearing his clothes. It was obvious why he hadn't shown up at the Gentle Winds like he said he would. He had been killed before the appointed time.

But if that were true, then it meant that he had to have been murdered before midnight. And the man with the gun had still been around an hour and a half later. Alone.

What did it add up to? The murdered man had definitely said *them*. But the man with the gun had been a *him*. So what had happened to the others?

And why had one of them stayed around the murder scene so long? And why had that same someone fired at *him*? And how had the man missed shooting Cuff from such a short distance? And why had the dead man been killed with a knife instead of a gun?

None of it made any sense, especially so since nothing in the house pointed towards robbery. No things were strewn about. There was no mess of any kind. Everything in the home was so tidy, so peachy clean.

The only exception was the one very dead man with a knife handle sticking out from his chest. But why had the killer with a gun used a knife? There were so many ways to muffle the sound of a shot. It made no sense.

Cuff found the card near the telephone. Mean anything?

Cuff picked it up, and read: Samuel F. Berylson. Consultant. 809-777-1426.

Cuff stuffed the card in the front pocket of his guayabera shirt. "Let's get lost, Rosie."

And back in the distance, across the way, lush Caribbean foliage, bright and fragrant in beauty, their colors majestic to behold in the bright daylight, completely obscured the eyes that were watching through the powerful binoculars as Cuff and his girl scrambled from the house and back to the rusty Honda. The eyes liked what they saw. They marveled at the elaborate ingenuity they had so painstakingly put together. Yes, things were moving along just as planned. Everything was just right, like a perfectly tuned engine, churning its way to a final destination known only by the owner of the powerful Swarovski Optik binoculars.

The eyes. The deadly eyes of St. Croix.

#

They were back on the North Shore Road before Rosie said anything.

"We should call the police."

"We will. But anonymously."

"Why anonymously?"

"You know as well as I do, Rosie. If we become a part of this, officially, who knows where it will get us? With the bureaucracy the way it is here, it's like living in the Third World. And, somehow, we'll lose."

"But we've got to tell them."

"And we will. I'll call from a pay phone. I don't want anybody tracing me through my cell phone."

"Maybe you're right."

"I *am* right. Remember what happened when I applied for my V.I. driving license? After standing in line for half a morning just to pick up the application, and then after making a doctor's appointment for my physical exam, and then after waiting to have my blood typed, and then after going back to Public Safety and standing in one line once again for hours on end, I finally get the lady who does the actual typing up of my license. And what happens? My birth certificate says James Cuffy, and my Iowa driving license says Jim Cuffy. So what's she do? Says I have to pick up another form and have it notarized, saying that James Cuffy is Jim Cuffy. I tell her, over and over, that Jim is short for James. I show her all of the cards in my wallet. I plead with her. I do everything but tell her what I really think of her and her inefficient system.

"But no go. She won't bend. Probably can't. She must have weighed two hundred pounds. So off I go, back into town to find someone to notarize that I am who I am.

"But that's not the end of it. I pull out of the driveway at Public Safety, and guess what happens?"

"I know what happened. You told me."

"I get pulled over for not having a V.I. driving license. The damned guy gives me a twenty-eight dollar moving violation. Can you beat it?" He pulled to a stop at the junction of North Road. "At least they had gotten their man. For once. Probably proud as hell about it too. Can't stop real crime in Paradise, but they'll get you every time for the little thing."

"Yes," Rosie said, "you better make the call from a pay phone. Anonymously."

Chapter 9

Cuff dialed 915, the Virgin Islands emergency number. "Yes, I'd like to report a murder…. I *know* this is the policy emergency line. That's why I dialed it. A murder. As in a man dead. By another's gun." Cuff raised his eyebrows in Rosie's direction. Her face remained expressionless, but her eyes were on Cuff. "I said I'd like to report a murder. No, I won't give my name. I'm not involved. I'm only doing my public duty, like any red-blooded American should. I'm reporting a crime so that you guys can get on the case. I don't want a killer on the loose. Not another one. We've got enough as it is. Right?"

Then he listened, shaking his head back and forth and fidgeting from one foot to the other as he did so.

Cuff cut in. "Will you listen to me for a minute? I'm trying my best to—"

But it was no use.

Cuff slammed the receiver down.

"They're more interested in me than in a murder," he said.

"It's a good thing you didn't go in to the station in person or call on your cell phone."

"I told you so, didn't I, Rosie?"

They walked back to his rusty four-year-old Honda Civic. The sun was hot, as was Cuff, not a guy to trifle with, even under the best of circumstances, which these obviously were far from being. He kicked at a rusty can that had probably been lying there for who-knows-how-long, sending it into the near distance, where it would probably remain for who-knows-how-long, if not longer.

\#

This time he called the Christiansted sub station.

"Yes, I want to report a crime. That's right. Murder. Caucasian male, approximately sixty years of age. Knife to the abdomen. Happened around midnight…last night. Guy's lying dead in his bedroom, Plot 78, Betsy's Jewel. The house right up the hill from the victim's dog, dead also, shot in the head, lying two feet or so from the road."

Click.

"That's that, Rosie."

"What now?"

"Gotta find out who shot at me. It won't leave my mind."

"You gonna go it alone?"

"I hope not, Rosie. I really hope not." He turned to look back over his shoulder. "You with me?"

"You bet!" she said, but the expression in her eyes totally betrayed the ebullience and, especially, the lack of apprehension in her words.

Chapter 10

"You have any more roti left?" asked Cuff.

"Yes, Honey, I've got one chicken and one conch."

"We'll take 'em. With plenty of your hot sauce." Cuff fought to not drool as he waited for his first taste of the fiery Scotch Bonnet pepper sauce.

"Okay, Honey."

"The best on the island." And Cuff meant every word of it.

"Thank you, Dearie." The woman pulled two of the thick tortilla-like wrappings from the stack at the back of her cart, spread one out in front of her, and began filling it with the remainder of that day's homemade portion of conch. She had had a pretty good day. She was sold out now, and it was just after three.

Cuff and Rosie stood in the shade of one of the large trees bordering the south parking lot of the Sunny Isle Shopping Center, St. Croix's largest. The roti cart they stood beside served some of the best food on the island, at least to Cuff's taste buds it did. He was a regular customer, with rarely a week going by before being drawn back again, the spicy combination of meat, vegetables, and fiery hot pepper sauce pulling at him as if it were gravity itself.

Under the nearby trees young Rastas sold tropical fruits, mangoes, papaya, genip, soursop, mammee apple, and breadfruit. When they had no customers, they often danced in place, making their own music with their homemade instruments and homegrown voices. They were quite a sight to see, especially for the tourists from up north who were in the Caribbean for the very first time. Dreadlocks swung in time with the loud rhythm, long cotton blouses whirling in the air as the bodies whirled on the grass, and colorful cotton dresses, flowing in the ever-present breeze, perfectly matching the floral colors of the island's ubiquitous plant life. Their dance was almost a ritual, something coming from both the heart and soul, very spiritual in nature. Watching the young people dance made one think about one's own life, about what was really important, about how to make the best of what life has to offer.

Everything that was good was right there before the eyes. It was such a powerful thing to see, mesmerizing to the core.

"The conch's on the bottom, Honey." The woman's voice broke Cuff's concentration on the dancers, bringing his hungry mind back to what he was soon to eat, his taste buds now on full alert, his mouth beginning to water. The woman handed over the small paper sack, and Cuff paid her. "Have a nice day, Dearie."

"You too." Cuff returned her smile. He couldn't wait to get that first taste of conch. He knew he would swirl it around his mouth a bit, as he always did, taking in the complexity of delectable flavors before finally swallowing. The first bite was almost like a gift from heaven. It tasted *so* good. the scrumptious flavor was so powerfully addictive.

They walked across the parking lot to Peter's Cellars, the outrageously priced gourmet shop, where Rosie sat at one of the outdoor tables. Cuff went inside to purchase a bottle of Elephant beer and a small white wine for Rosie.

Rosie had the roti unwrapped when he joined her. She was wiping somebody else's crumbs off the edge of the table. She was beautiful. Cuff watched her wipe. She had long black hair, which whipped about her shoulders in the breeze, and her teeth were the whitest he had ever seen.

The first time he had laid eyes on her was shortly after his arrival on the island. He had entered the small bar near the downtown wharf to whoops of laughter. Three or four men were gathered around a table where she sat arm wrestling a big brute of a man, whose buddies were really razzing him since he could not put her arm down. He looked twice her size. The tattoo on his right bicep, a fierce looking man-eating shark, was stretched to the limit, the razor-sharp teeth eager to clamp onto its next meal, as the big man put everything he had into his struggle, but to no avail. It was clear that he was going down. It was just a matter of time. She had him, and he knew it, as did his buddies, whose loud mixture of laughter and teasing permeated every inch of the bar. All eyes were on the struggle.

And then it was over, amid even louder laughter from his buddies.

"Fork it over," she had said, and the guy had taken out his wallet and handed her a twenty-dollar bill, which she sniffed, kissed, and waved in the air for all to see, before she plunged it down her plunging neckline.

Soon after, the big man at the losing end of the bet and his good buddies whooped their way out of the bar, and Cuff, sitting all alone, had turned his attention back to his bottle of Beck's.

The nod on his shoulder had startled him. He looked up, and there she stood, Rosie, as lovely as can be.

"What about you?" she had said.

"What about me?"

"You game?"

"Game?"

"Twenty bucks," she said.

Cuff understood. "You challenging me to an arm wrestling match?"

"For twenty bucks," she said. "You good for it?"

"I'm good for it," Cuff had said, "but are you sure about this?"

That's when she showed him the brightness of her teeth for the very first time, white as ivory and just as pretty. "I'm as sure of this as anything I've ever been sure about," she said.

They both laughed. It was that kind of moment. And then they had arm wrestled. Both hands were held steady in place for so long that first Cuff's began trembling a bit, and then Rosie's followed suit. No matter how hard they tried, neither could move the other's arm from the starting position. Winning was out of the question, and each knew so.

Cuff had strained until he thought his arm would burst, but he could not budge her arm. Finally he said what needed to be said. "You up for calling this a draw?"

Rosie struggled a bit more, just to make sure. Then she flashed him her gorgeous smile once again. "I can live with that," she finally said.

That is the day that Cuff had met his match, and Rosie hers, he in his T-shirt and she in her tease shirt.

Her father, she had said, had been Puerto Rican, or was it her mother? And some black blood ran through her veins, or had she said Indian blood: Arawak, Carib, Taino? Her skin, soft, smooth, and radiant, was the color of caramel and mocha that had been blended together with a touch of whipped cream.

She stood just over five-three, and she weighed, after a particularly filling meal, a tad under one-seventeen. She had a smile that could send the world spinning, but she could swear like an angry fisherman. She appeared deceptively frail, but her small frame was lithe, very well toned, and it covered a great inner strength. Her breasts were not large, but her legs were long for her size, and quite muscular, especially her calves, which seemed to go crazy whenever she moved, bouncing up and down like billows on a player piano.

She looked up at him. She had such beautiful eyes, the very same eyes that had made the song *Brown-Eyed Girl* so popular. The million-dollar sensation was practically tailor made for her. Cuff could feel a shiver run the length of his spine as she smiled at him, in the way that only Rosie could, her nose, eyes, and mouth all playing a major role. She was absolutely way beyond drop-dead gorgeous, and her personality was the mirror image of her outward beauty.

"You're wonderful, you know that, Rosie?"

"I'll bet you say that to them all."

"You're on for twenty," Cuff said.

#

After lunch, they started their search. The Sunny Isle shopping center, their first stop, was a big disappointment. The only real department store on the island did not carry the exact mask Cuff was after. He tried Mini World and People's Drug Store, but neither place carried the same witchdoctor mask the man with the gun had been wearing.

"How about the Land of Oz?" But Rosie got no immediate response.

Cuff's eyes were on the heavily muscled security guard with the gun in his holster and the large Billy club in his hands who was patrolling the sidewalks of the shopping center. St. Croix might be paradise, but the emphasis had to be placed on American. It was *American* paradise, wonderful weather with all of the poverty and resulting crime of a large inner city area. The socio-economic conditions of the little tropical island were not too dissimilar to a poor neighborhood in a place like Detroit or Gary, Indiana, and, in some ways they were worse.

The day federal welfare checks were distributed was always hectic, people jostling to get a heads up in line at the bank, elbows and tempers flaring every which way, especially loose. People were entitled to their entitlements, and the day they were paid was the one day when relaxation and the slow, casual pace for which the island and the rest of the Caribbean was so world famous was thrown completely out the door for the rush to the bank was on.

St. Croix was a peaceful place, but sometimes that peace would be bent just a bit. Since everything needed to be shipped in to the small island, there was a scarcity of goods at times, resulting in some frayed tempers, although Virgin Islanders were well known for their gracious nature most of the time. The high costs of almost everything on the island, with the exception of alcohol and luxury items, both of which were high-taxed on the mainland, coupled with frequent power outages, brought about annoyance and irritation to some who came here to live or visit, but those people obviously did not belong on the island. Life in St. Croix was best suited for those of even temperament who looked to move slowly. A casual, easy way of living was what life on St. Croix was all about, where relaxation was the name of the game. Though the tropical island was a true paradise in many ways, tourists were still reminded not to venture into certain areas after dark. Stern but attractive, St. Croix was the queen of the Virgin Islands.

"You still here, Cuff?"

He put his arm around her shoulder. "I'm here."

"How about checking the Land of Oz?"

Cuff stopped. "You know, Rosie, you never cease to amaze me. You *are* a wizard."

"When I want to be." And she grasped the hand he offered her.

#

The Land of Oz was located in King's Alley, one of the most picturesque areas of the entire island. It lay right off the water and was shaded by overhanging trees and vines. Rosie waved at her friends in the café as they passed. She would be joining them for the dinner hour. The hours were lousy, but the tips were often good.

Tourists loved the place, and when they were happy they didn't mind spreading their vacation funds around. Within reason.

They went into the crowded Land of Oz. Toys everywhere, hanging from the walls and the ceiling. There were two other customers in the store, and they seemed to be together. Cuff, Rosie at his side, browsed…waiting.

The door jingled, and the two customers were outside.

"Hi, Rosie!" The owner was standing next to them.

"I'd like you to meet Cuff." She made the introductions, and the two men shook hands.

Cuff picked up the mask, one of three lying on the overstocked table. "How are these moving?"

The man shrugged.

"I'm interested." Cuff fingered the mask, studying it. "I'm in the business."

The man made no comment.

Cuff put the mask back down on top of the other two. "I'm a distributor."

The man looked at him for several seconds. "What's your game?"

"I'm not playing."

"What are you trying to find out?"

Cuff picked up the mask. "Like I said, I sell these things. I'm interested in knowing how they've been moving."

"Not only do you not sell them, you're not a very good actor, Mr. Cuffy."

"Cuff. Let's just say it's personal."

"To me it's business. What are you up to?"

"Well, it's like this. How many of these masks have you sold recently?"

"Why?"

"Personal. Like I said."

"That's privileged information, between me and my accountant."

"Anybody else on the island sell these?"

"I seriously doubt it."

"Good." Cuff set the mask down. "That's good." He looked about the store, then back at the man. "What's the big deal?"

"That's what I'd like to know."

"All I want to know is how many of these you've sold. Ten? A dozen? Seventy-three? It'd make my job a lot easier."

"And just want exactly is your job, Mr. Cuffy."

"Cuff. At the moment I'm unemployed."

The man laughed.

Cuff watched him laugh. "It's no laughing matter," he finally said.

The man turned to Rosie. "Who is this guy, anyway?"

"Jim Cuffy."

"Rosie…"

"He needs your help," she said.

"Please." Cuff looked at the floor.

"As I said, Mr. Cuffy, you're not a very good actor."

"How many?"

"Two."

"Only two?"

"That's right. And I'll be lucky to sell the other three. They're not the greatest masks on the market. They seem to be a bit too scary looking for most people."

Cuff was deep in thought. He turned back to the man. "You have any idea who bought them?"

"Why?"

"Because whoever bought one of 'em tried to kill me."

"What!"

"Shot at me. Twice. I'm lucky to be standing here now."

The man looked at Rosie.

"He's telling the truth."

"Impossible," the man said. "Tom Bennett would never do such a thing."

"The lawyer?"

"One and the same, Rosie."

Cuff was on full alert. "A lawyer by the name of Tom Bennett bought one of these masks?"

"He bought both of them."

"My God," said Rosie.

"When was this?"

"About a week ago, Mr. Cuffy."

"My God," Rosie said again, her gymnastic features flexed, all ready for action, her body one sexy but formidable muscle, her hardened eyes on the future—one that she hoped it would not be but feared it would be because she was well aware of what was what. Rosie was no dummy.

Besides, she knew Cuff.

And all the while, the eyes, those terrible eyes, far down the street, once again maintained the distance that made the naked eye unable to discern their position, let alone their very existence, the powerful Swarovski binoculars zeroed in on Cuff's face, biding time, waiting patiently, once again, observing closely, leaving nothing to chance. Everything was so meticulously planned, down to the smallest detail. It was truly a wondrous thing these eyes had so carefully constructed, the people like chess pieces, their movements completely controlled by the eyes focused now on the central chess piece, on Cuff, the king of the chessboard, the very piece that would, in time, be checkmated. Once and for all. For good. For all eternity. And these thoughts made the eyes twinkle with absolute delight.

The eyes. The deadly eyes of St. Croix.

Chapter 11

Bennett's office was on King Street, not far from the Bombay Club, where Cuff and Rosie had spent a couple of glorious nights in the courtyard listening to fantastic jazz under the stars.

Bennett's office was closed.

"Wouldn't you just know it," said Rosie.

"Nothing surprises me anymore. Not after having lived here in the Virgin Islands so long."

She goosed him.

"Excepting you, of course, Rosie."

She glanced at her watch. It's about time I start making tracks to work."

"That time already?'

"You got it."

"You're right, Rosie, but you don't see me going around flaunting it now, do you?"

She goosed him again.

#

He was sweating monsoon drops, but nothing unusual for St. Croix living. A cold shower would perk him up. When he felt better, he thought better. And he had a lot of heavy thinking to do.

Cuff walked back and got his car, and was lucky this time, finding a parking spot right in front of the Pink Fancy.

He was practically to his room when he heard the cackle.

"Where you been keeping yourself?"

He saw her in the water, her big blue eyes looking up at him, her breasts fighting their way out of her top, two sizes too small for her. One thing about Suzy, she wasn't subtle. She knew what she wanted while on vacation in the Virgin Islands, a world away from her Denver classroom.

"I've been getting myself shot at."

"That a fact now?" Her tongue played with her lips.

"Yeah. Nearly got killed."

She searched his face, then up and down his body. Then she was back to his face. "You're a real laugh." She cackled.

He waited patiently for her to get it over with. "Ain't that the truth?" Cuff said. He unlocked his door and went into his room.

#

He sat down wet, letting the fan dry him. He leaned over and retrieved his wallet and removed the card he'd found in the dead man's house in Betsy's Jewel. He tossed the wallet back to the small writing table, but missed. The wallet fell to the floor but didn't bounce. Cuff fingered the card, holding it out in front of him so he didn't drip on it.

Samuel F. Berylson. Consultant. 809-777-1426.

What was a consultant? Plain consultant? On what?

Why the imprecision? Was the card intentionally ambiguous? If so, then why? But the *if so* took top billing.

Cuff stood up and bent down to get his wallet, when it suddenly hit him.

He looked at the card again. There was no doubt about it. The card *did* say 777. But there was no triple seven in the Virgin Islands. All numbers began with 77, but the third seven was non-existent here.

He went to the phone, dialed. As per usual, it took him several moments of dialing to finally get the inner workings of VITElCO working for him. Using a phone down here required an inordinate amount of patience and persistence.

No luck. A somewhat sweet, but taped, voice informed him to please try again, that the number he had dialed was not a serviceable number.

Why the triple seven? It just didn't make any sense.

He checked the phone book. No Berylson listed. He called the operator. No Berylson listed.

#

Nearly dry, he started towards his closet for a fresh pair of shorts and a clean guayabera, the perfect cotton shirt for the islands.

The knock on the door startled him. Rosie?

"Just a minute!" He scooped up a towel, wrapped it around his waist and went to the door.

"Hello again." The bottom half of her bathing suit was even skimpier than the top, which seemed an impossibility.

"Suzy."

"In the flesh." She giggled. "You up…for a drink?" Her eyes spelled tease. The lingering pause complemented it perfectly.

"I'm not dressed."

"You got more on than I do."

He looked at her. She was right. Cuff wondered how he would have fared as a growing boy, having a teacher like Suzy. "I'm really sorry, Suzy, but—"

But she had gotten past him, somehow, and had plopped down on the edge of his bed. "What you got to drink?"

He turned to her, the door still open. "Not much."

She eyed him as only Suzy could. "I think differently." She had   I've-only-got-three-more-days-here-before-I-return-to-my-Denver-classroom written all over her face.

"Let's say I meet you in the bar…in about ten."

She waited, finally rose. She walked to the door. She closed it with a bang. But she was still inside his room.

"About that drink," she said.

"All I've got is rum."

"All I *want* is rum."

"Help yourself," he said, unsmiling. "I'll be just a minute."

"Where you going?"

"If you don't mind, I'd like to put on my pants."

"But I do mind." She laughed. Two octaves too loudly, cackling to her heart's content.

He was halfway between the closet and the bathroom, his shorts slung over his arm, when she got him.

One quick, unexpected jerk and the towel lay at his feet.

\#

Suzy scooped it up. "Come and get it," she said. Her breasts, like two large coconuts, danced before his eyes, more outside of her top than within. Her skin was flawless, and she looked sweet eighteen, as inviting as the beautiful Christiansted harbor at sunset.

Cuff wheeled around, his shorts held in front of him as a cover up. "I'll give you to three to be on the other side of that door." He pointed. His eyes exuded terrible anger. "And I'm already on two."

Suzy wasn't stupid. She froze, reading his face perfectly, then left, quickly, without a word.

Cuff closed and locked the door. He was shaking as he went to the rum. He took two large swigs right from the bottle. Cruzan dark. In Cuff's book, this was the world's best.

Then he fell onto the bed, too drained to do anything but just think. With his eyes on the ceiling, he thought of Dubuque, of all he had worked so hard to achieve, of lost places and faces, of what might have been. And finally on what had just transpired, which had been just like adding a ton of salt to his still open wound.

\#

Thirty-four minutes later, Cuff stepped outside. Suzy was nowhere to be seen. Maybe one of these days he'd explain. Maybe he'd tell her all about Dubuque. Then she'd understand. Maybe.

Later.

He decided to walk. The exercise would do him good, help him to rid his body of the tension that had overtaken it. It wasn't far to town, and, besides, the hot sun had gone off somewhere else for the night.

Loud Puerto Rican music blared from the bar across the street, loud calypso blared from the bar around the corner, and loud reggae blared from the house beside the bar.

Cuff began whistling "Don't Fence Me In," something he believed in very strongly. He reached the King's Alley Café on the third stanza.

He caught Rosie's eye as she navigated her way through the sea of hungry tourists, carrying two platters of seafood to the elderly couple at the far railing. Cuff sat at the bar, ordered a Heineken, and exchanged small talk with the bartender.

"What's up, Cuff?" Rosie carried a dirty plate and an empty glass in her hands.

"I was practically attacked," he said.

"Again!"

"This time by a beautiful woman in a skimpy bikini."

"But you fought her off, right?"

"I told her to get out of my room pronto, Rosie."

"And she was a horny sexpot." Her facial expression exuded a childish playfulness.

"Right again, Rosie."

"And she was after your body."

"Ditto."

"And you wanted nothing to do with it."

"You got it, Rosie."

"It must be contagious then." She laughed. "So where you been really?"

"In my room."

"Fighting off the sexy woman?"

"Yeah."

"I can believe it," she said. "Gotta get back to the tips…I mean to work." And she flashed her fantastic white teeth at him.

#

"You ever heard of Tom Bennett?"

The bartender kept wiping the glass. "The lawyer?"

"Yeah. You know him?"

"Who wants to know?"

"Bing Crosby." Cuff fingered his own glass. "You know him?"

"I've got his Christmas album."

"Funny," said Cuff.

"Why do you want to know?"

"No big deal."

The bartender finally set the glass down. "By sight. Never talked to him, though."

"He ever come in here?"

"Why?"

"For a drink. Maybe for a bite to eat."

"Funny." The bartender picked up a second glass and started wiping it dry. "Not that I know of. But a lot of Vuppies like to eat at the Tivoli."

"Vuppies?"

"Made it up myself," said the bartender. "For young, well healed residents here in the Virgin Islands. But lunch only. Dinner's too expensive here for most locals."

"Tell me about it," said Cuff, as he forked over his dollar tip.

\#

No one at the Tivoli knew Tom Bennett. The bartender was new, and the waitresses didn't have time to talk. Cuff decided to try the place for lunch tomorrow. The Tivoli had the best scallops on the island. Just thinking about them made his mouth water.

He went back to his refrigerator for dinner, buying two bottles of Beck's along the way with which to wash down his two-day old tuna surprise.

Suzy was seated at the bar talking with a local. She frowned when she saw Cuff enter the courtyard, but when she crossed her legs she showed him that she wasn't wearing any panties.

Cuff ignored her. For just as Suzy had flashed in his direction, it had hit him.

Inside his room, he went to work with the phone. He tried 776, 774, 773, and then, on the next try, Bingo!

"Samuel F. Berylson, consultant, wit service to you from me." The voice was obviously West Indian, the clipped words coming out almost like a song. "At the tone, please leave name and number and I will—"

Cuff hung up. Had he uncovered a lead?

Possibly.

But what kind of person hands out business cards with the phone number—the most important part—incorrect?

Cuff had no idea of what was what—but it was the what-was-to-be that kept his mind in focus. For he was a man with a mission—and he would complete it. Nobody took a shot at Cuff and then walked away without suffering the consequences.

Nobody!

Chapter 12

"Wife," Cuff said. They sat under a Casablanca fan near the bar.

Rosie tapped him on the elbow. "What's that you just said?" She was beaming. She felt goose bumps all over her lithe body.

Cuff looked at her. "Wife."

Her broad smile hadn't changed a bit. "Am I hearing what I think I'm hearing?"

"It slipped my mind. Somehow."

Rosie studied his face. His eyes were focused inward. "You gonna let me in on it or what?" Her face exuded the excitement of a little girl reaching for her birthday present, not able to stand the suspense of having to unwrap it. Her eyes twinkled.

Cuff, looking across the way, in thought, didn't notice. "The man had a wife," he said.

The warm evening air gasped, almost audibly. "The guy who was...who we...?" Rosie looked completely crestfallen, like a spirited Mustang that had finally been broken, everything, all of it, being swept away in an instant, the rebirth bringing about the death of the past. And then came a long silence, the calm before the terrible storm.

Cuff was looking at her now, trying to decipher the meaning of the convoluted message written all over her face, attempting to fathom why the sudden frosty chill had thundered out the humidity of the Caribbean warmth that he thought existed between them.

"Are you all right?" he asked her.

She looked away, watching a bird chase another bird through the sky, fighting to control herself, her emotions tearing away at her insides. Finally, she got up. "I'll be right back," she said, and Cuff watched her backside as she angled her way to the powder room.

When she returned everything seemed to be forgotten. "I'm sorry," she had said. "I guess I just misunderstood." But when Cuff had inquired about what she had misunderstood, she had merely replied, "It's nothing. It really doesn't matter," and Cuff had studied her face, pretty and cheerful as can be once again after her almost forever stop in the women's room, and then he had finally taken her at her word.

"So, what were you saying?" she finally asked, their drinks now half gone.

"The night I met the guy, he said that he had a wife," Cuff said.

"And?" She was waiting for more, but nothing came.

"Don't you see?"

"No."

"The man had a wife."

"So?"

"So where was she? Where is she now? Why didn't she call the police?"

"Three down, seventeen to go."

Cuff watched her watch him, but he didn't comprehend. "I don't get it."

"Twenty questions," Rosie said. "You're on a run."

"But where is she now?"

"You've already asked that one, Cuff. But it still counts as four."

"I really think I might be on to something, Rosie."

"And who knows? You might just be. *On* something," she said.

But Cuff didn't get the joke. Instead, all of his faculties were now back at the scene of the murder, where a guy who had hired him to do a job of protecting him lay dead, and where, nearby, somebody had shot at him. And that was something he could not shake from his brain.

The man's money, a down payment for a job he trusted Cuff to carry out, was in his wallet, which was just like shaking hands to seal a deal while looking each other straight in the eyes. Cuff, because of who and what he was, was certain of one very crucial point: he would not forget.

The sound of an empty beer bottle meeting its death by shattering into pieces somewhere behind the bar suddenly brought Cuff back to Rosie, his loveable Rosie, the cutest, sexiest woman he had ever met. His girl. And she had said that she was with him. She had made that abundantly clear.

"Oh, Rosie," he said, looking into her eyes, "you and I have some work to do." And, as she nodded in total agreement, he could see the puzzlement on her face, an extremely quizzical expression invading all of her beautiful features, love, hope, anguish, despair, and fear all intermingled, like young puppies seeking out the comfort of each other as they lay together in their soft bedding completely oblivious to the fact that a pair of powerful binoculars was focused on them at that very second.

The eyes. The deadly eyes of St. Croix.

Chapter 13

Cuff looked at the headline for the third time. *Police suspects mudder*. Not bad really, considering some of the things he'd read in the local paper. What'd they do, anyway? Hire rummies as proofreaders? The more zonked they got, the more work they were given? Cuff shook his head, settled back, and turned to the short article.

"Daniel Steadley, the internationally acclaimed financier, was discovered dead last night at his newly purchased vacation home in Betsy's Jewel. Police were tipped off by an anonymous caller. Mr. Steadley had planned to make the island a semi-retirement home. There were multiple knife wounds to the body, according to a police spokesman. An autopsy is pending.

"Mr. Steadley was the owner of Steadley Enterprises, a worldwide conglomerate. He is one of the hundred most wealthy and influential men in the world, according to *Forbes* magazine. Police say they have a good lead."

Cuff ordered a refill to his coffee. He sat at the large round table near the entrance to the King's Alley Café. He watched a tourist couple go into Southerland Tours, across the way. There wasn't much of a breeze as yet, but he was still in the shade. He felt good.

But then he went back to the article.

Daniel Steadley. Steadley Enterprises. My God! The name rang just about the biggest bell Cuff could imagine. He couldn't believe it! The guy he'd met at Cathy's Fancy was actually Steadley, a man whose wealth and fame made even rich Wall Street gurus and political giants with enormous clout kowtow to him in jealous envy. Wow! Daniel Steadley! Cuff just couldn't believe it.

Anonymous caller. He liked that. He felt like the invisible man. Heard but not seen. And in this case that was like gold in his pocket.

But why had such a wealthy man, a guy who could buy entire companies let alone people of all stripes and affiliations, come to him for help? It made no sense. Such a powerful man had powerful friends. Hell, hadn't he almost single handedly engineered Newt Gingrich into Congress back in the 80's? What was this small peanut protection he had hired Cuff to provide all about? The guy could have had the most sophisticated monitoring equipment in the universe, both inside and outside his home. Hell, he could have hired a platoon of bodyguards to ensure his safety. So what was going on, anyway? Why would such a man hire a guy like Cuff to do such an important job? It just made no sense at all.

And the police say they have a good lead. Not a lead, but a *good* lead. Was the *good* the police, or was that merely a journalistic whim?

Whim? Good lead was quite a bit different from lead. Good versus mere.

Cuff picked up his coffee cup, and suddenly it hit him. He spilled some of the coffee on his white guayabera shirt as he returned the cup to the table.

Again! No mention of a wife. How come? Where was she? The media was all over the murder of Daniel Steadely. So why hadn't there been any mention of his wife. Surely every reporter in his right mind would be angling to get her story. They would be all over her like bloodhounds. Isn't that the way it always worked? So why all the hush-hush in this case?

Was there a she?

There had to be, somewhere. What reason had the man to lie about such a thing? So where was she? How had she stayed out of the newspapers?

Cuff needed answers. Somebody had taken a shot at him. He would *get* answers. Someone had taken a shot at him.

\#

Cuff finished his last bite of scallops and emptied his glass of Beck's. The food at the Tivoli was as delicious as ever. In his book, the place afforded the best value on the island, but only at lunch. And the scallops were the tastiest on St. Croix.

He watched the V.I. Seaplane Shuttle race across the yacht-filled harbor in the near distance. The sound of calypso rose from somewhere on the street below. Cuff was content. For the moment. The meal had been superb.

The slight nudge on his arm brought him face to shoulder with his waitress. She was young, very thin, almost skinny, but her biceps were very developed. For a second Cuff imagined she was challenging him to an arm wrestling match.

"Frank wants you," is all she said.

"Frank?"

She nodded in the direction of the bar. Cuff's eyes followed and found Frank watching him.

"Thanks."

"You're welcome. Will that be all?"

"Yes." Cuff left a good tip. He went to the bar.

"He just came in," the bartender said. "He's at the far corner table, against the railing. To the left."

"Thanks," said Cuff. "I appreciate it."

"No problem." Frank began mixing rum punches for a tourist couple from New Jersey.

No problem, thought Cuff, as he started towards the railing. Ten easy bucks was never any problem.

He stepped up to the table. "You Tom Bennett?"

The man looked up from the menu. He was probably fifty. Well-dressed, distinguished features. The kind of man younger women are often attracted to.

"Could be."

"And then again couldn't? If need be?"

The man had a nice smile. Cuff had to give him credit for that.

"What can I do for you?"

"May I sit down?"

"I was just about to order lunch."

"Don't let me keep you from it."

Tom Bennett waved to the waitress. He ordered a burger with grilled mushrooms. Cuff sat down. The waitress departed.

"So, what's this all about? You need a lawyer?"

"I don't think so. It's about two masks you bought from the Land of Oz."

Tom Bennett's eyes were over the rail on the street below. He watched a group of tourists cross the intersection. "What's this all about?"

"Two masks you bought at the Land of Oz."

"Where'd you hear that?"

"Straight from the horse's mouth."

"And what's it got to do with you?"

"Plenty."

Bennett picked up the saltshaker, then just as quickly set it back down. "Who are you?"

"Jim Cuffy. Friends call me Cuff."

"And just who are you?"

"Cuff."

"Look, I'm—"

"Where are the masks, Mr. Bennett?"

"What are you talking about?"

"The Land of Oz."

"Is this some kind of—?"

"It's important."

"To who?"

"Whom," said Cuff. "It follows a preposition." He waited for Bennett's water to be placed before him. The thin girl's upper arms were thicker than his own. Her bicep became quite a large mound with her up and down movements to the table. How'd such muscles end up on such a thin body?

But then she was gone. Cuff turned back to the lawyer. "It's important to me," and he paused for emphasis, "and it'll probably prove important to the police."

A yellow and black sugarbird landed on the railing near the table, where it pointed its beak in the direction of the packages of sugar in the bowl beside the salt and pepper.

"You a lawyer?" Cuff said.

"That's correct."

"Then I'll simplify it for you. A crime was committed by somebody wearing one of the two masks you yourself bought from the Land of Oz." He waited, but Bennett merely stared, blankly, with nothing to say and with nothing to show on his face. A lawyer's ploy, Cuff thought, to get them to talk. Let them spill their guts. Find out what *they* know.

Bennett's food arrived. The burger was huge. How he planned to get his mouth around it, Cuff had no idea. The thing stood half a foot high.

The waitress left, but still nothing. It was as though Cuff himself had left.

But he hadn't. "Do I need to repeat myself, counselor?"

No need. Bennett was studying his burger, formulating a plan of attack. He used both hands, opened wide, but only got two-thirds of the width of the loaded bun into his mouth. A mixture of mayonnaise, mustard and ketchup, along with a few scraps of bun and pieces of lettuce, fell to the plate along with a handful of grilled mushrooms. In his haste to rectify the situation, by clamping the burger more tightly and holding it steady, not allowing it to tilt to one side, he directed the leakage down the front of his Jordache top.

He set the burger down, wiped his hands, then looked around for another napkin. Cuff leaned over, took two from the vacant table behind him and handed them to Bennett. The lawyer dipped the end of one into his glass of water and began rubbing at his Jordache top.

Cuff waited. And waited.

"What crime?" Bennett was still dabbing at the mess he'd made on the front of his shirt.

"Someone wearing one of those two masks shot at me, tried to kill me."

Bennett, satisfied with his cleaning job, set the napkin down. "Oh."

"Oh!"

"What do you want me to say?"

"Say you at least give a shit. Somebody was trying to kill me."

"You know how many masks there are like that on this island?"

"Five. Two in your hands and three waiting to be bought."

Bennett looked impressed. But then the expression was gone. "I have no idea who you are or what you want, but I do want to get one thing clear. The masks I bought were in my hands for no more than two hours. They were a gift. For a friend."

"Who?"

"Whom," said the lawyer.

"No," said Cuff, "who."

Bennett shrugged. The guy didn't miss a thing.

"Well?"

"A friend."

"I need to know. And I will, with or without your help. Do I need to go to the police?" Cuff had on his best poker face. He'd won more hands than he'd lost with it over the years.

"You're on the wrong track, but it's your time. Right? Madge Wilburn. She's in the book."

"Thanks." Cuff stood. He watched Bennett lean down towards his burger for a second shot at it and winced in empathy with the guy as the oily mixture began dripping all over the lawyer again, all over the front of shirt, this time around blotting out the *ord* of Jordache.

Cuff took in the mess, shook his head at the lawyer's eating incompetence, and started towards the door.

And the eyes saw it all. That's why the binoculars had cost close to two thousand dollars. The power they oozed was worth every penny spent on them. They were truly the mother of all binoculars. They ruled the roost. They were worth their weight in gold, even at today's terribly inflated price.

Besides, money was no object. Not now. Not any more. Not for these eyes. Not when what had to be done must be done. And the eyes would see to that, but only when the time was ripe.

The eyes. The deadly eyes of St. Croix.

#

"Madge Wilburn?" Cuff was back at the Pink Fancy. He was hungry. He wanted answers, and his stomach growled. He stood in his kitchenette before a large chunk of Parmesan cheese. He was looking for his favorite steak knife set. For some reason, he couldn't find it. Both were missing. How odd was that?

"Speaking?"

"This is Jim Cuffy."

"Who?"

"A friend of Tom Bennett's."

"Oh."

"I'd like to talk to you, if you can spare me a few minutes. It's important."

"What is it you want?"

"Just to talk. Only a few minutes." Cuff fumbled around the small counter top. Where in the hell was the steak knife set?

"So talk."

"I think it'd be better if we met. The phone gets in the way."

"What about?"

"Tom Bennett."

"What about Tom Bennett?"

"Like I said, this would be a lot better in person. Face to face."

"If you've got something to say, then say it. I've got work to do."

"It's really rather personal."

"I think you've got the wrong number."

"No, wait…don't hang up. Please. Hear me out."

"I'm all ears. Go ahead."

"It's about the two masks he gave you as a gift. What I wanted to—" But she had hung up.

Cuff dialed her number, but it was busy. He waited, dialed again. Still busy. Five minutes later he tried it, but again the same result. And fifteen minutes after that.

Either she didn't want to talk about it, or that was exactly what she *was* doing: talking about it. But to whom?

What had made her hang up on him so abruptly? And what had he done with the steak knife set?

Cuff was as frustrated as could be—none of it made any sense—but when he remembered the shot fired at him, he suddenly realized that he was more frightened than perplexed, but madder than both. And the thought scared him no end.

This might be just the beginning, but Cuff was in for the ride, no matter where it might take him. Someone had taken a shot at him, and he would see this thing through to the bitter end, come what may.

Dubuque or no Dubuque, life here in St. Croix was all that mattered now. The past was past, the future was yet to be, but the present was still very much alive, the only reality that really counted.

But then it hit, like a lead pipe to the solar plexus, or a swift kick to the family jewels. He couldn't believe it. Why hadn't he seen it at the time? How had he missed seeing such a thing, a thing big as life staring back at him from Steadley's death? His own steak knife set had gone missing, a matching set, both of which looked identical to the knife that he had seen sticking out of Daniel Steadley's lifeless body. But how could that be?

What in the hell! And suddenly *scared* could in no way fully describe the way Cuff felt. His insides churned like a cement mixer gone haywire, and drops of perspiration fell to a watery death from his forehead, his body shaking as if he were having an epileptic fit.

Chapter 14

Cuff phoned from the Comanche Bar, where he sat nursing a Beck's. He had had to ask the bartender to use the bar's phone since he had, once again, left his own new Samsung Infuse smartphone back in his room at the Pink Fancy. Wouldn't he ever learn? Cuff felt like a dumb guy with a smart phone as he sat there waiting impatiently for the guy to pick up. "Mr. Samuel Berylson?"

"Berylson." With the *r*, *y*, *l*, and *s* twisted together, but in slow motion, the way of the easy-going islands.

"I'm glad I caught you in. I've been trying to get hold of you."

"How can I be servin' *you*?" Cuff couldn't help but marvel at how the Crucian intonation was so musical, reggae style.

"Good question. That's exactly what I need, your services. You see, I'm in the market for a consultant." Cuff waited, but he couldn't wait forever. So he added, "And you've been recommended to me."

"I see. Who tole you bout *me*?"

Cuff took a stab in the dark. "Tom Bennett."

There was a pause, long enough for Cuff to hear the wheels churning. "Tom Bennett, you say." It wasn't verbalized as a question. "And what exactly kind service I provide you wit?"

"You're a consultant, right? I'd like to consult with you."

"Bout what?"

"That's what I'd like to consult on. Not over the phone, if you get my drift."

"How long you gonna need *me* servin' *you*?"

"That depends."

Berylson made some kind of sound over the line, but Cuff couldn't quite make it out. It wasn't really an *ah*, and it certainly wasn't an *um*. More of a hodgepodge of tones. Calypso style.

"You still there?" Cuff asked, providing Berylson with about as much time as he would have needed to go to the refrigerator, get a Beck's, scrounge around for the bottle opener, open the bottle, and guzzle the beer.

"Who you say you be, again?"

"I didn't. But it's Jack Conroy," Cuff said. "Friends call me Roy." He'd almost said Con, but recognized immediately the inappropriateness of it. He had just barely caught himself in time.

"And what's our consultation all about, Mr. Conroy?"

"Roy. I'd really rather talk about it, ah, privately, if you know what I mean. The phone, you know."

"If you want."

"I want."

"My fee's not low, you know."

"How steep?"

"Depends. What you say we meet here at my place at five." And Samuel F. Berylson hung up.

Cuff was taken by surprise. Before he knew it he was listening-talking to a dead line. And the guy hadn't given him his address. Where in the Sam Hill was Berylson's place?

Cuff called him back. This time he got the taped message.

#

He tried Madge Wilburn again. But no domino. The phone rang and rang and rang. Twenty-three times by Cuff's count.

What was wrong with all these people?

In frustration, Cuff finished off his Beck's and tipped the bartender eighty-six cents, the last of the coins in his pocket, unaware that his every movement was being closely observed at that very moment, that he was the center of some else's full attention.

The binoculars were so powerful, even from such a far distance, down the street a block and a half, that they easily were able to register the exact amount of their prey's tip. And this despite the fact that the sole penny in the handful of coins was so worn that it had turned a sickly green.

The eyes. The deadly eyes of St. Croix.

#

In the courtyard of the Pink Fancy, where Cuff had returned for a greatly needed cold shower and change of guayabera, he was greeted by Suzy. She sat at the bar, two uniformed policemen standing behind her.

Suzy's greeting was wordless. She did her talking with her eyebrows.

The two uniformed policemen said something to the bartender, then started in Cuff's direction. They caught him at his door, just after he had switched on his ceiling fan, something he couldn't live without in the tropics. "You Jim Cuffy?" the taller of the two asked.

Cuff fumbled with his keys, dropped them, bent down and picked them up. "No. Wrong man. I'm James Cuffy."

"We got ourselves a smartass," the second policemen said to his partner.

Cuff looked at him and shook his head, slowly. "No way. Want me to get it notarized for you?"

"You trying to be a wise guy?" the taller one asked.

"If so, then I'm doing a lousy job of it, wouldn't you say?"

The overhead fan whirled loudly, the squeaking in the room only adding to the tension seen in the eyes of all present.

Chapter 15

"What do you know about Daniel Steadley?" Now that they were settled at a table in the courtyard, out of earshot of the bar, the taller partner became the dominant questioner.

"What's this all about?"

"Just tell us what you know about Daniel Steadley, Mr. Cuffy."

"Why me?"

"Don't make it hard on yourself."

"Is that a threat?"

"We don't make threats," the shorter cop said. "We're the good guys." His smile was not a smile.

"Why me?"

"Please, Mr. Cuffy. We're trying to be as—"

"Why me?"

"Look, Mr. Cuffy, this is just an informal little chat. We have reason to believe that you can, uh, be of some help to us."

"Why me?"

The shorter, much stockier policemen mouthed *shit*, though the word didn't come out all the way. "What's the big deal?" he finally got out. "We're just doing a bit of friendly questioning. No," he added quickly, "that came out wrong. What I meant to say is that we're only interested in asking you a few questions." He waited, but Cuff didn't say anything. "It's really no big thing. Really."

"Why me?"

"Is that all you can say?" The taller one was back taking control.

"Why me?"

"Jesus…"

"Why me?"

The two policemen tried the silent treatment, but that didn't work either. All it succeeded in doing was bringing about a prolonged silence. The sounds of the V.I. Seaplane Shuttle making its way back into the water, across the street and down a block, was the only thing heard for another twenty-three seconds, drowning out life on the St. Croix waterfront as it raced across the harbor.

"Okay," the tall one said. "It's like this. We know you were engaged in a lengthy conversation with him at Cathy's Fancy." He looked for a second as if he would add more, but then he closed his mouth. He stared at Cuff's face.

So that was it! Cuff wanted to laugh. Was this the good lead they had? The infamous good one?

"So what do you want to know?"

The tall one smiled. "There, that's smart, Mr. Cuffy." He was obviously pleased with himself. His face was aglow with the neon-lit message that the police had their information. That they knew how to uncover leads and tips. We aren't people to take lightly, his face said. We get our man. Despite what the local media might say to the contrary. "Let's go back to our original question, shall we?" The *shall we* only emphasized the fact that he was now in full control of the situation, that Cuff was beaten.

"What question?"

"What do you know about Daniel Steadley?"

"I know he's wealthier than hell and that he was muddered the other night?"

"What's that?"

"I said I know that he was muddered the other night."

"I wouldn't take this matter lightly, if I were you, Mr. Cuffy."

"I read about it in the paper. *Police suspects mudder.*"

"And?"

"And what?"

"Go on?"

"Go on where?"

"Continue."

"Continue what?"

"Look, Mr. Cuffy—" the short, stocky policemen started. His brown cheeks were red, but he was built like a pit bull, his body almost square, one compact muscle of a man.

His partner cut in. "I must inform you that this is serious police business, Mr. Cuffy."

"I should hope so. I wouldn't like my tax money being spent so you guys could do non-serious police business."

The short man was openly glaring now. The tall one spoke. "We are trying to be patient with you, Mr. Cuffy."

"And I appreciate it."

"We would like you to please continue what you're saying, about Mr. Daniel Steadley."

"Wire bend, story end," said Cuff, remembering the Cruzan saying that a local had once used on him. "I told you the whole thing."

"Let me get this right. You mean that you do not know a Mr. Daniel Steadley?"

"Very good, captain."

"Sergeant."

Cuff shrugged. The sergeant turned to his partner, whispered something, and then went back to Cuff. "Are you saying that our information"—he emphasized the word—"is incorrect, and that you have never spoken with the man?"

"I'm saying no such thing—about not having spoken with the man. About your information, as you call it, I can't say, because I have no idea what you think you know."

"Then you did speak to him at Cathy's Fancy…several hours before his death?"

"Yeah, we talked a bit."

"About what?"

"Things."

"What things?"

"Small talk. Hell, he didn't even tell me his name. I had no idea who he was. In fact, I wouldn't have ever known, probably, if I hadn't read about him in the paper."

The tall one turned to the shorter one. "You think we've got enough?"

"Yeah, we've got enough."

Cuff got to his feet. "Then I guess that's that. It's been nice. We'll have to do this again sometime." He reached in his pocket for his keys.

"I'm afraid you don't understand, Mr. Cuffy. You're under arrest."

Cuff swung around. "Under arrest! For what!"

"Murder, Mr. Cuffy. Have you got yourself a lawyer?"

Chapter 16

Cuff sat in a back room at the police headquarters, which had moved here to Times Square many years ago in order to help improve the image of the known crime-ridden area. But it was still the busiest all-day and all-night sing-shout-loiter-and-drink spot on the island. The young girls of the evening plied their trade right around the corner, and loud music always blared from each of the many bars in the area. The area was crowded, at all times, with men sitting on the sidewalk drinking, with men standing on the sidewalk and street drinking, with men dancing on the sidewalk drinking, with men and a few women sitting or standing in any of the bars drinking—and loud calypso never stopped here. Times Square lived up to its name.

Cuff sat on a hard chair. The man addressing him stood, but several cops, two of whom were young women, sat facing Cuff. The air was stifling. Either somebody had switched off the air conditioner, or else it had broken down. But no one seemed to be bothered by this, nobody except Cuff. He kept wiping at his forehead with the back of his hand.

"There's no reason to get upset, Mr. Cuffy. We're just interested in what you and Mr. Daniel Steadley spoke about."

"Why not replay the tape? I've repeated myself a hundred times. We talked about nothing. It was small talk. We shared a couple of drinks together. That's all there was to it."

"Why?"

"Because that's the way things happen."

"I mean why did you share a couple of drinks together?" There was obvious annoyance in his voice now.

"Because I was there and he was there. It's a normal thing for two people to chat when they find themselves together in a bar."

"You go there often?"

"Often enough."

"You ever meet Mr. Steadley there before?"

"That's a laugh," said Cuff. "How in the hell do you expect a guy like me to meet a guy like him? Hell, when that man sneezed, the whole world was his Kleenex."

"We're waiting, Mr. Cuffy."

"How many times have I got to tell you? Give me the number, and I'll go to it. Seventy-eight? One hundred and twenty-three? I never met the guy before."

"You only met Mr. Steadley once in your life?"

"Yes."

"And that was the day in question at Cathy's Fancy, where you and he shared a couple of drinks?"

"We didn't do any such thing. He drank his, and I drank mine."

"You're making things more difficult, Mr. Cuffy."

"Am I?"

"You never saw or spoke to Mr. Steadley at any time other than that one late afternoon at Cathy's Fancy. Is that right?"

"Yes that's right."

"Then how come we found your fingerprints in his bedroom?"

Cuff wiped at his forehead, as much to cover his eyes as to get to the perspiration, which continually gathered there.

"Tell us, Mr. Cuffy? How do you explain that?" His voice rose, as if ascending a steep mountain. "And how do you explain the fact that your vehicle, license number C 43579, was seen in the vicinity of Mr. Steadley's home on both the night of the murder and on the morning, uh," and he glanced at the paper in front of him, "and on the afternoon after the murder, just before the police were notified about the crime?"

Cuff couldn't believe it. Was this the same V.I. Police Department of which so many rumors of incompetence floated throughout the islands like loose ballast on a stricken ship?

"Tell us, Mr. Cuffy. We're waiting. We've got the knife too. We had to send that off to Miami. Seems the person who killed Steadley used gloves or something to keep his fingerprints off the weapon. But we'll get our man. You can count on it. Those folks in Miami can pull off miracles."

Cuff didn't know what to say. But he had to say something. He was getting in too deep. A case was rapidly being put together against him. But before he could get his thoughts into words, the policemen totally zapped him, like a taser to the stomach.

"Tell us about Dubuque, Mr. Cuffy."

Dubuque! My God. Where in the…how in the…?

It was as though he were being kicked to the body and head instead of being left for dead. This was overkill. How could he get himself out of this?

"Dubuque, Mr. Cuffy?"

The wheels in his mind churned like a hurricane at sea. "What took place in Dubuque has no bearing on what has happened, uh, on what is taking place here."

"We think differently, Mr. Cuffy."

"It's a free country," said Cuff. "Think what you will."

"You see, it's already been established that you have a history of violence."

"A history of violence! Are you crazy?"

"It's all on the record. We know all about Dubuque, the violence and all."

"You know damn well that's not the truth."

"So tell us about your relationship with Mr. Steadley."

"What relationship? We didn't have any relationship. We met once, small-talked, and that was it."

"So tell us about Dubuque."

"I didn't do a thing in Dubuque. Nothing. Nada. Zilch. You can read it for yourself. It's all in the record."

"We have read it, Mr. Cuffy."

"So there's nothing more to say about it."

"Oh, we think there is. There's still the matter of the murder of Mr. Daniel Steadley."

"I don't know anything about that. Other than what I've read in the papers, that is."

"But we have the fingerprints, Mr. Cuffy."

"Those can be easily explained."

"So explain."

"It's not that easy."

"We're waiting, Mr. Cuffy."

But how could he tell things the way they were? Even Rosie had taken a lot of convincing. But if he changed things around, even just a bit, they'd probably find out, somehow. Hell, they'd found out practically everything else.

"Okay. I'll tell you what I know. Everything." Cuff wiped at his forehead. "I was sitting there at Cathy's Fancy, minding my own business, when Mr. Steadley approached me. I'd never seen the guy before. I had no idea who he was. I have no idea what a guy who could practically control everything and everyone around him like a puppeteer wanted with me."

"And?"

"He wanted to hire me for a job he wanted done. Why a guy whose sneeze could move mountains wanted me to do it, I can't say. It really makes no sense at all. I don't get it. But he wanted *me*. He was pretty clear about that."

"Why you?"

"You gonna let me tell you my story?"

"Go ahead."

"That's just it," Cuff said. "Why me? The world was his oyster. Hell, he had all the money in the world, and we all know what money can do. Right?" Cuff wished they'd do something about the lack of fresh air in the room. "He said that somebody had been snooping around his house for the past few days and that he was afraid that they were going to hit his house. *Hit* was his word."

"Who?"

Cuff looked at the man, allowing his facial expression to say it all. Then he continued. "He wanted me to guard the place from midnight until six in the morning. To scare them off."

"Why you?"

"I don't know. He'd heard about me…from someone? Maybe he wanted to keep things kind of quiet, or some such thing. I have no idea."

"So you're known for doing things quietly?"

"Not exactly," said Cuff.

The room itself sighed. "So what'd he heard about you?"

"I don't know," said Cuff.

"So what happened?"

"Somebody killed him. That's what happened."

"Please, Mr. Cuffy."

"Nothing happened. I waited for him. He said he'd meet me at eleven-thirty at the Gentle Winds entrance. But he didn't show. So I went looking for him. That's why my car was spotted."

"And you found him, right?"

"Yeah, I found him."

"So why didn't you call the police?"

"Why didn't his wife?"

"What wife? Steadley was divorced. Several times over."

Cuff rubbed at his forehead. "He told me that he had a wife."

"Why would he do that?"

"Why not ask *him*?"

"Funny, real funny." The cop had obviously had enough of this already. "Let's get back to you, Mr. Cuffy. Why didn't you call the police?"

"Put it this way," Cuff said. "Your anonymous tipster is no longer anonymous." There was no way he was going to tell them about his missing steak knife set. It just didn't feel like the smart thing to do at this particular time.

"You got something to hide?"

"No. But if I'd given my name, well, then I'd probably have been brought down here like this talking to you like this and would have been accused like this of something I didn't have any—"

"No one's accused you of anything. Let's get that clear, Mr. Cuffy." But the *yet* hung in the air, like a cloud of cigar smoke, circling, biding its time.

"I hate to disappoint you, but your two sidekicks over there put me under arrest earlier. But then on the way down here they apparently had second thoughts. That's when they *un*arrested me. Said things would be much easier on me here on the island if I just came in and chatted. Like I'm doing. An implied threat of sorts. But what I don't quite—"

The man was no longer listening. He had turned to his two officers. "Did you at any time arrest Mr. Cuffy?"

The short bulldog look-a-like did the talking. "No way. It was probably just a misunderstanding."

"Probably," said Cuff.

"Did you at any time threaten Mr. Cuffy?"

"Us?" The stocky man tried a smile, half succeeded. "No way. You know better than that."

"May I go?"

The policeman turned back to Cuff. "We've got no reason not to let you go. Not at the moment. But we do thank you for coming in and talking to us. You've been a great help. We'll talk again, if need be. "

"If need be," said Cuff. "Have a nice day," he said to the short, mean-looking cop who had first approached him back at the Pink Fancy. Cuff hustled from the stifling room, crossed the hall, and vacated the police station. He went into Bentick's Grocery, at the corner, where to buy a cold Heineken.

Damn. His wallet was empty. When he took out his credit card, the guy behind the counter said, "That's all you're gonna buy while using your card?"

So Cuff was forced to grab a whole six-pack, which still didn't suit the cashier, whose face was as stern as the rear of the battered boat outside that had not seen water in years. The thing was rotting away, deteriorating much like the cashier's good humor was vanishing with age.

Cuff stood there waiting, his thirst strong and his mind still back in the police station.

"You gonna swipe your card or not?" the aging cashier asked, his tone somewhere between Crucian sweet and mainland impatience.

Cuff looked up from the counter, where his six-pack lay. "Why would I swipe my own card?" he said.

"What's that?"

"I said why would I steal my own card?"

The cashier simply didn't get it. "What are you talking about?"

"Forget it." Cuff swiped his card, picked up his six-pack of Heineken, and went back outside to the street, where he polished off the first of six beers before he had gotten a block from bustling Times Square.

But the combination of barley, hops, and water did not do much to improve his mood. He was tired, restless, angry, and scared. He felt like screaming, but who would really hear?

But the eyes, which had been following his every move, from down the street, from across the street, from up the street, but always from a safe vantage point where they themselves would not be seen, but always within clear telescopic range for the beautifully ornate binoculars to pick up everything, were pleased. They were so pleased, that the mouth below them began to drool with delight. Life was so grand. Everything was going along so splendidly. The evolution of events was moving ahead like perfectly timed clockwork. The fatal end would be something to behold, the subtle complexities something to be truly cherished, the finality to be the end to all ends.

Yes, this was truly a masterpiece being constructed, and the eyes were so proud of what they were witnessing, of the diabolical beauty of what was to come, but later. Why hurry? There was still time to enjoy what was happening right now, this very second even, before climaxing with what would eventually come. This was artistry at its best. The scenes unfolding were like those of a playwright who had created perfection, every player and piece doing precisely as written.

No, this was more godlike. Yes, that's what it was, godlike. The power, the majesty, the unimaginable becoming the believable—the eyes saw it all, and, even though they knew that it all had to come to an end, eventually, that end was still down the road a piece, so they were out to gain all the pleasure they could while the thing strung itself out, before the beautifully choreographed denouement brought the curtain crashing down. Yes, this was excruciatingly sublime, and the eyes were tickled pink with pleasure as they sparkled their way through the powerful binoculars.

The eyes. The deadly eyes of St. Croix.

Chapter 17

The three dots way out to sea were barely visible, but as they continued towards St. Croix, they gradually grew in size. As they approached the island, the human eye could discern that they were helicopters, large helicopters, as black as midnight.

Then they could be heard, and their sound grew louder. As they flew in over the secluded beach just north or Fredericksted, the noise they made grew in such intensity that they would have even greatly over shadowed the loud Virgin Islands seaplanes as they raced across the Christiansted harbor.

The three helicopters flew low, so low that they nearly touched the treetops as they made their way across the island towards the town of Christiansted. As they loudly made their way overhead, every pair of eyes on the island looked upward to see the strange sight. Nobody on St. Croix, not even the oldest of the old timers, could remember ever having seen such a sight before, three gigantic black helicopters flying straight across the tropical isle, their propellers whirling majestically, but forcing many people to cover their ears as the mysterious machines noisily flew by.

The three helicopters reached Christiansted in practically no time. The island was that small. One landed, while the remaining two hovered overhead like bodyguards. The frenetic sounds of the giant creatures held the populace in both fascination and dismay, their sudden appearance so mysterious but their sound so deafening.

The island's coroner had nervously been waiting their arrival. This was so out of the norm, but he knew he had no more say in the matter. That had been made as clear as the vodka that he knew he needed at that very moment.

"But the autopsy," he finally had the strength of character to say, as the men in black-striped suits, red and blue ties, and pressed white shirts began moving Daniel Steadley's body onto the helicopter.

"That's already been taken care of," was the only reply.

The coroner, who thought he had seen and heard just about everything in his time, found himself speechless at this. But he eventually found his voice.

"This is most unheard of," he said.

The eyes of the well-dressed man in the suit, towering over him, narrowed. "You have heard and seen nothing." His face was like granite. "Am I right?"

The coroner tried to object. "But practically everyone on the island has heard the helicopters."

The facial expression on the man in the expensive suit did not waver. "Nobody heard or saw a thing. Believe me. Right?"

The coroner's face was one big blank stare.

"Right?" And the tone this time around meant that there could be no evading the question.

"Right."

And that was the exit line for the men in the suits.

Within seconds the helicopter carrying the remains of Daniel F. Steadley joined its two brothers, and the three quickly ventured off into the sunset, quickly becoming dots on the horizon, and then disappearing altogether.

No mention of the three black helicopters was ever made in the local paper, not the next day or for any day after their sudden departure from St. Croix, which really got the citizens' tongues wagging. Crucians are sociable, and they like to talk. The unexpected arrival of the three helicopters and then their quick departure was the talk of the island. For days on end. Everyone had a theory, the most accepted one being that it was some type of military training mission being carried out by forces stationed on nearby Puerto Rico.

That seemed to make the most sense to people.

\#

Tom Bennett was on Cuff's mind as he stood under the shower nozzle. Cuff felt like a new man, the cold water on his body, a second Heineken in his stomach.

But Tom Bennett was still there, like a festering sore. The lawyer had given the two masks to Madge Wilburn. But she wouldn't talk about them to Cuff. And Tom Bennett had seemed wary, as if he were covering himself in some way or another.

And then there was the consultant, one Samuel F. Berylson. How were these three people connected?

Were they connected?

What did he mean by *connected*?

How did the masks fit in? Where were they now? Who had them? And what did the calling card of Berylson's add up to?

And the masked man who had shot at Cuff? Who was he? Where was he? Where was Daniel Steadley's wife?

But Cuff had chosen not to verbalize any of this to the police. Why tell them? It would only drive Cuff himself more deeply into whatever he was now in the middle of.

Middle of? Yes. Someone had fired a shot at him. And Cuff would never let it go.

Cuff let the water run through his hair one last time before turning it off. He stepped from the shower and stood before his small air conditioning unit, allowing his body to drip dry.

But Tom Bennett was still there—right at the upper level of his brain, like a bloodsucking leech holding on for dear life.

\#

Tom Bennett, the lawyer, couldn't be disturbed at the moment. He was with a client. His secretary didn't smile when she told this to Cuff.

Cuff walked past her and opened the lawyer's office door.

Tom Bennett swung his head around suddenly and frowned when he saw who it was that had barged into his private meeting unannounced, unwanted. "I'm busy," he said to Cuff, his tone saying a lot more than his words.

"If you want him to hear this," Cuff said, nodding towards the balding man sitting at the lawyer's side, "then that's your choice. I'll give you to thirty to decide. But I've got to tell you, Mr. Bennett, I'm already up to twenty-seven."

Bennett rose, tried to say something, and finally turned to his aging client. "Will you please excuse us for just a second. I'm terribly sorry about this. I'll be just a moment."

The man went out to where the secretary sat. Cuff closed the door. He turned to Bennett. "I need Madge Wilburn's address."

Bennett's face was angry now. "I'll dare you to—"

"I wouldn't do it, if I were you. I always take a dare. I need her address, like right now. As in *pronto*."

"I have no idea what you—"

"And that's how it will remain. Somebody tried to kill me the other night. Whoever it was, he was wearing one of the masks you yourself purchased from the Land of Oz, and which you say you gave to Madge Wilburn. I've got to talk to her about this, face to face. If I've got to, I'll take it to the police." His poker face again.

"You're not really a very good actor, Mr. Cuffy. Anybody ever tell you that?"

"I'm not acting."

"Be that as it may, I see no reason why you persist in bothering me about something I know nothing about. Besides, she's in the book."

"Her complete address isn't."

"Call her."

"I have."

"I see." Tom Bennett smiled. It came out just as it would if he were a used salesman trying to pawn off a lemon on somebody's grandmother. But his shirt was badly stained from lunch.

"I'm waiting."

Tom Bennett thumbed through a brown book he withdrew from his side drawer. "53 William's Delight," he finally said. "What's it to me?" He shrugged and put the book back where he kept it.

"That's just what I'm going to find out," Cuff said. He turned back to the lawyer as he reached the door. "If I were you, I'd get into the habit of keeping a spare shirt in my office, for after lunch. Or at least get yourself a bib." And then he made damned sure to slam the door on his way out.

\#

Getting to William's Delight was like driving across country, though it lay only fifteen miles from Christiansted. People's perceptions became warped after a while. Cuff had heard of people who never drove from Christiansted to Frederiksted because they considered it too long a journey since St. Croix's only two towns were located on opposite sides of the tiny island. Perception was everything.

Cuff parked down a couple doors. He slumped into the seat so that he could not be seen from Madge Wilburn's front door.

Rosie was gone about fifteen minutes. Cuff hummed to himself as he waited. He tried "I Love You Truly," but then switched to "Don't Fence Me In."

"She'll give you five minutes," Rosie said, her head poking through the passenger window of Cuff's rusty four-year-old Honda Civic. "That's it, though. Period. *Her* words."

"How'd you do it, Rosie?"

She returned his grin. "How do I always do it?"

"You're something else, Rosie. You know that?"

She winked at him in reply.

Madge Wilburn had gone back into her house.

Cuff got out of his Honda and let Rosie lead him to Madge Wilburn's front door. They knocked, waited. Knocked again. Waited.

"Change of heart?" Cuff asked.

Rosie shook her head. "Give her time. She'll talk. But only for five minutes."

They knocked again.

Madge Wilburn's hairdo was as wild as the goose chase Cuff seemed to be on. Her hairdresser must have been part of a voodoo rite of some type. It kind of stood on end, but the top curls were like bright banners. The ends were crimson, a far cry in color from the tinted brown at the sides and the dirty beige on top.

Cuff studied her face. There was nothing there to indicate why such a woman would wear her hair in such a style. Maybe the Jumbies, who some here on the island claimed were the spirits of the dead, had actually taken up residence in her floppy hair. Who knows? Superstitions can be very real, especially here in the Caribbean. No native in his right mind would walk under a ladder on Friday the 13th, and none ever scoffed at the mystical power of the Jumbies, supernatural beings as prevalent on the island as were witches at one time on the mainland. Was that it? Was Madge Wilburn some kind of witch?

Weird.

"Mrs. Wilburn?"

"Ms."

"Sorry. Ms. Wilburn?"

"Madge."

"Sorry. Madge?"

"You've got four minutes and thirty-seven seconds left."

"I'm here to ask about the two masks Tom Bennett gave you." Cuff couldn't take his eyes off her hair.

"What about them?"

"Have you got them?"

"Who wants to know?"

"Who's asking?"

She wasn't a bit fazed. Her hair stood combat ready. Not a strand in place. "Why do you want to know?"

"Because somebody wearing one of them tried to kill me."

"Are you crazy?"

Cuff couldn't pull his eyes from her hair. "Certainly not."

"I don't know anything about any masks."

"That's my very point, Ms., uh, Madge. I'm not asking about any old masks. I'm referring specifically to the two masks Tom Bennett gave you."

"Who told you that?"

"Straight from the horse's mouth."

Madge Wilburn laughed. Her hair plopped around uncontrollably as she did so. "That's good," she was finally able to get out. "Real good. But I would have said it had come from the horse's behind, myself, if you get my drift."

"Yeah," said Cuff. "I get it." He watched her hair settle back to where it had been prior to her laughter. "You don't much care for the guy, right?"

"An understatement if I ever heard one."

"Then why did he give you the two masks?"

"How should I know? You think I'm a clairvoyant or some such thing?"

Cuff had to agree that she certainly looked the part. "If you don't like the man, then how come he just told me that you two were friends?"

"Used to be."

"Used to be?"

"You heard me." She looked at her watch. "Time's just about up."

"Where are the masks right now?"

"Disappeared."

"Where to?"

She shook her head. Her rolling eyes relayed the message that she thought the question stupid and the person who asked it about the same, if not more so. "If I knew that, they wouldn't have disappeared, would they?"

Cuff started to speak, but she cut him off with the wave of her hand. She started to close the door. The five minutes were up.

"Just one more thing, uh, Madge. When did they disappear?"

She looked him in the eye. "After Tom Bennett, the creep, gave them to me." Then she shut the door.

Cuff's knocks did no good. Time and again, they did not. Not a rustle could be heard behind the closed door. Cuff, finally realizing that Madge Wilburn, the woman of the flaming trapeze hairstyle, had him beat this time around, so he finally give in to her doggedness. His knuckles hurt as he followed Rosie back to his four-year-old rusty Honda Civic.

#

Back at Cathy's Fancy, they sat together at the bar.

"You ever get the feeling you're talking to a wall?"

Rosie half smiled. "Sure," she said. "But mostly when I'm talking to you."

"Funny. I mean the people and the masks. Nobody seems to know anything, but everyone seems to be hiding something. First Tom Bennett won't say what he did with the masks, and then when he does he says he gave them to a friend, Madge Wilburn. Then she says she can't stand the guy. Well, then, why did he call her a friend, and why can't she stand him?"

"And who has the masks?"

Cuff looked at her. "Right. At least the one worn when I was shot at."

"You think they're lying?"

"I think all of them are keeping *some*thing back. *What*, I have no idea. *Why*, who knows? But it's really scary. Somehow I got myself mixed up in the murder of Daniel Steadley. Can you believe it? Daniel Steadley." He watched a sailboat in the distance. Cathy's Fancy was such a beautiful place, with a wide sandy beach, clear turquoise weather, and palm trees swaying in the gentle Caribbean breeze. But everything was so ugly at the moment. Why was everyone so evasive when it came to the mask?

And don't forget Samuel F. Berylson, the so-called consultant. Why the strange business card? What was *his* game? What was his connection?

Was there a connection? Between whom? As to what?

"Why not just let it be, then?" Rosie asked.

He looked at her a long time before he spoke. "You know I can't do that, Rosie. Somebody took a shot at me." He looked in the direction of a small dog chasing a larger dog along the water's edge. The funny thing about St. Croix was that a great deal of the fauna consisted of its dogs, no two that ever seemed to look alike. "And you know what's so funny, Rosie? The guy haggled the price he wanted to pay me. One of the world's richest men trying to save a buck or two. And look what happens to him in the end? Priceless, isn't it?"

"Maybe that's how he got so rich, haggling like that."

"Yeah, sure thing, Rosie. Go figure, huh?"

"Go finger," she said, and she showed him what she meant.

More sailboats began to dot the horizon, and everything looked the way it was supposed to, the sand white, the water turquoise, the palm trees swaying in rhythm to Nature's beat. Paradise surely lived up to its name. St. Croix was as beautiful as any place on earth.

The nudge on his shoulder brought him back to the moment at hand. Cuff looked up into the unsmiling eyes of the shorter of the two policemen who had earlier arrested him and then had quickly undone what they had done.

"I'm gonna get you," the man said. He looked like a Sherman tank.

Cuff picked up his empty Beck's bottle and handed it to the policeman. "Thanks. I appreciate that. I'm drinking Beck's."

The policeman, dressed now in civilian clothes, put the bottle on the table. He set it down so hard that it tipped, landed on its side, rolled to the end of the table, and fell to the floor. But it didn't break.

"I mean what I say," he said to Cuff. "We both know what you did. And I'm gonna be a pit bull on this case. I'm not letting you go. Consider yourself locked behind bars. There's no getting away from me this time."

Cuff waited, and finally said, "You through?"

"No way," said the policeman. "I'm just beginning." With that, he turned, and started to huff away.

Unfortunately, he had forgotten about the Beck's bottle. He hit it just wrong and began sliding across the beach bar out of control. Fighting to keep his balance, he reached for the table, for support. His frantic tug at the table sent Rosie's rum punch into her lap. She squealed involuntarily, jumped up, and the colorful drink ran down her legs on its way to the floor.

The policeman finally steadied himself. He took a deep breath.

"You owe the lady a drink," Cuff said to him.

The man looked over at Cuff, then at Rosie. His curled lips said it all. The stocky cop turned and hurried from the bar, his eyes on the wooden floor ahead of him as he moved. He was like an angry pit bull on the go.

Cuff was playing with his coaster when Roger, the bartender, stepped up. "What was that all about?" He handed Cuff a fresh bottle of beer.

Rosie spoke up. "The guy's a cop, and he thinks Cuff killed Daniel Steadley."

"What!"

Cuff nearly fell out of his chair. "Rosie, can't you ever learn to keep things to yourself?"

"You don't want me to speak, I won't speak." She sat there for a couple of silent seconds. Soon the seconds became more than a minute. Then she got up and walked off towards the beach.

"I wouldn't go too far, if I were you," Cuff called out to her backside. "Some very unsavory characters like to hang around the cove there."

"Just let them try something," she shot back at him.

"Quite a gal, that Rosie," said Roger. "Fantastic pair of legs."

Cuff nodded.

Roger looked across the beach bar to see if the pair of snowbirds there needed anything, but they seemed to be fine. "Is it true? What she said?"

"Probably. But she's sure got a way with her tongue, though, that Rosie. Words just seem to come out without thinking."

Roger studied Cuff's face. "You two having a bit of trouble?"

"Nothing out of character really. I just wish she could be a bit more tactful at times."

They both heard the movement of chairs across the bar.

"Thanks for dropping in," Roger called out to the two elderly snowbirds who were now headed back across the sand to their room.

Cuff emptied his bottle of beer. "I think I better go get Rosie."

"Good luck," said Roger. "By the way, is there anything I can do to help?"

Cuff thought about it. "Yeah," he said, "there is. The next time that short cop comes in here for a drink, serve him something that'll give him the runs. Compliments of me."

Roger laughed, but Cuff, on his way after Rosie, did not.

And the eyes, well out of sight, but well within range, ate it up. They glistened in the humid Caribbean sunshine, humidity so pronounced that it grabbed you by the neck, trying to squeeze the life out of you, relentless in its choking pursuit. But the eyes weren't a bit affected by the terrible humidity. In fact, they were so engrossed in what they were watching so intently that they had no idea there even was any humidity.

They were cool, calm, and collected.

The eyes. The deadly eyes of St. Croix.

#

Cuff caught up to her at the cove. Rosie had taken off her sandals. She stood at the edge of the water, waves gently swishing around her ankles, which were slim and firm and absolutely out of this world.

"Surprise, surprise."

Cuff stood beside her. "What are you so sore about, anyway?"

She kept her eyes on the distance. "I'm hurt, that's all. I really care for you, Cuff."

"I know you do, Rosie, and I do for you. A lot."

Rosie kept her eyes on the Caribbean. "You've got a funny way of showing it."

"I'm sorry, Rosie. It's just that this thing is driving me up the wall. I can't afford to have my name bandied around the island as if—"

She wheeled around, on one ankle, like a ballerina. "Bandied around? I'm not even sure what that means, but I sure don't like the sound of it."

They stood there staring at each other, the waves rolling ashore in cadence. Neither spoke for quite a while. Every now and then the nearby palm trees would flutter in the breeze, which seemed to be almost as erratic today as the spelling in the local paper was on almost a daily basis.

"Rosie," Cuff said at long last, the sun smiling their way.

"Yeah?"

He cleared his throat. "Rosie," he started again. He was not about to pull his eyes from hers, especially not at this moment.

"So say it," Rosie finally said. "What is it? We haven't got all day."

Cuff's expression didn't change. "Rosie," he said, "I think I'm falling in love with you."

She tottered a bit in the sand, caught her balance, then blurted out, " You *think!*"

Cuff, for once in his lifeless, was speechless. He was certain that the expression on his face must resemble that of a puppy seeking understanding and forgiveness from his human. Cuff stood there like a statue, his eyes saying what words could not. Then he held his arms out to her, and, as a seagull screeched somewhere off in the distance, she finally reciprocated. What would be would be, but what was did not have to be. There was always tomorrow, so tomorrow it would be. They both knew this as they hugged one another, as tightly as can be, on the white sand, the deadly eyes long gone, having called it a day.

Chapter 18

What name had he used? Cuff paced his room at the Pink Fancy. Rosie had left for work several hours ago. Cuff had showered, downed a shot of Cruzan dark, and then taken a short nap.

But now he needed the name. How could he call the so-called consultant if he couldn't remember?

Shit. He should have written it down. Or he should have used a code of some sort. Or he should have used a—

Should haves wouldn't help. Not a bit. They would only bring him wrinkles before his time. He didn't worry about developing an ulcer. If Dubuque hadn't brought one on, then what could?

But the wrinkles were another thing. He lived where the sun always shone. St. Croix. Blue skies year round. Sunshine everywhere. There was no need for Vitamin D supplement here on the island.

Such weather brought on early age. To the face it did. Cuff had seen it in middle-aged people from up north who had long ago made St. Croix their home. Wrinkled beyond their years since the sun always shone nearly three hundred and sixty-five days a year.

But Cuff wasn't a sun-worshiper, by nature. The thought of the big *C* had frightened him early. He had known many who had caught it, and many who had died from it. So he sat under a tree when he went to the beach. He had no desire to change the color of his skin, which was very pale for one who lived where the sun always shone. Tan in the tropics just meant trouble down the road.

If he were to catch the big *C*, which statistically was a strong possibility, then it would be because he had reached that age. The elderly caught something, eventually. Often the big *C*.

But he wasn't one to help the process along. He watched what he ate, he didn't smoke, and he did get a lot of exercise.

Another thing: if the big *C* got any aid from the way he lived, then it would be from the fact he did like to drink.

Not to overdo it. No way. He'd given up hangovers long ago. They just weren't worth it any more.

But he had a thing for beer. Imported beer only. He loved the taste of hops. The taste of Scotch. The maltier the better. Single malt preferred. Particularly Campbeltown, the tasty West Highland smoke tasted much like malt and hops did to a Bavarian.

And don't forget cognac. A good sparkling wine. And—

But he needed the name. What had he used on Samuel F.? Conroy. That was it.

But try as he could, he couldn't recall the first name he had given the consultant.

It didn't matter. He sat down on his bed, where he dialed the number from memory.

"Hello?"

"Samuel F. Berylson?"

"Berylson." The unique West Indian mixture of tonal consonants again.

"Samuel F., this is Conroy."

"Who?"

"Roy. Remember? We scheduled a meeting a couple of days ago. I'm in the market for a consultant. Remember?"

"I remember. You didn't show."

"How could I?" Cuff slapped at a mosquito that had landed on his leg, but missed. "You didn't give me the address."

The pause went on…and on…and on.

"You still there, Samuel F.?"

"Who this?"

"I told you. Roy. We talked just a couple of—"

"Who you?"

"I told you. Name's Conroy."

"Don't mean a thing."

"Does to Rosie."

"Who's Rosie?"

"What's your address, Mr. F.? I'd like to consult with you."

"Where you get my number?"

"From police headquarters." Cuff was growing irritated.

A long pause again. "Who give it you?"

"A short cop. Drives a big blue and white Olds. Moves like a pit bull. Likes to—"

"Yeah, yeah. Shorty Rawlins. Why he give you it?"

"He didn't. He gave me your card. Your number's on it. But it's wrong, right? Why so, Mr. F.? I just can't figure that one out. Why would a businessman hand out a business card with his phone number listed incorrectly?"

"I'm hanging up now."

"I'd advise against it. If I were you, I'd listen to what I want to consult with you about. There could be trouble ahead." Cuff, always the poker player, was bluffing.

The silence seemed to strengthen his hand.

"Are you threatening *me*?"

"No such thing, Mr. F. But I am certain somebody will be soon. For real. No games with these guys." The plural seemed like a full house. Good cards. Cuff waited.

And waited. "Why Shorty give you my card?"

"He's a nice guy."

"I no born yesterday," Berylson said.

"I was pretty sure of that," said Cuff.

"Okay, I meet you," the consultant said, "but only in public place. I pick the place and time."

"I'll see you," said Cuff.

"Wait. You don't want to know the place and time?"

"Of course I do. That was poker talk. I'll *see* you, partner. Like in show me your hand."

Berylson waited, then talked. "In two hours. Exact. Not Cruzan time. My watch say it's now seven-turdy. At Pelican Cove, at end of public access road." He hung up.

So did Cuff. Four seconds later. Didn't make much sense to hang onto a dead line.

\#

Cuff arrived ten minutes early. It never hurt to be alert. He parked and then walked on the beach. No one was in sight. He kept moving. He ended up in the trees behind one of the newly installed security lights put in by the new owners of the old Pelican Cove, a St. Croix landmark. Why the new owners would want to change such a fine name, he had no idea. And of all names, why call it Cormorant Beach Club, when there were no cormorants in the Virgin Islands, but there were plenty of pelicans?

Pelican Cove had been such a beautiful name.

Cuff stood in the shadows, his eyes on where he had parked his car. Berylson would be arriving any time. The secrecy of the meeting had put Cuff on full alert. Why take chances?

Just didn't make sense. He'd know where Berylson was before the consultant knew where *he* was. He'd keep his eye on the man for a time before showing himself. Case him out, as it were. Something didn't smell right about the guy. The wrong number on the business card. The secrecy of the meeting place. The mystery in the man's tone of voice when divulging the stocky policeman's name.

Cuff had to smile at that one. Shorty Rawlins. So the bulldozer of a man had a name. Cuff would have to look into this a bit further.

He was pleased by his actions. But he wasn't going to take any foolish chances. Ever. That's why he waited now in the dark, his eyes on where—

The pain came from nowhere. Cuff grabbed at his side and crumpled to the sand. Two arms held each of his. His legs, kicking wildly at air, were useless in this position. He was firmly held to the ground.

Sand in his eyes. Pain, itching, grating, and more pain. But his own hands were immovable, so he could do nothing for his eyes.

The pain was terrible.

And it kept getting worse. Sand was everywhere, in both his eyes *and* mouth. Gagging, his eyes watery with pain, his legs kicking at nothing, his upper body clamped to the sand, Cuff felt as helpless as he had ever felt before in his life.

"I'm gonna say it once, Bozo, and once better be enough." The man's voice was raspy, as if he were disguising it in some way. Maybe with a ball of cotton in his mouth. Or a handful of pins.

And Cuff was blinded. He couldn't see a thing. He stopped kicking at air. He lay still. He wished he could rub the pain from his eyes.

"There, that's much better, Bozo. What I have to say is this: leave it alone. You hear? Just leave it alone." The voice stopped, and more sand was added to the torture-chamber of Cuff's face. "It's nothing to do with you. You hear? You keep it up, and you're dead. That's a fact, Bozo. You're dead. You got it?"

The night was still. The sound of the palm trees blowing gently in the wind was the only thing heard. It was closer to ten in the evening than it was to nine, and the temperature, as usual at this time of night, was still in the high seventies to low eighties.

It was truly paradise, the thing of which dreams are made, a honeymooner's place in the sun, where the lovely Caribbean Sea displayed colors known to very few other places on earth. Palm trees, white sandy beaches, colorful seas, but still there was the terrible pain in his eyes.

Cuff thought for sure he was blinded for life. Is this how it was to end? He was resigned to the fact. Take me, his inner mind shouted. Now! The pain was unbearable.

"I'm counting to three hundred." The ugliness of the voice just didn't fit in with the beauty all around it. "And I'm a slow counter. We'll be backing off now. But I'll still be counting. You move one muscle before I've reached three hundred, and you're dead. You don't leave us alone, you're also dead. You leave it be, lay still till I reach three hundred, then maybe you're not dead. And remember, I'm a slow counter. One, two, three..." The arms were removed from Cuff's body. The man with the gnarly voice began his getaway.

Cuff lay motionless. He already felt as if he were dead.

"Seven, eight, nine..."

Tears gummed up the sand around Cuff's eyes. But the lovely Caribbean breeze lulled its way through the trees, rustling the palm leaves in the direction of the misnamed luxury hotel fifty yards behind where he lay, still motionless, wishing with full throttle that he had never gone to Cathy's Fancy that fateful day he had been propositioned by the wealthy man whose life had ended while clutching an investment book that would never again do him an ounce of good.

And there in the dark distance, hidden by the swaying palm trees, were the eyes. They had arrived much earlier than had Cuff. They had secured the best position in which to take in that night's action. They stood inside the fencing of the fancy hotel, in an obscured place in the dark, where not even the moon could penetrate. Shorty Rawlins had performed admirably. Give the guy credit. What a performance he had put on, an Oscar nomination one for sure. And the eyes removed the binoculars. That night's act was over. It had been a thrill a moment, a real crowd pleaser, and the eyes, the audience, now that the beach was deserted once again, clapped with utter joy as they blinked their way out of the dark. Another day would come, and with it would come more of the same, but *much* more.

The eyes. The deadly eyes of St. Croix.

Chapter 19

Shorty Rawlins was royally agitated with himself. Had he done anything to give himself away? Was there any way possible that he could have been recognized? He tortured his brain as he fought for answers, pacing back and forth in crowded Times Square, making sure that all eyes could plainly see him, would see that he was indeed working where he was supposed to that time of the night. He had not been gone *that* long. The drive to Cormorant Cove had been short, and the business there had taken practically no time at all. The surprise had been complete, the task done in quick order, and nobody, he hoped, would ever know that he had left his assigned post.

But had he made any mistakes? He remembered everything, although it had taken place so fast, and he could come up with no miscalculation on this part. Still, he was agitated. With what he had hanging over him, tightly controlling what he could do and say, practically forcing his every move, like it or not—and he hated it!— he simply could not take a chance. He knew full well that if anything ever went wrong, then his world would come to an abrupt end. Yes, his own actions, under complete scrutiny at all times by eyes that seemed almost too evil to be real, but, unfortunately, were as real as life and death itself, were predetermined, as if he were a puppet in a master's hands, which, in effect, he now was.

What a dangerous world his had suddenly become. Life was supposed to be so easy going in the tropics. The joke used to be that if a tourist looked around at the slow pace of living on St. Croix and asked what the people did for relaxation, then that tourist was definitely in the wrong place and time. Life was lived at a leisurely pace down here, where time really meant very little at all. Who cared if someone showed up an hour late, for instance, for an appointment? After all, Cruzan time was lived down here on the island. The hectic pace, the stress of everyday living, was for the mainland, to be carried out there, and to be left there, on the mainland. Here on St. Croix everything was run by Cruzan time. Live, party, drink, dance, sing. That's what life was all about on the islands.

And yet Shorty Rawlins was as stressed now as he had ever been, just as a mainlander might be, say, back somewhere such as in New York City. Shorty Rawlins was a native, born, raised, and educated on the island, having left only several times for training on the mainland. He was terribly proud of his accomplishments, the first in his family to ever graduate from high school, and the first and only one in his large family to have earned a position with the Virgin Islands government. As a public safety officer, he earned a pretty good pay and had nice benefits, and he was guaranteed a lifetime pension. But that lifetime now seemed a lifetime away. He had so far to go, and yet the chances of his reaching that point were becoming slimmer the more involved he became.

But what was he to do? He had been in the thing way too long now, and he knew too much. If he ever did decide to talk, then what would become of him? Where could he go? How could he live? Where could he hide?

The *thing*? What a term to use for it. But being more precise, more articulate about what to call it was far too painful to be endured. What it was, it was. What he had done, he had done. He had to live with it. There was no way of getting around that. The past could not be erased. What was real, was real, and nothing, no one, could change that.

But it was the what-is-to-come that hurt the most, so he tried not to visualize it, tried to block it out the best he could, tried to force it to the back of his brain by not calling it by its name, if such a thing had a name.

Monstrous! The thing had taken on such a life of its own, that he could hardly remember a time before he was part of it. He had been a proud young man when first sworn to duty, and he thought the world of himself as he began his duties of providing peace and safety to the people of his beloved island paradise. But then Tom Bennett had entered the scene, and that was that. How he had been so cleverly manipulated that he himself was now part of this terrible thing, he simply couldn't fathom.

Shorty Rawlins was convinced that he was not a bad man, and yet he found times when he had trouble living with what he had become. Good men can do evil things, he knew, but then how do they reconcile this within themselves, in the eyes of their loved ones?

He knew little about Catholicism, but he wished that he himself could somehow confess and then be forgiven, if that is how it operated. Hell, he'd change religions right on the spot, if it were so. But he knew that, for him, it would be impossible to be forgiven. How could anyone ever fully understand? Who would listen? Who would help? Who would comfort?

How he wished that he had never before met Tom Bennett, the famous—the infamous?—lawyer. If only they had never met. If only—

The *if only* bore into him like a knife, his life's blood spilling out all over raucous Times Square, to be trampled upon by people of all ages dancing along to the loud beats of reggae and calypso resonating all around him from the hopping beer and rum joints surrounding his place of work.

"What have I done?" he asked himself. "What *can* I do?" And Shorty Rawlins, the short public safety officer with the fireplug body, standing there in his official uniform, his fellow islanders joyfully whooping it up all around him, wished that he could just curl up in a little hole somewhere and enter eternal sleep.

But he knew very well that that was not an option. Not after all that had already transpired. And that realization is what was killing him from the inside out.

Chapter 20

Nobody at the hotel had heard or seen a thing. Cuff had washed his face in the men's room beside the open-air bar, which was closed for the night. The men—at least two he calculated—had probably come from around the opposite corner from where Cathy's Fancy lay, from the darkened beachfront that led back into Christiansted. They had planned well. There was no one to see them at that hour. They could have parked in any number of places, made their way through the brush and trees to the beach, and walked undetected along the sand until they had reached the security lighting of Pelican—that is, Cormorant—Beach. Then they could have taken their time, slipped in behind the lights, hidden themselves in the darkness of the trees.

Whatever they had done—and Cuff was pretty certain he wasn't too far off the mark—they had certainly caught him by surprise, totally so.

Cuff would have laughed, if it had been possible for him to do. And all the time he had thought he was pulling off the smarts by getting there early and checking things out.

Stupid, stupid, stupid.

His eyes were red, and sore, but at least the sand—most of it—had been washed out and away. And at least they hadn't broken his ribs, even though he knew the attackers had done something to them. His sides were as sore as his eyes.

He looked like he felt, and he felt like hell. Too bad the bar was closed. A Heineken or two might not have helped, but it sure wouldn't have hurt.

He trudged through the sand back to his car.

"Damn you, Samuel F.!" he screamed through his windshield. The consultant hadn't seen the last of him. No way. Cuff wasn't one to forgive and to forget. He would remember. Just as he would the masked man who had shot at him, and just as he would the threats made by one Shorty Rawlins.

With determination crowding out the pain, he dug in his front pocket.

Damn!

His keys were gone. Of all the—

#

It took him much longer than he thought it would to locate his keys. They had gotten themselves buried under several inches of sand. He finally retrieved them, stuck them in his shorts for safe keeping, until he could get back to his Honda, and then he did something he hadn't done in years.

He cried. Loudly and openly, for all the world to see.

#

At this hour, the courtyard back at the Pink Fancy was deserted.

"Hiya."

Cuff, his brain at feverish pitch, was startled. He turned a bit too abruptly, and he felt the pain in his side. "Suzy. What are you doing sitting there? The bar's closed."

"Waiting for you. Tonight's my last. I'm leaving on the first flight tomorrow to Puerto Rico, and then from there back to Denver."

Cuff started to say something, but then stopped suddenly. There was something there...in her eyes. She looked about how he felt. Partners in pain. The world upside down. The mind adding to the pain. Life so ugly, so unfair.

People doing terrible things to people. In the name of that and in the name of this.

This and that. All the same. It all added up the same. It all meant nothing. None of it.

Her eyes looked pained, but there was something beneath the pain. Something waiting. Hoping. Something that needed to be touched. Nurtured. For hope. For all of us. The world spinning off its axis. Nothing really mattered.

And yet, it all mattered. Terribly.

He was surprised when he heard the words come from his mouth, and yet he wasn't all that surprised. "I'm glad you waited, Suzy."

She smiled as Cuff helped her through his door, his eyes on the present, his mind only on the now, since the then and the what-will-be needed blocking out—if only for a second—almost for survival's sake.

The pain he felt had taken on a life of its own, and it was far more than merely physical. That's just the way it was at that very moment in time.

Life. The way things go down at times, and that is precisely what was happening.

Chapter 21

Cuff kept his back to her as he turned on the light. He didn't want her to see his face. Not yet. "Make yourself at home," he told her. "I'll just be a minute."

He felt foolish doing it, but he did it anyway. He locked the bathroom door. His eyes were still red, but it wasn't really all that bad. He undressed, took a long shower, checked his face again in the mirror, and wrapped the towel around his waist.

Suzy was sitting up in bed. She was nude from the waist up. The sheet was pulled up to her hips. She leaned against both pillows, which she had propped up behind her. She was sipping a Cruzan dark, no ice. Her breasts were lovely.

Cuff poured himself a drink, finished it quickly, then poured a second. "You need a top on that?"

Suzy shook her head. "I won't need it," she said.

Cuff turned on the lamp beside the bed, then turned off the ceiling light. Then he sat down in the chair near the bed.

"Your eyes are red," Suzy said.

"I've been crying."

"Over my leaving?" And she laughed…cackled.

But Cuff didn't mind. Not now. "You're a lovely woman," he said. "A good person."

Suzy smiled. She set her drink down. "Thank you." She saw him look at her breasts. But her eyes held steady.

"I'm sorry I've been so…so…" but he couldn't come up with the right word.

"You don't need to do this." Her voice was pleasant, but her eyes showed sadness.

"It's not what you think."

"And what is it that I think?"

"It's not important." Cuff took another drink. He fingered his glass as he spoke. "It's not you. It's me. It's not really me," he said, "it's something that happened to me. That's why," and he finished off his drink and tossed the glass along the rug, where it ended up in one piece near where he kept it, underneath the table containing his now half empty 1.75 litre bottle of Cruzan dark rum.

"It happened long ago," he said, "and yet it really wasn't too long ago. But it's had an effect on me. I'm different now, leery. Wary. Unsure. I'm a changed person."

She settled back on the pillows to better face him. "Tell me," she said, and her voice was soft, but insistent.

"Two years ago," Cuff said, "I was an assistant professor of English at the University of Dubuque. In Iowa. And a funny thing, my specialty was Chaucer. My God, Geoffrey would have—" Cuff got up, got himself another drink, and sat down. "I was a good teacher, Suzy, a damn fine teacher."

"I bet you were, Cuff."

He looked as if he had just suddenly realized she was there listening to him. "I really was. A fine teacher. I had the best student evaluations in the department for five years straight. I'd published a few things, and even nearly finished a book on Chaucer. Everything was going my way. Good job, a lot of time off to make up for the low pay, doing what I wanted to be doing. Good medical and dental plans, a nice retirement plan in place." He drank two gulps of rum in quick succession, sighed. "But all good things must end." He studied his glass, and then his hands.

"What happened?"

He looked up. "I was up for tenure. My career held in the balance. The right word, and I was set for life. And everything said that the word *would* be right. I had everything going for me. Everybody liked me, and they respected me."

She watched him sip at his drink. "So what happened?"

"Lisa Smithers. She happened. Sweet little Lisa Smithers." He drank loudly. He set his glass down even more loudly. "In my introductory lit. class. Front row center. Always a smile on her face. Somebody's sister. What more could you ask for in a daughter?" He looked back at his glass, more to steady himself than anything else. Every time he thought of her…of Lisa Smithers…

"So one fine day," he said, "Lisa Smithers comes into my office. For a conference. About her term paper. She needs some direction. She's stuck. Doesn't know which way to go." He gritted his teeth, leaned back, and breathed deeply. "So what happens? Next thing I know she's ripping at her blouse and yelling bloody murder."

"My God…"

Cuff looked into her eyes and nodded. "She said I'd tried to…that I'd…said she'd had to fight me off." He was staring at the floor, at his feet. He looked back up. His eyes were still red. "Anyway, to make a long story short, I was denied tenure. Getting another job, after that, would have been difficult, to say the least. I sort of snapped, told off too many important people.

"So I said the hell with it. The hell with being a part of all that crap. I picked up and left. I drifted for a while, lived off some of the twenty-seven thousand dollars I'd had in my TIAA/CREF retirement account. Retired early, you might say.

"I ended up down here. Still have about six thousand dollars left, but this time I got smart. I put it into an IRA. Won't touch it until I'm fifty-nine. If I live that long. Hell, it's the only thing I've got left from all the years I had put into my chosen profession."

The stillness of the room screamed. But both waited. Suzy was the first to say anything. "Why'd she do it?"

"Who knows why people do what they do? A better grade. A pushy parent. Who knows? But even my lawyer couldn't get her to budge from her story." He shook his head. "If only I'd left my office door open that…that fine day. If only…oh, the hell with it. What's past is past. And there's nothing I can do to change it. I sometimes get my insides all hopped up about it, but most often, now, I can write it off. To bad luck. Some such thing. It's not the end of the world. I'm still me. And I'm still breathing. I'm in paradise, aren't I?" Eyes searching. For an answer that wasn't there.

Suzy returned his attempt at a smile. "You have a cute smile. It shows your dimples."

"I try," Cuff said. He stopped smiling. "You're the first person I've opened up to about this. I wanted you to know. After Lisa Smithers…well, I just haven't been very good company."

"I understand."

"I wanted you to."

"I do."

They stared at each other, he in his chair, she propped up on her elbows, in the bed.

"If I've been…" he began, trying to keep eye contact with her, "then I hope you will understand why. I didn't ever mean to…"

"I know you didn't." She leaned towards him. "Thank you," she said.

"For what?"

"For telling me."

Cuff nodded. "You see…" he tried.

"Yes," Suzy said, "I see." She reached out for him.

And Cuff stood. He slipped off his towel and went to her.

Her body was as firm and fine as it looked, and to Cuff their lovemaking was like a lifetime annuity from heaven.

For Suzy it was even better.

Chapter 22

They had loved and grappled playfully and hugged and kissed and lay in each other's arms forever and ever. Their bodies had experienced sensations only the most fortunate can achieve. They had whispered into each other's ears, said things that made their bodies tingle with even more satisfaction. It had gone on and on. Forever and ever.

But it was nine in the morning now and Suzy was gone. Forever. She had taken a taxi to the airport. She had not wanted Cuff to see her off. She had insisted.

But he had called for the taxi. He had insisted.

Cuff lay in bed, on his back, his eyes on the ceiling. He watched his life. He watched Dubuque. He watched his anger, then his aimless trek across country. He watched his person-to-person talk with himself one lonely night in a bad hotel room somewhere in west Texas.

Or had it been east Oklahoma?

It didn't matter. What mattered—the only thing that mattered—was that he had managed to save himself that night. From despair. Deep and festering, on the verge of exploding. From destruction, total and irrevocable.

He had taken a good look at himself, hated what he saw, what he had become, and how he had become.

St. Croix?

He couldn't say exactly where the specific place had come from, how it had managed to enter his mind-set, but when it had come, there was no turning back. St. Croix it would be.

And was. Soon he'd met Rosie. Leery and wary as always, since Dubuque, Cuff had gone through some rough times with her. He had put her through some rough times. But he cared. He cared a lot. They had gone out seventeen nights in a row, and they did not make love until their seventh date. They both knew that this was something special. In fact, Rosie had once told him that she had called her sister in Baton Rouge the very night she and Cuff had first met and had told her, "I think I've met the one." And that had been only after being with him a little over three hours. That had been months ago. And now this…

No, he had not told Suzy the complete truth. For there were now *two* people who had heard Cuff open up about how his life had been mangled in Dubuque. Suzy had been the second. Rosie had been the first.

Cuff wasn't really sure anymore what the word *love* meant, whether or not it really meant *any*thing, but he sure knew one thing, and he knew it well: Rosie was special! If he knew nothing else, he did know that. How in the hell he had done what had done last night, with Suzy, the lonely school teacher from Denver, he had no idea. But it was a fact that it *had* happened, and he knew full well that he had to man up to it and be honest with Rosie. Never again would he allow any human weakness of his to get in the way of the total commitment he felt for Rosie. There simply was no excuse for what had happened last night, and he knew it. But now he had to deal with it. They had had their many ups, and a few downs, but nothing like this, and it was all his fault. He had given in when giving in was absolutely the very worst thing he could have done.

Rosie.

Rosie.

He had to spill his guts, get it all out, and confess his sins. Their very relationship, which was just starting to be, required this, screamed for this.

Cuff jumped from bed, showered, didn't shave, and half jogged to the Scotia. But Rosie was out. Nobody knew where.

The way of the world.

He found her at the wharf, window-shopping in front of Wadsworth's.

"Rosie."

"Up a bit early, aren't we?"

"Couldn't help it. She woke me when she left. Couldn't get back to sleep after that."

Rosie showed him her teeth. She too knew they were fine-looking teeth, white as coral. "The sexpot again?"

"You got it, Rosie."

"The one with the beautiful body?"

"That's the one."

"The one who's after your body? Is that her?"

"She."

"Yes, ex." This time she showed him her tongue. "She finally succeeded, huh? Got you in the sack."

"That's exactly right, Rosie."

"But now it's over. A thing of the past. Finished."

"Right again, Rosie. About this time she's somewhere between San Juan and Miami. On her way back to Denver. Where she lives."

"That a fact?" The tease in her voice, for which Cuff had at first resisted but eventually, after his telling her about Dubuque, had fallen head over heels for, was back again big as life. It was her signature personality trait.

"It's a fact, Rosie. The whole story."

"Thanks for telling me." Her eyes were smiling, filled with tease, with challenge. She was really enjoying their little word game.

"You're welcome." His eyes, though, were deadly serious.

It was out. Cuff was still sore with himself for his inexplicable behavior of the night before, but he did feel good about himself that he'd told Rosie about it. Even though she might not have really heard what he had verbalized to her, at least it had been said, and now it could be shelved forever, to be used as a learning tool for the future. Live and learn, even the hard way, was the new mantra he would follow.

"That it?" Rosie wanted to prolong the game. She was having fun. Her eyes flirted as only Rosie's could. Had she heard what he had said?

"Not quite. You see, I was feeling sorry for her, for me. I guess I was feeling sorry for the state of the world. That's why it happened."

"She finally got ya, huh?" Rosie was still grinning as she punched him on the arm. Her teeth were so white that Cuff needed sunglasses to return her gaze. "That's for telling stories." She punched him again. "And that's for if you ever really do meet up with Miss Sexpot. You savvy?" Tease and love were silently mingled now in the salt air. "You had breakfast yet?"

"No. And I'm starved, Rosie. But there's something else I've got to tell you. I was attacked last night."

"The sexpot again?"

They were on a roll this time around, their little teasing game seeming to go on longer than ever.

"Not this time. Two men jumped me, probably more."

She studied his face for a time, concern creeping into her features. "You're serious, aren't you?"

"Yes."

"My God, Cuff…" She wrinkled her forehead as her eyes bore into his. "I thought you were storytelling again."

"No. Everything I've told you is the truth. All of it. I'll fill you in as we eat." They bought food in the Grog and Spirits and went across the wharf parking lot to one of the benches alongside the water. They sat, staring across the multi-colored harbor at Protestant Cay, a small island in Christiansted harbor that now sported a luxury hotel, the little isle so named during the time of the French, when the burial of non-Catholics had been prohibited on the main island of St. Croix.

"Well?"

Cuff looked at her. He swallowed the pieces of cheese he had been working on. "It has to be Berylson. I just can't come up with any other explanation as to how they knew when and where I was going to be."

She watched the Seaplane Shuttle hurdle its way along the surface of the water, and, at seemingly the last possible second, finally lift itself into the air. "What have you gotten yourself into?"

"Murder."

"But why?"

"I have no idea."

She looked at him. "You have no idea why you've made yourself part of this?"

"I've no idea why Daniel Steadley was murdered."

"But why get involved—especially now, since things are getting so rough?"

"Somebody tried to kill me. I told you."

And that was something not easily forgotten. His eyes were like two angry fists, and Rosie, who knew him well, maybe even better than he knew himself, saw it all. Determination had finally gotten the upper hand and had overpowered agitation, in a hard fought battle, and had emerged as the victor, to be able to proclaim that it, and it alone, was now Cuff's Alpha facial expression.

Rosie stared into his expressive eyes forever, happily ever after, and then wrapped her strong arms around him and hugged him as hard as she could. She couldn't help herself.

Rosie now knew for certain that she was truly in love with the guy.

Chapter 23

Madge Wilburn was not happy to have to open her door. "Yeah?" she said. But then when she recognized Cuff, she said, "What do *you* want?" But there was very little questioning in her tone but lots of annoyance. Her hairdo was as wild as ever, maybe even moreso than the last time Cuff had talked to her. She looked like she had just stepped into a multi-color strobe light and had somehow danced her big toe into a live wall socket.

"We'd like to talk."

"Well, I wouldn't. I'm busy." She slammed the door, but Cuff's outstretched leg stopped it from closing.

"We really would like to talk."

"And I'd really like you to get your foot out of my—"

"What's the problem?" The voice came from somewhere within her home.

"It's nothing," Madge called back over her shoulder.

"That's where you're wrong," Cuff said. "It is something, and it's important." He couldn't quite make out the voice that had come from inside Madge's home, but it was familiar. Very familiar.

"Look," Madge Wilburn began.

"No, you look," Cuff butted in. "What we have to say is very important. We're not about to—"

"Who's there?"

Such a familiar voice. Cuff knew it, from somewhere.

Madge Wilburn started to answer, but her mouth moved for several seconds before the words came out. Cuff hadn't noticed the idiosyncrasy before. But now as he watched, he became fascinated. Her mouth twitched and then went to work an easy three to four seconds before her vocal cords became synchronized with her lip muscles.

"I want to go. Do you understand me? I have nothing to say to either of you. Ever. So if you will please allow me to close my door—"

"What is it?"

And suddenly Cuff recognized the voice.

"Excuse me," Cuff said, and he pushed the door open with his foot, and then with his hands, and slipped into the house, pushing Madge Wilburn to one side, Rosie right behind him.

"What do you think you're doing?"

Cuff ignored Madge Wilburn. First things first. There was a time for this, and there would be a time for that. Cuff would see to it.

Samuel F. Berylson, the consultant, was sprawled out on the sofa, his shoes off and his feet over the arm of the couch, which showed as much age as did he himself, his head cradled back on a pillow, his eyes half shut, a gentle wheezing coming from his sleepy face.

Cuff looked down at the red-eyed consultant, and Madge Wilburn waddled into the scene. She started to say something, but Cuff didn't let her get started. She had barely begun moving her facial muscles when he turned to her, abruptly, in order to startle her, a good tactic in his book.

"What's *he* doing here?"

She looked at Cuff, avoided Rosie's eyes, then focused on Berylson, who was clearly fighting to keep his eyes open. "That's none of your business." Her hair looked like a painted porcupine.

"It's all of my business, Madge. You mind if I call you Madge? You see, somebody tried to kill me. And I swear to you—"

"Not in my house, you don't."

Berylson groaned, sat up, slowly, then fell back to where he had been.

"He's drunk as a skunk," said Rosie.

"Very original, Rosie."

"I'm giving you five seconds to get the hell out of my house."

Cuff turned to Madge Wilburn. "You're not giving anybody anything, Madge."

The big woman huffed, and then she started towards the phone.

"I wouldn't do that if I were you," Cuff said to her back.

"I'm calling the police. I gave you fair warning."

Rosie could be fast when it counted. Before Madge Wilburn could react, Rosie had pulled the Radio Shack Tone Dial Mini-Fone from its plug-in phone jack. She tossed the cord across the room.

"I told you," Cuff said. "Rosie can be one tough woman."

Madge Wilburn opened her mouth as wide as she could, thrust her arms into the air, focused her eyes on Rosie, then promptly sat down, where she buried her head in her hands.

Crickets could be heard from the louvered windows at the back of the house.

Samuel F. Berylson began the painful process again of trying to sit up. Cuff gave him a hand and then propped up some pillows behind him.

Berylson blinked several times, but he couldn't get his eyes to focus properly. "Where Shorty?" he finally got out, before he began his terrible coughing spell.

They watched him cough. Then they heard the crickets again.

"Where Shorty?" Berylson asked again. Then his eyes began to work, and he recognized Cuff. "Who invite you?" Berylson tilted is head to get a better look at Cuff, but he could only get one eye open, and only halfway at that. Then he tried to see who else had come into the room, but he just could not get his head turned in the right direction.

Madge Wilburn picked her head up from her hands. "He invited himself. He shoved his way in here."

The consultant tried to say something, but his overworked lungs wouldn't cooperate. He slumped back against the pillows, where he concentrated on ridding his body of its hacking.

"Nice party," Rosie said.

Madge Wilburn gave her the finger.

Cuff turned to Berylson, who had stopped coughing. "I've got a score to settle with you."

"Score?"

"You know what I'm talking about."

"Score?"

"The beach party you arranged for me."

"Party. We goin' have a party?" How he kept his one eye open Cuff had no idea. Then the consultant spotted his half-filled glass of Scotch and milk. "Drink," he mumbled. But, for some reason, the glass wouldn't budge. He looked at it sideways, through his one half-opened eye, but he just couldn't make sense out of any of it. That's because Rosie's hand was clamped around his, holding the glass to the tabletop.

"You've had enough," she said. She moved the glass out of his reach.

Berylson stared in her direction, trying to make heads or tails out of what he was seeing, but all he saw was a blur. Then his head began swaying to and fro.

"You got any coffee?" Cuff asked Madge Wilburn. "I want him sober when I get even with him."

"Not in my house, you don't."

"Coffee," Cuff repeated.

"Coffee yourself," said Madge Wilburn.

Outside the crickets were chirping up quite a storm.

Cuff won the contest of angry stares. Madge huffed and puffed her way to the kitchen. She returned soon enough with a cup of instant coffee. She handed it to Cuff.

"Here," he said to the consultant. "Drink up."

"Drink up, drink down," mumbled Berylson.

"Either way, do it," said Cuff, and he forced the cup into Berylson's hands.

The guy slurped so loudly that it grated on Cuff's nerves, but he forced himself to keep quiet until all the bitter instant crap that Madge Wilburn called coffee had gone down Berylson's throat.

"About your card," Cuff said to the drunken consultant, "just what kind of consultant are you?"

Berylson set down his empty coffee cup. He had been given only a minute or two to empty it. "What kind you tink?"

Cuff waited, but got no further response. "About your telephone number."

"What about it?"

"Why was it printed wrong on all your business cards?"

"To fool 'em."

"To fool whom?"

"Dem dat try to bug me. I add a seven to fool 'em."

"Somebody bugged your telephone?"

Berylson nodded vigorously. "Yeah, yeah. Dat's right. And day bug my new number too."

"How do you know about that?"

"Easy," said Berylson. "If you didn't tell anyone about where we were gonna meet on the beach, and I didn't tell, den how dey know?" He looked particularly pleased with himself.

"That's another thing. How come you didn't show up when you told me you would?"

"I tole you. I late. When I reach, you gone."

Cuff leaned forward. "But you made a point of telling me to be on time. On the dot."

"But me Cruzan, man." He looked around the room. "Where Shorty go?"

Rosie stood up. "I'll be outside. I'm gonna check around the yard."

Cuff nodded. "Good idea." He turned back to Berylson. "What were you all up to here tonight?"

"We talkin'."

"What about?"

"We talkin' business."

"What kind of business?"

"*Our* business." Berylson laughed at his own joke, which brought back his coughing. When he was through hacking, he laughed a bit more until spittle began to drool down his chin.

"Funny," said Cuff.

"Tanks."

But Cuff's face plainly showed that humor was the furthest thing from his mind.

Silence. Crickets. A car in the distance. Then a dog barking, bringing about the barks of one more dog, and then another.

"Well?" Cuff said.

"Well run dry," said the consultant, breathing heavily from all the work his lungs were undergoing. "I ain't saying another ting. You can even break my arm, if you want."

Cuff sighed. "We're not that kind."

"I'll bet."

"You're on for fifty," said Cuff.

#

Rosie crept through the yard, started around back, and that's when he jumped her. She fell to her knees, swung her elbow back as hard as she could, catching him right in the middle of the forehead. Caught completely off guard, he slipped to the side, and Rosie leaped to her feet. She turned, just as Shorty Rawlins got to his feet.

She gasped when she saw who it was, but the bulldog-like head formed a grin, as he started towards his prey. He would show the little lady no mercy.

Rosie was fast. Kicking out with her right leg, she got him squarely in the mouth, then abruptly came back with her left leg to his face. Short Rawlins, the human refrigerator, was literally stunned, and Rosie sent him back onto the grass with a quick kick to the family jewels and another to his chin. Taking no chances, knowing full well, despite their enormous weight differential, that she had him, Rosie pounced on the man, got her wiry legs around one of his arms and pulled it tightly against his neck, clamping her feet behind her, and lay her body on top of his other arm. Shorty Rawlins, still in terrible pain from the kicks, especially the one where a lady should never kick a man, was completely under Rosie's control. To a bystander, the situation would look almost humorous, a thin little woman completely overpowering a massively muscled dump truck of a man. But it had happened quickly, rhythmically, and almost effortlessly.

Rosie's leg scissors was as tight as a vice, Shorty Rawlins' one arm, along with his head, trapped by her powerful legs, and the other completely useless under her backside, plastered to the grass. He lay on his back, his face starting to turn red from the unbreakable and painful hold he found himself imprisoned in. He knew full well that he was finished, that she had clobbered him in just a matter of seconds, that there was no way for him to get up, that she could hold him there like that until she decided to let him go. Abject terror was written in his eyes, and there was absolutely nothing he could do about it.

"I can't breathe," Shorty was barely able to get out.

Rosie showed him her pearl white teeth. "In case you hadn't noticed, I've got strong legs. I bet I could even strangle you here like this now if I choose to? What do you think?"

"Please," he said, nearly at a whisper.

Rosie added a bit more pressure, for show, which brought forth a yelp from the pit bull of a cop. Then she backed off just a bit, but still keeping him under full control. "You talk, I'll let up. Is it a deal?" She squeezed full force for a second, to demonstrate her will, then let up again, but just a bit.

Shorty was almost gagging now. "I'll talk," he said, "but please let me breathe."

Rosie was thoroughly enjoying the moment. "Talk," she said, "but you better make it good. You hear?"

"I hear," said Shorty Rawlins, and he began to think fast. What he said now had life or death—his own life or death—written all over it. There was no way he could spill any of the beans, so the words that came out of his mouth went to the only possible place they could, considering the huge hole that he had dug himself into, one that would bury him alive if any inkling whatsoever of the thing he was now such a prominent part of surfaced prematurely.

The eyes, off in the distance, could see but could not hear. And they were thoroughly disgusted by what they were witnessing. After all, the bulldog of a cop was supposed to be the muscle of the operation. And there was no telling what he was blabbing his mouth off to that skinny little bitch now. This was not supposed to be the way it went down.

The eyes knew that something had to be done. And soon. Loose lips had to be silenced. Physical pain was no excuse. Wasn't the guy built like a granite slab, one huge muscle of a man, the perfect candidate for a bouncer at the roughest beer joint imaginable?

The eyes had seen enough. They were angry slits as the binoculars were finally set aside.

Chapter 24

Cuff accelerated, passing a slow moving rust heap that sounded as if it were running on one cylinder. They were on Centerline Road, nearing the St. Croix branch of the University of the Virgin Islands.

Cuff chose to speak first. "We now definitely know that Madge Wilburn, Shorty Rawlins, and Samuel F. Berylson are in business together. At least we got that much out of them before Madge clammed up and Berylson passed out. It's a start, anyway."

Rosie grunted in reply, but she kept her eyes through the front windshield.

"What's wrong, anyway?"

This time she snorted in reply.

"I've got it!" Cuff said. "Haven't let you goose me lately. That's it, isn't it?"

"You keep it up, I'll cook your goose one of these days."

"You probably would, wouldn't you?"

"Yeah, I just probably would. On second thought, why not just take out the *probably*."

"That time of the month for you, Rosie?"

"It's that time of my life, is more like it."

Cuff shifted into third, then second and rounded the sharp corner. "What brought all of this on, Rosie?"

"All of what?"

"All of what!"

"We playing Repeat What I Say?"

"I'm not playing at all."

"What about *around*?"

Cuff shifted back into fourth. "You're speaking gibberish, Rosie."

"You think so?"

"I *know* so. I've got ears."

He sighed. "Look, Rosie, I have no idea what's eating at you. Why not come right out with it?"

She turned back to the windshield, then quickly swung her head back towards Cuff. "I'm not stupid, you know."

"Stupid? Of course not." He slowed down a bit and looked over at her. "Just what is it, Rosie? Tell me. Please."

"It's you. There. I've said it. You satisfied now?"

He glanced at her again. "I have no idea what you're getting at."

"Don't you?"

"How could I?"

Rosie nodded. "Yeah. You had no way of knowing that Shorty would talk. To me, that is. Did you?"

"Shorty talked to you?"

"Yeah he talked to me."

"When?"

"When do you think? Back there. He jumped me in the yard, and I beat the shit out of him." She nodded with a flick of her head. "What choice did he have? I had him in an unbreakable strangle hold," she added. "I could have broken his neck."

"I had no idea," Cuff said. "So Shorty was still there?"

"Yeah, but I bet he sorely regrets that fact now."

"You are something else, Rosie. You know that?" But she didn't respond. Something was wrong, but Cuff had no idea what. The silence that had come between them was killing him. "So what did he say?" Cuff finally asked. "What did you learn about his connection to Bennett, about why he threatened me, about who took the shot at me?" There was excitement in his voice, anticipation now flowing like Cruzan rum down a thirsty throat.

"I didn't get the chance, not after he told me plenty about you."

Cuff slowed down. He pulled into the Sunny Isle parking lot, stopped, and turned off the ignition. He turned to her, but she refused to look at him. "What's going on, anyway, Rosie? Just what is it you're trying to tell me? What exactly did Shorty Rawlins tell you?"

She kept her eyes away from him, but finally she spoke. "What a fool I've been. Just to think that all the time I thought we had something special going for us, like caring and honesty and...and..."

"And we do."

She turned on him. "Do we?"

"Of course."

She turned away. She watched a car in the distance. "That's what I thought. I really did."

"Look, Rosie, I have no idea what Shorty Rawlins said to you, but whatever it was—"

"Sometimes I really wonder," she said. "I really do." She studied the darkness out of the window, she urned back to Cuff to say something, but thought better of it, and quickly returned her eyes to the car window. Then she got out of the car and started walking across the empty parking lot, leaving only silence in her wake. Cuff, having no idea what was happening, got out and went after her. She turned abruptly, her fists hard, her body in a boxing stance, ready for combat. "You know I can take you," she said.

Cuff stopped in his tracks, just out of her reach. "What's this all about, anyway?"

"Say it, Cuff."

"Say what?"

"Say that you know I can take you. Go ahead. Say it."

Cuff tried a smile. "Rosie, you can take me anywhere."

She lurched forward, striking out, but he backed up just in time. "Say it," she said. She was in the ring and ready to rumble.

"I don't get it." Cuff continued to stay just out of her reach.

"Say it, Cuff."

"Why?"

"Because it's true, and you know it."

Cuff studied her face, but he still had no clue what was going on between them. "Okay," he finally admitted.

"Okay what?"

"Okay, Rosie, I know you can take me."

"Do you mean it?"

"You know me, Rosie. My word is my bond."

"Bullshit!"

"What's got you so fired up, anyway?"

"Come on," she replied. "Let's have it out, here and now. Just you and me. Right now." Her dukes were ready, and legs were just itching to go.

Cuff reached out to her, but she pulled back. "Tell me. Please. I've got a right to know."

"Oh, my God," she said. "Now he talks of rights." She tossed his hand aside and backed away, slowly unclenching her fists, her eyes steely hard but on the verge of tears.

"Please," said Cuff. "Tell me. Open up. What's going on here?"

Instead, she turned and silently jogged back to the rusty Honda, and got in. Cuff had no choice. He followed. They sat there in the dark for several agonizing minutes.

Time did its thing. The night was both dark and still. Nothing could be heard. Silence, all around, almost like a morgue. And time kept ticking away, second by second, relentless, determined, unwavering. And then Rosie had it all together once again, so she slowly turned to him. And then she spoke, slowly by decidedly. "Here I thought that we meant something to one another, that honesty counted and look what happens: he goes creeping behind my back."

"I did no such thing. We *do* have something special going for us. Hell, Rosie, you're my girl." He studied her expression, but he kept his hand away. "My woman, I mean," he said.

She finally looked at him, face to face. "Why, Cuff? Why? How could you have done such a thing to me?"

"Talk, Rosie. What exactly did Shorty tell you?"

She kept her eyes on his, and finally turned back to the front windshield. "He tailed you. He's determined to get you. Those are his words. Anyway, he saw the woman, the sexpot, go into your room. And he saw when she came out. He was there, Cuff. He told me all about it. He sat out there in his car all night. He was tailing you, like I said."

Cuff hesitated. He leaned forward and waited until the words finally came. "I can't explain it, Rosie, because I don't even understand it myself. Yes, it happened. I admit it. I just don't know why it happened. Hell, I was feeling like shit. I'd just been mangled at the beach. My head was…no, I won't try to explain it, because I know I can't. I have no excuse. It happened, but it's over. She's gone. It was a one-night…no, it wasn't that at all. It was just one of those things. It happened, and there's nothing I can do to change that." He leaned in closer. "Rosie, there's no one but you. You should know that."

"Please, just leave me be, okay? You've said enough, all right? Give me time to sort it all out. We'll talk when I'm ready." She began fumbling through her fingers.

"I told you all about it, Rosie, right after it happened. I didn't try to hide anything from you. It happened, and I'm sorry for that, but I was open with you. Right upfront."

She thought about it. "That's not how I remember it."

"But that's what happened."

"Not in my book, it isn't."

"Do you mean to say you don't remember my telling you about the lonely school teacher from Denver?"

"The sexpot?"

He thought about it. "My mind wasn't right. I'd been beaten on the beach. I wasn't thinking clearly. But I did tell you about it. I had to. I don't want to keep anything from you, Rosie. You mean too much to me."

"Yeah, you told me. But telling isn't always the same as telling."

"What do you mean by that?"

"I mean your tone. You didn't seem to be serious. I thought you were playing some kind of word game with me, just getting your kicks or something."

"Rosie, you know me better than that."

"Yeah, I know you. And I think that's the problem."

"What problem?"

"Us. I don't think I really know you, although I know you."

Cuff started to laugh, but he stopped suddenly. "Sorry. But now you're talking crazy."

"Am I?"

"To my ears you sure are."

Rosie shifted her legs around on the seat, so she now sat facing Cuff. "Just how much do I mean to you, Cuff? Tell me straight. I need to know. It's important."

"Without you, Rosie, I've only got me. That's it. You know what I've been through, Dubuque and all. Sometimes I…sometimes I do and say things I later regret. I've always been that way. I'm trying my best. You know that. Or at least I hope you know that. I'm working my way forward, the best I know how. Hell, I make mistakes. I know I do. But I care, Rosie. I care about life and living and about me and about you. Especially about you and me as a couple, as one. I really care, Rosie, and I want you to know that. I slipped up, badly, and it hurts me as much as it probably does you. It can't be undone. But it's done and over with. And even when it was happening it was nothing, nothing at all. It didn't mean a thing. It was like it wasn't really me. I was a physical wreck, a psychological mess. I was hurting. Really hurting. It wasn't pretty. It was a bad dream, like a…like a…" He couldn't come up with the right words, so he stopped. He shook his head, sadly, his eyes hurting.

The silence that took hold between them screamed. Neither knew exactly what to say or what to do.

Only time would tell.

Chapter 25

The water felt fantastic, the saltwater filling his pores, helping to soak away the aching in his body, massaging the redness of his thick neck, which still showed signs of redness. Shorty Rawlins, an athlete at heart, was an accomplished swimmer, a rather unusual feat for a Virgin Islander since, surprisingly, so few natives actually know how to swim, even though they live within eyeshot of the ocean, the Caribbean surrounding them in all directions.

The turquoise water, as clear as ever, was almost flat today, and the sun glistened off it like a moving shadow on a mirror. He took powerful strokes, swimming out quite a distance from shore, and then back towards the sandy beach. He was all by himself, having driven through the small rainforest, through Rasta country, past the patches of darkness under tall slumps of tress, past ramshackle homes with smoke coming out of their chimneys, though the day was sunny and hot, finally finding a clearing in the trees that afforded him his own secluded beach, the sand almost white. He toweled off at water's edge, his eyes on the horizon. What he saw, he did not like. His future lay somewhere out there, somewhere up ahead, and things had turned so sour, like vinegar, spoiling everything he had dreamed of since the very day he had entered the police academy. His mother, bless her soul, had raised him on the good book, and she had made sure that he had visited the Lord's house every Sunday, and punctually, at that. What would she have to say…if she knew?

The thought pierced him like a Carib arrow hitting its target as Christopher Columbus had foolishly attempted to land on St. Croix, worlds ago. What if his own mother could see him now? What if she were looking down from on high on his every move?

Oh, Mama…

And what about the old man? He still got around, but how would his frail body get around trying to comprehend what his only son had become? How could he even try to explain anything at all about it to his own father?

Shorty Rawlins was in turmoil, like an inexperienced swimmer caught in a riptide, his brain in overdrive, thinking, planning, hoping…praying.

But was it even possible for God to hear him, let alone to listen to him any longer? He shuddered at the thought.

Why he hadn't just disappeared from Madge Wilburn's house when he had had the chance, he couldn't say. What a mistake. He would have been completely in the clear.

Except for Berylson, the lush. The damned alcohol had eaten away most of his brain cells. The guy was now more of a liability than an asset. The guy could hardly think straight anymore. The booze had caused him to slip up one too many times, and now this. The guy had been there at Madge's house, drunk as usual, and he probably had been made to talk.

Was that why he himself had hung around like that—to try to get Berylson out and away before he started blabbering away? Don't take so much credit, he chided himself. That notion hadn't even come to mind at the time.

Talk about slip ups. Hell, he himself had been the big slip up this time, leaving Berylson in that condition, to be probed, and prodded, and who knew what else. Loose end, loose end, loose end. Just what Bennett preached to them to avoid at all costs.

Preached! What a laugh. Bennett was anything but a preacher, the lowdown—

Shorty Rawlins was suddenly too scared to complete the sentence. He tossed his towel aside, and, as he began to pull on his shirt, he thought of the deadly little thing who had whipped him so thoroughly. What had he been thinking, anyway? He had actually attacked her. But why? For what reason? Had he really intended to physically hurt her?

Another laugh! Ha! She had literally beaten the crap out of him—him! And it had probably taken no more than ten seconds or so to get him helplessly tied up like a pretzel.

What was happening to him? He fully realized, and regretted, the terrible decisions he had made, getting himself mixed up with Tom Bennett and all, but here he was now trying to beat up a petite little female, who, somehow, had turned the tables on him instead. Wasn't he one of the Virgin Islands' best, trained to uphold and defend?

Defend what? Hell, he couldn't even defend himself against a young woman he outweighed by probably eighty-five pounds or more.

Shorty Rawlins wanted to scream, but he was afraid that screaming might lead to crying. Just what he needed, on top of everything else.

"My God," he was thinking, "what have I done?"

Chapter 26

They had gotten to the King's Alley Café an hour before Rosie had to report to work, simply so she could have the thrill of having her colleagues wait on her for a change. Things had been strained between them for the past day and a half, but time has a magical way of eventually allowing people to mend things between them. Though Cuff's indiscretion was still there—big as life—it now had been relegated to the back burner, so that life could go on for both of them. There had been a lot of joking at lunch, and now it was about time for Rosie to get to work. Their table had been the center of attention for the past fifty-seven minutes, but now, with the real lunch crowd about to arrive, Rosie and Cuff were alone.

Rosie poked him on the arm. "I wonder how Shorty's feeling today?"

"Like hell, I hope."

"I tried my best."

"And he's probably gonna be gunning for you now, too. He's probably not too happy about a skinny girl beating him up like that."

"Skinny girl!" She gave him a harder poke on the arm.

"Just a figure of speech, Rosie."

She gave him the finger. "Just a finger of speech," she said.

Cuff reached out as if to poke her, but she made a fist and waved it in his face.

"Be careful with that," he said. " I'm not Shorty Rawlins, you know."

"You better remember that too. He's supposedly highly trained, and I kicked the shit out of him. With you, it would a piece of cake, and you know it. Right?"

She was as cute as could be, and he told her so.

"I'll bet you say that to them all."

Cuff was on the verge of saying, "You're on for twenty," but then he thought better of it and instead said, "There are no others. It's you and me, Rosie. Just you and me."

Rosie waved to her young boss and gave him the word she would be right there. She checked her watch. "See you at the Moonraker for drinks?"

"You're on. The Moonraker. Tenish?"

"I'll be there," said Rosie. She flashed him her huge grin for which she was so famous. She was feeling much better about things between them now.

Cuff hung around a few minutes, mulling over his possibilities. His options were plentiful, and yet what exactly could he do? But the *could* took back seat to the *would*. Somebody he tried to kill him, somebody had physically assaulted him, and the cops were still suspicious of him. Besides, the dead man, Daniel Steadley of all people, had paid him to do a job. Even though the duties he had been paid for could never be performed, Cuff was still in debt to his employer, though now deceased. That's the way things were, and always would be. At least for Cuff.

So what should he do, immediately? What course of action? Rosie had said that Shorty had been tailing him. That's how the whole crazy situation with her had come about. So why not turn the tables and become the tailer? Tailee?

Tailee. Legal talk? Which brought up one Samuel F. Berylson, consultant. Why not tail him? The guy was in the thick of whatever he was in the thick of. And he did not strike Cuff as the extra cautious type of guy. He seemed one to take chances. Maybe the drink would be his downfall. Besides, Shorty would be too difficult to tail, his being a cop and all.

Shorty? Cuff slowly looked around, trying not to be obvious about it. What if Shorty were out there right now? But the guy couldn't always be out there, could he? He had to work sometime. Or was tailing Cuff part of his work? And for that matter, did Shorty use others for the leg work? Could Shorty be out there, in person or in the person of others, just waiting, watching, snooping? It was possible. Anything was.

Cuff studied the small café, the streets, the faces, the expressions. But he couldn't spot a thing that indicated the presence of Shorty Rawlins or cohorts. He went through the process again, and several times more, first one way, then the other. Sometimes he covered his eye movements with gestures, such as scratching his forehead, or dropping a napkin and then bending to retrieve it. But again he came up with zero. Still he wasn't entirely convinced. Shorty could be out there, somewhere, waiting.

Waiting for what? Why was Shorty Rawlins so intent on getting back at him. Why? Getting back for what? What had he done to so antagonize the gung-ho cop? Shorty must have known that he hadn't killed Steadley. Or did the cop really think that he had murdered the guy?

What if? What if not? There were so many possibilities. One led to a host of others.

First things first, though. Somebody had to lead him somewhere, to something. So Cuff pushed away from the table.

Samuel F. would be his man.

But on his way out, and then down the street, Cuff kept his eyes peeled for any sign of Shorty Rawlins. He had no way of knowing that Shorty was not the problem. He saw no eyes on him, though the eyes were intently watching him, as always. And, as always, they were impossible to spot.

Chapter 27

Company Street, as usual, was a mess. It was St. Croix's answer to traffic congestion in a large city. The tiny road was the major east-west thoroughfare out of town. It was always hot, slow going, bumper to bumper. The street brought out the worst in people. Impatience had found a permanent home here.

But Cuff had learned long ago that life was different in the Caribbean, that simplification was the key to survival. A person had to realize that efficiency no longer existed, and that the only certainty was that nothing was really ever certain. Everything on the island had to be shipped in from somewhere, and when a person finally acknowledged exactly what that meant, then, and only then, could flexibility enter his mind, and he would no longer be bothered by things such as tardiness, unavailable items, and inefficient bureaucracy, the standards of the islands. If these things bothered you, then life here was not for you.

Whenever Cuff drove—snailed his way—through this area, he swore he would get the air conditioning fixed in his four-year-old rusty Honda. But with the prices the way they were down here, who could afford it? He tried leaning his head out of his side window whenever this car came to a halt, but the famous Caribbean trade winds had a way of never quite reaching Company Street.

Cuff hit the gas, hit the brake. Moved, stopped. Started forward, came to an abrupt halt. Waited. Moved. Stopped. Waited. Moved. It wasn't pleasant, but at least things, traffic-wise, got much better when one reached Times Square, which was only several blocks away. Coping was the name of the game. And Cuff did so once again, this time helped along by the clear view he had of the backside of Berylson's station wagon, about nine cars in front of his own.

The slight breeze that filtered down the street as he turned into Times Square brought some much needed relief to Cuff's soaked body. He slipped past the police cars illegally double and triple parked in front of the police headquarters building, and rocked to the sound of the calypso blaring out from the bar across the street, which appeared to be devoid of customers at the moment.

Cuff was now only five cars behind Berylson. The consultant was a slow driver. He played it safe. He drove the same way he probably made love. Smart really, in this day and age.

The consultant gave a hand signal—his blinker lights undoubtedly did not work, as was the case with a large percentage of automobiles here on St. Croix—and then turned to the right.

The drive to the St. C. Condos was spectacular, particularly just when entering the property. Each unit had a superb view of the Caribbean, with the town of Christiansted in the distance, across the bay. Berylson drove to the upper level. Cuff took the lower road. He parked beside the steps leading up to the swimming pool. He climbed the staircase, and suddenly froze. The consultant stood on the balcony of a unit two or three from the end. He was with a couple, a younger woman and an older man. All three looked out into the Caribbean, where the view from the balcony was priceless.

Cuff edged himself back down the stairs. That had been too close. Berylson had come within seconds of spotting him. Cuff returned to his car and drove back down the entrance to the condominium complex, turned right, in the opposite direction the consultant would have to turn, and parked near the gate leading into Judith's Fancy, where uniformed guards monitored all traffic into the exclusive residential area. He would have a clear view here of Berylson when the consultant retraced his way to the main road.

As Cuff had suspected, Berylson's station wagon appeared several minutes later. The consultant turned left, heading back to North Shore Road. He led Cuff back through town, about five miles away, and then clear to the east end of the island, where he stopped at Coakley Bay Condo, which afforded a wonderful view of Buck Island, a colorful reef that daily drew hordes of scuba divers to its turquoise waters and its living museum of coral just below the surface of the clear water. Cuff pulled into a spot near the outdoor restaurant and bar, where he could look down on Berylson's station wagon.

Cuff waited and waited but nothing happened. When he returned from using the men's room in the lobby, the consultant's car was no longer there. Cuff nearly laughed, but it was really no laughing matter. The call of nature had gotten the consultant off the hook, free and clear. Go figure.

\#

They sat overlooking the street, which was bustling with tourists who felt no pain. The Moonraker was on the second floor and, like many such establishments in the islands, which boasted of having the world's most perfect weather, it was open to the air. Ceiling fans were constantly at work, and, if that didn't help, you could always lean a bit over the balcony to catch the evening breeze, which is what Cuff was doing.

They ordered another round, settled back, and listened to the duo singing continental favorites, the songs from the mainland. The bar was small but lively, with nearly every chair occupied. It was like that on St. Croix.

"So what are you gonna do next?"

"Me? I thought it was us, dear Rosie. My, my, how soon they forget?" He finished off his bottle of Heineken. "But first things first, okay? So finish up, and I'll take you home."

"And then?"

"Put you to bed."

"And?"

"And what?"

"And what comes next?"

"Is that you speaking, Rosie? The same Rosie who's out to cook my goose?"

She stuck her tongue out at him and wiggled her nose. "Who do you think?"

"Yes, that's my Rosie."

"So?"

"So what?"

"So what happens next?"

"I told you."

"Not about after putting me to bed, you didn't."

Cuff picked up her glass. He sniffed at what she was drinking. "What is this, anyway?"

"What's wrong? Can't a girl wonder a bit?"

"Rosie, you *are* a wonder," said Cuff.

Somewhere off in the distance thunder could be heard, though the sky above them was still clear, twinkling with stars just happy to be alive high up in the night sky, far out of reach of human hands, safe and content to be at home where they were.

But the eyes were not happy. The face they belonged to frowned. Deeply. It was distressed. The drama they had so carefully created suddenly called for a bit of improvisation.

So the wheels began churning, the brain hard at work, while the eyes stayed focused on a pair of lovebirds sitting on the balcony of the Moonraker. Yes, it was time. The ante needed to be raised, and by a lot.

The eyes. The deadly eyes of St. Croix.

Chapter 28

"Shhh."

"Shhh yourself," said Rosie.

"You know," Rosie, "you really exasperate me at times, you know that? And your mouth sometimes only exacerbates the exasperation." You could tell that he took pride in the creative way he in which he had strung the words together, as if he had been waiting for just the right time to show off his ex-prof juices, though this really appeared to be the very worst of times to do so.

"Exacerbate this," Rosie said, as she stuck out her tongue, moving it wildly from side to side, like an insect caught in a crazy crosswind.

"But I must admit that I do love it," and Cuff was smiling at her.

"Shhh," said Rosie.

"How about we both shhh."

"Now you're talking." She goosed him.

Cuff squealed in surprise.

"Shhh," said Rosie.

They had parked the Honda on the lower level, just in front of the stairs leading up to the swimming pool. St. C. seemed to offer hope of their seeing or hearing something. Each unit had its private balcony overlooking the ocean, and since the view was so magnificent, the balcony got a lot of use. It was a relaxing place to be after a day of work or play. In addition, most units received a nice breeze from the water, so louvered windows and doors were often left open, not necessarily enough to be able to see into the unit, but enough to hear the voices coming from within the condo.

They crept now on their knees, keeping their heads from appearing above the balcony of each condo they passed. Cuff indicated with his hand which unit they sought, the one Samuel F. Berylson, consultant, had led him to earlier. He and Rosie got in close, lay flat, so that they could not be spotted from the units on the lower level. They had two points to their advantage: it was dark, and the ledge they lay on was considerably higher than the roof of the lower units, since St. C. was built on the edge of sloping terrain.

All was quiet for several long minutes, except for the constant sounds of the ocean, which at this time of night was hidden by darkness, except for the patches of water in the far distance, which shone at the foot of the lights of Christiansted. The musical rhythm of the breakers was a godsend in two senses: it calmed the nerves since there are very few things in the world as soothing as the sound of waves gently lapping upon the shore, and they provided some cover for any inadvertent noise they themselves might make.

"Cuff?"

"Shhh."

"You think there's really somebody in there?"

"Shhh."

They listened to the ocean for a time. The breeze felt good. It always did at St. C., which was known to get more than its fair share of the famous Caribbean trade winds.

Then Cuff felt it, a hand, nearing his crotch.

"Not now, for God's sake, Rosie. Are you crazy?"

"Shhh."

Cuff wiggled a bit in the grass. He got his crotch free of her hand. "Geez, Rosie, you've really got an awful sense of timing, you know that? Anybody ever tell you that?'

She reached for him again.

Cuff twisted but she held on. That's when he heard it. Suddenly his body sprang into full alert. "Shhh," he commanded Rosie, as he hugged the ground.

Rosie also lay still now, not moving a muscle. She had heard it too. Somebody was inside the condo.

The waves lapped up against the rocks just beneath St. C., but nothing else could be heard. All was still, and most was dark. Lights flickered from across the bay, and then suddenly they shone on the balcony in front of which Cuff and Rosie lay, only half successful in shielding themselves from view of anyone who might decide to walk to the railing and peer downward.

Soon there were voices.

"I said it's not quite time yet, and I mean it? You savvy?"

Silence.

"You savvy?"

"Yeah, if you say so."

"I say so."

"Okay, if that's the way it's going to be."

"That's the way it's going to be."

"Okay. Don't be so testy."

"Screw you!"

"You'd like that, wouldn't you?"

"In your dreams."

"Well, I'm not dreaming, am I?"

Rosie nearly gagged, but Cuff used his hands to keep her quiet. They waited for what seemed forever, but no more voices could be heard. Soon after the lights went out in the condo, there was a squealing of tires from the driveway out front, but there was no way for them to discern the car or the driver from their vantage point. Frustrated, they played tongue tag with one another before they slowly crept up towards the sliding glass door. They moved slowly, on their tiptoes as much as possible, making very little noise. The sand and then the grass muffled most of any sound they might make, but there were also fallen leaves to contend with, so each step was torturous. They were like ballerinas as they tiptoed in the dark, almost as one, their bodies gazelle like, but in slow motion. Every few steps they would stop in their tracks just to be sure that their presence had not been spotted or heard by a soul.

They pulled themselves onto the balcony. Rosie, with her unbelievable arm strength, her competitive spirit well and alive in situations such as this, got there first, and Cuff was not a bit surprised. Rosie's face told Cuff in no uncertain way that her gender had bested his, so there. Cuff tried to ignore the pride her face was exalting over his, so he looked away.

Both the balcony and the condo were dark. They crept towards the door, slowly, slowly, one small baby step at a time, their adrenalin on highest alert, their bodies flexed, ready to hightail it in short order if need be.

Then they were there. The salt air in the breeze smelled so refreshing and felt good on their skin, but neither could be enjoyed to their full potential. Not now. Their attention had to remain completely focused on the potentially dangerous task at hand.

Cuff tried the handle of the sliding glass door, pulling it ever so slowly. It moved, surprising them both. The door was unlocked.

But then he hesitated.

"Are we going in or not?" said Rosie, whispering in his ear.

"Or not," Cuff whispered back. "I don't like it. Look what happened last time we broke into someone's house. Remember Steadley? Remember the cops dragging me downtown? Remember the—"

"Yeah, yeah, I remember."

"Shhh," he said.

"Shhh, yourself," said Rosie.

Even after the slow trek to where they now stood, even though the door was unlocked, even though the condo was in complete darkness, it suddenly just didn't seem right. If anything happened to go wrong now, then there was no telling how deeply into hot water they could get. Cuff hated to do it, but he knew it was the best course of action. He tugged at Rosie's blouse, to indicate they should leave, and she tugged back at his shirt. Then his eyes met hers, and hers met his, and, after a short standoff, they both knew, silently, what they had to do. They were in full agreement as they slowly backtracked their way off the private property of who-knew-who, but of someone who definitely knew something or someone. The answers would have to wait a bit. There was always tomorrow.

Back at the rusty Honda, Cuff finally told her what he was thinking. "Look," he said, "we can't just hang out here all night like some kind of stakeout. So let's get our butts back here first thing in the morning. We can find ourselves a spot were we ourselves won't be spotted, and we can bide our time and see who comes and goes from the condo. We can even prepare ourselves by bringing along food and drink. What do you say about that, Rosie?"

"I think we gotta get our butts in the car instead of standing out here talking all night." And, just for emphasis, she goosed him again.

No it was Cuff's turn. "How about we spend the night together?"

"How about it?"

"Your place or mine?"

"Whose do you think?" And Rosie gave him her all-American smile.

Chapter 29

"I'll take a shower and slip into something a bit more comfortable," Rosie said. "You know what I mean?"

"I hope I do," said Cuff.

"Help yourself to a beer in the fridge while you're waiting," she tossed back over her shoulder.

"Will do." Cuff went to the fridge as Rosie closed the door to the bathroom and prepared for her shower. To his disappointment, all he found in her fridge was *a* beer, the lonely bottle of Beck's surrounded by an array of vegetables, every possible color finding a home in Rosie's refrigerator. That woman sure knew what was good for her.

He popped open the only bottle of beer in the apartment and returned to the living room, where he waited for Rosie's return. Her small Scotia apartment did not exude a good-to-be-at-home-at-last look. It had scant furnishings and hardly anything hanging on the walls. After all, it served mostly as just a place for the hardworking Rosie to lay her head at night. Cuff marveled at how she got through so much in one twenty-four-hour period. Her days were long, her minimum-wage pay just a notch or so above okay, thanks to the sometimes plentiful tips the tourists to the island gave, especially after encountering more than one of the island's potent drinks, where alcohol cost less than any mixer requested by vacationing mainlanders. She scraped by, and that's about it. Her small Scotia apartment was a testament to that fact.

Cuff played with his beer, the only one he would get that night, taking his time, sipping much more than usual, savoring each drop of hops as he swished every mouthful around his thirsty taste buds in order to get the full flavor with each swallow, taking his time to really enjoy.

Rosie finally opened the door from the bath. She was wrapped in a white towel.

"Nice," said Cuff. He finished off the last of his Beck's and set the empty bottle aside.

"Come and get it," Rosie said.

Cuff rose from the chair, and that's when Rosie swirled the towel from her body and snapped the end of it at Cuff, like adolescents are fond of doing in school shower rooms. She was wearing only a pair of red bikini panties.

Cuff tried to grab the end of the towel that came his way, but he missed, so Rosie struck him again. She was laughing. She was definitely in the mood.

"What are you going to do about it, big guy?"

He came closer, and she snapped the towel again. This time he was able to get a hand on the end of it, and a brief tug-of-war ensued, which ended with Rosie's suddenly letting go, causing Cuff to lose his footing. She raced through the room and hopped on the bed. She was on her knees now, facing him.

"Come and get yours," she said.

Cuff slid onto the bed. He slipped his shirt off. But before he could get to his shorts, Rosie needled him. "Let's see what you've got, big guy." She stood her ground, her knees on the mattress, her stance showing clearly what she had in mind.

Cuff was surprised. "You mean you want to tussle?"

Rosie flashed her teeth his way. "You scared, big guy?"

"No way."

"Then show me what you've got." Tease filled her eyes, but something else was there too, right beneath the tease, something that spoke in volumes though it could not be readily seen or heard.

Cuff sized up the situation. He clearly had her in size, by a long shot. He weighed a lot more than she, and he was taller by more than half a foot. He also had her in muscle size. Though she was femininely firm and workout hard, her musculature, though impressive for one her petite size, was no way the equal to his. But Rosie had the advantage in a number of ways. She was faster, more agile, much more flexible, and she had the heart and spirit that it took to never give in.

"You ready?"

"If you say so."

"I say so," said Rosie. "But the real question is, are *you* ready, to go down to defeat that is?" Gosh, she had pretty teeth.

"If you say so," said Cuff.

"I say so," she said.

They faced each other, and Cuff counted to three. His heavier frame forced hers to the bed, but she landed with an arm around his neck and her legs entwined around his as they fell back onto the mattress. They lay there for several seconds. Cuff's body was more on top than not, but she clearly had him clamped in such a way that he could not move.

"Say it," Rosie said, "and I'll let you go."

Cuff squirmed, but he could not break free.

"Say it," she said. But although she had the upper hand, they both knew that they were at a standstill. She might have him, and only after a few seconds, but there was no way he was about to admit it. He was in no pain, even though he was held tightly in place. It was clear to both of them that he was not enveloped in a submission hold.

"Well, here goes nothing," said Rosie, and she quickly kicked outward and upward, getting her legs around his neck. Making full use of her strong leg hold, she was able to force his body to turn until he was flat on his back. The only thing that saved him was the fact that his chin was turned downwards towards his chest, which kept her powerful legs from squeezing his windpipe into submission. Though he couldn't break free, he could hold on. It wasn't over yet. He was under her control at the moment, but he was not in dire straits.

"You had enough, big guy?"

"No way." He struggled, but they were once again at a standstill. He could not make a move on her, tied up as he was, so he would bide his time, patiently waiting for her to make a mistake.

Then suddenly Rosie let him go, but, quick as a flash, she was back on him, lying on his chest, one of his arms held firmly by both of hers, high above his head, and she got her ankles twisted around his, spreading her legs so that Cuff was now held securely in a painful grapevine.

"You're pinned," Rosie said. And Cuff knew he was. He struggled, but he was not going anywhere. She had him. He was clearly out by the count, but there was no referee, and he wasn't about to admit defeat.

Rosie held him there for half a minute or so. He could feel the pain, but he was able to bear it, though just barely. Just as he thought he could no longer take it, Rosie made her first mistake. She let him go.

But as he fought to sit up, Rosie flung herself sideways across his head and upper chest, forcing him back onto the mattress. She moved like lightning. Cuff kicked in the air, his two legs trying to buck her off of his chest, and Rosie, who had all the leverage she needed now and the wiry strength in which to back it up, got one leg around his, and her arm around his other leg and pulled as hard as she could in opposite directions, bringing an immediate sense of completely helplessness to Cuff, and excruciating pain.

Cuff knew it was over. He was in a classic banana split hold, his rear end a bit off the bed, his neck bent backwards, and his legs held uselessly in the air. He felt like a turkey wishbone at Thanksgiving. He was sure that she would break him in two. The pain was immense.

"Say it," Rosie said.

"I give!" Cuff said. "Let me go."

"Have I got you?"

"You know you have, Rosie. It's over."

"Say you submit, then."

"I submit then."

"Say it right."

"I submit."

"You mean it?"

"I mean it. Please let me go, Rosie. You're hurting me."

"You surrender?"

"I surrender," said Cuff. "You win. Okay?"

And that did the trick. Rosie let him go. As Cuff lay back rubbing the pain from his crotch, Rosie leaned over and kissed him on the cheek. "Well, whataya think?" she asked.

Cuff didn't quite know what to think or how to react. He kept his eyes on the ceiling, thinking, remembering, and trying hard to sort things out in his brain. He sighed, twice, and then he answered her question. "You've proved yourself, Rosie. You're the Alpha. Okay?"

"You think so!"

"I do," said Cuff.

She hugged him. "Good. I like that. I really do." Her smile was as pretty as the lights of Christiansted harbor at night.

Cuff felt as if he had just been run over by a snowplow. Every limb on his body hurt, and his neck ached. He had been put through the ringer, stretched to the limit, pulled in all directions. He eventually sat up. He stretched his sore legs and rubbed at his neck. "I can't believe what just happened."

"I can," said Rosie. "I licked you fair and square. Didn't I?"

Cuff looked over at her. She was the sexiest thing he had ever laid eyes on, as pretty as the daintiest flower, and she was his girl. How lucky could a man be?

But he had absolutely no idea how to respond. What *could* he say? He lay his head back on the pillow, his mind working overtime.

"Can you live with that?" she asked.

He thought about it for a couple of very productive minutes. He tossed the question around like a juggler at work, questions and implications bouncing around freestyle, covering every angle, until he eventually had things sorted out in his head to his own satisfaction. "Yeah, I can live with it," he finally said.

She curled up on his powerful chest, her head close to his. She stroked his hair, and then his cheek.

Their eyes met, and their souls touched. Their embrace was hard, yet soft, as gentle as a breezeless night.

"I just needed to know," said Rosie. She held her eyes steady, looking directly into his, strong, proud, and soft as can be.

"And I need you," Cuff replied. *More than ever*, he could easily have added. Love was the unspoken word that raced around the room like two cats at play, whooping and hollering from one room to the next, bouncing off the walls and right back at them, hitting each smack dab right where it counts.

And then their lips met, as their history together, as a couple, as one, progressed to an entirely new level.

Chapter 30

Shorty Rawlins was as quiet as a moose standing still, and the determination on his face was just as fierce. He stood silently in the closet, the door shut, waiting. He knew there was a good chance that Cuff and his girlfriend would enter the condo, and he had taken every precaution he could think of to not be found inside by them. Not after what he had just done. He figured that he had a good chance of getting away clean since his dirty work, in the next room, would surely drive them back out the door in a hurry. Just the sight of all the blood should be enough. But just to be totally certain that his name would not be connected to the crime, his weapon was ready for action. If one of them decided to open the closet door, then that would be the end of both of them, Cuff and the girl. It's not that he wanted to hurt them, but he knew there was no other way. His own freedom depended upon that. No way could his name be linked to the scene in the bathroom.

So Shorty Rawlins waited. He was all ears, but there was nothing to hear. He strained, but there was no inkling of any entry into the condo. He knew they were out there, but that's about all he knew. The vibration on his cell phone had alerted him to their presence. The eyes, those terribly deadly eyes of St. Croix, had sent him the text message. The two had been spotted near the balcony, so it was just a matter of time before they made their appearance.

One of the reasons Shorty had turned off the lights, turning the condo into complete darkness, was to provide them with the lead-time they would need to formulate their decision to investigate the premises further. Maybe after a short wait, they would think the condo vacated. Maybe they would think the occupants had gone to bed. Maybe they would wait for sleep to overcome anyone still in the condo, and then feel safe to creep inside to have a look. Maybe, maybe, maybe. The maybe was driving him bonkers. Shorty Rawlins was not the most patient of individuals, and this waiting, hiding in the closet like a scared rabbit, nearly brought his blood pressure to the boiling point. But what else could he do? He had been instructed to stay there until the coast was clear. Period. The eyes, the producer and the director of the drama, had demanded this on his part. So there it was. He was a like a trapped bunny rabbit. But at least he had his weapon in case worse came to worst.

Shorty Rawlins waited, and he waited. As he did so, he ran the events of the past half hour through his mind. As instructed, by the eyes from hell once again, he had gone to the condo for one purpose: to rid them of the weak link in their chain, the drunken fool Berylson, whose services were no longer needed. The drunken fool of a man had served his purpose, and now the guy was nothing but extra ballast, and a deadly one at that since his drunken stupors could lead to loose lips, which, in turn, would lead to big problems for all of them. Why take a chance? It just wasn't worth it.

Shorty Rawlins did not like the fix he was in, not one iota, but he had been told—told!—that Berylson must be put to rest and that Shorty himself was the one to do it. And that was that. No argument or disagreement allowed. Zilch. When the eyes spoke, the others listened, and when they commanded, the others carried out. Shorty, though a cop, had never killed a man before, and he hated both the idea and himself for having had to do so twenty minutes earlier, but there had been no alternative, no way out. The thing. Always the thing. It compelled, and it controlled.

Shorty Rawlins felt like curling up in the fetal position and crying his head off like a baby, but he also felt like fleeing the island paradise and going off somewhere halfway across the world to get as far away from what he had become as he could. But both ideas were ludicrous. There was no way he could stop himself from what he had become. Nothing or no one could help him. He was like a prisoner in a maximum-security cell, and yet he had lost all semblance of security the very second he had been enveloped by this terrible thing.

The eyes had made it clear. Take the gun with Cuff's handprints all over it, the one Steadley had handed him the day they had met at Cathy's Fancy. Shorty had worn white silk gloves, and he had been shown precisely how to handle the gun that would kill Berylson without as much as smudging the fingerprints of one James Cuffy, which would still be found all over the deadly weapon.

Shorty Rawlins had taken his time. He didn't want to make even the slightest mistake. He had gone way overboard in being as friendly and open to the heavily drinking Berylson as he could, not wanting the St. Croix grown lush to harbor even the slightest suspicion that anything was wrong.

The men had talked in friendly terms, argued a bit, in order to keep things real, shared jokes together, and laughed together. Everything had gone smoothly. Berylson had had no inkling that he was on his very last legs.

And the scene of the death could not have been more perfect.

Shorty Rawlins had taken his time. He had been as patient as can be, waiting for the most opportune time. And when it had come, he had struck fast. It was almost comical the way it had played out. Berylson, after who knew how many drinks, had had to pee. The inebriated consultant had just unzipped his fly and had begun peeing, when Shorty entered the bathroom, took aim, and pulled the trigger. Blood, urine, and the remnants of what used to be St. Croix's favorite lush lay all over the tiles of the bathroom floor. It was not a pretty sight, but it was closure at its best. Shorty Rawlins had carried out his duties as instructed. He knew the eyes would be glad. And for that—and *only* for that—Shorty Rawlins was grateful.

Suddenly his ears picked up something. They were on the balcony. They were good. He had to give them that much, but not good enough. He was a trained cop, and his ears picked up nuances not readily heard by the masses. He was like a statue as he waited there in the closet, his powerful body tensed for action, but nothing happened.

Shorty waited some more, but then he eventually realized that they were gone. When he finally stepped from the closet, crept through the deserted condo, peered outside to make sure the coast was clear, snuck back outside, and wandered down the road to where he had left his car, he felt good about himself, even though he felt absolutely terrible about what he had been forced to do.

But tomorrow would be another day.

Chapter 31

"What do you think?" They sat in Cuff's Honda, which was parked now at Sugar Beach, just down the road from St. C.

"I have no idea."

"You have no idea what you think? Is that what you're saying, Rosie?"

"So what do *you* think?" she said after gazing into the distance.

"Hard to say," said Cuff.

She eyed him, but finally turned from his profile. "Talking to you is like trying to eat an ice cream cone down here and not have it drip all over you. You know that?"

They sat in silence for half a minute or so. The ocean was barely perceptible from there. "Well," Cuff finally said, "you up for a walk? It might just do us both some good."

Giving herself sufficient time to think about it, Rosie finally said, "Why not?"

They walked hand in hand. The night sky was beautiful, and the weather picture perfect. Things could not have been more lovely, more perfect, the aroma of night blooming jasmine in the air, the faint strings of a love song off in the distance.

"Shit," Cuff said suddenly.

"Romantic," said Rosie.

Cuff glanced at her. "I couldn't help it, Rosie. It's just that sometimes I wonder if I'm on a wild goose chase after all."

"You took the words right out of my mouth."

The few scattered clouds scattered, and the moon became brighter.

"Absolutely gorgeous."

Rosie hugged him. "Thanks. I think I needed that."

Cuff, startled for a moment, finally got it. He grinned. "Sometimes you really surprise me, Rosie."

She returned his smile. "Sometimes I really surprise myself. And sometimes I really surprise everybody."

He turned to pinch her on the arm, but it was as if she could read his mind. She pulled away, her eyes frisky.

"I'm gonna get you, Rosie."

"Catch me if you can!" She kicked off her sandals, stooped and picked them up, and took off down the beach, her long legs pumping furiously.

Cuff kicked off his own sandals, left them where they landed, and went after her.

But Rosie was just too fast. He couldn't get her, let alone narrow the distance between them. If anything, by the time he stopped to rest, Rosie had managed to widen her lead. He plopped on the sand, in the dark, breathing heavily. He knew he was out of shape, but this was ridiculous.

"Too fast for ya?" She was grinning, and nearly breathing normally. She stood off to one side, about four feet from where he sat, her hands planted firmly on her hips, her sexy body challenging.

"My God, Rosie..." was all he could get out.

#

When they got back to where Cuff had kicked off his sandals, they were gone. He looked everywhere, even got down on all fours and dug around in the sand, but the sandals were no longer on the beach.

"Face it," said Rosie, at long last, "they're not here."

"Then where are they?"

"Not here, that's where."

"There's no way the ocean could have gotten them. They were clear up here."

"Then somebody picked them up."

"Who? There's nobody around."

"Not now, there's not," said Rosie, "but there was."

Cuff sat down on the sand. "I loved those sandals."

Rosie sat down beside him. She nudged her leg up against his. "I know you did, Cuff. You were always wearing them. But you have to admit that they were starting to show their age."

Cuff picked up a handful of sand and flung it towards water, where it fell way short of its mark. "What a day," he said.

"You got that right."

They held hands as they walked back around the building, to his car, where they found Shorty Rawlins, in his civvies, sitting on the hood.

"What do you think you're doing?" said Cuff.

The cop didn't lose a beat. "What do you think *you're* doing" He had to be tough. It couldn't be an act. Things had gone too far for that. His own life now depended on his carefully constructed new persona. Even though he was well aware that the eyes were on him, those deadly eyes, the eyes from hell, he figured a little bit of friendly banter wouldn't hurt. It could provide a little respite from the depression that was quickly drowning his body. A small diversion like this might just help his psyche, if even for just the shortest amount of time.

"Taking a stroll on the beach."

"Sure," said the cop. His facial expression was really pouring it on. Why not have a bit of fun at their expense?

"Get off my car."

"Sure, said the cop. But he didn't budge. If anything, he leaned back a bit more comfortably. For the first time in what seemed like forever, he was starting to enjoy himself. "By the way, you leave some sandals on the beach?"

"What'd you do with my sandals?"

"Nothing. I didn't do a thing. It's just that I found them. And I notice you're barefoot. The cop in me, you know." His smile sneered at them.

"Yeah, we know," said Rosie.

Shorty Rawlins jumped down from his seat on the hood of Cuff's Honda. "Have a nice life," he said, hoping he could pull the tough guy thing off flawlessly, knowing the ramifications if he failed to do so. Enough was enough. His little fun had been had. The talking was now over.

Cuff started after him. "Hey, where're my sandals?"

Shorty Rawlins turned around with what he called a grin on his face. "Oh, that's right, I forgot about that. Over here."

Cuff followed the cop to the swimming pool, where Shorty pulled a sandal from the garbage can.

Cuff grabbed it. "Where's the other one?"

"Only found one," said the cop.

"Where is it?"

"That's all I found. Just the one. The water must have carried off the other one."

"Where is it?"

"Can't hear very well, can he?" the cop said to Rosie.

"Where is it?"

"I told you, Bozo."

Bozo!

Cuff dropped the sandal. "What's that you called me?"

"Got sand in your ears? You heard me."

"What's that you called me?"

"Is he hard of hearing?" the cop asked Rosie, but she merely shrugged in reply.

"You called me Bozo."

"What of it?"

"That's the same word you used the night you and your friends jumped me on the beach."

"I don't know what you're talking about."

"I'm talking about you, Shorty. You know exactly what I'm talking about."

Now it was the cop's turn to shrug.

Cuff wasn't impressed. "I owe you one, a big one."

The cop shrugged again. "I have no idea what you're talking about."

Cuff grunted. He had had enough. He waved Shorty away. "Don't worry," he said, "you'll get yours."

"Is that a threat?" The pit bull was now back in his groove.

Cuff shrugged, but didn't take the bait.

"So what are you gonna do about it, Bozo?" It was working like a charm, as always. Lots of practice definitely did make for perfect.

Cuff clenched both his fists and tightened his jaw, his eyes narrowing in anger. "I'll think of something," he said.

The cop half laughed. "Yeah? Well, I wouldn't count on it."

Cuff took a step forward. "One of these days, Shorty, and I mean it, I'm going to see to it that it all comes back to you."

"I'm shaking." Shorty laughed again.

"Laugh if you want, but it's going to happen."

"What are you going to do, take a punch at me or something? I wouldn't advise it, Bozo. But learn the hard way, if that's what you want. It's no sweat off my body."

Rosie stepped forward. "If you call that thing a body. Junk heap is more like it."

Cuff nudged her and turned to go, but quickly swung back towards Shorty Rawlins. "If you're not careful, Shorty, one of these days I'm going to sic Rosie here on you again."

#

Back at the car, Rosie said, "You forgot your sandal."

Cuff was still hot. "The hell with the sandal."

"And thanks for nothing, about bringing me up like that to Shorty."

But before Cuff could come up with a good comeback to her last remark, the still St. Croix night was suddenly shaken by a single gunshot. Bang!

The eyes had seen enough. The pit bull of a cop, with a brain size to match, had been warned about talking, and then what's he do, he does it again. There was no telling what he would divulge. Talk was the last thing they needed. What was wrong with him? The guy just didn't get it.

But then the eyes chuckled because this time he *had* gotten it. Once and for all. For good. Besides, he had already served his purpose. What good was he now, alive? None whatsoever.

Shorty Rawlin's body was sprawled face up in the parking lot, lifeless. Blood poured from his forehead, where the gunshot had found its mark and also from the back of the stocky cop's head as it had crashed into the asphalt.

And then the stillness of the warm Caribbean night returned.

Chapter 32

They had no idea where the shot had come from or who had fired it, but they did know that the bulldog of a cop was as dead as was the death that had started this nightmare, the murder of one Daniel Steadley.

Without the need to think or talk, they both knew precisely what to do, the only option they had. They piled into Cuff's rusty Honda and hightailed it as fast as they could from the latest murder scene. After what had taken place after his fingerprints were found at Steadley's house, they could take no chances this time. They wouldn't even call the police. There really was no need to call them. The dead cop's body sprawled like that in the parking lot would easily be spotted soon by someone. Why take a chance being implicated in something in which they absolutely had had no hand in whatsoever?

Having driven for fifteen minutes or so, a considerable distance on such a small island as St. Croix, they pulled to a stop as near to the deserted water as they could. Cuff found a dirty rag in the trunk and two empty beer bottles.

Together, they scooped up water from the bathtub-warm Caribbean and rubbed out any evidence that might later show that Shorty Rawlins had sat on and had touched the car. The last thing they needed were fingerprints again at the scene of a murder. It took time, but then they were satisfied. They felt certain that there was no way that they themselves could be linked to the final moments of Shorty Rawlins' life.

Rosie was the first to speak. "What in the hell is going on here, anyway?"

"You tell me and then both of us will know."

"Do you think Madge Wilburn knows? I know she knows something, but do you think she knows enough to give us a clue as to what is happening?"

"I do indeed," said Cuff. "But do you think we can get her to talk?"

"I *know* we can," said Rosie. "After all, I made Shorty talk. Right? No way I can't get her to talk."

Cuff knew she was right. When Rosie wanted to get someone to talk, she could do it. There was no doubt in his mind about that. That fiery little woman had what it took. And if it took more than verbal persuasion, then that was no problem either.

"We better get to her before word gets back about Shorty not being around anymore."

"Then why are we standing around here talking like this?" She half shoved him towards the car, which now was devoid of any fingerprints other than their own.

#

"Do you know what time it is!" Madge had greeted them with when she opened her door after seventeen or eighteen very loud, persistent knocks. Her face was blotchy red, and her hair stood straight up in some places, straight down in others, and pointed sideways elsewhere, always straight out with an array of mismatched colors everywhere. She looked as if she had a multi-colored Mohawk that had just had a brawl with an octopus, getting the raw end of the deal, each strand having been pulled to its limit.

"It's time to talk, that's what time it is," said Rosie.

"Ugh," said Madge Wilburn. But her voice had been so low that maybe they had misheard her. It's possible she had voiced an "F" in front of the *ugh.*

"We mean it," said Rosie, and she meant it.

Madge tried to slam the door shut, but Rosie's muscular leg prevented this from happening.

"Why you—!"

But Rosie had shoved the door backwards with such force, that Madge Wilburn, hairdo and all, was sent backwards, against her will, and she had to fight to stay on her feet, finally having to grasp at a nearby table, where a loud crash was heard as a prized vase of hers, made of famed Murano glass, was sent splattering to its death on her brightly tiled floor, bits and pieces finding a home all over the entrance way to her sunken living room. Madge Wilburn, beside herself in anger at what had just taken place, her expensive vase now nothing more than garbage, began to scream, startling both Cuff and Rosie by the intensity of her pain.

The big woman staggered back one or two steps, her head held at an odd angle, her body bent backwards, and then, suddenly, in one big blur of a moment, Madge Wilburn fell face first onto her tiled floor, hitting it nose first. She hit so hard that the cracking noises that emanated from her body sent chills down Cuff's spine.

Then there was a deathly silence. All was still.

Cuff got to her first. "My God," he blurted out, "she's dead. She's been shot straight through the forehead."

"But how…?" Rosie mumbled. "But who…? But why…?"

Cuff wasn't taking any chances. He kicked the door closed behind them and hurried Rosie along as they flicked off the light, bringing immediate darkness to the deathly living room, banging their way to safety behind Madge Wilburn's oversized leather sofa, where they kept their heads down and breathed silently, their bodies as one as they clutched at the floor, hoping that whoever had shot Madge would quickly disappear.

Their lives, they knew, depended upon that hope.

Chapter 33

The body in the black ninja suit moved quietly through the yard, one short step at a time, not allowing even the tiniest sound to be heard. The deadly eyes, the only part of the body not covered in black, were almost super like in their ability to clearly discern people and objects in their night vision mode. The eyes were like two professional hit men. They were pros. They had had a lot of practice following, frightening, and stalking. With the powerful Swarovski Optik binoculars hanging securely now from a strap around the neck, and with the deadly military sharpshooter's best friend in hand, this ninja definitely controlled the night. This ninja was the alpha of all comers, an adversary not to be tested or bested. This ninja was a force to behold. This ninja had now added the first three of several other such notches to the string of deaths that would eventually become a quite a lengthy rope.

The eyes crept to the house and waited, listening, reconnoitering. When the time seemed right, the eyes peered through the far window. The room was very dark, but the eyes knew what it was seeing even though what it saw was hidden out of sight. The eyes knew that Cuff and his squirrelly girl were hidden in the house somewhere, most likely behind a piece of furniture, or in a closet, such obvious places to look. What a crock of stupidity to think that they were doing the outwitting. It was almost laughable, but there was nothing laughable about any of this. This was serious business, deadly serious business. The eyes of the ninja were little slits as they surveyed the front room of the home of one Madge Wilburn, recently deceased, one of the unwilling but very willing minor partners in this scheme.

Scheme! This was very far from being any such a thing. What a disgrace to even verbalize such a vulgar word. It was so degrading. No, this was something extraordinarily special. This was a true master at work, and the ninja was the one in charge. And the eyes of the ninja opened with pride at what it had already accomplished, and in such a short time. But just wait, they seemed to be saying. You ain't seen nothing yet! And they smiled at the thought, as only eyes can.

#

Cuff and Rosie hadn't moved, let alone made a sound, in over thirteen minutes. They heard nothing, and they saw nothing.

"You think the coast is clear by now?" Rosie finally whispered.

"Shhh," said Cuff.

"Shhh, yourself."

"Not this again."

"Shhh," said Rosie.

And then breakers, down below, swishing their way onto the St. Croix sand, sloshing their way against and above the rocky shore, were the music of the night. The mompies, better known as "no-see-ums," had retired for the night, and the stars had taken their place in the moonlit sky outside the window.

They returned to the waiting, which was terrible, especially knowing that Madge Wilburn lay dead not more than a few feet from where they hid. But where was the killer? And was he the same guy that had killed Shorty Rawlins? And what about Steadley? Was there a serial killer out there? If so, why had Shorty Rawlins and Madge Wilburn both been shot while Cuff and Rosie had been right there, well within spitting distance of each, practically touching both victims at the moment of their violent end? What was the connection? *Was* there a connection? There *had* to be. But what? And why?

Rosie suddenly sneezed, breaking the silence with a boom, like a firecracker at a funeral.

"Sorry," she whispered.

"Shhh."

She punched him on the arm, hard enough this time to probably leave a bruise.

"Ouch!"

"Shhh," she said. For several seconds only their thoughts could be heard. All else was eerily still.

They both heard the sirens in the distance at about the same time.

"Like or it or not, we better get the hell out of here, like right now," Cuff said, hoping that whoever had shot Madge Wilburn was not still out there just waiting for Rosie and him to appear.

Rosie moved first, and Cuff followed, slowly, slowly, creeping their way across the living room, around the dead, and then onto the front porch.

No way did they want to be anywhere around the place when the cops arrived.

Cuff was the first to notice the small red laser beam. It sat there big as life and death right in the middle of his chest. He moved, and it moved along with him. He shifted position, and the laser did too. He moved back, and then sideways, but the laser beam stayed right there in the middle of his chest.

"Oh, my God! I think somebody's out to kill you," Rosie said in alarm, her usually steady and controlled voice starting to crack.

Cuff was a bit more composed. "I think not he said." No trigger had been pulled. "I think somebody's playing with us."

Rosie's tone was still filled with fear. "But why? Who?"

Cuff tried to move out of the aim of the red laser beam, but it stuck to him like an aggressive virus. He hadn't a clue to either of Rosie's questions, and he had no idea what to say. So he remained silent, the red beam on him for several terribly long seconds. And then it disappeared into the St. Croix night, leaving ugly fear in its wake.

#

Lisa Smithers had a clear view of Cuff and his squirrelly girl as they crept from Madge Wilburn's house. With just two quick pulls on the trigger, they too, like the others, could be history. Lisa smiled at the thought. The others had all been helpful, in their own way, but each had been expendable. It wasn't any concern of hers if they hadn't realized that at the time. No, this was her operation, all hers, and hers alone. The others were like ballast on a ship: they were a godsend when needed, but when they became nothing more than added weight, they were tossed overboard. And that's exactly what had happened to Steadley, Berylson, Rawlins, and now Wilburn. They had all done their job, and now that they had, they had become expendable, obsolete, not much more than human garbage to her way of thinking. What good were any of them to anyone anymore?

Lisa Smithers, like the python she had become, was all-powerful. She was like a god, a god dressed like a ninja. She determined life or death. She was in complete control of whether Cuff lived or died. Fate had nothing to do with it.

No, that was not quite correct. Fate had *everything* to do with it. The very second, long ago, that Professor James Cuffy had snubbed her advances, fate had intervened. Cuff's outcome had been determined at that point in time. His death had been ordained. And the entire process would be so delicious. The taste of his demise melted in her mouth. She couldn't wait, and yet the journey was such wonderful entertainment that there was no great rush, because when the deed was done, then what? Wasn't anticipation of a trip a lot of the pleasure? And this was the ultimate trip, the journey of a lifetime, and just thinking about it sent delighted chills the length of her curvy body, tingling the very femininity that Professor Cuffy had chosen to scorn.

The rage she had felt at his rejection had been immediate, but the plan for revenge had come in bits and pieces over time. She had left school for a semester and had waited for the scandal to die before returning. On her first day back, the formulation of her cat and mouse plan took hold. It was right there before her eyes, along the wall of her biology class, the very motivation she had needed.

The huge python snake, in its enclosed glass cage, seemed to regale in the fact that its next delicious meal was right there for its taking, any time it chose. The small live rodent was paralyzed with fear, not able to do anything other than breathe. It sat there motionless day after day, knowing that its end was up the very second the python made that decision. The scene mesmerized Lisa Smithers. She always made sure she was one of the first to class, so she could choose her seat at the side of the classroom, nearest where the python held complete control over the terrified rodent. Sometimes Lisa would not even hear the words of the lecture that day since she was so engrossed by the power of the scene in the python's cage. Imagine, being able to instill complete fear in another, and maintaining it day after day, without let up, both the predator and the victim completely certain of the final outcome. It was the waiting that brought about the paralyzing stress, the waiting, knowing that not a single thing could be done to alter the awful yet delightful finality to come.

Lisa Smithers swore revenge then and there. She had been tinkering with the idea for months, but now it was a done deal. She would be the python and Professor James Cuffy would play the part of the rodent. She would, early on, prove her masterful control of his own fate, and then the lingering waiting, juicy for her but so agonizing for him, would eventually add up to the well-deserved denouement. It was such a simple plan, and yet its complexities were what made it so creatively masterful. She had watched the movie *Fatal Attraction* two times before she had first met Professor James Cuffy, but after he had dismissed her overtures, after the scandal and all had died a slow death around campus, she had watched the movie for the third time, and it was as if she were seeing it for the first time. This time around Lisa Smithers had really *seen* the movie. She hadn't missed one nuanced detail. She had learned a lot. She had been fascinated, her eyes glued to the screen, and, since she had recorded the movie on her DVR, she was able to play back parts of it over and over, and she often did, her mind and body completely absorbed by the evilness displayed by Michael Douglas, the way he scorned the woman who wanted him. Glenn Close was definitely a great teacher. And Lisa was her best student. She even learned from the Hollywood star's mistakes, a great education in itself.

Lisa Smithers had fallen in lust with Professor James Cuffy the very second he had entered the classroom on her first day of college. His body, and the way he felt so comfortable in it, and the way he moved it, so gracefully and yet forcefully, had brought her loins to a tingling sensation as she sat there watching this gorgeous hunk of a man take roll. She simply could not get over the initial effect his appearance had had on her.

And his voice! Oh, how she loved the way he could put words together. Even the very sound of his voice could put her into a state of ecstasy. So her young mind began working overtime in order to come up with the perfectly appropriate reasons why she so often needed to seek him out in privacy during his required office hours. She needed help with this, and she needed help with that, but what she really needed was to be in his presence, to watch his manly lips as he spoke, to fanaticize about their lovemaking as she sat there so near to him, listening to the answers to her well-prepared questions.

She just could not get him out of her mind. Nobody in her life had attracted her so, not even close. Professor James Cuffy was a like a sexual magnet, and he pulled her with a force that she could not resist. And she just knew that he also found her to be attractive. She still remembered the time she had practiced her signature act at home before performing it on stage for him in his office. She had chosen the perfectly loose blouse, low cut to tempt him with some cleavage, and it had worked. She had noticed him glance once or twice at her cleavage when he thought she wasn't looking. But she knew. Lisa Smithers knew. Hell, yes she knew.

And then the big move. She had practiced this to perfection beforehand in front of her floor length mirror in her bedroom. She had accidentally dropped her textbook on the floor right there between where they sat. When she had slowly bent down to retrieve it, he had been afforded the perfect opportunity to see what Lisa knew was her best body feature. To top it off, she had purposefully worn no bra that day. She knew he had had an eyeful, and she took her time sitting back up. When she did, Lisa Smithers' eyes looked into those of her professor, and they told him exactly what she was thinking, precisely what her thoughts and motives were. There could be no doubt about that whatsoever. Her eyes did that to people. They spoke. And when they spoke, people listened. She had such power in those eyes.

But then came the day when calamity had struck, a day that would forever live in Lisa Smithers' unforgiving mind. She had asked Professor Cuffy a rather complex question, one that had taken quite a bit of mind thought on her part the night before. As he started in with his lengthy answer, Lisa had sat back. She was wearing a dress that day, and, much unlike how her mother had taught her to sit when she was a young girl, Lisa had smiled sweetly at her professor as she showed him in no uncertain way that she had drop-dead gorgeous legs, sexy as all get out. She even looked away from him several times, feigning a cough here, a small twist in her neck there, a seeming interest in something in his crowded bookcase—affording him the time he needed to see just how beautiful, sexy, and willing she was.

When it came time to take her leave, they had both stood. Lisa Smithers had sent her powerful eyes deeply into his, she had smiled in the sexiest way she knew, and then she had reached down to rub him right where there could be absolutely no misunderstanding of what it was she was offering him, of what it was she wanted from him since she knew he wanted the very same from her.

But to her shock, Professor James Cuffy, the love of her life, the very center of everything as a young woman she would ever want or need, had pushed her away. He had actually gotten angry with her. He had ordered her out of his office.

That's when she lost it. That is what had brought about her tearing at her own blouse and screaming bloody murder at the top of her lungs. And now, as she thought back on it, reminiscing about the good old days, her eyes narrowed a bit as the memories brought such pain to her. Then suddenly, the pain was replaced. Yes, Mr. Cuffy, you definitely did the wrong thing to the wrong woman. And now it was payback time. After all, the python was getting very hungry.

Chapter 34

"I'm positive I'm being played with," Cuff said.

Rosie looked up. "Don't' you mean *we*?"

"I'm not sure. But the laser beam was focused on me."

"But I was at your side."

"True," said Cuff. He was quite restless. He was pacing his room at the Pink Fancy. It was late morning. The sun, as usual, was shining brightly outside, the little island all aglow in its colorful magnificence, but here inside it was a dark. Cuff had closed all the blinds. Why? He couldn't rightly say. It was just a feeling. Someone had obviously been watching him…them…at Madge Wilburn's place. The red beam of light that had practically followed him all the way back to his rusty Honda was proof of that.

"You know what?" he suddenly said. He stopped his pacing and whirled around to face her. "I think somebody is trying to set me up?"

Rosie's face did show the concern that suddenly had slapped its way onto it. "What do you mean?"

"What I mean is that somebody wants the police to think I killed Daniel Steadley."

"They let you go, though, remember? You explained about the fingerprints."

"But what about the knife?"

"What about it?"

"Well," said Cuff, "I'm starting to think that Steadley was killed with one of my steak knives. Both are missing."

Rosie nearly fell off her seating position on the edge of the flimsy sofa. "What are you talking about, anyway?"

"What I'm talking about," said Cuff, "is that my steak knife set is missing."

"So?"

"It's not here in my room anywhere."

"What are you trying to tell me?"

"What I'm trying to tell you, Rosie, is that the steak knife we saw sticking out of the Steadley guy's chest looked a helluva lot like the ones I'm missing. In fact, it's identical."

"Oh, my God," said Rosie. "What do you think it means?"

"What I think it means, Rosie, is that someone, somehow, came into my room here, stole my steak knife set, and then murdered Steadley with one of my knives. That's what I'm thinking."

"But why would somebody do that, especially to you?"

"Exactly what I was wondering, Rosie."

Somebody outside, probably across the street, yelled something to someone else further away, breaking the silence that had come between them. But at least it had done some good. Cuff had had time to sort things out a bit better.

"You know," he said, "I'd *bet* that somebody is trying to plant Steadley's murder on me. But what I don't get is the who and the why."

"And what about Shorty Rawlins and Madge?" Rosie blurted out. "We were both there when they too were murdered. What do you think is going on, anyway, Cuff. I'm not a bit ashamed to admit that I'm beginning to get scared. Really scared."

"Me too," said Cuff. He went to the window and separated the blinds and looked out, but what he saw made him freeze. But only for a short time. He quickly let the blinds fall back into place, and turned to Rosie. "You're not going to believe this, but guess who's right outside."

With panic scrawled across her forehead, Rosie asked, "Who?"

"The FBI," said Cuff. "The FBI is watching me."

"Why do you say that, Cuff. You're scaring me, you know."

"I know, Rosie, but have yourself a look see."

She did. "I see the man in the suit across the street. So how do you know he's FBI, and how do you know he's watching you?"

Cuff thought about it for a few seconds. "Rosie, an FBI agent can be spotted a mile away. They don't fool anybody. Why they all dress, look, and act the same way, I have no idea. Not very smart in my book. And they always drive a car that even the most unobservant of people can easily spot. Did you see his car, Rosie?"

"I saw it," she said. For once, she knew, rather than thought, that Cuff was spot on, and this only served to bring about greater alarm. "I'm really scared now, Cuff."

"But what I don't get," he finally said, "is who trained the laser beam on me. And who killed Shorty and Madge."

"And don't forget Steadley," said Rosie.

"No way I'll ever forget *him*. He started the whole thing in the first place."

"My God," Rosie said, "three dead people and a laser beam trained on us."

"On me," Cuff corrected her.

Rosie would have none of that. "On us," she insisted. "Remember, we're a team. Right?"

"Right." A fly buzzed his nose, and Cuff, quick as ever, captured it in his hand. He got up and went to the front door, opening it and then allowing the fly to soar off into the darkened night. Then he shut the door, and sat back down beside Rosie.

"You're a good man, Cuff. Maybe even too good for your own good."

"What's that supposed to mean?"

"I'm not sure," she said.

"A left-handed compliment, huh?"

Rosie rose to the occasion, as only she could. "More like a left-handed whack to the side of your head if you don't watch your lip, buddy boy." Then she flashed her pearl white teeth his way.

Cuff put his arm around her, and they hugged each other tightly. He kissed her on her neck, just the way she loved it, making sure to take his time.

Rosie spoke up first. "Why not just turn yourself in. You haven't done anything wrong."

Cuff shook his head. "I know I haven't done anything wrong, and you know I haven't done anything wrong, but what do they know? Hell, Steadley's murder is a big thing. The man had powerful connections. And then these other murders to go along with his. And now the FBI is here. And their eyes are on me, of all people."

"I don't get it."

"Just look at it their way of thinking, Rosie. They'll soon know that the steak knife that killed Steadley is mine. The cops, the day they brought me in, told me that they had sent it off to Miami to be checked there. They'll have fingerprints, all the fingerprints they need. And they know that Shorty Rawlins and I didn't get along, to put it mildly. And they also know that I was in touch with Madge Wilburn. I probably left fingerprints all over her place, too. Hell, this is the FBI now, for God's sake, not the Keystone Cops who police this island. The FBI doesn't get involved unless it's really big. And this is big, Rosie. Three murders."

"You think they suspect you of being a serial killer?"

"I wouldn't doubt it," Cuff said. He started to laugh, although there was absolutely nothing laughable about the situation.

"I really hope you're not losing it."

"Losing it?" said Cuff. "Don't you see, Rosie. The FBI thinks I've done something I haven't, and then there's the matter of somebody taking shots at me and then aiming laser beams at me. It's like I'm a target from both ends."

Rosie, the fighter, the strong one who could hold her head up high despite her short stature, the unbendable dependable one, suddenly burst into tears, something that completely caught Cuff off guard. He was so startled, that it took him a few seconds to realize that the red laser beam was showing up big as ever once again right in the middle of his chest. And this with an FBI man nearby.

"Oh, Rosie!" he cried, and he found himself nearly bawling his own head off.

"What is it, Cuff?"

"We didn't get the blinds shut all the way. Look at this."

Rosie's eyes ballooned up as though they had been filled with helium. "My God," she said, following the red dot on Cuff's chest until they got the blinds closed properly, shutting out the outside world.

#

"I've got a plan," Cuff said. They were sitting together on the sofa, and their eyes were now dry. It was time for serious thinking. "You got your cell phone with you?" She had. "Good. Then here it is. I'm going to go out the back way, through the bathroom window. Since there's no back door, I doubt that anybody will be looking for me there. But just in case, you keep your eyes on the FBI man across the street. In fact, keep your eyes on any movement at all from anybody after I get outside. I'll take the roundabout way, but I've got to get to the lawyer, Bennett. He'll know something. I'll make him talk or else."

"Or else what, Cuff? You going to kill him?"

Cuff started to laugh, but stopped on a dime. "That's not a bit funny, Rosie, and you know it."

She pouted. "I know it. I'm sorry."

"You with me then?"

"Always, Cuff. And that's a promise. But how are you going to find Bennett?"

"I'll find him. I know where he likes to hang out for lunch."

"Be careful. Okay?"

"Don't worry about me," said Cuff. "You just keep your eyes peeled and call me if you see anything, anything at all. You got it?"

"I got it," Rosie said. Then she looked into Cuff's face, love painted all over hers. "And him," she added, her lips waiting.

Cuff kissed her passionately before he vacated the Pink Fancy. He did not speak French, but that's the way he kissed, as did Rosie.

#

The waiting time for Bennett, the lawyer, to show was only one and half bottles of beer. Cuff grabbed the half empty second bottle of Beck's and hurried to where Bennett was about to be seated.

"Not there," Cuff commanded, the tone of his voice surprising them both. "We've got to talk."

Bennett sat.

"Not there, I said," said Cuff.

The lawyer looked agitated. "Just who in the hell do think you are telling me what to do?"

Cuff didn't miss a beat. "I'm the guy who's going to talk to you over there in that corner table where it's more private, the one by the sidewalk." He indicated the place with a nod of his head.

"Why you—!"

"Why not me?"

"What's that?" Bennett looked startled.

"Over there," said Cuff. "Now."

"Look, I'm gonna call the cops if you don't get the hell out of my face. You hear?"

Cuff moved in closer, his face nose to nose now with the lawyer, whose own was nearly twice as big as Cuff's and redder by one hundred shades. "What are you going to tell them? That your partners are all being killed off like flies?"

Bennett's face, surprisingly, showed little emotion. Was he a poker player? "Okay," he finally said, "have it your way." He got up and followed Cuff to the chosen table.

"What's this all about, anyway?" Bennett asked.

"The usual?" the lovely waitress with the arm wrestling championship arms asked. Her veins popped out on her muscular forearms, but she was nearly as skinny as the railing they sat beside. Weird. Such powerful arms on such a thin body.

"Yeah," that'll be fine, and an iced tea, please."

"And you, sir?" She waited, but, getting no response, she had to ask again.

Finally Cuff realized that she had been talking to him. It had been a long time since anyone had addressed him as *sir*. "A Beck's, please. And on *his* tab."

Bennett nodded in the affirmative, and the young waitress with the extraordinary arms went off to turn in their order.

"We're talking death," Cuff finally said.

"You're talking," said Bennett.

"Yeah, but I'm talking about you."

The lawyer's eyes narrowed. Maybe he wasn't that great of a poker player after all. "Are you threatening me, young man?"

Cuff smiled. He couldn't help himself. Maybe the *young man* had done it. He really couldn't say. "No way. I'm talking about Daniel Steadley, Shorty Rawlins, and Madge Wilburn."

"Who?"

"Don't try to play me," Cuff said. "Your gang, or whatever it is."

Bennett started to laugh, but stopped abruptly. "Are you crazy?"

"Definitely not." Cuff watched a small sugarbird chase another small sugarbird from the stash of sugar packets on the table across from where they sat, against the railing. The little birds loved nothing more than to peck away at the packets of sugar that tourists, in turn, liked to put into their coffee or tea. Whoever came up with the phrase, "She eats like a bird," to describe a picky eater, sure didn't know what he was talking about because these little guys had sugar on the brain; hence, their name.

Cuff watched as the pecking commenced on another packet. The little bird seemed ravenous, though his protruding belly showed that he was well fed. Finally turning his eyes away from the empty table across from them, Cuff focused his attention back on the lawyer, whom he looked directly in the eyes as he asked his question. "Why are all your friends suddenly dead, anyway?"

"People die," said Bennett.

"Not like that," said Cuff. "Aren't you just a little bit scared yourself?"

Bennett sighed. "Why should I be? Scared of what?"

"Murder," said Cuff. "Your gang, or whatever it is, is falling one at a time."

"What gang?" For the first time, Cuff noticed that the lawyer's hands had begun shaking. Was the guy's nonchalant attitude merely a cover for the fear he must be feeling?

"Look," said Cuff, "I know that all of you are connected somehow. I just don't know the how or the why. But believe me, I'm gonna find the answers, Mr. Lawyer."

Bennett did have a nice smile. "It's a small island. I know people, and people know me."

"Yeah, but it seems the people you associate with are getting themselves killed. First Steadley, then Shorty, and now Madge."

Bennett looked up from his lap, where his hands were readying a couple of napkins for the upcoming battle with his cheeseburger. "You left out Berylson."

"What about him?" Surprise had taken over Cuff's chiseled features.

Bennett leaned back. He placed a third napkin in his shirt color. "You haven't heard yet?"

Cuff was on full alert. "Heard what?"

"He's gone too," the lawyer said.

"Gone where?"

That's when the thick juicy cheeseburger with a heap of fries arrived.

"Gone where?" Cuff asked, after the waitress had left their table.

"Probably to hell, for all I know. I doubt he was a very good candidate for the other
direction, if you know what I mean."

Cuff couldn't believe his ears. "Do you mean to say that Berylson's dead too?"

Bennett picked up his cheeseburger. He had to use both hands, and the fact that they were still shaking a bit didn't help matters any. "I mean to say," he said. He took his first bite, and already the thing began dripping down his front. The guy was fortunate to have placed a napkin there this time around. He chewed and swallowed. Then he wiped at his chin with one of the two napkins resting in his lap. "Dead as dead can be," he said, and he didn't seem a bit bothered by the fact.

Cuff sat there in total shock. He had so much to say, so much to ask, but he couldn't form the words. He watched in horror as mustard and mayonnaise and ketchup and relish all found a new home somewhere on Bennett's shirt. When he had had enough, he stood up. "I'll be right back," he said. He walked across the open-air restaurant to the bar, where he asked for a cloth napkin for Bennett. Paper napkins just didn't get along with the guy. He waited for the bartender to return with the cloth napkin, thanked him, and walked back across the still nearly empty restaurant.

He couldn't believe what he was seeing as he got closer. Somehow the lawyer had managed to get ketchup all over the side of his face and his shirt. How the lawyer managed to do that, Cuff had no idea. The guy ate like a blender without a top. Food seemed to get all over him, even despite his elaborate preparations beforehand. Napkins were no defense in the hands of this eater, who reminded Cuff of his one-and-half-year-old nephew a couple of years ago who seemed to get food everywhere except where it belonged: in his mouth.

All of a sudden a lady passing by on the sidewalk began to scream hysterically. Several other people ran up to join her.

And suddenly Cuff knew exactly what was what. There was no ketchup. Bennett was covered in his own blood. The knife, protruding from the side of the ex-lawyer's neck, had undoubtedly been thrust into his now lifeless body by someone passing by on the sidewalk.

Nobody, of course, had seen a thing. But Cuff's eyes bulged up like a pair of bowling balls. He could not believe what they were seeing. There was no doubt at all in his mind's eye. He felt like screaming himself.

That is because he recognized the steak knife immediately.

Chapter 35

"Captain Jeremy O'Brien," the police officer said. He had a grandfatherly face, West Indian to the core, black and proud.

Cuff couldn't resist. "Black Irish, huh?"

O'Brien wasn't a bit rattled. "You should see me on St. Patrick's Day. Biggest day of the year here on the island." And it was. The intermingling of Irish supervisors and African sugar cane workers had resulted in many Irish surnamed families on all three of the American Virgin Islands. Yes, Caribbean history lived in the captain's name.

"I've had the experience," Cuff said. "This year." And it had been remarkable. The town of Christiansted, a West Indian gem in the middle of the Caribbean, where over 75% of the population was of African descent, was Irish through and through every St. Patrick's Day. The town became one huge green mass, everyone dressed in green, green tarps and banners hanging everywhere. Cuff had marveled at the beer stands throughout town offering free beer for the day, but only in bottles that were green, Beck's and Heineken. To top it off, a dozen restaurants scattered around town offered free corned beef and cabbage all day long.

It might be the Caribbean, but on St. Patrick's Day, St. Croix outdid Galway, Killarney, and even Dublin in its Irish fervor, no matter that slavery had played such a big part in its own history.

"I just don't believe in coincidences," Captain O'Brien said, who was trying with everything he had to keep his cool, which was excruciatingly difficult given the circumstances for he sat right across from not only a probable serial killer, but also a cop killer. Shorty Rawlins was one of theirs. And the guy had also murdered Daniel F. Steadley, a man whose picture stared back from the first page of practically every newspaper everywhere. Not an hour went by that Daniel F. Steadley's murder wasn't mentioned on news channels throughout the world. Their killers would be found and dealt with in due time. You can bet your marbles on that, Mr. Cuffy, he was thinking, fighting with all his might to keep things in check for the moment.

Cuff had waited at Bennett's murder scene because he had had no other alternative: he had been seen at the scene. Leaving it would only add to the suspicions the cops already had. Not a good idea. He sat in a small office, in front of a crowded desk, behind which sat Captain O'Brien. In the corner stood a lone figure, a man of average height in a dark suit. His presence had not been mentioned by O'Brien, so Cuff just took it in stride.

"Well, this you *can* believe," said Cuff. "I was merely an innocent bystander. My back was turned when the guy was killed. I was getting him a cloth napkin at the bar."

"And why were you doing that, Mr. Cuffy?" the captain's intonation hinting very clearly that Cuff could very well have been the one who had stabbed the lawyer to death.

"Cuff. Because the guy is...was...the world's sloppiest eater."

"And what about all the bits and pieces of evidence we keep picking up, including fingerprints, that all point right at you know who? How do you explain that?"

Cuff stared back. He had covered this ground already so many times.

"Don't you think it's just a bit suspicious?" Captain O'Brien's Irish was beginning to rise. "What about it?"

"What about the slithering snake up your ass that's keeping you from seeing straight, the one that's driving you to all the wrong conclusions?"

Captain O'Brien prided himself on his even temper. His colleagues admired how he never lost his cool. He was the perfect person to have around in a panic situation. He was known for being level headed, for never allowing emotion to cloud his judgment. If anyone could be termed a calming presence in a scene of utter confusion, where others said and did what they might later regret, it was Captain O'Brien. He was like a sea of tranquility in the midst of a hurricane. His calm, rational demeanor could always be relied upon. But this time his buttons had been pushed much too far. "We've got lots of clues," he said to Cuff, annoyance and even bitterness clearly evident in his voice "and you know who they all point to?"

"I know you're just dying to spit it out."

Captain O'Brien was not about to lose a staring contest, especially with someone who had started his blood pressure to boiling. "Take a good look in the mirror. That's who."

Cuff waited, but he couldn't wait forever, so he broke the lingering silence that had crawled itself up the wall. "You say you don't believe in coincidences, is that right?"

"You got it," Captain O'Brien said.

"Then what about the helicopters?"

"What helicopters?"

Sal Garza's voice was much deeper in tone than his wiry body would suggest. "That's enough, Jeremy." He moved out of the corner in which he had been standing quietly.

"FBI, right?" said Cuff.

Garza's eyes flickered with surprise.

Cuff continued. "And you think that I'm a serial killer, right?"

"The FBI doesn't get paid to think," said Garza.

Cuff nearly laughed. "That sure is reassuring to hear."

Garza, a bit flustered, cleared his throat. "The FBI gets paid to prove. And proof is what we'll get. We always get our man."

"You deal in just the facts, right?"

Garza seemed to smirk at Cuff. "Like they say, just the facts."

"Then the fact is," said Cuff, "that you are all barking up the wrong tree."

Garza turned to O'Brien. "Anybody hear any barking?"

No one did.

Just then a dog, a big one, a Rottweiler by the sound of it, began barking somewhere outside the window.

Cuff couldn't help it. He laughed out loud.

Captain O'Brien, the patient type, waited for the laughter to die. Then he said to Cuff, "I wouldn't laugh about it, if I were you."

"Oh no?"

Sal Garza, the FBI man, broke in. "That's enough." Something in his voice showed that it *was* enough.

But the Rottweiler, somewhere on the St. Croix street outside, obviously did not agree.

\#

Mr. James Cuffy had left the office several minutes before. Everything they could get from him, which was really next to nothing, had been painfully extracted, leading up to not much more than they had on him before he had accompanied them back to the police station, this time voluntarily.

Sal Garza, based in San Juan, Puerto Rico, only forty minutes away by seaplane, but a world away in size and prominence, had been carefully selected to head the task force assigned to this possible serial killing case in St. Croix. He was quite familiar with the little island. His grandmother, like so many other Puerto Ricans, had moved to the island in her youth, and she had died here. She was buried, however, back in San Juan. Although the vast majority of residents of St. Croix were West Indian, nearly 19% were native Puerto Ricans, so Spanish could be heard on the island and the dishes Sal Garza loved, the spicy food with which he and his eight siblings had been raised, could be found scattered around the little island. There were pockets of Puerto Ricans and their culture all around St. Croix. So homesick, he would not be here on the small island. He had some roots planted here, and in places the lovely island looked a lot like home, just on a much smaller scale.

St. Croix was a bit like one of its most popular dishes, kallaloo, a seasoned mixture of meat, crab, and fish boiled with kallaloo greens and okra, a little bit of this and a little bit of that, all stirred together as one. And Sal Garza fit the bill perfectly.

He had been handpicked for the job because one of the very few in the know knew him well, knew that he was absolutely the right man for the job. Sal Garza had big ambitions, and good connections, and he was completely trustworthy. He had a well-earned reputation as a man who always did whatever it took to get his man. His no-nonsense approach to getting done what needed doing had earned him many an accolade. His record of success was absolutely second to none. Sal Garza would be the right guy at the right time and place to faithfully ensure that the local authorities did their job, and expeditiously so, pure and simple, the complexities of the real world notwithstanding.

Sal Garza had been sent to St. Croix to help ascertain what was going on with all these murders on the island, including the unforgivable murder of a fellow law enforcement officer and the murder of one of the nation's most powerful and influential men. The conclusion he had reached, and he had done so quickly, was that, yes, there is a serial killer out there. He was also pretty certain that he knew who that serial killer was. He had been provided bits and pieces, like a dog thrown a bone, just to whet his appetite, and it had worked. He was famished, hungry to get to the bottom of the case and close it shut. What ate at him, though, was that he could come up with no motive. What possible reason could the guy have for killing these people? How were the deaths all connected? It was too early to tell, but tell they would. The dead don't lie. The truth can be found in their remains. It just took time.

"You think he's our man?" Captain O'Brien asked.

"My nose and my gut both say yes." Agent Garza watched a spider crawl its way up the wall. "Miami will let us know for sure. They've got the knife, the gun, and the sandal. And they've got plenty of fingerprints from all the crime scenes. And they know it's marked urgent. The Steadley murder is headlines all around the world."

"And don't forget the knife that's on the way."

"The Bennett murder? No, I haven't forgotten that either."

"I think it's a done deal," Captain O'Brien said.

Agent Sal Garza thought so too, but, being the FBI professional that he was, waiting for the reports from Miami, he chose not to verbalize those feelings just yet. "Just don't let him out of your sight until the definitive proof we need gets back to us from Miami."

"No worries there," said Captain O'Brien, hoping against hope that they had seen the last of the guy's killings.

Chapter 36

Daniel F. Steadley's funeral was a worldwide event, televised throughout the world. It happened quickly, just days after his death. The story ran rampant on all social media. Facebook, Twitter, LinkedIn—everybody was talking about the murder. His untimely death had shocked the world. Here was a guy with no enemies, and being as powerful and influential and wealthy as he was, that was almost a miracle to behold. He was known as Mr. Philanthropy. His money had literally been spread around the world. His name was synonymous with caring. He had funded so many humanitarian projects in Africa that doctors and scientists would need a calculator to keep count. His money had helped build dams and bridges in Asia, to help combat flooding, and it had helped feed millions throughout Eastern Europe, the Middle East, South America, and both Asia and Africa. His reach knew no end. If someone in needed help, then Daniel F. Steadley had been the man to turn to, the good-hearted man whose wealth provided aid and comfort to every part of the world.

On the mainland, Daniel F. Steadley was like a god. His name evoked only good. His commitment to help stave off starvation in the world was unparalleled. He was beloved by all political parties, from the most extreme on one side to the most extreme on the other. To the delight of Republicans, he made it clear that his money would not support any type of stem cell research, and he was adored by Democrats for his staunch stance on not offering a dime to any type of military weaponry. In the eyes of practically everyone, from the northernmost settlements of Alaska to the depths of Antarctica, the name Daniel F. Steadley was the good Samaritan incarnate. So many people depended upon him, and now he was gone.

Readers could not fathom why anybody would ever want to do to this great man what somebody obviously had done. It made no sense. And the pressure to find the person responsible, and then to convict him and give him the punishment he deserved came from all quarters. People clamored for the killer's head. They wanted the guy caught, and right now.

The funeral was a thing of pure majesty, almost like a royal wedding from across the pond. The National Cathedral was packed, endless throngs of well wishers wanting to say goodbye to the Mother Theresa of Dubuque. As a role model, Daniel F. Steadley was the best of the best. There were very few in the world like him. His mold was unique, one of a kind. With his enormous wealth, he could have lived anywhere, from the largest castle in Ireland to the plushest condo in Manhattan. What he had done, however, in keeping with who he really was, he had stayed in the first house he had ever bought, an unassuming four-bedroom in the town where he had been born, Dubuque, Iowa.

Everyone who was anyone in the book of *Who's Who* attended the massive celebration of his life, a two-day rally that culminated in the ceremony at the crowded National Cathedral, where the scenes had been so emotional that even Vladimir Putin's usually stoic face was captured for all to see in that days' press rubbing at the sadness in his eyes. Daniel f. Steadley was that kind of man. He would be sorely missed, by millions, if not more.

His sudden cremation surprised some, but it was quickly forgotten in all the commotion surrounding his death. His ashes were separated into seven equal portions, so that his remains could be scattered on all seven continents, so that his life after death would live forever worldwide.

But his killer was still out there, and people were agitated. Editorial columns everywhere deplored the slowness of the case. Catch his killer. Do it now. People wanted blood, and they would have it. Send the murderer to where he rightly deserved to go.

The pressure mounted to near boiling point, and the hunt for his killer continued to be the leading story everywhere, from Nome to Barbados, and everywhere in between and to all sides.

TO PROVIDE FOR INDIVIDUAL READING PREFERENCE, THIS BOOK HAS SOMETHING NEW: TWO ALTERNATIVE ENDINGS, THE SECOND ENDING MUCH DARKER THAN THE FIRST. TO GO NOW TO THE DARKER ALTERNATIVE ENDING, PLEASE SKIP TO PAGE 239, CHAPTER 37A. OTHERWISE, FOR THE FIRST ENDING, PLEASE CONTINUE READING NOW.

Chapter 37

Cuff was tired, really tired. And he was frustrated, irritated, annoyed, angry, and scared. He flicked on the light to his Pink Fancy room and headed straight to the bathroom, where he would get himself ready for his well-deserved night's sleep.

He gasped when he saw it. What the hell! He had to grab onto the door to keep his balance. The shock was such that he was no longer one bit sleepy. Any hint of it had flown away in alarm. Not one iota remained. His body was tense, and his blood rushed through his veins like floodwaters, demolishing everything in its path. He fought for air, sucking for dear life. He had no idea who had done it, or why, but he knew exactly what it meant. Death was staring back at him big as life, for on his bathroom mirror, in large black letters, somebody had scrawled, "Remember me?"

And beneath this cryptic message sat a large red dot, just like a laser beam. And the thing pointed right back at him through the mirror, right at eye level.

#

The pounding at the door startled her. It was well past midnight. Rosie crept from her bed, and then slowly made it across her small Scotia living room, finally reaching the front door. Just in case, she had a baseball bat in her hands.

"Who is it?" The baseball bat was held in a ready position. If need be, Rosie would hit a grand slam, one that would make even Babe Ruth sit up and take notice.

"It's me."

"Who's me?"

"What's that supposed to mean?"

"Cuff? Is that you?"

"It's not you," he said in reply.

"Is that you Cuff?"

"Who do you think it is?" He was starting to get irritated.

"It better be you, Cuff, or else. You hear?"

"I hear, Rosie. Now let me in for God's sake."

Rosie opened up. In the moonlight, Cuff's face was almost pale. He looked as frightened as a person could be. She quickly closed the door behind him, and locked it securely. "My God, Cuff. What happened?"

"It's what's going to happen? That's the real question, Rosie." And then he told her what he had seen both on and in his mirror, where his hardened face had portrayed the fear that the words staring back at him had sent racing through his veins.

"My God," said Rosie.

Cuff studied her beautiful face for quite some time. Ever the gambler, he knew what he needed to do. They needed help. The stalker, whoever he was, was getting much too close for comfort. This whole terrible nightmare had to be stopped before he or Rosie, or both of them together, became the psycho's next victims.

#

They had spent a restless night in Rosie's small Scotia apartment, tossing and turning things over in their minds as they tossed and turned in bed.

"Are you sure of this?" Rosie asked him as they lay in each other's arms, the West Indian sun rising from its own night's sleep.

"I'm not sure of anything," he said, "but I think the cops have to know about this. It might just help get them off my back for a change and set them on the right track. Who knows? Right?"

"Shit," said Rosie.

Cuff nuzzled at her neck. "You took the words right out of my mouth."

They had a hurried breakfast, and then Cuff was off. He was able to walk the several blocks through town to Times Square, which was bustling with rum-drinking, happy-to-just-be-alive Crucians, even so early in the morning. Living on St. Croix was like living in a constant Carnival. Though much smaller in size and in population, the small tropical isle could make even Rio Carnival and New Orleans Mardi Gras revelers envious.

Just as he was about to cross the car-infested street and head into police headquarters, Cuff spotted the red beam. First it was on the pavement in front of him, dancing around as if a cat or dog owner were teasing his pet with a laser. Cuff stopped and looked around. The red dot followed him, slowly, playfully, and then it began creeping up his pants and then his shirt, where it finally honed in and found a home in the middle of his chest.

And then he saw him. What the hell! The guy was dressed as a ninja. A ninja!

But just as quickly as he had shown himself, the ninja vanished. Cuff knew there was no way to catch the guy, not at this distance and not in this crowd. There were too many obstacles and too much space between him and where the ninja had been standing. There were just too many hiding places. There were simply too many options for hiding, or for quickly leaving the scene.

Cuff was scared, but he was more angry than scared. What was a ninja doing here in the middle of St. Croix? And why would the guy be stalking him, of all people? It made no sense, but it was terrifying as hell. Cuff looked around, studying the faces of the people around him, but what he saw in the human activity all round the active square hit him like a steel club to the stomach: it was quite obvious that no one else had seen a thing.

\#

"Look," said Cuff, "I told you that the guy who is stalking me is dressed like a ninja."

"A ninja?" Captain O'Brien's face was beginning to show traces of the exasperation that Cuff always seemed to plant on it. "*You* look," he said, "this here ain't Japan."

"I tell you he's dressed as a ninja."

"And I tell you," said the head cop on the island, "you better just watch yourself real careful like. You hear?" It was amazing how the cop's voice sounded as if he could be from anywhere on the mainland. There was not the slightest trace of the West Indian calypso like tonal qualities in his speech. Captain O'Brien sounded like a law enforcement officer from anywhere from Miami to Detroit.

"Check out my room at the Pink Fancy if you don't believe me."

Captain O'Brien's eyebrows rose a bit. "We'll find a ninja there?"

Cuff shook his head. "I told you a million times already what you'll find there. Talking to you is like—"

And for the first time Sal Garza, the FBI agent, who had been standing quietly in the corner once again, spoke up. "Sit still, give us your keys, and we'll check things out."

"Am I under arrest?" Cuff said.

Sal Garza shrugged. "Should you be?"

Cuff lost the battle of stares. He handed over the key to his Pink Fancy lodgings. And then waited, for over forty-five minutes, while two detectives were sent to check out his place. When they returned, they reported that they had found no ninja there. They looked quite smug as they relayed this information to their superior.

"So there," said Captain O'Brien, " what do you know. No ninja in your room."

Cuff leaned forward, his knees pressed against Captain O'Brien's desk. "Are you crazy? Who in their right mind would expect the guy to just be waiting for you like that in my room? Are you imbeciles?" He couldn't contain himself. "I'm being stalked, I tell you. Are you listening? Do your ears work?" He leaned even closer, his nose within easy reach of Captain O'Brien's. "How do you explain the writing on my mirror? The who's after me obviously put it there as a threat. The guy's playing with me, I tell you, like a cat with a mouse."

Only the whirling of the ceiling fan could be heard for several seconds.

"What writing on what mirror?" one of the two detectives who had just returned from Cuff's Pink Fancy room said. "The mirror was wiped clean as a whistle."

"Oh, shit," said Cuff.

And Sal Garza stepped back out of his corner. He stood beside Cuff and looked down at him. "And shit is what you'll get if you don't stay put on the island. You hear? Don't even think of going anywhere. Period. You hear me? We'll be watching you like hawks until we get word from Miami. You understand?"

Cuff didn't quite know what to say, but what he was thinking was that *vultures* was probably a more appropriate word choice than hawks.

#

Cuff lay low all day. He had to think clearly, rationally, but he was neither clearheaded nor rational. "The guy actually got back inside my room to wipe his evidence away. I just can't believe it. What in the hell have I done to be stalked like this? The damn guy is killing people all around the island, and he's making the cops think that I'm the one responsible."

"Who would do such a thing, anyway?"

Cuff looked her squarely in the eyes. "Someone who would kill just for pleasure, that's who. Someone who would shoot a man in Reno just to watch him die, like in the Johnny Cash song. Somebody's after me, and I don't think it's just the cops. But they suspect me of being who the someone out there probably is. Somehow I'm mixed up in something, but I don't know how or why."

Rosie, though as pretty as a peach, as always, had worry written all over her forehead. "So what'll we do now, Cuff?"

"Breathing room," he said. "We need some breathing room. I've got to think things through. I have to be given time to think, just to think. All these clues against me are adding up, and I know how a cop's mind works. They'll nail me the minute they get word back from the mainland. My fingerprints are on both knives." He pounded the top of his head with both hands. "I can't believe it. I just can't believe it." He paced the room, sat down, but then quickly got back to his feet. He was as restless as a big cat in the wild. "Somebody, for some reason, wants to pin a series of murders on me. And that someone is now stalking me. But why? One pull of the trigger when the laser beam was on my chest, and I'd be a goner right now. So why didn't he do it? If he wants to kill me, then he just blew the perfect opportunity to do so. What's he up to? What's he thinking?" He kicked at the air, nearly losing his balance. And then his brain came alive.

"Remember those three helicopters?"

"How can I forget?" said Rosie. "They nearly burst my eardrums."

"I think they have something to do with this."

Rosie reached out and touched his arm. "What makes you say that?"

"At the police station," Cuff said, "it was as if the helicopters were hush hush."

"Well, they sure made a hell of a racket for being hush hush," Rosie said.

Cuff thought about it. "You know what I think is going on, Rosie?"

"What?"

"Some son of a bitch out there is stalking me. The crazy guy in the ninja outfit is playing with me. And all the time he is making it look like I have committed the murders that he's probably responsible for. Why he's doing this, I have no idea. It's some kind of game to him. I'm sure of it. And whoever he is, he's sure got some high-powered contacts, the helicopters and all."

"But who would do such a thing?" Rosie's eyes were like two globes.

"A psychopath, that's who, a well-to-do one."

Rosie reached out to him, but he was a tad out of her reach. "You're really scaring me, Cuff."

Cuff sat down beside her, and he stared off into space, but he couldn't come up with a thing, no matter how hard and how long he tried. Then he sighed, and as their eyes met, they clutched to one another as if there were no tomorrow.

"We need space," said Cuff, "and time."

"You mean like in hiding?"

"From both the cops and from the psychopath. It'll just be temporary, maybe a couple of days or so. Just time to try to sort things out, to get a handle on things. So, are you with me, Rosie?"

She hugged him so hard that he could barely breathe. "I'll always be there with you, Cuff. I just hope you know that."

He looked at her, and he smiled, and then he said the two words that sent her heart racing, the two most precious words he could ever say to her, the very ones she had hoped to hear him say for too long now. "I do," he said.

Chapter 38

The Buccaneer Hotel, according to both *Travel and Leisure* and *Conde Nast Traveler* magazines, is one of the top resorts in the entire Caribbean. This institution on St. Croix, established way back in the 17th century, and family run for generations, provides the best of everything the Caribbean has to offer. It is St. Croix's premier destination for water sports, golf, tennis, weddings, every type of family vacation imaginable. Very simply put, the Buccaneer is legendary in this part of the world, offering the gracious and relaxing respite from the mainland that makes St. Croix such a magnet for vacationers.

Lisa Smithers knew exactly what she was doing and what she wanted when she had first booked her luxurious room at the famous resort. She was on a working vacation now that her husband was dead. She needed a place where she could really relax after working her butt off all day, a place where nobody would ever know who she really was. Tailing, stalking—the mere having to be on one's feet all day—was hard on a body, so the resort, with its world-class spa, its great cuisine, its luxurious accommodations, and especially the privacy it afforded one in its gated grounds away from the crowds of Christiansted, was just the ticket. Here she could let her hair down, so to speak, and just be herself, Joan Hascomb, the name she had used to secure the room, which she had done so the day she had killed her husband.

She couldn't believe how stupid people thought she was. Her uncle, her deceased husband, had taken her at her very word, and he had paid Professor Cuffy to step into her trap, although the stupid sap himself had always been the intended victim. How gullible could a person be?

Her uncle, who liked her to call him Papa Dan, had begun fondling her when she was only five. And she had been told to never tell anybody about this. His lavish gifts to her were his insurance policy against her talking. He bought her so many gifts that it became a family joke. Just how many stuffed animals could a little girl own? Her well-stocked bedroom looked like an ornate zoo, like a Noah's ark with nearly every animal known to man finding a loving home there, and most often in multiples. Everyone knew that Papa Dan doted on his little niece. Her every wish was practically his command. If she wanted to visit Disneyland, then off the two of them would go, often spending a night or two together on the road. They visited the world famous San Diego Zoo, Disney World, and Niagara Falls. She was one lucky little girl to have such a doting uncle, especially one as filthy rich as he.

And not one word was every said about his favorite game, the one he had taught her at a very young age: swallow the leader. As she grew older, the game continued, and they played it often, on the road, in the best suites of the most luxurious hotels, and in both his home and hers, when her parents were not around. He loved playing the game, and as she got older they played it more often, and Lisa tolerated it. She lacked for nothing. Anything in the world she wanted, it was hers for the asking, as long as she never told and as long as she continued to play.

As a maturing pre-teen, she was told about the living trust that he had drawn up for her. She learned that at the age of twenty-one she would be the sole beneficiary of the ten million dollar trust, and that every year after that, one million more dollars would be added to the trust. Papa Dan also told her that it was a revocable living trust, and he carefully explained what that meant. In plain English what it meant was that the trust could be revoked at a second's notice, and that it would be if any other person found out about their arrangement. Lisa was okay with this. Besides, Papa Dan usually came pretty fast, and she made it a point to never swallow a drop.

Lisa Smithers never told a soul about their game, and she never left a clue about it. Nobody ever suspected a thing. Papa Dan, childless, had taken it upon himself to lavish love and kindness on the daughter of his only sister.

And, then, before they both knew it, Miss Lisa Smithers was twenty-one, and she now had ten million dollars to do whatever she wanted with, and a promised one million more for each year she continued to play, which was much less frequent now since she had moved off to go to college, and Papa Dan wasn't around so much. But he was around enough. And it was at this age that Lisa determined that the trust she had been provided with was insufficient. No, ten million dollars was just not enough. She wanted it all. Papa Dan missed her madly, and he wanted nothing more than to spend much more time in her company. That's where her real planning took root.

She spent hours online, and eventually she was able to track down Professor James Cuffy, who had moved to the little island of St. Croix. Knowing that Papa Dan was growing ever restless since they had not seen each other in several months now, Lisa reached out to her doting uncle. She proposed that they take a vacation to St. Croix, to the lovely Caribbean, where they could spend time together just enjoying the delights of the island and of each other.

Papa Dan got right on it. To secure their exclusivity, he purchased the property in Betsy's Jewel sight unseen. Money was no object when his niece was involved, although in all other aspects of his life he was known to be quite careful money wise, ever the respected businessman with a knack for making and keeping hold of a dollar.

The first couple of days on St. Croix, they had hardly ventured from their luxury estate on Betsy's Jewel. But Lisa, who had researched everything on the Internet before flying off to the island, was growing a bit impatient. It was now time, her time in the sun, both figuratively and literally. Her proposal of marriage to her Papa Dan did not surprise him in the least. If anything, it reinvigorated him. His love of the game had not diminished in all of these years, even though his age was beginning to show and take a toll. What better dream to come true than to spend the rest of his life in the arms of the only female who could turn him to mush with one blink of her sexy eyes?

But there was one thing that needed to be settled first. Always alert, and ever vigil, particularly when it came to his wealth, Papa Dan made it clear that she would need to sign a prenuptial agreement, but that this should not alarm her in the least. She would be well provided for, come what may. She had the money in her trust, and in his will she would also be given quite a handy sum, but just not the bulk of his holdings, which, of course, were somewhere between six and seven billion by his last count.

Lisa Smithers, all smiles, had agreed. The $50 Virgin Islands marriage license fee was paid, they completed the required two-page application form, and then they observed the eight-day posting period before the ceremony could officially be held, mainly by pleasuring each other in their private retreat in Betsy's Jewel.

Papa Dan quietly made all the arrangements. The lawyer Tom Bennett drew up the prenuptial agreement, and after both of them signed it, the lawyer kept under lock and key in his office. The lawyer had recommended the man to the legalize the union by performing the required ceremony, which was held in the living room of their beautiful estate. Samuel F. Berylson was a clergyman in name only, but he did have the paperwork necessary to meet government scrutiny here on the island. As for the two required witnesses, Berylson's on-again and off-again sweetheart, Madge Wilburn, and Shorty Rawlins, a cop that Bennett himself would trust with his own life, were happy to do their part. Who could turn down the lavish spread the small group would be devouring on the plush grounds of Daniel F. Steadley's estate?

Lisa Smithers was remembering it all. Her alert, ever-present antenna told her that she knew how each of these individuals would deal with her own proposal, which she had made to them in Bennett's office four days before the marriage ceremony. With the prenuptial agreement, she told them, she would indeed be set up for life if something were to happen to her soon-to-be husband, but the millions she would have access to were nowhere near the billions she would see coming her way, upon her husband's death, if there were no prenuptial agreement. All present knew of the existence of the prenuptial agreement, but they were the only people aware of it. Tom Bennett had drawn it up, and the other three were witnesses to Lisa's signing of the document.

So her deal was simple. When Steadley died, and he would soon, she assured them, though she offered no further details, then the prenuptial agreement would disappear and each of them sitting before her now in the lawyer's crowded office would see five million dollars coming to each of them. But after the shock had vanished from the room, the debating had begun, so an hour later Lisa Smithers was forced to relent and guarantee double the amount to each of them, Tom Bennett, Samuel F. Berlyson, Madge Wilburn, and Shorty Rawlins, ten million dollars apiece upon her husband's death.

But there was just one other thing: Lisa Smithers told them about Mr. James Cuffy, about how the man had violently molested her, and how she needed their help in making the sexual predator as uncomfortable as possible as she herself sought revenge on him for what he had done to her back in Dubuque. After hearing her tell of the horrific things her professor had done to her, they had all agreed. The guy needed to be taught a lesson, to be made to feel as she must have felt when he had attacked her. They would do all they could to frighten the guy, to scare him shitless, to avenge the terrible wrong he had done to her. Here the guy had been a trusted teacher, and just look at what he had done. His unforgivable actions had torn away the innocence of who she had once been, shredding it into a thousand pieces. She was now a mere facade of happy girl she had once been. Professor James Cuffy— damn him to hell—! had turned her into a nothing more than a frightened shell of the person she had been before his unprovoked attack.

And to top it all off, the guy had lied about the whole thing and then had gotten off scot-free. How fair was that?

They were convinced. They would help her scare the guy all the way off their beloved island. And besides, there was the ten million dollars apiece to think about, much better than the slap in the face that life had seemed to be giving each of them up until this point.

The shock of Papa Dan's sudden and untimely death must have stunned them, she knew, but they learned to take it in stride. They had little choice. The next day Lisa Smithers had let it be known that each of their voices had been recorded agreeing to the ten million pay off despite the fact that they had been fully cognizant of her implied death threat of her husband. Thus, a good prosecutor could undoubtedly construe that each of them had, indeed, been compliant in one way or the other in Daniel F. Steadley's unseemly death. Yes, Papa Dan had finally paid the ultimate price for all those years he had played his so-called game, but, unfortunately, for him, in the end, all the time he had been playing with the wrong person.

For two days before his death, Lisa Smithers had moped in bed, all alone, seemingly so overpowered by depression that she was unable to function. She was like an Academy Award actress. Papa Dan was beside himself with worry. He missed her so much. What could he do to make things better? He would do anything, anything at all, to get her back to being the only girl he had ever loved, the only girl he would ever love. Just tell me, he had pleaded. Please. He had even gotten down on his knees before her, pleading, begging, beseeching.

And that's when she had told her husband the big lie. Believe it or not, she had seen Professor James Cuffy, the horrible man who had sexually molested her back in her college days. The horrible creature had come back in her life. He was on the island, probably stalking her. She was scared. Deathly so. That terrible man of her past who had caused her such irreparable harm was back now. All the therapy she had undergone to remove the awful episode from the top of her brain had suddenly been thrown out the door. She simply could not be herself with that horrible man around. He had to be dealt with, pure and simple. It was a matter of life and death. The guy was obviously out to get her, but who would believe her story? Just look at what had happened in Dubuque, all the lies and more lies.

Papa Dan remembered. He remembered how incensed he had been when he had heard about the incident and then by how the guy had gotten off scot-free. His little niece had suffered such terrible things at the guy's hands. Papa Dan remembered it all. He was now as worked up and agitated as she, his now beloved wife.

It was at that moment that Lisa told him of her plan. Lure the guy up to the privacy of their estate, in the dark of night, and she could once and for all bring an end to the terrible toll the guy's molestation of her had glued to her psyche. This would be the end, the final curtain, and then their life together, Papa Dan and his loving bride, could continue forth with love and happiness until death do them part.

It would be made to look like an intruder had attempted to break into their house, and they had only done what any red-blooded American would do: they had protected their home and property. And then when the dead man's identity was learned, think of the glorious way in which she would be able to avenge the terrible things he had done to her back in Dubuque. The media would eat it up. The guy had been stalking her all this time. The awful excuse for a man had been pursuing her all this time. Now that he had found her, there was no telling what such a monstrous mind such as his would concoct. All she knew, she told her dear husband, her uncle, Papa Dan, was that Professor Cuffy liked to hang around the bar at the Tivoli, and that he seemed to be real friendly like with a certain waitress there, a cute little thing named Rose, or some such thing.

Everything was so neat. Lisa had seen to that.

She remembered Papa Dan's final seconds. He lay there in bed, she beside him, the knife under her pillow. "I love you so much," he had said, and she had smiled so sweetly in reply. "You know I would do anything for you, don't you? And I have, haven't I, leading the guy up to you tonight so that you can have the last word?" Papa Dan had had such love and affection in his eyes. "I would even die for you, you know?" he had said.

And that's when she had really perked up. "I know you would," she had said, sitting upright, thrusting her breasts straight out towards him, smiling as sweetly as she knew how, and then swiftly plunging the knife into the middle of his chest.

And Bennett, the fool, thinking that the prenuptial agreement that her uncle had had the lawyer draw up could be held safely in his hands. How simple-minded people could be? Getting her hands on the document, and then destroying it, was really not that difficult for someone as determined as she. And the topping on the cake was the fact that her legal marriage to Daniel Steadley, her uncle, one of the wealthiest men in the world, but now deceased, meant that she herself would soon be joining the wealthiest of the world club. The legal marriage papers, all signed and notarized and filed, would be made very public soon. And the whole world would stand up and take notice. Little Miss Nobody from Nowhere would suddenly be Mrs. Somebody.

The world didn't yet know that she was her uncle's wife. He had insisted on that point. Hence, the small wedding on the secluded island. He had said that when they returned to the mainland, they would have the celebration of the century, inviting everybody who was anybody, and that they would then announce to the world that they were husband and wife. It would be her big moment, her coming out party, for she would be the wife of one of the world's best-known faces. Lisa was quick to agree with him. They would stay mum for the time being. Not until it truly served a purpose would their marriage be made public.

And the plan was perfect for Lisa, who needed to remain unknown and unseen as she carried out her mission. It suited her purposes to a T. There was no conceivable way that her name could be connected in any way to Professor James Cuffy, a guy who suddenly had gone berserk.

Eventually, the fact would get out, now that her husband was dead, that they, in fact, were a married couple. And sooner or later, someone in the Virgin Islands bureaucracy was bound to notice the names on the recent marriage certificate. But when that happened, that too would work in her favor. It would be obvious that she had somehow left the island, she had the money and means to do so now, and quietly, and that she had probably gone into seclusion somewhere in order to grieve over her husband's untimely demise. The shock of the startling turn of events, from marriage to murder, had simply been too much for her to handle. She needed complete privacy in order to deal with everything that had come her way so suddenly.

When the time was right, she would make her reappearance, the grieving young widow, a part she would play with perfection. Joan Hascomb, who she was known by here at the ritzy resort, would become a lost footnote in history, just a woman who had stayed a few days on the island, a lady barely noticed by anyone since she had stayed pretty much to herself the entire time she had been on St. Croix. Lisa Smithers would be Joan Hascomb for a few more days, at the most, just as cover until Lisa's own deadly deeds were a fait accompli. And then Lisa Smithers, too, would leave the island, reappearing back on the mainland where she had supposedly been privately grieving the entire time Mr. James Cuffy had continued on his killing spree on a little island far removed from where she herself had been immediately after her husband's death.

But Lisa Smithers was now in a quandary. How soon should she act? Should she keep Professor Cuffy dangling on the end of her laser beam for old time's sake, for another day or two, just to rub more terror into the fear she knew she had instilled in him already, or was it time now for the final plunge, the last kill? Which way should she go? Give Professor Cuffy another day or so of fright, or end his life ASAP?

She just could not make up her mind. Both options tasted so good. Adding lots of salt to the wound she had now ground into the good professor sounded so good to her ears, the fact that he also knew that he was soon to be charged for several murders, and the fact that he must feel like a frightened rabbit, being chased from all sides. Wow! The awful fear he must be feeling was like a dream come true.

On the other hand, though, her final act in this episodic nightmare in her still young life, his death at her hands, and his seeing it as it happened, his knowing precisely why it was happening and who was making it happen, was like liver to a starving tigress in the wild. So which way should she go? Both alternatives sounded equally terrific.

And when the end came, it would be so deliciously ironic. The professor who had snubbed her would die by her hands. How tasty! Irony at its best!

Lisa was a clear-cut type of person. She despised times such as this, when she was forced to choose between two equally fine alternatives. But she knew that she had to make up her mind soon since she could not keep up the pretense of the grieving wife in total seclusion too much longer. Besides, she needed to stake her claim on the money that now was rightfully hers.

The more she thought about it, the more pain the too-tough-to-make decision caused in her brain, the exact opposite of why she had come to the island in the first place. She closed her eyes for a short time, the two evenly pleasant options in her brain going back and forth like a teeter-totter, and then she finally made up her mind.

The time for the denouement had arrived!

Chapter 39

It was still dark as they stepped outside of Rosie's small Scotia apartment. The sun wouldn't be showing its face for several more hours. The dark provided cover, and that's precisely what they needed. They had gathered up as much food as they could from Rosie's stock, including the case of bottled water she had had the good fortune to buy a couple of days ago. Water was so precious on St. Croix that all buildings, by law, had built-in rooftop cisterns to capture all the rainwater they could, each cistern having to meet strict capacity quotas per square foot of roof, including porches and garages. The cistern, in fact, accounted for approximately 10% of the cost of a building. Bottled water, like many other items taken much for granted on the mainland, were prohibitively expensive on the island, whereas luxury items, because of its nearly tax free status, were ridiculously cheap on St. Croix.

Along with the precious food and water, they tossed blankets, pillows, eating utensils and all essential toiletries they could think of or get their hands on into her car, and finally they were ready for their trek to the great unknown, to a safe house, so to speak, where maybe they would be able to make heads or tails out of the two-pronged attack now besieging them.

They drove for several blocks, Rosie turning her head in all directions to see if anyone was following them. Then they stopped the car and waited.

"What was that?" Rosie suddenly asked.

"What?"

"Didn't you hear it?"

"No, I heard nothing," said Cuff. They sat there in silence for a couple of more minutes, their ears straining but hearing nothing.

"False alarm, I guess."

And Cuff restarted the engine.

#

Lisa Smithers waited a bit longer, allowing them to gain a bit more ground on her. She was in no hurry. After all, they were like two mice, well within her python grasp.

And her taste buds were salivating!

#

They stopped again, both of them searching in all directions, but no one seemed to be following them. It sure seemed that way. Finally as certain as they could be that they were not being tailed, they turned onto North Shore Road, which meanders around some of the most isolated parts of the island, almost at shoreline in places, truly living up to its name. If anyone were following, they would surely be spotted from here on out. But taking no chances, they pulled to the side of the road, cutting the engine and their lights, waiting, observing, praying. They appeared to be in the clear.

#

Lisa Smithers was no dummy. She was as cautious as she was determined. Her black Volkswagen bug, lights turned off, kept a safe distance. At this late stage of her mission, she was not about to take any chances at all.

She was in no hurry. The time for the kill would appear sooner than later, and she would know precisely when the perfect time was at hand. Yes, two more kills, and that would be it. Then the thing would be done, and Lisa could get back to living her own life once again.

The bastard! He would be made to watch, as the pathetic bitch he now hung around with would die right there before his eyes. And then Professor Cuffy would have another murder on his hands, just before he then took his own life. The evidence would speak for itself. She would see to that, just as she had seen to everything else thus far. Her rage suddenly became a smile. The bastard deserved what he would get: a few seconds to see his little bitch die, and then a very deserved shortened lifetime of his own.

#

At one of the most desolate areas of the entire island of St. Croix, they pulled off the road and took a few very windy undeveloped roads, a couple of which were really nothing more than unpaved trails and eventually drove along on no trails at all. The had entered a new dark world, but at least they were now in a place where they would be provided with time to think, to plan their next move, to sort things out before returning to town.

#

Lisa Smithers could not quite see them now in the distance, but she knew they were there. She waited as they waited, her engine off, her ears and mind ever alert, her brain on full alert.

#

Cuff finally restarted his engine, and they moved on. Soon they found themselves in a rainforest, not like those gigantic monsters of South America, since St. Croix was such a tiny island, but a rainforest nonetheless. The world around them was a world apart from the rest of St. Croix. The trees here were like those surrounding the ornate graveyards of Savannah, their mossy limbs hanging down from a high, providing perpetual dampness and shade on an otherwise sunny and humid tropical isle. This was the perfect spot to beat the heat, which is precisely what they needed, in both senses of the word, and it was an ideal place in which to become lost if one needed to find a hiding place.

"This is the place," Cuff declared.

Rosie couldn't help herself. "Who do you think you are, anyway? Brigham Young?"

Cuff pulled the car as far into the forest as he could. "Yes, Rosie, you definitely have a way with words."

"Look who's talking," she said.

"Touché."

#

Lisa Smithers' ears could not quite make out their words, but she definitely could figure out what they were doing. She crouched in silence, calmly biding her time, much like a hurricane slowly making its way towards the island, where only death and destruction would be left in its wake.

They buried the car as deeply in the brush as they could. Then they spent time gathering up more materials to ensure that the car would be completely hidden from the human eye. Finally satisfied with their work, they looked around, trying to come up with a plan to tide them over, to give them a bit of breathing room, until they could come up with a more permanent strategy.

"Hey, you!" The voice was loud and piercing, and it sent chills down the backs of both Cuff and Rosie. Where had it come from? "What you tink ya doin?" The calypso like West Indian tonal quality and word structure floated towards them like a butterfly in a soft breeze, flitting up and down and sideways.

They waited, hearts pounding as if they might burst any second. What had they gotten themselves into? Was this it? Had their short run been all for naught?

Then the voice stepped out of the darkened rainforest, dark even now at midday. It belonged to a tall, thin male with dreadlocks that hung down well below his waist, his beard long and untrimmed. For a second, Cuff thought he was looking at a young Bin Laden. But the dreadlocks and the rainbow striped shirt made it very clear to anyone in the know, and that meant everyone who resided in the Caribbean, that this young man was a Rastafarian, a member of the Jamaican born religious sect that held that Ethiopia is Eden and that blacks, who had been forced from their homes and into slavery, would someday be repatriated to live happily ever after in Africa.

"What you tink ya doin'?" the young Rasta asked again. He came closer. And then he stood there right before them.

Cuff decided to gamble, something that was in his blood. "We're hiding," he told the Rasta.

The young guy didn't seem a bit fazed by this bit of information. "Who you hidin' from?"

Another gamble. Cuff was on a roll. "The police."

Still the young Rasta did not seem at all uncomfortable to learn this bit of information. "Why you hide from police?"

Cuff thought for a second, ever the gambler. "I stole the wife of the head honcho in the Frederiksted station." He gestured towards Rosie.

"That right?" The young man seemed quite amused by this.

"It's a fact," said Rosie. "We were going to be married."

The young Rasta laughed. "I like you, white man. But the man, he gonna be plenty mad."

"Who?' said Cuff.

"The policeman you steal she from," came the clipped West Indian response.

Cuff recovered quickly. "You better believe it," he said. "He's got practically the entire police force here on the island out looking for us."

The young Rasta was loving every bit of it. You could see it by the sparkle in his eyes. "And you hiding from da police now?"

"You got it," said Cuff. "But at least I got the girl." He beamed, but the beam was quickly replaced with an "Ouch!" as Rosie gave him a punch on the arm. That gal had quite a wallop. With a little training, she could probably be a contender for the women's professional lightweight division world championship in boxing. "At least I got the *woman*," he quickly corrected, not wanting to be on the receiving end of another of Rosie's infamous right hooks.

The young Rasta was as gracious as can be. "You can stay wit me," he said. "You can hide out wit me. I live up there." He pointed. "Nobody look for you here."

Cuff looked at Rosie, and she looked back, and they nodded as one. "We thank you so much. We will be happy to take you up on your offer. It'll just be for a couple of days."

"You can stay wit me as long as it takes," the young Rasta said.

Cuff thanked him profusely. "I'm Cuff, by the way, and this here is Rosie. What's your name?"

The young Rasta embraced them both, and as he pulled away he said, "Rasta. Everybody call me Rasta."

"Rasta?"

"That's my name, white man." And his shiny white teeth showed them that they were now at a place that they could call home.

#

Lisa Smithers unsheathed her knife and quickly went to work. She deflated all four tires of Cuff's car. Then she slowly crept onwards towards her prey.

#

"We've got it!" Captain Jeremy O'Brien's face was radiant. "The results just came in from Miami." He looked as if he could blind a mongoose with just his smile. "Here, take a look for yourself." He handed the folder to Sal Garza, who took the materials to a desk, where he sat down and read through them like a professor through a set of research papers. His eyes missed not a syllable, not a letter. When he had finished, he looked up, his own face stoic, being the FBI professional that he was, but inside he was jumping up and down like a little boy in line for the Ferris wheel.

"Perfect," he said. "We were right. We've got him. His fingerprints are on the knife that killed Steadley and on the knife that killed Bennett. His fingerprints are on the gun that killed Steadley's dog, and on the gun that killed Berylson, the same gun, by the way. And he was present at every crime scene. His fingerprints are all over Steadley's bedroom, they were found on both a coffee cup and a glass at Wilburn's house as well as on her furniture, and they were found on the sliding glass door to the condo where Berylson was murdered, and then we have the sandal, with his fingerprints all over it, that was found in Detective Rawlins' car at the place where *he* was murdered."

"Wow!" Captain O'Brien too was elated. There was nothing like an early wrap up to a serial killer gone loose case. This had been almost too easy.

Agent Sal Garza, in his best FBI poker face, frowned. "A motive. We still need a motive."

Captain O'Brien nodded, but then he said, "Who knows why people kill people?"

"Yeah," said Sal Garza.

"You think we've got enough?"

"More than enough," said Sal Garza.

Captain O'Brien turned to his left, and called out into the main office. "It's a go, folks. Get on it. Right away. Mr. James Cuffy's number is up. Bring him in, book him, and put him under lock a key. We've got a big one here, folks, a serial killer at the worst. So get hopping. You hear? Let's get ourselves a cop killer."

They heard. Sure grit and determination swirled around the room in hurricane force, ready to sweep up everything in its path, and the road on which they were headed was very well paved.

"If only we had the motive," mumbled Sal Garza, but mainly to himself.

#

The smoke circled Rasta's nose, and then danced around his head, eventually taking flight towards the sky, blue as can be, as always here on St. Croix. Weather forecasters hated their work down here in American paradise where the weather seldom changed. They sat in the dirt, their backs propped up against Rasta's little shack.

"You sure you no want some, white man?" Rasta extended the remnants of his chosen pleasure, a religion to him really, toward Cuff.

"I'm sure."

"It good stuff, man. I ought to know." Rasta laughed until he hacked. He wiped some spittle from his black flowing beard. "It make everything beautiful. It make the world a pretty place."

Cuff took time to look around at the scene laid out before him. He marveled at the slow swaying palm trees, the white sand in the distance, the turquoise ocean, the sweet fragrances of the lush vegetation all around him, the hanging vines and coolness they produced in this tropical rainforest within the beautiful tropical island.

"It's already beautiful," he said. "Who needs ganja to see it that way?"

Rasta chuckled. "You a strange man, white man."

"I can't say I haven't heard that before," said Cuff.

Rosie chimed in. "Like ten times a day."

"Here, try," said Rasta in his clipped West Indian way.

"No, I've got to think," said Cuff.

Rasta lit up. "Ganja make you tink real good. Here try."

Cuff refused. "I think not, but thanks."

Rasta shrugged. "Then I tink for both of us, okay?" He took a leisurely drag of his rapidly disappearing ganja.

Their laughter finally at an end, they sat in silence for a time. Birds, of all sizes, shapes, and colors, chirped and chirped, their cadence steady like the soft swishing sound of the trees as the Caribbean trade wind gently moved them to and fro like ancient pillars in a time gone by.

"You believe in God?" Rasta asked.

Cuff paused, "I'm not sure."

"What about you?" Rasta asked Rosie.

"Same-same for me."

Rasta thought about it, taking the last couple of drags of his ganja. "You believe in Bob Marley?"

"That I do," said Cuff.

"He God."

Cuff laughed, but stopped when he deciphered the look on Rasta's face.

"He God," Rasta said. "He everywhere. He in trees, ocean, sand, everywhere. Bob Marley everywhere."

Cuff, knowing full well that Rasta's eyes were studying him, nodded in reply.

Seagulls in the distance broke the silence. Rasta stretched, then yawned, then leaned back even further. "Bob Marley my God. He go wit me everywhere. He wit me right now."

Cuff nodded again.

Rasta spoke up. "See what I mean?" He pointed. Cuff looked, but he could see no evidence of Bob Marley.

"See what I mean?" Rasta's voice was filled with exuberance, like Eddie Murphy's excitement on the big screen. "I told you, right? Bob Marley here wit us right now."

Cuff's eyes followed the end of Rasta's extended finger. He saw the three little birds beside his doorstep.

"See?" Rasta said, his voice animated. "I tell you the truth, man. Bob Marley everywhere. He wit us now. Just like he sing."

Cuff nodded again.

And Rasta began singing, first rather quietly, gently and softly, but getting progressively louder as he got fully into the song. "Don't' worry, about a thing, cause every little thing's gonna be all right....I woke up this morning...three little birds beside my doorstep..." Bob Marley's words streamed into the Caribbean sunshine, and their meaning was so nice, so called for, so hoped for, so soothing.

And when Rasta was finished, it was the birds' turn to sing, and they did, ever so sweetly.

"Why you worry so?" Rasta asked. "Don't worry. Bob Marley, he protect you."

"Hell, Bob Marley couldn't even protect himself," Cuff blurted out.

"What dat?" Rasta's face had annoyance graphically painted all over it.

"Nothing," said Cuff, but really it was something, something really worrisome. With all that he had experienced recently, those worries seemed to have found a permanent home in his brain, and they had no intention of moving out soon.

"Don't worry, about a ting..." Rasta's voice started in once again, booming this time around, much like a megaphone. But as Cuff's own mind worked overtime, his own worries began to magnify.

And this time when the song ended, the birds were silent.

Chapter 40

"Shit," said Cuff, "I forgot my smartphone again."

"Dummy."

"Did you say rummy?'

"Dummy rummy."

"I can't believe I did it again."

"I can," said Rosie.

"I wanted to give Frank a call."

"The bartender?"

"The one and only. I wanted to see if he's heard anything?"

"About what?"

"About anything," said Cuff.

"Why Frank?"

"He's a bartender, isn't he? If anyone's heard anything."

"I got it," said Rosie.

Cuff winked. "You took the words right out of my mouth. You've got it. That's for sure." They played tongue wiggly with each other from a short distance, and then Cuff turned to Rasta, who appeared to be meditating with ganja in hand. His eyes were closed and his hands were folded on his lap. "I think I already know the answer, but do you have a phone, Rasta?" But there was no movement or any reaction from their new friend. "Rasta," Cuff said again, "do you have a phone?"

Rasta stirred, but just a bit. He opened his left eye, slowly, but did not move his head. "I heard." But that's all he said.

Cuff asked a third time. "Have you got a phone, either landline or cell?"

Rasta opened his other eye. He lifted his head from its original slumped position. "I got ganja, man. I got ganja." And then he closed both his eyes.

"Just as I thought," said Cuff.

Rosie feigned a pout, but some sincerity showed through, the corners of her unpainted lips curling upward ever so slightly.

"I got good ganja," Rasta said. "Good ganja. You want?"

"I don't need any ganja," Cuff said. "I've got Rosie."

Rosie's immediate reflex was to give him the finger, but she thought better of it, this time, and caught herself just in the nick of time for Cuff's face showed only sincerity, all joking long gone, vanishing in the sky like the short puffs of smoke that disappeared from Rasta's curled lips.

Instead, Rosie blew him a kiss, one that found an immediate home on his own lips, forming a mirror like image of the rose-colored glow emanating from the lips on which it had been born.

And then there was love and music in the air, all around them, Bob Marley style, with not a worry in the world about a thing because they both knew that every little thing was going to be all right.

\#

Lisa Smithers was a well-oiled piece of machinery. She patiently studied the scene before her, the perfect place to proceed with her plan. The isolation of the rainforest provided the perfect cover. Of course there was now an extra person she would have to deal with, but the way the young Rastafarian smoked incessantly should only serve to work to her advantage. In his drugged-state, the guy shouldn't pose a problem at all.

She slowly removed her ninja suit, tying it in a bundle and laying it behind the trunk of a tree. Lisa Smithers was now dressed in what she considered her sexiest outfit, a tiny pair of thigh hugging shorts, and an eye-popping half blouse, extremely low cut, with no bra underneath.

Yes, the final scene would be delicious. Mr. Cuffy would be made to suffer in more ways than one.

\#

The centipede, which looked like a large worm in a caterpillar's body, slugged its way along the sand. It did not like the heat, and it was determined to find a darker, more moist spot to rest for the day. The shadow of the shack just ahead looked perfect. The centipede meandered around a fallen palm branch, and then navigated itself past several ugly ganja stubs, which had been haphazardly tossed into its way, but long before the centipede itself had been on this path.

It had a stomach full of bugs, lunch had been great, and it was time now for a siesta. But there was a protrusion blocking its way to the shade it sought, so the centipede did what comes so natural. It took a bite out of the obstacle in its path.

Cuff screamed bloody murder, jumping to his feet in a panic.

Rasta was the first to spot the centipede. He attempted to get to his feet in order to kill the little creature with the toxic bite, but Cuff, hobbling on his painful foot, got to the crawling source of all the commotion before Rasta, in his slow-moving, ganja-loving state, could stand up.

Cuff looked around and finally found what he sought. He picked up the rotting piece of wood, which had obviously come free from the shack in which he and Rosie had been living for the past couple of days. It took patience, but Cuff was eventually able to scoop up the centipede. He walked slowly, gingerly, and not just because of the pain in his foot. He wanted to be doubly sure that the centipede remained on the board in his hand.

Far enough away from Rasta's shack now, Cuff tipped the board sideways, and the centipede slipped into the sound and started off, for safety's sake, in the opposite direction, wiggling its way to freedom.

When Cuff returned to where Rasta and Rosie now stood, both alarmed by what had just happened to Cuff, all three of them checked his foot. Fortunately, there was no inkling of any toxicity at all, no swelling, and not even a bit of redness.

"You a lucky man," Rasta said.

"Yeah," said Cuff, but *lucky* is the last word in the world that he would consider using to describe himself, not the way he was feeling at the moment, not since his life had suddenly been forced to crawl into a box that seemed to have no outlet.

\#

Agent Sal Garza suddenly seemed so out of character. His usually stern facial features were devoid of all that had helped to project the ultimate professional that he was. He was practically grinning like a little boy.

"What's up with you?" Captain O'Brien asked as he watched the FBI man waltz his way into the office.

"You better sit down to hear this," Garza said to O'Brien.

Captain O'Brien's reaction to this was to raise his right eyebrow. He was already sitting. He had been sitting there for the past half hour. "So what have you got?"

Agent Garza was almost smiling. He could hardly contain himself from spitting out the news, but he also was well aware of the great drama of the moment. "You're not going to believe this. I just got word myself." He stood before Captain O'Brien's faux oak desk. He was too excited to sit down.

Captain O'Brien leaned back a bit in his big swivel chair. "So are you going to tell me?"

Sal Garza was on cloud nine. His voice was as animated as if he were an eighteen-year-old kid on a hot date. "Guess what?"

"What?"

"Daniel Steadley was recently married, for the fourth time. You know his story, the court scene dramas, the alimony, the headlines in every newspaper in the country, ad nauseam, all that shit."

Captain O'Brien knew that this was not it. There was a lot more to this, and Agent Garza was taking his sweet old time spilling the beans. "Yeah, I read all about it. Day after day. Week after week."

"So guess who he married this time around, who he was married to until death did part them?"

Captain O'Brien waited, and then he gave in. "I give up," he said.

Agent Sal Garza beamed as he said, "His niece. Can you believe it? He married his niece, his sister's only daughter."

Captain O'Brien was convinced that there was a lot more. "Strange," he finally said in an attempt to move things along just a bit.

"But that's not the weird part," Agent Garza finally got out.

"No?"

"Not by a long short. His niece is nearly forty years younger than he is…was, than he was when he died. And you want to hear the juiciest part of this whole thing?"

Captain O'Brien nodded. "Sure do," he said.

"Well," said the FBI man, "here comes the crème de la crème. Remember the scandal back in Dubuque?" He waited until the recollection hit full force in the brain of his partner sitting across the big desk.

"You're shitting me." Captain O'Brien had suddenly come to full alert.

"I'm not," said Agent Garza. "Daniel Steadley was married to his own niece, the same girl who accused one Mr. James Cuffy of sexual battery, the same James Cuffy now right in our own scopes."

"Wow!" and Captain O'Brien leaned back so fast that he nearly tipped the swivel chair over.

"Yes wow," said Agent Sal Garza. "We've finally got ourselves the motive."

#

Cuff was restless and growing more so with every passing hour. Time ticked away, but his brain was like a ticking time bomb, ready to explode to the high heavens at the smallest notice, taking the tops of the swaying palm trees with him. He felt like a cornered rat in a maze, and he hated the feeling. This was not living. Hiding was not the answer. He knew full well that the authorities thought him guilty of terrible crimes he had not committed. He felt as if he were held in a vice and could not get loose. His movements were severely restricted, and this small rainforest had become his cage. How long could he live like this?

Live! This was not living at all. You call this life? He laughed out loud at the thought.

Rosie looked up. "What's so funny?"

"Look around you, Rosie. You see anything to laugh about. Nothing's funny. Absolutely nothing." He sounded bitter, his tone more so than his choice of words.

"Well, you don't have to take it out on me." Rosie's rosy cheeks were turning a brighter shade of red. She picked up a handful of sand and scattered it in his direction, not hard, but clear enough to leave her message.

"Okay, okay," said Cuff, mindful of the fact that he had unwittingly raised Rosie's ire. "Here's taking it *back* instead of *out*.

How's that for an ex?" The expression on his face showed that he was delighted by his own perceived cleverness.

"Ex, smex, you're still an ass in my book."

"And what is it you're reading, outdated historical fiction?"

"Read this," she said, extending her finger towards him.

Cuff winced, and then blinked, but the thing was still there. "Down girl," he finally said.

"You speaking to me?" Her eyes narrowed.

Cuff shrugged. He couldn't come up with the right words.

Rasta came to the rescue. He blew a bit of smoke their way. "She she, and you he," he said, his West Indian way with words sounding a lot like calypso. "Me me. She, you, and me. We all the same. Right? You like she, and she like you. And I like both. And the weather nice. The sun shine, just for us. Right? So be happy. Smile. Laugh. Enjoy what life give us. Everything is going to be all right, just like Bob Marley say. Right?"

"If *he* gets off his high horse," Rosie said.

Cuff scrambled for the perfect retort, but it just wouldn't form itself the way he wanted this time around. "You, you..." is all he could get out.

"You're the you-you, you know, not me."

"I," said Cuff.

"You want an eye for an eye, is that it?" But the handsome look he gave her melted her to the core. She scrunched her nose in the way that only she could, appearing so churlishly forlorn but, at the same time, since she could not help herself, her eyes were flirting with him as only hers could. He just had that effect on her, always had and always would, even at times when he made her so mad that she could scream.

Cuff took a few deep breaths. He recognized her look at once, and it was so cute he wanted to laugh, but this was not the time for laughter. He knew full well what she was after, and so he complied. "I'm sorry, Rosie. Truly sorry. I really am. It's just that I feel like a cooped up animal. I apologize. Okay? I just don't know what to do?"

Rosie just stared back at him in reply, saying nothing. Time did a cartwheel and landed flat on its back.

"Okay. Okay. Enough now. My home, your home," said Rasta, who leaned against a swaying palm tree across the way, but well within hearing distance. "Making up is a good thing. Right?"

It was if she hadn't heard Rasta. She had been thinking hard about Cuff's last words, which had really hit their mark. "And how do you think *I* feel about all of this, Cuff?" This time her nose kind of wiggled at him. She couldn't help it. "But what can we do about it?"

"That's just it, Rosie, we've run out of options. We can't hide out here forever. Hell, St. Croix is so small, that we'll eventually be found. And there's probably no way to get off the island. They made that point quite clear to me. It's not too difficult for the authorities to see to that. There's only one airport, and there are only so many docks. And besides, everyone knows everybody else's business. It's such a small world here. Like one big family. Word of our escape, if such a thing were even possible, would get out faster than snot from a sneeze."

"You know, Cuff, you sure have a way with words," Rosie said.

He eyed her. "I sure have a way period," he said.

Rosie couldn't help herself. She tossed her head back and laughed, but not for long. "So what's the plan then, prof?"

"Ex," he said, "and this time around let's just leave it at that. No *ass,* okay?"

"Okay, no ass for Mr. Ex." She threw him her coquettish smile. "Have I got it?" her eyes dancing now like two bridesmaids.

"You've got it, Rosie, that's for damned sure. You get it?" Was that a twinkle in his eye?

"You really are…" but she hesitated just a bit.

"I know," said Cuff, "something." He blew her a kiss, which she sent right back to him. "Anyway, the more we hide out like this, the more guilty it makes me seem in their eyes. And they already have so much pointing in my direction."

Rosie held his hand. She held it firmly. She pulled him closer. She rested her chin on his neck. "I think you're right," she finally said.

"You do?'

"I do." She clung to him even more tightly. "I know what you're thinking, Cuff."

"You do?"

"Yes. You know full well that I can read you like a book. And I think you're making the right decision." She decided against adding *this time.*

He leaned down and tenderly kissed her on the cheek, then on the neck, and then their lips and tongues were as one, as they swayed in time to the romance of the St. Croix sun, sea, and sand.

Rosie was the first to speak. "I need you."

"And I need you," said Cuff. "I really don't know how I would be coping with this thing without you here at my side."

"No," said Rosie. " I don't think you heard me. I said I *need* you."

Little birds began singing, and the rays of the Caribbean sun shone through in a few spots in this tropical rainforest they now called home.

Rasta finally chimed in. "She say she need you, man. You two use my shack. I stay here and smoke my ganja. Okay?"

The silence was like a symphony, the key, mood, and tempo all so grand. Cuff hugged Rosie. The harmony brought forth the music of the gods, and then came the crescendo as he whispered in her ear, "I need you too. Shall we?"

Rosie licked at his neck. "We shall," she said.

\#

It was time to act. The young Rastafarian was stoned out of his mind, practically lying in the dirt now, and Professor Cuffy and his little whore had gone into the ramshackle shack for a romantic interlude, the last of his life.

Lisa Smithers waited for a couple of excruciating minutes. When Professor Cuffy and his little whore were at their most vulnerable, undressed, lying in each other's arms, that's when she would strike.

\#

Lisa Smithers crept past the sleeping Rastafarian and poked her head into the one-roomed shack. Just as she thought: the two lovers were entangled with each other in bed. The floorboards creaked rather loudly as she entered the lovers' nest.

"Remember me, Professor Cuffy?" She stood erect, her head held high, her semi-clad body on display, the deadly rifle in her hands.

Cuff's head shot up off the pillow. "Oh, my God." He couldn't believe his eyes. It just didn't make any sense. What was going on? Could this really be for real? "Lisa?" But then suddenly it made all the sense in the world. "Lisa!"

"Yes, Lisa." And the red laser of her high-powered rifle began circling his forehead.

"I don't believe it."

"You better start believing, because time's running out." She continued to fan his forehead with the red laser beam.

"Who in the hell is she?" asked Rosie, quickly taking in the woman's strange outfit, but then concentrating on the rifle in her hands.

"I'm your worst nightmare, honey." And Lisa Smithers flashed her teeth and then turned the laser on her, before quickly turning it back to Cuff's forehead.

"The ninja!"

"Correction, honey. I'm your worst nightmare. Welcome to Hell."

"My God," said Cuff.

"Praying won't help you a bit," said Lisa, toying with the trigger of her rifle.

Cuff moved slowly. He leaned back against his pillow. "But why?"

Lisa Smithers laughed, but she kept the rifle pointed at her prey. "You know full well why. Don't play games with me."

"Games!"

"Life and death ones," and Lisa was forced to smile at her own choice of words.

Cuff tried to stay calm, attempting with every fiber of his body to not show fear, to keep her at bay until—

Until what? What *could* they do? Here he and Rosie were up against a deadly force that had already killed time after time, one that held all the cards. He had to think.

Lisa Smithers broke the spell. "I'm sorry it had to end like this." She waved the laser beam back and forth from Cuff to Rosie. "You know, it didn't have to be this way, Professor Cuffy."

"Look, Lisa, I have no idea why you have become what you have, but I did nothing to—"

She laughed. "That's just it. Don't you get it? You did nothing, and just look at what you missed out on." She posed for Cuff, assuming the sexiest posture she could act out, considering the restrictive conditions in which she now found herself. She smiled sexily, showing off her legs, thrusting her breasts towards him, then dipping towards him, and finally turning slightly to show him her best profile. "I just wanted you to see what you gave up...for her, your skinny little whore," and she pointed to Rosie. "Before you kill her, I mean."

Rosie started to move, but the laser beam stopped her dead in her tracks.

Cuff needed to act fast to prevent Lisa from pulling the trigger then and there. He needed an immediate distraction. "Where's Rasta?" he asked.

"Rasta? You mean the stoned out zombie outside. He's on death's bed."

"What!"

"*You've* killed him," said Lisa Smithers. She smiled; her powerful rifle was the 800-pound gorilla in the room. "Don't worry, Professor darling. All the evidence that the authorities need will be right there for them to find. I can assure you of that." Lisa Smithers laughed. "But first you're going to kill your little whorish girlfriend here." She licked her lips, slowly, tauntingly, savoring every second of the end of Professor Cuffy's life. "Then you are going to do yourself in. A bit of a change of plans for me really, but I like it. And I think it will provide a perfectly packaged case for the police. A lover's quarrel gone wrong."

"You are one sick woman," said Cuff.

Lisa Smithers steadied the rifle.

"You really are crazy."

Lisa held the rifle steady.

"You're mad."

Lisa still held the rifle steady.

"You're a crazed lunatic, you know that?"

Lisa Smithers nodded. "And you, dear Professor Cuffy, are one dead man," she said.

Cuff tried to say something, but Lisa Smithers cut him off.

She glared at her former professor and then at the skinny little whore lying there beside him. "Do you love her?"

"Hell yes I love her!" said Cuff.

Lisa Smithers' feigned a smile, but quickly gave up. "Then say goodbye to her." She pointed the gun point blank at Rosie.

"Who dere?" Rasta's voice startled them all. As Lisa Smithers turned to see just where the voice was coming from, Rosie's kick came out of nowhere, a blur or power, which sent the gun flying across the room. Lisa Smithers quickly turned back to face the bed, but Rosie's second kick caught her completely by surprise. Stunned by the force that had knocked her silly, Lisa Smithers staggered backwards one or two steps, and then slumped to the ground, shocked by the strength possessed by the skinny little whore, whose face now even looked possessed.

Rosie was so fast, that she was on her feet in one fluid movement. "I'm gonna kill you!" she shouted, as she threw herself towards the still dazed threat on the floor.

It was clearly evident to Lisa that she would be no match for the infuriated Rosie, even with the steak knife she had somehow been able to pull from its holster around her waist. She was well aware that the tide had abruptly changed, so quickly so, that Rosie was fully capable of carrying out what she sought. Knife or no knife, her brain quickly realized the terrible mistake she had made by allowing herself to end up like this, especially when she had been in complete control of the situation. Her thoughts churned and whirled around much faster than even Rosie could move, tumbling around in a maze, flailing madly for breathing room.

Thud! Rosie had arrived for the kill, so up came the knife, quickly and deadly. It was now or never!

"I think not, bitch," said Lisa Smithers, as she angrily plunged the steak knife into her own chest, preventing Professor Cuffy's little whore from gaining the satisfaction at doing so with her own hands.

#

After lots of shaking, sweating, and total shock, after fighting back tears and nausea, after slowly backing their way outdoors in order to get away from the death scene, after gagging and fighting to breathe in the fresh tropical air, after what seemed an eternity, Cuff and Rosie and Rasta were now in much higher spirits. They hugged and hugged and hugged, the trio, Cuff, Rosie and Rasta, until all the shaking had stopped. The adrenalin rush they had all experienced took a long time passing, but eventually it was overpowered by their own elation at just being alive. Even though they still had to deal with the police, they now had the evidence they needed in order to prove their own innocence and to show the authorities just who had been behind all the killings. They were safe now, and their nightmare was behind them, though they knew they would be severely tested by the authorities.

After all, wasn't Bob Marley right there beside them, just as Rasta had told them as they had waved their see-you-laters to their newfound friend? Cuff had declined one last offer from Rasta for a hit on his ganja, and hand-in-hand he and Rosie had gone off to Rasta's rusty Volkswagen bus, his Rasta wagon, as he called it, since Cuff's Honda, they had discovered, was inoperable at the moment. Rasta would leave the body and the crime scene untouched while they went to get the police. He would make his presence known to them again right after the police had done their thing and had left the scene, he had explained. When they hadn't quite understood, he had blown some ganja smoke their way.

"No worries, man," he had told them. "I be watching everything, but from afar when da police come."

"You saved our lives," Cuff said. "We'll never forget that."

Rosie hugged him like a long lost brother.

Rasta smiled, his yellowing teeth big as life for all the world to see. "Life worth saving," he said.

#

The trusty old car, though badly dented, rusted and soiled, having been neglected for who knew how long, but being the proud model of German efficiency that it was, rust and all, came alive at the third turn of the ignition key.

They were both quiet on the drive back to Christiansted, where they would contact the authorities, and then, when the time was ripe, go shopping for four new tires for Cuff's rusty Honda, each lost in thoughts of where they now were in life and where they were heading. Theirs would be a bright future, one filled with lots of laughs and plenty of loving. The past was the past, and the terrible storm clouds they had faced together, the threats made against Cuff's good character, the doubts and recriminations so unfairly directed at him, the diabolical nightmare they had had to face and then defeat, the anxiety and stress of it all, the threats against their own lives, despite all of that, love was now the only thing in the air, all around them, bubbling around their heads, bouncing out the trepidation of what might have been that still lingered there, the sheer terror of what they had encountered.

It may be a dog-eat-dog world, but they were like two large cats, careful and cautious, but fully capable of taking care of themselves when threatened. Life was good, but soon it would be beautiful, glorious, the weight of the wait and doubt fully removed from their shoulders and tossed into the past, where it might never be forgotten but it most definitely would be laid to rest, like a bad nightmare that was simply that: a nightmare and nothing but, to be placed in the far recesses of their memory banks where it would lie dormant for all intents and purposes, and for all time. Yes, indeed. If Bob Marley, as Rasta had said, was God, then God had spoken and had told them not to worry because every little thing was going to be all right, and this they both believed.

Suddenly Cuff broke the silence, and Rosie made faces of feigned pain directed at him, which only urged him to sing a bit louder. So what if he couldn't carry a tune. So what if their broken-down Rasta wagon was filthy, dirt like frosting on the metallic paint. Bob Marley's soothing lyrics flitted through their heads, the positive vibes like reassurance from above that all was fine and dandy now, that, in their case, the calm had succeeded the storm, the weather ahead already brightening their way onward. Life was good again.

Cuff pulled off North Shore Road and came to a halt on the shoulder. "Just look at that view," he said.

"Don't you just love it, Cuff?"

"It's you I love, Rosie."

She leaned over and gave him a big kiss on his cheek.

"Let's take a closer look, you want to?"

"I want," said Rosie.

They got out of the car and walked across the narrow road. They stood just above the sand. They were looking at a world-class vista. The sky was as blue as Cuff's eyes, the ocean as pretty as Rosie's cheeks. The gentle lapping of the waves at their feet was a lullaby, and the swaying of the palm trees was a dance. The sand was as white as sugar, the horizon a world away. This indeed was paradise. St. Croix was definitely the perfect place for living, laughing and loving. The moment was perfect.

Cuff put his arm around her shoulder and gently pulled her body into his. He cupped her chin with his two hands, and bent his face towards hers, their lips nearly touching, eyes on eyes, two hearts beating as one, time at a sudden standstill as the special moment gave birth to the glory of caring, sharing, and loving until…

"Rosie," he finally asked, "will you be my wife?"

"Oh, Cuff!" and her hard embrace nearly sent them both tumbling into the sand. "I will! I do! I do! I will! Yes! Yes! Yes!"

And then came the sweet rhythm of the waves lapping onto shore intermingled with the lovely sounds of true love and happiness forever after that circled right above them, like a halo.

THE END

NOTE: THE ALTERNATIVE ENDING IS A MUCH DARKER VERSION THAN THE FIRST ENDING. IT BEGINS NOW. FOR THOSE READERS WHO WOULD LIKE TO SKIP IT, PLEASE GO DIRECTLY TO THE PREVIEW OF MICHAEL MEYER'S SUSPENSEFUL THRILLER *COVERT DREAMS,* WHICH BEGINS ON PAGE 299, RIGHT AFTER THE FOLLOWING ALTERNATIVE CHAPTERS 37A-41A.

Chapter 37A

Cuff was tired, really tired. And he was frustrated, irritated, annoyed, angry, and scared. He flicked on the light to his Pink Fancy room and headed straight to the bathroom, where he would get himself ready for his well-deserved night's sleep.

He gasped when he saw it. What the hell! He had to grab onto the door to keep his balance. The shock was such that he was no longer one bit sleepy. Any hint of it had flown away in alarm. Not one iota remained. His body was tense, and his blood rushed through his veins like floodwaters, demolishing everything in its path. He fought for air, sucking for dear life. He had no idea who had done it, or why, but he knew exactly what it meant. Death was staring back at him big as life, for on his bathroom mirror, in large black letters, somebody had scrawled, "Remember me?"

And beneath this cryptic message sat a large red dot, just like a laser beam. And the thing pointed right back at him through the mirror, right at eye level.

#

The pounding at the door startled her. It was well past midnight. Rosie crept from her bed, and then slowly made it across her small Scotia living room, finally reaching the front door. Just in case, she had a baseball bat in her hands.

"Who is it?" The baseball bat was held in a ready position. If need be, Rosie would hit a grand slam, one that would make even Babe Ruth sit up and take notice.

"It's me."

"Who's me?"

"What's that supposed to mean?"

"Cuff? Is that you?"

"It's not you," he said in reply.

"Is that you Cuff?"

"Who do you think it is?" He was starting to get irritated.

"It better be you, Cuff, or else. You hear?"

"I hear, Rosie. Now let me in for God's sake."

Rosie opened up. In the moonlight, Cuff's face was almost pale. He looked as frightened as a person could be. She quickly closed the door behind him, and locked it securely. "My God, Cuff. What happened?"

"It's what's going to happen? That's the real question, Rosie." And then he told her what he had seen both on and in his mirror, where his hardened face had portrayed the fear that the words staring back at him had sent racing through his veins.

"My God," said Rosie.

Cuff studied her beautiful face for quite some time. Ever the gambler, he knew what he needed to do. They needed help. The stalker, whoever he was, was getting much too close for comfort. This whole terrible nightmare had to be stopped before he or Rosie, or both of them together, became the psycho's next victims.

\#

Suzi's plane landed back in Denver about eight minutes ahead of schedule. She was feeling no pain. And, being the professional she was, she felt no guilt at all. If anything, she felt extreme pride in what she had accomplished on St. Croix. She had gotten exactly what she had gone to the island to get. School teacher! Don't make me laugh. The only teaching she had ever done was to show the newcomers a few of her hard learned tricks of the trade, but never revealing enough to give them any advantage they might have on her as they worked the streets of Denver. After all, it was certainly a rub-my-back-and-I'll-rub-yours kind of world. It *was* in Suzi's little world.

The first thing she did when her plane landed back in Denver, after her one-stop flight back from her working assignment in American paradise, was to make the cell phone call back to St. Croix, as she had been directed to do.

Lisa Smithers, because she could see on the face of her phone who the call was from, answered after the first vibration.

"The deed is done," Suzy said.

"As planned?"

"Even better," said Suzi, "much better. We were able to exchange lots of body fluids. I made doubly sure of that. If anybody's infected, that man surely is."

Lisa Smithers was pleased, ecstatically so. She nearly peed in her pants. HIV was like honey from heaven. Revenge was tastier than the sweetest fruit. And it smelled so good, like a fresh spring after the winter snow had vanished. It was like sunshine after a terrible storm. This was one of the big moments she had been waiting so long to take place. And now things had gone off without a hitch. She wanted to shout out loud and tell the world about her exploit, her comeuppance, her sweet-tasting revenge. But that was out of the question. Not here in this place and at this time. The celebration would come later, after every last detail had been seen to. Then the party would begin, and what a party it would be.

Lisa Smithers nearly whispered the following words into the phone. She could hardly contain herself waiting for Suzi's reply. "How was it?" she asked. "Is he good?" She nearly trembled as she waited for the reply.

Suzi, the ever practical, but also the seasoned professional, did not have to spend much time sorting out her words. They came so naturally. "I must admit that he is a damn fine ride in the sack. That guy knows what he's doing, and he knows how to give a girl what she wants and needs."

There was a long pause on the St. Croix end of the line. "I'm glad to hear it," the voice of Lisa Smithers said, but her tone betrayed her choice of wording. She felt terrible tingles of envy and regret. Time would never be able to erase that from her psyche. She wanted Professor James Cuffy as much now as she had back when she was his student. That would never change. Her brain was helpless to obliterate the what-could-have-been. Sometimes she wished that she could just reformat her brain, like a hard drive on a computer, but she knew that was crazy. Lisa sighed and then, for the moment, sucked it in. Then she said the words that Suzi had waited so long to hear. "I thank you for your services. You can rely now upon my holding up my end of the deal. You have my word on that. Okay? The whole enchilada, all medical bills, hospital stays, medicine, and hospice when the time comes. Okay?"

"Okay," said Suzy, exuding wonderfully refreshing relief, as she stood there at the Denver airport. She would be taken care of when the time came, and that was all that mattered. Suzi felt like dropping to her knees, right there in the middle of the airport lobby, and showing her blessings for the day that the Lisa woman had first approached her about the odd proposition. The whole thing had been like a heaven-sent gift. "You know," she finally added, feeling really good about herself for the first time in what seemed to be ages, "I could have been an actress. You know that? The guy really ate it all up."

"Well," Lisa Smithers said, "aren't you an actress in a way? You do have to fake it a lot in your chosen profession, right?"

Suzi thought about it for a while. "Yeah, I like that. I guess you're right. But," she added quickly, words that unknowingly pierced straight through the heart of Lisa Smithers, "with this guy there was no faking it. Believe me, he's the real deal." After all these unfulfilled years, she had finally gotten lucky, and on the job, no less.

Lisa Smithers flinched, because she did believe, and it was so painful to be forced to do so. It hurt; it really hurt. She worked to compose herself, to get beyond the thoughts she was thinking, to get back to the present, where she was definitely a born again woman. She had no words to add. So she said the only thing she was capable of saying, "Goodbye, Suzi. And thanks again."

For several seconds Lisa Smithers stood there without moving, without knowing what to do. Then she brightened up considerably as she remembered Suzi's words about the large exchange of body fluids. *Take that!* she nearly shouted out loud, but she caught herself in time.

Now she felt better, lots better. She was back on top of the world, the world her own two hands had molded. She felt as if the weight of her earlier world of humiliation had finally begun to be lifted from her shoulders. It had taken a long time coming, but what Suzy had just told her made everything worth it. That Professor James Cuffy was now most certainly infected with the HIV virus, everything in the world was good again. Everything. The python had shown its teeth, and painfully sharp they were.

Lisa Smithers was still on a mission as of yet not totally accomplished, so the real celebration would have to wait until this thing was history. But this was such a grand ending to the beginning. Or was it the other way around. It didn't really matter. What mattered was that one James Cuffy was getting his, exactly what he deserved.

The almost uncontrollable excitement Lisa Smithers now felt inside of her bounced around like a carnival, the sounds and sights bringing her almost to a climax herself.

#

They had spent a restless night in Rosie's small Scotia apartment, tossing and turning things over in their minds as they tossed and turned in bed.

"Are you sure of this?" Rosie asked him as they lay in each other's arms, the West Indian sun rising from its own night's sleep.

"I'm not sure of anything," he said, "but I think the cops have to know about this. It might just help get them off my back for a change and set them on the right track. Who knows? Right?"

"Shit," said Rosie.

Cuff nuzzled at her neck. "You took the words right out of my mouth."

They had a hurried breakfast, and then Cuff was off. He was able to walk the several blocks through town to Times Square, which was bustling with rum-drinking, happy-to-just-be-alive Crucians, even so early in the morning. Living on St. Croix was like living in a constant Carnival. Though much smaller in size and in population, the small tropical isle could make even Rio Carnival and New Orleans Mardi Gras revelers envious.

Just as he was about to cross the car-infested street and head into police headquarters, Cuff spotted the red beam. First it was on the pavement in front of him, dancing around as if a cat or dog owner were teasing his pet with a laser. Cuff stopped and looked around. The red dot followed him, slowly, playfully, and then it began creeping up his pants and then his shirt, where it finally honed in and found a home in the middle of his chest.

And then he saw him. What the hell! The guy was dressed as a ninja. A ninja!

But just as quickly as he had shown himself, the ninja vanished. Cuff knew there was no way to catch the guy, not at this distance and not in this crowd. There were too many obstacles and too much space between him and where the ninja had been standing.

There were just too many hiding places. There were simply too many options for hiding, or for quickly leaving the scene.

Cuff was scared, but he was more angry than scared. What was a ninja doing here in the middle of St. Croix? And why would the guy be stalking him, of all people? It made no sense, but it was terrifying as hell. Cuff looked around, studying the faces of the people around him, but what he saw in the human activity all round the active square hit him like a steel club to the stomach: it was quite obvious that no one else had seen a thing.

#

"Look," said Cuff, "I told you that the guy who is stalking me is dressed like a ninja."

"A ninja?" Captain O'Brien's face was beginning to show traces of the exasperation that Cuff always seemed to plant on it. "*You* look," he said, "this here ain't Japan."

"I tell you he's dressed as a ninja."

"And I tell you," said the head cop on the island, "you better just watch yourself real careful like. You hear?" It was amazing how the cop's voice sounded as if he could be from anywhere on the mainland. There was not the slightest trace of the West Indian calypso like tonal qualities in his speech. Captain O'Brien sounded like a law enforcement officer from anywhere from Miami to Detroit.

"Check out my room at the Pink Fancy if you don't believe me."

Captain O'Brien's eyebrows rose a bit. "We'll find a ninja there?"

Cuff shook his head. "I told you a million times already what you'll find there. Talking to you is like—"

And for the first time Sal Garza, the FBI agent, who had been standing quietly in the corner once again, spoke up. "Sit still, give us your keys, and we'll check things out."

"Am I under arrest?" Cuff said.

Sal Garza shrugged. "Should you be?"

Cuff lost the battle of stares. He handed over the key to his Pink Fancy lodgings. And then waited, for over forty-five minutes, while two detectives were sent to check out his place. When they returned, they reported that they had found no ninja there. They looked quite smug as they relayed this information to their superior.

"So there," said Captain O'Brien, " what do you know. No ninja in your room."

Cuff leaned forward, his knees pressed against Captain O'Brien's desk. "Are you crazy? Who in their right mind would expect the guy to just be waiting for you like that in my room? Are you imbeciles?" He couldn't contain himself. "I'm being stalked, I tell you. Are you listening? Do your ears work?" He leaned even closer, his nose within easy reach of Captain O'Brien's. "How do you explain the writing on my mirror? The who's after me obviously put it there as a threat. The guy's playing with me, I tell you, like a cat with a mouse."

Only the whirling of the ceiling fan could be heard for several seconds.

"What writing on what mirror?" one of the two detectives who had just returned from Cuff's Pink Fancy room said. "The mirror was wiped clean as a whistle."

"Oh, shit," said Cuff.

And Sal Garza stepped back out of his corner. He stood beside Cuff and looked down at him. "And shit is what you'll get if you don't stay put on the island. You hear? Don't even think of going anywhere. Period. You hear me? We'll be watching you like hawks until we get word from Miami. You understand?"

Cuff didn't quite know what to say, but what he was thinking was that *vultures* was probably a more appropriate word choice than hawks.

#

Cuff lay low all day. He had to think clearly, rationally, but he was neither clearheaded nor rational. "The guy actually got back inside my room to wipe his evidence away. I just can't believe it. What in the hell have I done to be stalked like this? The damn guy is killing people all around the island, and he's making the cops think that I'm the one responsible."

"Who would do such a thing, anyway?"

Cuff looked her squarely in the eyes. "Someone who would kill just for pleasure, that's who. Someone who would shoot a man in Reno just to watch him die, like in the Johnny Cash song. Somebody's after me, and I don't think it's just the cops. But they suspect me of being who the someone out there probably is. Somehow I'm mixed up in something, but I don't know how or why."

Rosie, though as pretty as a peach, as always, had worry written all over her forehead. "So what'll we do now, Cuff?"

"Breathing room," he said. "We need some breathing room. I've got to think things through. I have to be given time to think, just to think. All these clues against me are adding up, and I know how a cop's mind works. They'll nail me the minute they get word back from the mainland. My fingerprints are on both knives." He pounded the top of his head with both hands. "I can't believe it. I just can't believe it." He paced the room, sat down, but then quickly got back to his feet. He was as restless as a big cat in the wild. "Somebody, for some reason, wants to pin a series of murders on me. And that someone is now stalking me. But why? One pull of the trigger when the laser beam was on my chest, and I'd be a goner right now. So why didn't he do it? If he wants to kill me, then he just blew the perfect opportunity to do so. What's he up to? What's he thinking?" He kicked at the air, nearly losing his balance. And then his brain came alive.

"Remember those three helicopters?"

"How can I forget?" said Rosie. "They nearly burst my eardrums."

"I think they have something to do with this."

Rosie reached out and touched his arm. "What makes you say that?"

"At the police station," Cuff said, "it was as if the helicopters were hush hush."

"Well, they sure made a hell of a racket for being hush hush," Rosie said.

Cuff thought about it. "You know what I think is going on, Rosie?"

"What?"

"Some son of a bitch out there is stalking me. The crazy guy in the ninja outfit is playing with me. And all the time he is making it look like I have committed the murders that he's probably responsible for. Why he's doing this, I have no idea. It's some kind of game to him. I'm sure of it. And whoever he is, he's sure got some high-powered contacts, the helicopters and all."

"But who would do such a thing?" Rosie's eyes were like two globes.

"A psychopath, that's who, a well-to-do one."

Rosie reached out to him, but he was a tad out of her reach. "You're really scaring me, Cuff."

Cuff sat down beside her, and he stared off into space, but he couldn't come up with a thing, no matter how hard and how long he tried. Then he sighed, and as their eyes met, they clutched to one another as if there were no tomorrow.

"We need space," said Cuff, "and time."

"You mean like in hiding?"

"From both the cops and from the psychopath. It'll just be temporary, maybe a couple of days or so. Just time to try to sort things out, to get a handle on things. So, are you with me, Rosie?"

She hugged him so hard that he could barely breathe. "I'll always be there with you, Cuff. I just hope you know that."

He looked at her, and he smiled, and then he said the two words that sent her heart racing, the two most precious words he could ever say to her, the very ones she had hoped to hear him say for too long now. "I do," he said.

Chapter 38A

It was still dark as they stepped outside of Rosie's small Scotia apartment. The sun wouldn't be showing its face for several more hours. The dark provided cover, and that's precisely what they needed. They had gathered up as much food as they could from Rosie's stock, including the case of bottled water she had had the good fortune to buy a couple of days ago. Water was so precious on St. Croix that all buildings, by law, had built-in rooftop cisterns to capture all the rainwater they could, each cistern having to meet strict capacity quotas per square foot of roof, including porches and garages. The cistern, in fact, accounted for approximately 10% of the cost of a building. Bottled water, like many other items taken much for granted on the mainland, were prohibitively expensive on the island, whereas luxury items, because of its nearly tax free status, were ridiculously cheap on St. Croix.

Along with the precious food and water, they tossed blankets, pillows, eating utensils and all essential toiletries they could think of or get their hands on into her car, and finally they were ready for their trek to the great unknown, to a safe house, so to speak, where maybe they would be able to make heads or tails out of the two-pronged attack now besieging them.

They drove for several blocks, Rosie turning her head in all directions to see if anyone was following them. They even stopped the car several times, and waited, both of them searching in all directions, but no one seemed to be following them. It sure seemed that way. Finally as certain as they could be that they were not being tailed, they turned onto North Shore Road, which meanders around some of the most isolated parts of the island, almost at shoreline in places, truly living up to its name. If anyone were following, they would surely be spotted from here on out. But taking no chances, they pulled to the side of the road four or five times, cutting the engine and their lights, waiting, observing, praying. They appeared to be in the clear.

At one of the most desolate areas of the entire island of St. Croix, they pulled off the road and took a few very windy undeveloped roads, a couple of which were really nothing more than unpaved trails and eventually drove along on no trails at all.

Suddenly they found themselves in a rainforest, not like those gigantic monsters of South America, since St. Croix was such a tiny island, but a rainforest nonetheless. The world around them was a world apart from the rest of St. Croix. The trees here were like those surrounding the ornate graveyards of Savannah, their mossy limbs hanging down from a high, providing perpetual dampness and shade on an otherwise sunny and humid tropical isle. This was the perfect spot to beat the heat, which is precisely what they needed, in both senses of the word, and it was an ideal place in which to become lost if one needed to find a hiding place.

"This is the place," Cuff declared.

Rosie couldn't help herself. "Who do you think you are, anyway? Brigham Young?"

Cuff pulled the car as far into the forest as he could. "Yes, Rosie, you definitely have a way with words."

"Look who's talking," she said.

"Touché."

They buried the car as deeply in the brush as they could. Then they spent time gathering up more materials to ensure that the car would be completely hidden from the human eye. Finally satisfied with their work, they looked around, trying to come up with a plan to tide them over, to give them a bit of breathing room, until they could come up with a more permanent strategy.

"Hey, you!" The voice was loud and piercing, and it sent chills down the backs of both Cuff and Rosie. Where had it come from? "What you tink ya doin?" The calypso like West Indian tonal quality and word structure floated towards them like a butterfly in a soft breeze, flitting up and down and sideways.

They waited, hearts pounding as if they might burst any second. What had they gotten themselves into? Was this it? Had their short run been all for naught?

Then the voice stepped out of the darkened rainforest, dark even now at midday. It belonged to a tall, thin male with dreadlocks that hung down well below his waist, his beard long and untrimmed. For a second, Cuff thought he was looking at a young Bin Laden. But the dreadlocks and the rainbow striped shirt made it very clear to anyone in the know, and that meant everyone who resided in the

Caribbean, that this young man was a Rastafarian, a member of the Jamaican born religious sect that held that Ethiopia is Eden and that blacks, who had been forced from their homes and into slavery, would someday be repatriated to live happily ever after in Africa.

"What you tink ya doin'?" the young Rasta asked again. He came closer. And then he stood there right before them.

Cuff decided to gamble, something that was in his blood. "We're hiding," he told the Rasta.

The young guy didn't seem a bit fazed by this bit of information. "Who you hidin' from?"

Another gamble. Cuff was on a roll. "The police."

Still the young Rasta did not seem at all uncomfortable to learn this bit of information. "Why you hide from police?"

Cuff thought for a second, ever the gambler. "I stole the wife of the head honcho in the Frederiksted station." He gestured towards Rosie.

"That right?" The young man seemed quite amused by this.

"It's a fact," said Rosie. "We were going to be married."

The young Rasta laughed. "I like you, white man. But the man, he gonna be plenty mad."

"Who?" said Cuff.

"The policeman you steal she from," came the clipped West Indian response.

Cuff recovered quickly. "You better believe it," he said. "He's got practically the entire police force here on the island out looking for us."

The young Rasta was loving every bit of it. You could see it by the sparkle in his eyes. "And you hiding from da police now?"

"You got it," said Cuff. "But at least I got the girl." He beamed, but the beam was quickly replaced with an "Ouch!" as Rosie gave him a punch on the arm. That gal had quite a wallop. With a little training, she could probably be a contender for the women's professional lightweight division world championship in boxing. "At least I got the *woman*," he quickly corrected, not wanting to be on the receiving end of another of Rosie's infamous right hooks.

The young Rasta was as gracious as can be. "You can stay wit me," he said. "You can hide out wit me. I live up there." He pointed. "Nobody look for you here."

Cuff looked at Rosie, and she looked back, and they nodded as one. "We thank you so much. We will be happy to take you up on your offer. It'll just be for a couple of days."

"You can stay wit me as long as it takes," the young Rasta said.

Cuff thanked him profusely. "I'm Cuff, by the way, and this here is Rosie. What's your name?"

The young Rasta embraced them both, and as he pulled away he said, "Rasta. Everybody call me Rasta."

"Rasta?"

"That's my name, white man." And his shiny white teeth showed them that they were now at a place that they could call home.

#

"We've got it!" Captain Jeremy O'Brien's face was radiant. "The results just came in from Miami." He looked as if he could blind a mongoose with just his smile. "Here, take a look for yourself." He handed the folder to Sal Garza, who took the materials to a desk, where he sat down and read through them like a professor through a set of research papers. His eyes missed not a syllable, not a letter. When he had finished, he looked up, his own face stoic, being the FBI professional that he was, but inside he was jumping up and down like a little boy in line for the Ferris wheel.

"Perfect," he said. "We were right. We've got him. His fingerprints are on the knife that killed Steadley and on the knife that killed Bennett. His fingerprints are on the gun that killed Steadley's dog, and on the gun that killed Berylson, the same gun, by the way. And he was present at every crime scene. His fingerprints are all over Steadley's bedroom, they were found on both a coffee cup and a glass at Wilburns's house as well as on her furniture, and they were found on the sliding glass door to the condo where Berylson was murdered, and then we have the sandal, with his fingerprints all over it, that was found in Detective Rawlins' car at the place where *he* was murdered."

"Wow!" Captain O'Brien too was elated. There was nothing like an early wrap up to a serial killer gone loose case. This had been almost too easy.

Agent Sal Garza, in his best FBI poker face, frowned. "A motive. We still need a motive."

Captain O'Brien nodded, but then he said, "Who knows why people kill people?"

"Yeah," said Sal Garza.

"You think we've got enough?"

"More than enough," said Sal Garza.

Captain O'Brien turned to his left, and called out into the main office. "It's a go, folks. Get on it. Right away. Mr. James Cuffy's number is up. Bring him in, book him, and put him under lock a key. We've got a big one here, folks, a serial killer at the worst. So get hopping. You hear? Let's get ourselves a cop killer."

They heard. Sure grit and determination swirled around the room in hurricane force, ready to sweep up everything in its path, and the road on which they were headed was very well paved.

"If only we had the motive," mumbled Sal Garza, but mainly to himself.

#

The smoke circled Rasta's nose, and then danced around his head, eventually taking flight towards the sky, blue as can be, as always here on St. Croix. Weather forecasters hated their work down here in American paradise where the weather seldom changed. They sat in the dirt, their backs propped up against Rasta's little shack.

"You sure you no want some, white man?" Rasta extended the remnants of his chosen pleasure, a religion to him really, toward Cuff.

"I'm sure."

"It good stuff, man. I ought to know." Rasta laughed until he hacked. He wiped some spittle from his black flowing beard. "It make everything beautiful. It make the world a pretty place."

Cuff took time to look around at the scene laid out before him. He marveled at the slow swaying palm trees, the white sand in the distance, the turquoise ocean, the sweet fragrances of the lush vegetation all around him, the hanging vines and coolness they produced in this tropical rainforest within the beautiful tropical island.

"It's already beautiful," he said. "Who needs ganja to see it that way?"

Rasta chuckled. "You a strange man, white man."

"I can't say I haven't heard that before," said Cuff.

Rosie chimed in. "Like ten times a day."

"Here, try," said Rasta in his clipped West Indian way.

"No, I've got to think," said Cuff.

Rasta lit up. "Ganja make you tink real good. Here try."

Cuff refused. "I think not, but thanks."

Rasta shrugged. "Then I tink for both of us, okay?" He took a leisurely drag of his rapidly disappearing ganja.

Their laughter finally at an end, they sat in silence for a time. Birds, of all sizes, shapes, and colors, chirped and chirped, their cadence steady like the soft swishing sound of the trees as the Caribbean trade wind gently moved them to and fro like ancient pillars in a time gone by.

"You believe in God?" Rasta asked.

Cuff paused, "I'm not sure."

"What about you?" Rasta asked Rosie.

"Same-same for me."

Rasta thought about it, taking the last couple of drags of his ganja. "You believe in Bob Marley?"

"That I do," said Cuff.

"He God."

Cuff laughed, but stopped when he deciphered the look on Rasta's face.

"He God," Rasta said. "He everywhere. He in trees, ocean, sand, everywhere. Bob Marley everywhere."

Cuff, knowing full well that Rasta's eyes were studying him, nodded in reply.

Seagulls in the distance broke the silence. Rasta stretched, then yawned, then leaned back even further. "Bob Marley my God. He go wit me everywhere. He wit me right now."

Cuff nodded again.

Rasta spoke up. "See what I mean?" He pointed. Cuff looked, but he could see no evidence of Bob Marley.

"See what I mean?" Rasta's voice was filled with exuberance, like Eddie Murphy's excitement on the big screen. "I told you, right? Bob Marley here wit us right now."

Cuff's eyes followed the end of Rasta's extended finger. He saw the three little birds beside his doorstep.

"See?" Rasta said, his voice animated. "I tell you the truth, man. Bob Marley everywhere. He wit us now. Just like he sing."

Cuff nodded again.

And Rasta began singing, first rather quietly, gently and softly, but getting progressively louder as he got fully into the song. "Don't' worry, about a thing, cause every little thing's gonna be all right….I woke up this morning…three little birds beside my doorstep…" Bob Marley's words streamed into the Caribbean sunshine, and their meaning was so nice, so called for, so hoped for, so soothing.

And when Rasta was finished, it was the birds' turn to sing, and they did, ever so sweetly.

"Why you worry so?" Rasta asked. "Don't worry. Bob Marley, he protect you."

"Hell, Bob Marley couldn't even protect himself," Cuff blurted out.

"What dat?" Rasta's face had annoyance graphically painted all over it.

"Nothing," said Cuff, but really it was something, something really worrisome. With all that he had experienced recently, those worries seemed to have found a permanent home in his brain, and they had no intention of moving out soon.

"Don't worry, about a ting…" Rasta's voice started in once again, booming this time around, much like a megaphone. But as Cuff's own mind worked overtime, his own worries began to magnify.

And this time when the song ended, the birds were silent.

Chapter 39A

The Buccaneer Hotel, according to both *Travel and Leisure* and *Conde Nast Traveler* magazines, is one of the top resorts in the entire Caribbean. This institution on St. Croix, established way back in the 17th century, and family run for generations, provides the best of everything the Caribbean has to offer. It is St. Croix's premier destination for water sports, golf, tennis, weddings, every type of family vacation imaginable. Very simply put, the Buccaneer is legendary in this part of the world, offering the gracious and relaxing respite from the mainland that makes St. Croix such a magnet for vacationers.

Lisa Smithers knew exactly what she was doing and what she wanted when she had first booked her luxurious room at the famous resort. She was on a working vacation now that her husband was dead. She needed a place where she could really relax after working her butt off all day, a place where nobody would ever know who she really was. Tailing, stalking—the mere having to be on one's feet all day—was hard on a body, so the resort, with its world-class spa, its great cuisine, its luxurious accommodations, and especially the privacy it afforded one in its gated grounds away from the crowds of Christiansted, was just the ticket. Here she could let her hair down, so to speak, and just be herself, Joan Hascomb, the name she had used to secure the room, which she had done so the day she had killed her husband.

She couldn't believe how stupid people thought she was. Her uncle, her deceased husband, had taken her at her very word, and he had paid Professor Cuffy to step into her trap, although the stupid sap himself had always been the intended victim. How gullible could a person be?

Her uncle, who liked her to call him Papa Dan, had begun fondling her when she was only five. And she had been told to never tell anybody about this. His lavish gifts to her were his insurance policy against her talking. He bought her so many gifts that it became a family joke. Just how many stuffed animals could a little girl own? Her well-stocked bedroom looked like an ornate zoo, like a Noah's ark with nearly every animal known to man finding a loving home there, and most often in multiples. Everyone knew that Papa Dan doted on his little niece. Her every wish was practically his command. If she wanted to visit Disneyland, then off the two of them would go, often spending a night or two together on the road. They visited the world famous San Diego Zoo, Disney World, and Niagara Falls. She was one lucky little girl to have such a doting uncle, especially one as filthy rich as he.

And not one word was every said about his favorite game, the one he had taught her at a very young age: swallow the leader. As she grew older, the game continued, and they played it often, on the road, in the best suites of the most luxurious hotels, and in both his home and hers, when her parents were not around. He loved playing the game, and as she got older they played it more often, and Lisa tolerated it. She lacked for nothing. Anything in the world she wanted, it was hers for the asking, as long as she never told and as long as she continued to play.

As a maturing pre-teen, she was told about the living trust that he had drawn up for her. She learned that at the age of twenty-one she would be the sole beneficiary of the ten million dollar trust, and that every year after that, one million more dollars would be added to the trust. Papa Dan also told her that it was a revocable living trust, and he carefully explained what that meant. In plain English what it meant was that the trust could be revoked at a second's notice, and that it would be if any other person found out about their arrangement. Lisa was okay with this. Besides, Papa Dan usually came pretty fast, and she made it a point to never swallow a drop.

Lisa Smithers never told a soul about their game, and she never left a clue about it. Nobody ever suspected a thing. Papa Dan, childless, had taken it upon himself to lavish love and kindness on the daughter of his only sister.

And, then, before they both knew it, Miss Lisa Smithers was twenty-one, and she now had ten million dollars to do whatever she wanted with, and a promised one million more for each year she continued to play, which was much less frequent now since she had moved off to go to college, and Papa Dan wasn't around so much. But he was around enough. And it was at this age that Lisa determined that the trust she had been provided with was insufficient. No, ten million dollars was just not enough. She wanted it all. Papa Dan missed her madly, and he wanted nothing more than to spend much more time in her company. That's where her real planning took root.

She spent hours online, and eventually she was able to track down Professor James Cuffy, who had moved to the little island of St. Croix. Knowing that Papa Dan was growing ever restless since they had not seen each other in several months now, Lisa reached out to her doting uncle. She proposed that they take a vacation to St. Croix, to the lovely Caribbean, where they could spend time together just enjoying the delights of the island and of each other.

Papa Dan got right on it. To secure their exclusivity, he purchased the property in Betsy's Jewel sight unseen. Money was no object when his niece was involved, although in all other aspects of his life he was known to be quite careful money wise, ever the respected businessman with a knack for making and keeping hold of a dollar.

The first couple of days on St. Croix, they had hardly ventured from their luxury estate on Betsy's Jewel. But Lisa, who had researched everything on the Internet before flying off to the island, was growing a bit impatient. It was now time, her time in the sun, both figuratively and literally. Her proposal of marriage to her Papa Dan did not surprise him in the least. If anything, it reinvigorated him. His love of the game had not diminished in all of these years, even though his age was beginning to show and take a toll. What better dream to come true than to spend the rest of his life in the arms of the only female who could turn him to mush with one blink of her sexy eyes?

But there was one thing that needed to be settled first. Always alert, and ever vigil, particularly when it came to his wealth, Papa Dan made it clear that she would need to sign a prenuptial agreement, but that this should not alarm her in the least. She would be well provided for, come what may. She had the money in her trust, and in his will she would also be given quite a handy sum, but just not the bulk of his holdings, which, of course, were somewhere between six and seven billion by his last count.

Lisa Smithers, all smiles, had agreed. The $50 Virgin Islands marriage license fee was paid, they completed the required two-page application form, and then they observed the eight-day posting period before the ceremony could officially be held, mainly by pleasuring each other in their private retreat in Betsy's Jewel.

Papa Dan quietly made all the arrangements. The lawyer Tom Bennett drew up the prenuptial agreement, and after both of them signed it, the lawyer kept under lock and key in his office. The lawyer had recommended the man to the legalize the union by performing the required ceremony, which was held in the living room of their beautiful estate. Samuel F. Berylson was a clergyman in name only, but he did have the paperwork necessary to meet government scrutiny here on the island. As for the two required witnesses, Berylson's on-again and off-again sweetheart, Madge Wilburn, and Shorty Rawlins, a cop that Bennett himself would trust with his own life, were happy to do their part. Who could turn down the lavish spread the small group would be devouring on the plush grounds of Daniel F. Steadley's estate?

Lisa Smithers was remembering it all. Her alert, ever-present antenna told her that she knew how each of these individuals would deal with her own proposal, which she had made to them in Bennett's office four days before the marriage ceremony. With the prenuptial agreement, she told them, she would indeed be set up for life if something were to happen to her soon-to-be husband, but the millions she would have access to were nowhere near the billions she would see coming her way, upon her husband's death, if there were no prenuptial agreement. All present knew of the existence of the prenuptial agreement, but they were the only people aware of it. Tom Bennett had drawn it up, and the other three were witnesses to Lisa's signing of the document.

So her deal was simple. When Steadley died, and he would soon, she assured them, though she offered no further details, then the prenuptial agreement would disappear and each of them sitting before her now in the lawyer's crowded office would see five million dollars coming to each of them. But after the shock had vanished from the room, the debating had begun, so an hour later Lisa Smithers was forced to relent and guarantee double the amount to each of them, Tom Bennett, Samuel F. Berlyson, Madge Wilburn, and Shorty Rawlins, ten million dollars apiece upon her husband's death.

But there was just one other thing: Lisa Smithers told them about Mr. James Cuffy, about how the man had violently molested her, and how she needed their help in making the sexual predator as uncomfortable as possible as she herself sought revenge on him for what he had done to her back in Dubuque. After hearing her tell of the horrific things her professor had done to her, they had all agreed. The guy needed to be taught a lesson, to be made to feel as she must have felt when he had attacked her. They would do all they could to frighten the guy, to scare him shitless, to avenge the terrible wrong he had done to her. Here the guy had been a trusted teacher, and just look at what he had done. His unforgivable actions had torn away the innocence of who she had once been, shredding it into a thousand pieces. She was now a mere facade of happy girl she had once been. Professor James Cuffy— damn him to hell—! had turned her into a nothing more than a frightened shell of the person she had been before his unprovoked attack.

And to top it all off, the guy had lied about the whole thing and then had gotten off scot-free. How fair was that?

They were convinced. They would help her scare the guy all the way off their beloved island. And besides, there was the ten million dollars apiece to think about, much better than the slap in the face that life had seemed to be giving each of them up until this point.

The shock of Papa Dan's sudden and untimely death must have stunned them, she knew, but they learned to take it in stride. They had little choice. The next day Lisa Smithers had let it be known that each of their voices had been recorded agreeing to the ten million pay off despite the fact that they had been fully cognizant of her implied death threat of her husband. Thus, a good prosecutor could undoubtedly construe that each of them had, indeed, been compliant in one way or the other in Daniel F. Steadley's unseemly death. Yes, Papa Dan had finally paid the ultimate price for all those years he had played his so-called game, but, unfortunately, for him, in the end, all the time he had been playing with the wrong person.

For two days before his death, Lisa Smithers had moped in bed, all alone, seemingly so overpowered by depression that she was unable to function. She was like an Academy Award actress. Papa Dan was beside himself with worry. He missed her so much. What could he do to make things better? He would do anything, anything at all, to get her back to being the only girl he had ever loved, the only girl he would ever love. Just tell me, he had pleaded. Please. He had even gotten down on his knees before her, pleading, begging, beseeching.

And that's when she had told her husband the big lie. Believe it or not, she had seen Professor James Cuffy, the horrible man who had sexually molested her back in her college days. The horrible creature had come back in her life. He was on the island, probably stalking her. She was scared. Deathly so. That terrible man of her past who had caused her such irreparable harm was back now. All the therapy she had undergone to remove the awful episode from the top of her brain had suddenly been thrown out the door. She simply could not be herself with that horrible man around. He had to be dealt with, pure and simple. It was a matter of life and death. The guy was obviously out to get her, but who would believe her story? Just look at what had happened in Dubuque, all the lies and more lies.

Papa Dan remembered. He remembered how incensed he had been when he had heard about the incident and then by how the guy had gotten off scot-free. His little niece had suffered such terrible things at the guy's hands. Papa Dan remembered it all. He was now as worked up and agitated as she, his now beloved wife.

It was at that moment that Lisa told him of her plan. Lure the guy up to the privacy of their estate, in the dark of night, and she could once and for all bring an end to the terrible toll the guy's molestation of her had glued to her psyche. This would be the end, the final curtain, and then their life together, Papa Dan and his loving bride, could continue forth with love and happiness until death do them part.

It would be made to look like an intruder had attempted to break into their house, and they had only done what any red-blooded American would do: they had protected their home and property. And then when the dead man's identity was learned, think of the glorious way in which she would be able to avenge the terrible things he had done to her back in Dubuque. The media would eat it up. The guy had been stalking her all this time. The awful excuse for a man had been pursuing her all this time. Now that he had found her, there was no telling what such a monstrous mind such as his would concoct. All she knew, she told her dear husband, her uncle, Papa Dan, was that Professor Cuffy liked to hang around the bar at the Tivoli, and that he seemed to be real friendly like with a certain waitress there, a cute little thing named Rose, or some such thing.

Everything was so neat. Lisa had seen to that.

She remembered Papa Dan's final seconds. He lay there in bed, she beside him, the knife under her pillow. "I love you so much," he had said, and she had smiled so sweetly in reply. "You know I would do anything for you, don't you? And I have, haven't I, leading the guy up to you tonight so that you can have the last word?" Papa Dan had had such love and affection in his eyes. "I would even die for you, you know?" he had said.

And that's when she had really perked up. "I know you would," she had said, sitting upright, thrusting her breasts straight out towards him, smiling as sweetly as she knew how, and then swiftly plunging the knife into the middle of his chest.

And Bennett, the fool, thinking that the prenuptial agreement that her uncle had had the lawyer draw up could be held safely in his hands. How simple-minded people could be? Getting her hands on the document, and then destroying it, was really not that difficult for someone as determined as she. And the topping on the cake was the fact that her legal marriage to Daniel Steadley, her uncle, one of the wealthiest men in the world, but now deceased, meant that she herself would soon be joining the wealthiest of the world club. The legal marriage papers, all signed and notarized and filed, would be made very public soon. And the whole world would stand up and take notice. Little Miss Nobody from Nowhere would suddenly be Mrs. Somebody.

The world didn't yet know that she was her uncle's wife. He had insisted on that point. Hence, the small wedding on the secluded island. He had said that when they returned to the mainland, they would have the celebration of the century, inviting everybody who was anybody, and that they would then announce to the world that they were husband and wife. It would be her big moment, her coming out party, for she would be the wife of one of the world's best-known faces. Lisa was quick to agree with him. They would stay mum for the time being. Not until it truly served a purpose would their marriage be made public.

And the plan was perfect for Lisa, who needed to remain unknown and unseen as she carried out her mission. It suited her purposes to a T. There was no conceivable way that her name could be connected in any way to Professor James Cuffy, a guy who suddenly had gone berserk.

Eventually, the fact would get out, now that her husband was dead, that they, in fact, were a married couple. And sooner or later, someone in the Virgin Islands bureaucracy was bound to notice the names on the recent marriage certificate. But when that happened, that too would work in her favor. It would be obvious that she had somehow left the island, she had the money and means to do so now, and quietly, and that she had probably gone into seclusion somewhere in order to grieve over her husband's untimely demise. The shock of the startling turn of events, from marriage to murder, had simply been too much for her to handle. She needed complete privacy in order to deal with everything that had come her way so suddenly.

When the time was right, she would make her reappearance, the grieving young widow, a part she would play with perfection. Joan Hascomb, who she was known by here at the ritzy resort, would become a lost footnote in history, just a woman who had stayed a few days on the island, a lady barely noticed by anyone since she had stayed pretty much to herself the entire time she had been on St. Croix. Lisa Smithers would be Joan Hascomb for a few more days, at the most, just as cover until Lisa's own deadly deeds were a fait accompli. And then Lisa Smithers, too, would leave the island, reappearing back on the mainland where she had supposedly been privately grieving the entire time Mr. James Cuffy had continued on his killing spree on a little island far removed from where she herself had been immediately after her husband's death.

But Lisa Smithers was now in a quandary. How soon should she act? Should she keep Professor Cuffy dangling on the end of her laser beam for old time's sake, for another day or two, just to rub more terror into the fear she knew she had instilled in him already, or was it time now for the final plunge, the last kill? Which way should she go? Give Professor Cuffy another day or so of fright, or end his life ASAP?

She just could not make up her mind. Both options tasted so good. Adding lots of salt to the wound she had now ground into the good professor sounded so good to her ears, the fact that he also knew that he was soon to be charged for several murders, and the fact that he must feel like a frightened rabbit, being chased from all sides. Wow! It was like a dream come true.

On the other hand, though, her final act in this episodic nightmare in her still young life, his death at her hands, and his seeing it as it happened, his knowing precisely why it was happening and who was making it happen, was like liver to a starving tigress in the wild. So which way should she go? Both alternatives sounded equally terrific.

And when the end came, it would be so deliciously ironic. The professor who had snubbed her would die by her very own hands. How tasty! Irony at its best!

Lisa was a clear-cut type of person. She despised times such as this, when she was forced to choose between two equally fine alternatives. But she knew that she had to make up her mind soon since she could not keep up the pretense of the grieving wife in total seclusion too much longer. Besides, she needed to stake her claim on the money that now was rightfully hers.

The more she thought about it, the more pain the too-tough-to-make decision caused in her brain, the exact opposite of why she had come to the island in the first place. She closed her eyes for a short time, the two evenly pleasant options in her brain going back and forth like a teeter-totter, and then she made up her mind. She would go treat herself to the best dinner ever, she would drink a bit too much, and then she would come back up here and plop three aspirin in her mouth, and get a good night's rest.

Yes, it was a good plan, a safe plan. She would sleep on it.

Chapter 40A

It was dark here on the island of Grenada but it was even darker in northern Virginia, where he knew the next call must be made: to the top banana in the unnamed agency, whose middle name was *secretive*, a seemingly non-existent entity known only to a very select few. Dr. Mortory, satisfied that everything that could be done *had* been done with the quick cremation of Daniel Steadley's body, where mystery would remain forever but prying eyes would never uncover a clue, was now able to turn to more urgent matters. The latest word he had gotten from nearby St. Croix had alarmed him, so much so that he was forced to punch the speed dial on his cell phone.

"Hello," said the grandmotherly voice on the other end, but not a word more.

"I would like to talk to Smith."

"Code?" replied the soft woman's voice.

"Gentle breeze."

"Locator identity?" the woman said.

"Bloom on the fruit, not."

"Personal identity number?"

"59832647780024zebracotto."

"Tracer code?"

" Love menudo."

"Smith," said Lawrence Covington. He had picked up immediately after the first ring.

"The Lisa Smithers woman, she's proven herself," said Dr. Mortory. "I am convinced that the time is right. What if her next move is to kill him?"

"We can't have that," said Lawrence Covington from his secure office in northern Virginia.

"No, that's for sure. She's already crossed all or our T's and dotted all of our I's. She has taken care of all of the loose ends for us. She's done our work for us, and she's proven herself. She's it," said Dr. Mortory, "the real thing. She's the one."

"I believe you."

"Should we bring her in then?"

"Yes, do so. Bring her in. Now," said Lawrence Covington. He felt good about himself and about his work. Life was good, and it would get that much better. Lisa Smithers had definitely proven to be exactly what and who they had hoped she would be, the golden feather in their newly refurbished cap, a polished gem in the rough, so to speak.

\#

Getting inside the room was a piece of cake. At least it was for the man in the Hawaiian shirt, shorts, and sandals and, of course, his long white gloves. He had made certain that the all-clear-ahead sign had been broadcast before making his move. He was quick to get the hotel room door open. He slipped beside the far end of the queen-sized bed, carefully placed his parcel under the bed, and then sat there on the floor, waiting, something that his professional background had provided him with the training required in order to perform flawlessly. He would be able to lie down on the floor when the time demanded such action. And then the real show could begin.

The minutes became hours, but nothing else mattered but the waiting. His time—*her* time, really—would come soon enough.

The room, he could see, as he sat propped up against the side of her bed, was pure luxury, Caribbean style. He could see why it cost an arm and a leg to stay there. The furnishings were plush, and the room itself was pretty expansive. The mattress even felt plush. He wouldn't have minded staying here himself. Then he chuckled at the thought.

The view over the sandy beach and into the ocean was marvelous. He could imagine himself sitting on the balcony and drinking in the gorgeous view while sipping on an expensive cognac. Now that would be a vacation!

But the dream was but a dream, and what was to be is what was real. Ever the professional, a man who took great pride and satisfaction in his work, patience was a true virtue. Remaining still and out of sight, as he was now, just biding his time until his task at hand needed to be performed, he allowed his mind to visualize life as a tourist on this beautiful little island. Although a tourist is the farthest thing from what he was now on St. Croix, he did have the time and the imagination to dream of the utter relaxation both the island and this wonderful resort could provide him. And they did, for the entirety of his wait, for well over three hours, his mind freely wandering to fun and games in American paradise.

Then he heard it, the clicking of the key in the doorknob. His adrenalin flowing now like rum based specialty drinks at any number of outdoor bars at a St. Croix Happy Hour, he lay himself down, out of sight, his body hugging the side of the mattress.

She tossed her bag, the combination purse and handbag that contained her ninja suit, on the bed, and walked to the bathroom. He could hear running water from the sink. Everybody needed to cool down after coming in from the terrible humidity, but he found it funny that she had no inkling that she was, unknowingly, cooling herself down from St. Croix's heat for the very last time.

She vacated the bathroom, and he heard her kick off her shoes, one flung in one direction and the second in the other direction, each bouncing once or twice on the floor, before becoming as silent as the man lying at the side of the bed opposite to where they now lay.

She sighed, long and leisurely, and then yawned, a good one, which must have felt as great as it sounded. Lisa Smithers was feeling no pain, but her insides were churning with uncontrollable emotion. She had already accomplished so much, but her rage had not subsided one bit. She had finally made up her mind. Tomorrow it would be. Professor James Cuffy would finally pay the price he deserved. She hated the guy with a passion. If anything, the thoughts she harbored were more pronounced than ever. She sighed again, and that's when he pounced.

The man was so fast that he wasn't even a blur. The cloth, saturated, was clamped over her nose and mouth, and Lisa Smithers was out cold. He had been told that she would remain that way for several hours, a motionless statue oblivious to everything but the darkness that had suddenly been forced upon her brain.

Methodically, he went to work, ensuring that the crime scene the local cops, in collaboration with the FBI, would find and then search for clues would leave no doubt in their minds whatsoever about what had transpired in room 211. It would be made to appear to even the most well-trained eye that Mr. James Cuffy had murdered the young student he had for so long obsessed over. Even the best Hollywood makeup artists could not create a more lifelike murder scene. The man was that good at what he did. He was the consummate professional.

He retrieved his parcel from under the bed. The syringe was inserted seven times into Lisa Smithers' vein, and the seven vials of blood withdrawn from her were carefully poured out onto the bed and onto the carpet, leaving a random trail of death in their wake. Then he ripped at her blouse, tearing off a small piece, which he kicked under the bed, as if it had fallen there after a struggle, along with three buttons.

Her purse, which he now placed on a small corner table, would clearly identify her as who she really was, Lisa Smithers, from Dubuque. The authorities would know immediately that Joan Hascomb and Lisa Smithers were one and the same. There were many reasons why she could have decided to register in an assumed name. Maybe she thought the killer of her husband was also after her. Maybe that's why she could no longer stay in her own St. Croix home. Maybe she needed complete privacy from the notoriety that would ensue when it became known that she was the wife of Daniel Steadley. Maybe she was too scared to show herself to anybody, including the cops. Maybe she had simply panicked. Maybe her terrible grief had overburdened her so that she simply couldn't think straight. Maybe. Maybe. Maybe. There were so many possibilities.

But none of it really mattered much. The bottom line, as far as the authorities would be concerned, was that it was a clear-cut case of murder in the first degree. Mr. James Cuffy had insinuated himself back into her life, after careful plodding, and then he had killed her and dumped the body where it would never be found, into the depths of the Caribbean.

Next, the man put the worn and obviously well read clippings from the Dubuque newspaper, which had covered her allegations against Professor James Cuffy several years back, in her purse, beside her cell phone, which contained fake text messages from Mr. James Cuffy, a long string of such messages, as if he had been texting her for quite sometime. When he had learned that she was on the island, he had obviously made arrangements to meet with her, at her hotel. He needed to talk to her, a ploy, the authorities would later agree, in order to get his deadly hands on her. Somehow he had gotten her to let her guard down and agree to hear him out, some such thing. Whatever the case, the guy was good. Mr. James Cuffy's obsession with her had obviously never died.

Then the man gathered up Lisa Smithers' handbag, carrying her ninja suit, which would disappear along with her. He carefully removed from his parcel the new Samsung Fuse smartphone that Mr. James Cuffy had so carelessly forgotten back in his room at the Pink Fancy, the phone in which he had planted a series of text messages from Lisa Smithers' own cell phone, now in her purse, the last message finally giving in and finally agreeing to see him at the Buccaneer, the link needed to pull the plot together. Somehow, the two had made their amends and had ended up back in her room, and that is where he had killed her. All the clues were in place. They unraveled the pieces of the puzzle of how one man's deadly obsession and a young woman's innocence had met such an awful end.

The man looked around carefully, deciding upon the best placement for the phone. He finally settled on the bathroom sink, placing it under a soiled towel, making it appear that Mr. Cuffy must have washed up a bit after killing Lisa Smithers, and that's how he had misplaced his phone. As a crowning touch, he took out the photos that had been taken by telescopic lens of the wedding party celebrating together on the estate in Betsy's Jewel. These he placed them under a pillow, as if they had been overlooked. There, for the law officials to see were pictures of all the victims of Mr. James Cuffy, along with the woman, Lisa Smithers, whose body had simply vanished, and it would not be difficult to ascertain just who had been responsible for that too.

He looked around and was quite pleased with his work. The photos, along with all the previously planted clues, would show very clearly that this was not a random serial killer on the loose. No way. Mr. James Cuffy was obviously a crazed man avenging a perceived wrong. Not only had he stalked and then killed Lisa Smithers, but the guy had also murdered, in cold blood, her close friends, everybody who had attended her wedding, something that was supposed to be one of the great highlights of her life. What the crazed professor had committed was simply horrific in nature, but, fortunately, he would receive the very punishment he deserved. The world would be stacked against him and his female accomplice.

Satisfied that everything was just as it should be for the good folks who would be investigating the mysterious disappearance of Lisa Smithers, the man gathered up his parcel, and then he made the call on his company provided smartphone.

"It's done," he said. "Come and get her." And then he hung up. He knew full well that they would be thorough, methodical, professional, and speedy. Their great American ingenuity would ensure that nobody would be aware of anything out of the ordinary. They were that good. Hadn't they whisked Daniel Steadley's body away without much to-do? And that had been carried out in the light of day and by three loud helicopters. Hell, the word *impossible* simply didn't live in their world.

The man's job was now done, but he did not leave the room at the beautiful Buccaneer Hotel until he had given himself one more look around, one more time to dream of what could have been if only he himself had booked the room and had been able to take full advantage of all the amenities of the fantastic resort.

#

"Shit," said Cuff, "I forgot my smartphone again."
"Dummy."
"Did you say rummy?"
"Dummy rummy."
"I can't believe I did it again."
"I can," said Rosie.
"I wanted to give Frank a call."
"The bartender?"
"The one and only. I wanted to see if he's heard anything?"
"About what?"
"About anything," said Cuff.
"Why Frank?"
"He's a bartender, isn't he? If anyone's heard anything."
"I got it," said Rosie.

Cuff winked. "You took the words right out of my mouth. You've got it. That's for sure." They played tongue wiggly with each other from a short distance, and then Cuff turned to Rasta, who appeared to be meditating with ganja in hand. His eyes were closed and his hands were folded on his lap. "I think I already know the answer, but do you have a phone, Rasta?" But there was no movement or any reaction from their new friend. "Rasta," Cuff said again, "do you have a phone?"

Rasta stirred, but just a bit. He opened his left eye, slowly, but did not move his head. "I heard." But that's all he said.

Cuff asked a third time. "Have you got a phone, either landline or cell?"

Rasta opened his other eye. He lifted his head from its original slumped position. "I got ganja, man. I got ganja." And then he closed both his eyes.

"Just as I thought," said Cuff.

Rosie feigned a pout, but some sincerity showed through, the corners of her unpainted lips curling upward ever so slightly.

"I got good ganja," Rasta said. "Good ganja. You want?"

"I don't need any ganja," Cuff said. "I've got Rosie."

Rosie's immediate reflex was to give him the finger, but she thought better of it, this time, and caught herself just in the nick of time for Cuff's face showed only sincerity, all joking long gone, vanishing in the sky like the short puffs of smoke that disappeared from Rasta's curled lips.

Instead, Rosie blew him a kiss, one that found an immediate home on his own lips, forming a mirror like image of the rose-colored glow emanating from the lips on which it had been born.

And then there was love and music in the air, all around them, Bob Marley style, with not a worry in the world about a thing because they both knew that every little thing was going to be all right.

#

The unmarked car moved through the heavy vegetation covering both sides of the dirt road and finally stopped at the nondescript building off by itself in the middle of a beautiful tropical rainforest, completely hidden from prying eyes. Grenada was a lovely island.

Lisa Smithers, heavily drugged, was helped into the building, inside of which housed a state of the art research facility, thanks to the American taxpayers who, unknowingly, funded it. This was offshore research at its best, where the work at hand could be performed with no interference from anybody. Outsourcing it was not. This was a one hundred percent American place of work.

Dr. Jonathan Mortory was like a kid in a candy store when Lisa Smithers was brought inside his laboratory. He had been impatiently waiting her arrival from the very first time that he had been told of her. He was the Energizer Bunny of cutting edge science, always on the go, and his mind was as sharp as a sword and as quick as a wink. That's why he was the ideal person to be in charge of the secretive facility. He knew that only a few people in Washington were even aware of its existence, and he doubted that the President was one of them.

Lisa Smithers was helped into the bed that had been made ready for her. The room was really not bigger than a cubicle, but its walls were solid. She was placed on the mattress, where, for the time being, she would be allowed to sleep off the powerful drugs.

"Who is she exactly?" Dr. Mortory's assistant asked.

Dr. Mortory's voice clearly demonstrated that he was fully relishing that very moment in time. "She is one in a million, Alfred, the cream of the crop. She is the gem that we have been seeking."

"The jackpot, huh?"

"Yes, Alfred." Dr. Mortory's face broke out in such a big grin that his cheeks hurt. "The biggest of jackpots," he agreed. "And with that, I'm going to put in the call to Smith."

"He's sure going to be pleased," Alfred said.

Dr. Mortory looked at his younger assistant. "*That*, Alfred, is probably the biggest understatement I have ever heard."

And once again the good doctor got on the phone to his contact known only as Smith, a world away in his large office in the world's largest building, *the* man for all intents and purposes.

#

The centipede, which looked like a large worm in a caterpillar's body, slugged its way along the sand. It did not like the heat, and it was determined to find a darker, more moist spot to rest for the day. The shadow of the shack just ahead looked perfect. The centipede meandered around a fallen palm branch, and then navigated itself past several ugly ganja stubs, which had been haphazardly tossed into its way, but long before the centipede itself had been on this path.

It had a stomach full of bugs, lunch had been great, and it was time now for a siesta. But there was a protrusion blocking its way to the shade it sought, so the centipede did what comes so natural. It took a bite out of the obstacle in its path.

Cuff screamed bloody murder, jumping to his feet in a panic.

Rasta was the first to spot the centipede. He attempted to get to his feet in order to kill the little creature with the toxic bite, but Cuff, hobbling on his painful foot, got to the crawling source of all the commotion before Rasta, in his slow-moving, ganja-loving state, could stand up.

Cuff looked around and finally found what he sought. He picked up the rotting piece of wood, which had obviously come free from the shack in which he and Rosie had been living for the past couple of days. It took patience, but Cuff was eventually able to scoop up the centipede. He walked slowly, gingerly, and not just because of the pain in his foot. He wanted to be doubly sure that the centipede remained on the board in his hand.

Far enough away from Rasta's shack now, Cuff tipped the board sideways, and the centipede slipped into the sound and started off, for safety's sake, in the opposite direction, wiggling its way to freedom.

When Cuff returned to where Rasta and Rosie now stood, both alarmed by what had just happened to Cuff, all three of them checked his foot. Fortunately, there was no inkling of any toxicity at all, no swelling, and not even a bit of redness.

"You a lucky man," Rasta said.

"Yeah," said Cuff, but *lucky* is the last word in the world that he would consider using to describe himself, not the way he was feeling at the moment, not since his life had suddenly been forced to crawl into a box that seemed to have no outlet.

#

Agent Sal Garza suddenly seemed so out of character. His usually stern facial features were devoid of all that had helped to project the ultimate professional that he was. He was practically grinning like a little boy.

"What's up with you?" Captain O'Brien asked as he watched the FBI man waltz his way into the office.

"You better sit down to hear this," Garza said to O'Brien.

Captain O'Brien's reaction to this was to raise his right eyebrow. He was already sitting. He had been sitting there for the past half hour. "So what have you got?"

Agent Garza was almost smiling. He could hardly contain himself from spitting out the news, but he also was well aware of the great drama of the moment. "You're not going to believe this. I just got word myself." He stood before Captain O'Brien's faux oak desk. He was too excited to sit down.

Captain O'Brien leaned back a bit in his big swivel chair. "So are you going to tell me?"

Sal Garza was on cloud nine. His voice was as animated as if he were an eighteen-year-old kid on a hot date. "Guess what?"

"What?"

"Daniel Steadley was recently married, for the fourth time. You know his story, the court scene dramas, the alimony, the headlines in every newspaper in the country, ad nauseam, all that shit."

Captain O'Brien knew that this was not it. There was a lot more to this, and Agent Garza was taking his sweet old time spilling the beans. "Yeah, I read all about it. Day after day. Week after week."

"So guess who he married this time around, who he was married to until death did part them?"

Captain O'Brien waited, and then he gave in. "I give up," he said.

Agent Sal Garza beamed as he said, "His niece. Can you believe it? He married his niece, his sister's only daughter."

Captain O'Brien was convinced that there was a lot more. "Strange," he finally said in an attempt to move things along just a bit.

"But that's not the weird part," Agent Garza finally got out.

"No?"

"Not by a long short. His niece is nearly forty years younger than he is…was, than he was when he died. And you want to hear the juiciest part of this whole thing?"

Captain O'Brien nodded. "Sure do," he said.

"Well," said the FBI man, "here comes the crème de la crème. Remember the scandal back in Dubuque?" He waited until the recollection hit full force in the brain of his partner sitting across the big desk.

"You're shitting me." Captain O'Brien had suddenly come to full alert.

"I'm not," said Agent Garza. "Daniel Steadley was married to his own niece, the same girl who accused one Mr. James Cuffy of sexual battery, the same James Cuffy now right in our own scopes."

"Wow!" and Captain O'Brien leaned back so fast that he nearly tipped the swivel chair over.

"Yes wow," said Agent Sal Garza. "We've finally got ourselves the motive."

\#

Cuff was restless and growing more so with every passing hour. Time ticked away, but his brain was like a ticking time bomb, ready to explode to the high heavens at the smallest notice, taking the tops of the swaying palm trees with him. He felt like a cornered rat in a maze, and he hated the feeling. This was not living. Hiding was not the answer. He knew full well that the authorities thought him guilty of terrible crimes he had not committed. He felt as if he were held in a vice and could not get loose. His movements were severely restricted, and this small rainforest had become his cage. How long could he live like this?

Live! This was not living at all. You call this life? He laughed out loud at the thought.

Rosie looked up. "What's so funny?"

"Look around you, Rosie. You see anything to laugh about. Nothing's funny. Absolutely nothing." He sounded bitter, his tone more so than his choice of words.

"Well, you don't have to take it out on me." Rosie's rosy cheeks were turning a brighter shade of red. She picked up a handful of sand and scattered it in his direction, not hard, but clear enough to leave her message.

"Okay, okay," said Cuff, mindful of the fact that he had unwittingly raised Rosie's ire. "Here's taking it *back* instead of *out*.

How's that for an ex?" The expression on his face showed that he was delighted by his own perceived cleverness.

"Ex, smex, you're still an ass in my book."

"And what is it you're reading, outdated historical fiction?"

"Read this," she said, extending her finger towards him.

Cuff winced, and then blinked, but the thing was still there. "Down girl," he finally said.

"You speaking to me?" Her eyes narrowed.

Cuff shrugged. He couldn't come up with the right words.

Rasta came to the rescue. He blew a bit of smoke their way. "She she, and you he," he said, his West Indian way with words sounding a lot like calypso. "Me me. She, you, and me. We all the same. Right? You like she, and she like you. And I like both. And the weather nice. The sun shine, just for us. Right? So be happy. Smile. Laugh. Enjoy what life give us. Everything is going to be all right, just like Bob Marley say. Right?"

"If *he* gets off his high horse," Rosie said.

Cuff scrambled for the perfect retort, but it just wouldn't form itself the way he wanted this time around. "You, you..." is all he could get out.

"You're the you-you, you know, not me."

"I," said Cuff.

"You want an eye for an eye, is that it?" But the handsome look he gave her melted her to the core. She scrunched her nose in the way that only she could, appearing so churlishly forlorn but, at the same time, since she could not help herself, her eyes were flirting with him as only hers could. He just had that effect on her, always had and always would, even at times when he made her so mad that she could scream.

Cuff took a few deep breaths. He recognized her look at once, and it was so cute he wanted to laugh, but this was not the time for laughter. He knew full well what she was after, and so he complied. "I'm sorry, Rosie. Truly sorry. I really am. It's just that I feel like a cooped up animal. I apologize. Okay? I just don't know what to do?"

Rosie just stared back at him in reply, saying nothing. Time did a cartwheel and landed flat on its back.

"Okay. Okay. Enough now. My home, your home," said Rasta, who leaned against a swaying palm tree across the way, but well within hearing distance. "Making up is a good thing. Right?"

It was if she hadn't heard Rasta. She had been thinking hard about Cuff's last words, which had really hit their mark. "And how do you think *I* feel about all of this, Cuff?" This time her nose kind of wiggled at him. She couldn't help it. "But what can we do about it?"

"That's just it, Rosie, we've run out of options. We can't hide out here forever. Hell, St. Croix is so small, that we'll eventually be found. And there's probably no way to get off the island. They made that point quite clear to me. It's not too difficult for the authorities to see to that. There's only one airport, and there are only so many docks. And besides, everyone knows everybody else's business. It's such a small world here. Like one big family. Word of our escape, if such a thing were even possible, would get out faster than snot from a sneeze."

"You know, Cuff, you sure have a way with words," Rosie said.

He eyed her. "I sure have a way period," he said.

Rosie couldn't help herself. She tossed her head back and laughed, but not for long. "So what's the plan then, prof?"

"Ex," he said, "and this time around let's just leave it at that. No *ass,* okay?"

"Okay, no ass for Mr. Ex." She threw him her coquettish smile. "Have I got it?" her eyes dancing now like two bridesmaids.

"You've got it, Rosie, that's for damned sure. You get it?" Was that a twinkle in his eye?

"You really are…" but she hesitated just a bit.

"I know," said Cuff, "something." He blew her a kiss, which she sent right back to him. "Anyway, the more we hide out like this, the more guilty it makes me seem in their eyes. And they already have so much pointing in my direction."

Rosie held his hand. She held it firmly. She pulled him closer. She rested her chin on his neck. "I think you're right," she finally said.

"You do?'

"I do." She clung to him even more tightly. "I know what you're thinking, Cuff."

"You do?"

"Yes. You know full well that I can read you like a book. And I think you're making the right decision." She decided against adding *this time.*

He leaned down and tenderly kissed her on the cheek, then on the neck, and then their lips and tongues were as one, as they swayed in time to the romance of the St. Croix sun, sea, and sand.

Rosie was the first to speak. "I need you."

"And I need you," said Cuff. "I really don't know how I would be coping with this thing without you here at my side."

"No," said Rosie. " I don't think you heard me. I said I *need* you."

Little birds began singing, and the rays of the Caribbean sun shone through in a few spots in this tropical rainforest they now called home.

Rasta finally chimed in. "She say she need you, man. You two use my shack. I stay here and smoke my ganja. Okay?"

The silence was like a symphony, the key, mood, and tempo all so grand. Cuff hugged Rosie. The harmony brought forth the music of the gods, and then came the crescendo as he whispered in her ear, "I need you too. Shall we?"

Rosie licked at his neck. "We shall," she said.

#

Cuff and Rosie were in high spirits. What they were about to do now was the right thing to do, and that knowledge was the force that pushed them onward, the lift they had needed in order to see things clearly. Everything would work out in the end, they knew. After all, wasn't Bob Marley right there beside them, just as Rasta had told them as they had waved their see-you-laters to their newfound friend? It was sad to have to depart, but they knew they must. But they would be back to visit their gracious host when they had finished taking care of business.

Cuff had declined one last offer from Rasta for a hit on his ganja, and hand-in-hand he and Rosie skipped and hopped their way back to where they had earlier hidden his car.

Digging the four-year-old rusty Honda out from under the fallen palm branches and leaves where it had lived for the last couple of days was a bitch, but bitch about it they did not. Cuff and Rosie were both feeling good about themselves and their situation. They knew that they were doing what they knew they had to do, and that made the cumbersome work of pulling off the long, heavy, sharp palm branches that much less pleasant. Cuff even whistled as he pulled and tugged at the prickly fronds, Rosie making faces of feigned pain directed at him, which only urged him to whistle a bit louder. So what if he couldn't carry a tune. So what if his Honda was filthy, dirt like frosting on the metallic paint. Bob Marley's soothing lyrics flitted through their heads, the positive vibes like reassurance from above that all was fine and dandy, that, in their case, the calm would succeed the storm, the weather ahead already starting to brighten their way onward.

The trusty Honda, though soiled and though having been neglected for a couple of days, but being the proud Honda that it was, rust and all, came alive, as always, at the first turn of the ignition key.

They were both quiet on the drive back to Christiansted, each lost in thoughts of where they now were in life and where they were heading. Surely theirs would be a bright future, one filled with lots of laughs and plenty of loving. Even though their present storm clouds, the threats made against Cuff's good character, the doubts and recriminations so unfairly directed at him, the anxiety and stress of it all, despite all of that, love was in the air, all around them, bubbling around their heads, bouncing out the trepidation still lingering there, the fear of what they would find when they reached where the rusty Honda was now taking them, but knowing in their hearts that they really had nothing to fear because they had done no wrong. They were two innocents out to prove themselves once and for all.

It may be a dog-eat-dog world, but they were like two large cats, careful and cautious, but fully capable of taking care of themselves when threatened. Life was good, but soon it would be beautiful, glorious, the weight of the wait and doubt removed from their shoulders and tossed into the past, where it might never be forgotten but it most definitely would be laid to rest, like a bad nightmare that was simply that: a nightmare and nothing but, to be placed in the far recesses of their memory banks where it would lie dormant for all intents and purposes, and for all time. Yes, indeed. If

Bob Marley, as Rasta had said, was God, then God had spoken and had told them not to worry because every little thing was going to be all right, and this they both believed.

Cuff pulled off North Shore Road and came to a halt on the shoulder. "Just look at that view," he said.

"Don't you just love it, Cuff?"

"It's you I love, Rosie."

She leaned over and gave him a big kiss on his cheek.

"Let's take a closer look, you want to?"

"I want," said Rosie.

They got out of the car and walked across the narrow road. They stood just above the sand. They were looking at a world-class vista. The sky was as blue as Cuff's eyes, the ocean as pretty as Rosie's cheeks. The gentle lapping of the waves at their feet was a lullaby, and the swaying of the palm trees was a dance. The sand was as white as sugar, the horizon a world away. This indeed was paradise. St. Croix was definitely the perfect place for living, laughing and loving. The moment was perfect.

Cuff put his arm around her shoulder and gently pulled her body into his. He cupped her chin with his two hands, and bent his face towards hers, their lips nearly touching, eyes on eyes, two hearts beating as one, time at a sudden standstill as the special moment gave birth to the glory of caring, sharing, and loving until...

"Rosie," he finally asked, "will you be my wife?"

"Oh, Cuff!" and her hard embrace nearly sent them both tumbling into the sand. "I will! I do! I do! I will! Yes! Yes! Yes!"

And then came the sweet rhythm of the waves lapping onto shore intermingled with the lovely sounds of true love and happiness forever after that circled right above them, like a halo.

#

Captain O'Brien was in waiting mode. Everything that could be done *had* been done. There was absolutely no way Mr. James Cuffy and his girl would ever be able to get off the island. And they couldn't hide out forever. There was only so much space on the small island. They had very few options, and almost none, if any, for the long term. The more time that passed, the more likely they would be spotted.

"You think they might just turn themselves in?"

Agent Garza was quite skeptical. "I seriously doubt it. Unless they're not afraid of the frying pan. Just a euphemism," he added as he saw the question mark creep up Captain O'Brien's forehead. With what they had on the couple, their fate was probably not that much different from that of cattle being led into a slaughterhouse.

#

Cuff parked the rusty Honda on Times Square, the loud calypso and reggae coming from the plentiful bars in the area drowning out any doubt that what they were now about to do was the right thing. The sun was shining brightly, the air was clear, and the breeze was gentle on their skin. Life was so much more than good. Not only were they madly in love, but they were now engaged to be married. Nothing could be better than this. His future would be hers, and hers his. The bright future was theirs, and it all looked so grand.

Rosie noticed it first, the headline of the copy of *USA Today* staring up at them from the sidewalk where it had either been tossed or blown to by the gentle winds coming from down the street.

"My God, Cuff, look at that!"

He looked. "Prof. on Murder Spree!" the headline read, right above a picture of James Cuffy.   Cuff was momentarily held in place by the stunning headline, but then he bent down to retrieve the newspaper. He had to read the article, every word of it, over and over, and then again.

"Hold it right there, buddy!" the voice challenged, and when Cuff looked up from the newspaper he had tried to pick up off the ground, he was facing a handgun, which was pointed right at his head. And before he could say a word, another emerged from the front of the police station, and the uniformed policeman holding it had it directed right into Rosie's chest.

"Inside, you two. You are both under arrest!"

And the beats of calypso and reggae, so alive and so danceable, continued from across the street as Cuff and Rosie were led to their fate.

Chapter 41A

"No way we'll lose this case. It's cut and dried. All the evidence is right there for any and everybody to see. And besides, we've got Toomey prosecuting. We saw to that. And you know what that means?" Dr. Mortory looked over at his assistant to see if he indeed knew.

"Yeah, Mr. Cuffy's goose is cooked." Alfred looked particularly pleased with himself.

Dr. Mortory's expression was reciprocal. "Yes," he said, "he'll never see the light of day again. Not with all that Toomey's got to work with. Thanks to our dear little Lisa, the world will be shown that the guy turned out to be a vengeful serial killer. He planned meticulously, he stalked her for well over a year, and he killed everyone associated with her wedding. What he did was diabolical in the extreme. To have such venom and hate, and then to carry it such an extreme. Unbelievable. The members of the poor jury will be facing a complete sadist in the courtroom. They will have no option other than to convict him and then to send him along to death row. It's quite clear that the guy is sane. They'll see just how carefully he planned things out, all the preparations he made. No, the insanity plea won't see the light of day here. That guy's life on the outside is over and done with."

Alfred allowed time for his mentor's words to sink in before speaking himself. "What about the girl?"

"The girl? Well, as a willing accomplice, she'll serve her time too. Don't you worry about that." The ceiling fan whirled and whirled round and round, its barely discernable click-click bouncing off the walls as it moved in space.

"And Lisa Smithers?"

Dr. Mortory had been waiting for this question from his young assistant. "Well, Alfred, in the world's eyes, Lisa Smithers will end up as just another unfortunate female victim whose body has mysteriously disappeared from a small Caribbean island. Nobody will ever fathom the real truth, that she will be spending the remainder of her life here with us, under the microscope, so to speak.

Mr. James Cuffy will be prosecuted for her supposed murder, and eventually the search for her will be given up for good. By all appearances, it will look as if her body was probably dumped somewhere in the ocean, just another body lost in the Caribbean waters. You know the drill. You've read the papers. You know how these things go."

"Yeah," said Alfred, "I know how they go," and though he was an ambitious young man with high hopes for the future, a slight uneasiness had crept into his enunciation. But he quickly covered this up as he returned his mentor's high-five.

\#

"You've got the wrong man," Cuff pleaded. The veins in his neck were as agitated as he was. "I have absolutely nothing, zilch, to do with any of the killings. I wouldn't hurt a cockroach, and that must stand for something that you would personally understand."

"Sit," said Agent Garza.

"You sit," said Rosie.

"Look," said the FBI agent, "don't try to play me. You hear? I wasn't born yesterday."

"All I hear is shit," said Cuff.

Garza's eyes showed that he was not a happy camper. "Don't try that I'm-the-completely-innocent crap on me."

Cuff leaned forward until his nose was only inches from that of the agent questioning him. "You've got the wrong guy," he said. "It's as simple as that."

"Nothing's simple," said Agent Garza. "Hell, what do you take me for, anyway? A moron?"

Rosie perked up. "You sure look the part," she said.

Agent Garza had had enough. "Get them out of my sight," he ordered.

And the deed was done.

\#

Lisa Smithers was strapped to the bed. What in the hell! Where was she? Why was she strapped down? Who was doing this to her?

She blinked several times, but things did not get any better. The straps remained, and she was held fast to a bed in what looked to be a hospital room, but only God knew where. She hadn't a clue. She struggled, but it was no use. She was held securely.

She shook her head back and forth, trying with everything she had in a futile attempt to clear it of the cobwebs that seemed to have invaded it. She could feel the spiders climbing up and down, biding their time, just waiting for the kill.

Kill! That was a clue, but to what? She tried shaking her lower body, but nothing seemed to move. She watched the ceiling, where nothing at all was taking place. Her head was the only thing other than her fingers that she could move. What was happening to her? Why? She tried to remember, but it was hopeless. Where was she? Why was she strapped to the bed? Who was responsible for this? Her mind was like a rollercoaster, up and down, up and down, around and around we go, screaming all the way.

Her eyes followed the shadow on the wall. Then there was a blur, and then a human likeness, and then the man himself. Her eyes focused, and she saw him, and she did not like what she was seeing. She recognized him. The man in the doorway was the last person she had seen before being put under again. Death. Funeral home. Something like that. What was the name she had heard him called? Why couldn't she remember? Why? Why? Why?

"You feeling better?" the man asked.

Lisa Smithers glared at him. "I'm going to kill you," she said, spittle spraying about her angry mouth.

Dr. Mortory smiled in reply. "I don't doubt it for one minute," he said. "If you were given the opportunity," he added, still showing his best professional smile.

"I mean it! I will kill you! Do you hear me?" she shouted, her lungs ready to burst like a puffed up balloon. "I mean it! I will kill you! I will kill you! I will kill you!" She hacked, attempting valiantly to clear her clogged throat.

"Oh, Lisa," he said, his voice soft now, his hand patting hers, which was still strapped tightly to the bed. "If only you knew." He bent down and kissed her cheek. Then he turned away.

And he felt the spit dribble its way down his backside as he vacated her space.

\#

"Go to hell," Rosie told the jailer who brought her dinner, burnt fish and a few overcooked vegetables. He had just old her that Cuff was probably headed for the big chair, the one that would send him to where he belonged.

The overweight jailer just laughed. "Show me the way, baby, since you'll be getting there well before the rest of us."

"I'll show you this," said Rosie, extending her finger in the way that only she could, her eyes backing up the full import of her meaning.

\#

"It's ironic, really, that the great hunter was actually the prey all along, and she didn't have a clue. With all of her meticulous planning, she had no idea that we were on her like superglue the whole way." Dr. Mortory could see the dark humor in it.

Alfred was still in the dark about so much. His face highlighted the perplexity he felt, "Where did you find her?"

"We didn't. She found us."

"What do you mean?" Alfred, the inquisitive, was well aware that knowledge was power, and he, with hope of rapidly moving up the ranks, was desirous of having both.

"Baxter."

"The therapist in Chicago?"

"That's right. With the emphasis on *the* therapist. Hell, Baxter is probably the most highly regarded therapist in the world today. His resume is as long as a book. He was internationally famous by the age of nineteen when he developed his theory of total integration while only a freshman at Harvard. Just think of it. Even at that young age, he was considered by many to be a candidate for his first Nobel Prize. And, that, Alfred, was just the beginning. Not only did he rise from that lofty position while still a teen, the guy literally flew, almost out of the stratosphere, I guess you could say. His career took off like a rocket. And he's still soaring today, his background and experience second to none."

Alfred was impressed, and always had been, just by the mere mention of Baxter's name. "But doesn't it make you curious, just a bit, how she was able to afford do be treated by Baxter? The guy must charge a fortune just for one session."

Dr. Mortory had to chuckle. "Her uncle, Alfred."

"Her uncle?"

Dr. Mortory, sensing the drama of the moment, waited a few seconds before answering his young assistant. "Daniel Steadley footed her bill."

Alfred was really impressed. "Her uncle is Daniel F. Steadley? Wow! No wonder she could see somebody like Baxter."

"Was," said Dr. Mortory.

Alfred didn't understand. "Was what?" he asked his mentor.

Dr. Mortory put his arm around his young assistant's shoulder. "Steadley *was* her uncle," he said. "Right?"

Alfred nodded. His mentor was right again. But what was new about that?

"Anyway," Dr. Mortory continued, "she went to him for therapy after the Dubuque incident. She spent months with him, but the therapy, obviously, did not do her a bit of good. But for us, her failure at treatment was perfect. If Baxter had been successful with her, then we might not have ever gotten wind of her. So it was a lucky break for us, a very lucky break.

"You see, Alfred, Lisa Smithers has a capacity for hatred that no known form of anger management can touch. Baxter's work with her is confirmation of that. On the outside she is able to project herself as normal as you and I, but inside she is a seething wreck, her mind so obsessed by the need for revenge for a perceived wrong that nothing, absolutely nothing, can control it. Her brain is wired in such a way that her only release is the very act of revenge itself, orgasmic like. It is a compulsion that cannot be broken. This narrow-minded focus totally overpowers her, controlling her every thought. And what makes her case so special is that she is able to maintain an appearance of normalcy as this cancer like affliction in her brain leads her down the only path available to her: revenge. According to Baxter, she's virtually unique in her drive to exact her pound of flesh. Charles Manson, Ted Bundy, David Berkowitz, Jeffrey Dahmer, John Wayne Gacy—the pure evil of the inner workings of the brains of these guys, even all combined together, doesn't come close to reaching the diabolical depths inhabiting Lisa Smithers' brain. And that's directly from Baxter."

"Wow!" And from Baxter!

Dr. Mortory looked at his young assistant, and he knew precisely what was now on his mind. "Yes, I know what you are wondering, Alfred."

"Sir?"

"No, Baxter did break his professional oath, if that is what you were thinking. You see, Baxter was my roommate at Princeton. We were fraternity brothers. We have stayed in touch all these years. We try to get together at least once a year. Anyway, last year, after a couple of drinks too many, he began telling me about this new case he was working with. He never divulged her name, you know, the client privacy thing and all, but with our reach—hell, it was like child's play finding out who she was."

Alfred nodded, allowing his mentor sufficient time to gloat before speaking up himself. "But this isn't a game."

Dr. Mortory agreed wholeheartedly. "No, it's not. This is war."

"War?'

"We are at the forefront in the war against terrorism. We are Home Security at its finest, though the public we serve and protect will never know, which is why we are so effective in what we do. Hell, we're like the scientists who feverishly worked to create the atomic bomb in World War II before the enemy beat us to it. Just think what the world would be like today if Hitler had developed the bomb before we had. Too horrible to even contemplate, isn't it?" He shook his head as if to rid his mind of the awful thought still lingering there. "Yes, we're the good guys, the powerful silent partner of the visible public agencies out there doing their patriotic jobs. And although in the eyes of the public our agency simply does not exist, in the end, after all is said and done, the entire country will benefit from the great work we do here. All of us. Yes, the atomic bomb caused death and destruction, but it also prevented so much more death and destruction." He paused to catch his breath. "The only real difference between us and our colleagues back then at Los Alamos is that our scientific work is with the brain, instead of a bomb. And let me tell, you, Lisa Smithers is one in a billion. And I didn't say million. I said billion. Her obsession for diabolical plotting is second to none.

"There is no end to what our research with her will reveal. Just think of the psychological benefits, the brain of the one of the world's most diabolical people here for us to study in every conceivable way, and in complete secrecy, to do as we see fit. Scientific heaven, if you will." His voice exuded the very excitement he felt. "Think of the possibility in the future of using highly trained operatives with absolutely no repulsion whatsoever to carrying out the most gruesome of orders—all in this country's best interest, of course. Think of the possibilities of unlocking the darkest secrets of the human brain. The possibilities are enormous. Who knows to what end this knowledge will lead us? Just think about it. Let your imagination run wild. There is really no end to what we might achieve.

"And, besides. We've got to stay a step ahead of those who are out to do us harm. Who knows what our enemies are planning? The world is filled with evil, so we have to be prepared for anything and everything. Our enemies can be quite inventive, as you well know. So we have to do them one better—at all times. We can never let our guard down." He gave his young assistant a fatherly like pat on the back. "She's like a godsend to us."

"Or a gift from hell?" Alfred immediately regretted having verbalized as such to his mentor, but the words were out, so he contented himself by looking away, his dismay with himself displayed away from Dr. Mortory's challenging eyes.

"We'll learn a lot from her. Much good will come of it," said Dr. Mortory. "No animal on earth, even a thousand of the same species, could ever hope to give us anything even close to what she will. This is like having the golden lantern in hand. She'll go down in history, unwritten of course, as having served humanity in ways unfathomable to the average person. Having her here like this with us to study, uninterrupted, away from all prying eyes and potential naysayers—it's like the golden goose just laid a thousand eggs on our plate. Discovering the marvels of her working brain will be like finding life on Mars. It will add a whole new dimension—to everything we now know. It will open unlimited doors to us, doors that, today, don't even exist." He was quite animated. Alfred hadn't seen his mentor like this in months.

"Yes," he continued, suddenly pacing back and forth like a nervous rabbit, but then stopping suddenly, his face beaming with exuberance, "yes, Alfred, having her here with us is like a miracle. No, I take that back. It *is* a miracle. Most definitely. The one hundred percent genuine thing." Then he began pacing again, his adrenalin urging him to get to work immediately. He had waited years for such a coup to fall into his lap, and now that the miracle had taken place, it was as if he could wait no longer. Patience was no longer his middle name. He turned and started back towards where his young assistant still stood.

"What about the others, her victims on St. Croix?" Alfred asked, as his mentor neared.

"The others?" Dr. Mortory stopped, hesitated, and then talked. "There are always casualties of war. *You* know that. It's sad but true. Bad things happen to good people. Innocent people die. It's unfortunate, but it's always been that way and always will be. The war on terrorism is no different. Think of them as collateral damage. We had to let her play it out. That was the key, to see just how far her determination would take her. We had to let her brain take her where it would. The data we collect from her working brain will prove to be of immense value to our scientific studies, with an emphasis on later formulating practical applications of our research. I don't really like it any better than you do. But it had to be done. Also, we had to make certain that her culpability would go unnoticed, and she did brilliantly by making it look like a jilted lover had gone bonkers by not only killing her, but by killing those around her. We had to let her play the thing out to the end, at least right up to the end."

"She certainly gave an Oscar performance, if you ask me, sir."

"You ain't just a whistling *Dixie*," replied Dr. Mortory, as he headed back to the cubicle where Lisa Smithers now lay, undisturbed, in her drug-induced sleep.

Tomorrow the real work begins, he was thinking, and he began whistling his favorite song, *Dixie,* as he neared his prized possession, the brain that would have impressed even Einstein.

#

The sensational trial, blasted on the front page of every newspaper in the country, let alone most of the world, had gone the very route of its foregone conclusion. Mr. James Cuffy, with his accomplice, had stalked his ex-student and had brutally murdered her, her new husband, and all those present at her wedding ceremony. He had been checked and rechecked by the best minds in psychiatry, and his sanity was never an issue at the trial. In a calculated manner, well thought out beforehand, he had committed a series of cold-blooded, senseless murders. He had proven to be no less than a monster. And neither he nor his female accomplice in the horrific crime spree had offered one bit of remorse for what they had done.

He and Rosie had probably set a Guinness Book of Records achievement for how many times they had been told by the judge to observe the proprieties of the court, but they simply would not be silenced. They spoke up when they had something to say, which was nearly all the time, and they stood up, out of turn, objecting loudly to things they knew to be untrue, which was practically everything that was said. But the truth was not on trial here, and things went from very wrong to completely hopeless faster than Rosie could connect a sucker punch, and that gal was fast.

The prosecutor, a pompous ass in Cuff's book, began detailing how Cuff had been stalking his prey for well over a year. He had then killed, in cold blood, her husband and everyone who had attended her small wedding.

"That's a lie!" Cuff had shouted, but he was quickly silenced by the judge, who threatened to gag him if need be.

The prosecutor then detailed how Cuff had murdered Lisa Smithers and how he had dumped her body somewhere in the ocean.

"Lisa Smithers?" Cuff had said out loud, jumping to his feet. "Are you crazy! What in the hell is going on here, anyway? I never killed her or anybody. I wouldn't hurt a flea." But he did hurt his right knee as the burly guard forced him back into his chair.

"Any more outbursts like that, Mr. Cuffy, and we will be forced to—"

But Cuff cut him off. "Forced to convict me of something I had absolutely nothing to do with? Is that it?"

"That's it," said the judge. "I warned you. Take him away," he commanded.

The next day was Cuff's turn to testify. He pleaded ignorance of all of the crimes for which he was being tried. He was an innocent man through and through.

"Then why does all the evidence point to you having killed all of those named here?" The prosecutor was clearly enjoying his moment. "The knives, the fingerprints, the gun, the sandal, the bloody room at the Buccaneer Hotel, the cell phone messages—everything points right at you, Mr. Cuffy. Why is that?"

Cuff had no idea.

"Do you mean to say that the evidence just piled up of its own accord?"

"Hell, no!" said Cuff. "Do you think I'm a fool?"

"On the contrary," the prosecutor said. "You are a very calculating, determined man. The evidence proves that."

"The evidence be damned!"

"Damning is more like it," said the prosecutor. "So how do you explain it all?"

"I can't," said Cuff. "Somebody must have planted it."

The prosecutor laughed. "Come on, Mr. Cuffy. Do you really think that the jury here is going to believe that somebody planted evidence at six different crime scenes in order to implicate you?"

"I do," said Cuff. "There's no other explanation."

"I see," said the prosecutor. "And who would do such a thing? And why?"

Cuff had no answers. He tried, but he could come up with nothing. None of it made any sense to him. For one of the few times in his life, he found himself with a loss for words.

"You see?" the prosecutor asked the jury, and they definitely saw.

Then Cuff had it. "Lisa Smithers," he said.

The prosecutor wheeled around. "Are you saying that you think Lisa Smithers planted all the evidence?"

"Why not?" said Cuff.

"And that she then murdered herself?"

Cuff rubbed at his forehead, where a dull ache had taken root. "That part I can't figure out," he finally said.

"Well, then, let me help you, Mr. Cuffy. There's nothing for anybody to figure out. It's plain as day what has happened here on the island, and you know it. As do all of us, the jury included. The preponderance of evidence is right there in front of all of us."

"And it stinks," said Cuff, "because I had nothing to do with any of it. A ninja is out there somewhere. The guy was stalking me. *He's* probably the one who planted all the evidence."

"Probably," said the prosecutor. "And probably Donald Duck murdered Pluto." He laughed a bit, completely unaware of the nonsensical absurdity of what he had just said. "One thing is for certain, though, Mr. Cuffy, you sure know how to fabricate a story."

"Fabricate this!" Rosie said, and she gave the pompous ass the finger. "This is nothing more than a pile of donkey dung, if you ask me," but nobody had asked her. And that had been the next-to-last straw.

The judge had had it with these two, and he told them so, for the umpteenth time.

The last straw had been when Cuff, objecting to a ruling the judge later made, stood up and told him for all the world to hear, "This trial is a farce, as phony as the two-bit rug you call a hairpiece."

From then on, everything collapsed, as if a hurricane had swept over the courtroom. Their lawyer, appointed by the court, a man entirely overwhelmed by his much more experienced adversaries, from that point on was nothing more than a piranha in the eyes of the jury. The dye had been cast, and die they must, but in due time.

It took three men to get Cuff back into his holding cell after the final verdict was read, and that was with his hands cuffed behind his back. For Rosie leg chains were required in addition to the handcuffs. For both, words of fight, despair, irritation, and downright anger flew from their mouths non-stop, but no one was listening, and the silence all around them was deadly calm, like after a tornado that had swept through, its total destruction the only thing left behind.

#

It had now been almost a year since any mention of the trial of the decade had hit any newspaper anywhere. Even Daniel F.

Steadley's name had not found itself in a news story or media event in many long months.

The call to Smith was picked up, as always, on the first ring. "Smith here."

"Sullivan," replied the voice, quickly adding, "the warden out here."

Lawrence Covington remembered at once. "And?"

"And," said Sullivan, the prison warden, "you're going to just love this. It concerns Mr. James Cuffy."

"And?"

"And he just underwent our yearly physical, required by law—everyone gets one—even those on death row."

"And?"

"And it seems Mr. Cuffy has a full-blown case of HIV. That ought to cost the taxpayers a pretty penny. It's funny how things have turned out, isn't it?'

Lawrence Covington, still committed as ever, but mindful of everything that had gone down, thought about it for several seconds. He was a man who had been around the block plenty of times. He might not like the means to the end, but, as the scientific mind that he was, out for only one thing, to aid mankind in the long run, it was only the end result that really counted, never mind the means. His mind had learned how to live with the less tasteful means to that end. One person sacrificed for the good it would bring so many others in the future, when his work was completed, was a slam-dunk decision on his part. It was really a no-brainer. In his book, it was. He had come to terms with the terms of his work, which had one purpose: to serve humanity in the long run.

He looked over at a picture of his family that had been on his desk for as long as he could remember. His children, depicted there in all their glory, were older now, but they were still his children, and always would be, come what may. A sense of relief entered his body as his eyes took in his loved ones. Life had its misfortunes, but it also could be so grand.

He sighed, deeply and fully, exhaling slowly and loudly, then gradually brought his breathing back to normal. He had work to do, lots of work, important stuff, all for the eventual good of humankind. The good that would eventually result from his work far outweighed the negative. He was a firm believer in what he did. He had to be.

And yet he was a sensitive and caring individual filled with human emotion, just as compassionate as the next guy.

"Yeah, it's a real hoot," he finally said. "About as funny as a turd in the punch bowl." And then he hung up, sighed, frowned, and then quietly got back to his life's work.

THE END

For more exciting reading, here is a preview of Michael Meyer's suspenseful thriller COVERT DREAMS.

THE BEGINNING

It was 1984 and people were doing crazy things to other people in the name of one thing or another, and Dabbie Hodson could see it clearly. She had but seconds to live. And just because she had been in the wrong place at the wrong time.

She was helpless to do anything about it, but her eyes would be her weapon. They would remain open, probing, pleading, rebelling.

"I really don't know that much." She repeated this over and over, but seemingly on deaf ears, until she realized the terrible choice of words she had used. *That much?* What was that supposed to mean? How was he to take such a thing?

She knew something of Munich, of course, and of Berlin, but not that much about what was being planned for Saudi Arabia, but she really only knew bits and pieces, not enough to be killed for. What threat could she pose? The little bits and pieces added up to such a fragmented picture of the thing.

He stopped. He looked at her, and his face was kind. Her twenty-one-year-old face was truly beautiful. "Shhh," he said. He gently stroked her hair, her cheek. "It won't hurt a bit. I give you my word on that." He even smiled. He had terribly white teeth and boyish long hair.

She struggled harder, though she knew it was only wasted energy on her part. She was held securely. Duct tape and rope had seen to that. All she could do was resign herself to her fate. There was absolutely no reasoning with this man. She had already tried everything, but she had failed miserably each and every time.

But she was determined. She would go with her eyes open, despite whatever might come. She would see it all just as it happened. She would look him squarely in the eyes, force him to see that she saw, her only real weapon.

He went to work. He was meticulous. Dabbie couldn't tell exactly what he was doing, but she knew very well what the end result would be. If only she had stayed back home. If only she had not come to Europe. If only she had not stumbled into all of this. If only she had not met Gus.

Gus began to hum to himself as he worked. His hands never stopped. Dabbie tried to tilt her head, to get a better look, but she couldn't budge. She had to content herself with seeing his profile, with listening to his humming, with knowing that her eyes would be filled with defiance when the time came.

The Munich all around her was bustling with activity. She could hear it from all directions. Munich was a wonderful city, a fun-loving place, the live and let live ebullience of the city emanating from its every nook and cranny. She had had a lovely stay here. All of it had been so adventurous, so new, so unlike life back home in Arizona. She could vividly recall the first time she had ventured into a Munich beer garden, where the liter mugs had been so huge that she had had to lift hers with both hands, and the giggles, from him, until he too had had to use both hands.

The fumbling noises he had been making came to an abrupt halt. He began stroking her cheek again. Gus looked so happy, so young, so full of life. It was so hard to imagine that he could be so heavily involved in all this horror.

Gus smiled at her once more. His eyes were soft, so gentle, so caring, so loving.

Maybe this was some kind of huge mistake. Maybe he wasn't going to kill her after all. Maybe everything would turn out happily ever after. Maybe. Maybe. Maybe.

But then suddenly she saw it clearly. It was no fairy tale. There would be no maybe. This was real, as real as the mixture of sadness and fear that now flooded her brain.

And then she died, with her eyes wide open, challenging, piercing his to the end.

Chapter 1

She is gorgeous, tall, long legged and slender, with hardly any waist at all. She is powerfully made, with highly developed calves and broad shoulders. She reminds me of pictures I once saw of former East German swimmers, her face young and pretty and healthy looking, her body strong yet graceful.

I follow her up the steps of the Löwenkeller. We are happy and feeling good, and several of the customers turn to look at us as we head to one of the less crowded tables.

We order two half-liter glasses of beer. The band begins playing the third stanza of "Treue Bergvagabunden," and we sing along. Then come the loud cheers, the clinking of glasses.

We smile-talk, sometimes laugh. Soon two German men across the room begin to arm wrestle. The match ends quickly, amid drunken laughter.

Dabbie pokes me on the arm. "Come on, B.J. you wanta try me at arm wrestling, or are you chicken?"

"Are you kidding? It wouldn't be a match."

"You're chicken, huh?"

We arm wrestle. Dabbie surprises the male out of me with her strength. She steadily pushes my arm down towards the table. I grit my teeth. I am temporarily able to halt her advance, but only temporarily. With a phenomenal burst of strength, the sexy girl across from me forces my arm flat against the table.

Dabbie giggles and begins jumping up and down in her chair. "It wouldn't be a match, huh?" She giggles again. "And it wasn't, was it?"

"Pure luck." Then I spot the waitress. *"Bitte, zwei noch, und eine Brezen."* I turn back to Dabbie. "Bet I can take you at leg wrestling."

She smiles. "Forget it. I'm wearing a dress. Or hadn't you noticed?"

I wink at her. "Why do you think I'm challenging you? How about the Alter Botanischer Garten?"

"Where's that?" A slight twinkle comes to her eyes.

"Right off the Stachus. Up the street a couple of blocks."

She props her chin on her fist, the muscularity of her forearms smiling up at me, and she studies my face. "Well, here goes nothing." She empties her glass of beer in one fast gulp.

We stumble arm in arm up Bayerstrasse. The night is dark but the sidewalk glitters with neon. Beer is in the air and our arms sway up and down in rhythm with our bouncing feet.

We wander into the grassy area just to the rear of the outdoor beer garden. Dabbie suddenly plops to the ground. "You gonna join me, or what?"

We lie on our backs. At the count of three we lock our legs together. I am quickly forced backwards, helpless to do anything about it. Sexy Dabbie has beaten me again.

But then suddenly she goes limp, and I begin to push her leg upwards towards her upper body. I prolong flipping her completely over into a backwards somersault by suspending her midsection and lower body in the air. I lift my head from the grass, peering quizzically in her direction. She is wearing black bikini panties.

Finally I toss her to defeat. I sit up. "We're even."

"We're both winners now, huh? I can live with that?" She pulls her dress back into place, scoots to where I am sitting. "The beer's finally hit me. How many did we have, anyway?"

I am looking at her face, but I see her black bikini panties, her shapely thighs.

Then her question registers. "Who counts?"

"Just as I thought," she says. "Help me up, will you. It's getting late, and I've gotta be getting back."

"Sure thing." I get to my feet, and bend down to help her up. With a quick jerk, she pulls me down beside her.

"What was that for?"

"For nothing," she says. "Wait till you do something and see what you get."

We both laugh. I search her eyes, then slowly begin rubbing her knee, her thigh, upwards, under her dress, my other hand around her waist, probing. Her warm breath is against my cheek, our lips about to come together.

And suddenly there it is, on her face, in her eyes, especially in her eyes. It is deep. Festering. Smoldering. Raging.

I am terrified by what I see. I freeze, panic overtaking my body. I want to bolt. I've got to get away. Run. Fast. Now!

But then our lips come together, and a soft tongue begins exploring the inner reaches of my mouth.

#

B.J. opened his eyes, blinked himself awake, then looked over at Gina. She had worry written all over her face. The sheets were soaked, and his pillow lay across the room, on the floor, where it had been flung from the bed during the night.

"Are you all right, B.J.?"

He wasn't sure how to answer. He probed at his forehead. His hands were clammy. "I'm not sure."

"You had the nightmare again, didn't you?"

His head hurt. "Five nights in a row, Gina. What's going on? How can a person have the same dream five nights in a row? I'm talking exact."

She wasn't sure what to say. She loved him, even more than she could put into words, and his strangeness of late—she couldn't come up with a better word for it at the moment—made her deep feelings for him just that much deeper. She wanted to reach out, cuddle him—protect him from whatever it was he needed protection from. But how was she to do this? She had no idea what was going on. It was as though he was torturing himself into a state from which she feared she would never be able to safely extricate him, a place where her protective arms would surely have no effect. Each day that ticked by took him that much further from her. The way things were going, the unknown would be the death of them both.

But she would not fold up and fade away. He needed help, whether he realized it or not, and she would be there for him, for better or for worse.

She looked at the youthfulness still there in his face, tried a smile, to comfort him, but failed miserably. "Oh, B.J...." was all she succeeded in getting out.

He looked at her, then at the far wall. He was angry with himself. Why couldn't he make her understand? Something was taking place with his brain, like an invasion of some sort. It just wasn't normal to have the same exact dream night after night.

And now look at what all of this was doing to Gina.

He watched her smile, but his own eyes were sad. He loved her, but now he was on the verge of losing her. He could feel it, just as he could feel the immense power the dream held over him.

At night, while he slept, his mind was like an advanced home video system, and the picture was projected to him in living color on a sophisticated big-screen digital command center. For five straight nights now he had been one with the dream. Everything had been so lifelike, so real, so unlike any other dream he had ever experienced.

It just wasn't something out of the ordinary. It was so much more than that.

But how was he to make Gina understand? They both meant too much to one another to let something like this come between them. But that was precisely what was happening. The dream had a force of its own, and it wasn't about to let go. It was there all the time, waiting, burning, clutching at him with hands of steel. He couldn't dump it. Nothing seemed to work. There had to be a way. But what?

He probed again at his forehead, which had become one dull ache.

Gina studied his face, hoping her voice wouldn't betray her own anxiety. She reached out to him, hoping, praying, but failing once again. He turned away, ignoring her advances. She wanted to cry, but somehow she held steady, as always. He was going through something incomprehensible, but things would work out. They *had* to work out. All it needed was time, and a stiff upper lip. She must remain firmly in control, even when their lives were falling to pieces all around them. She knew it was in her hands. She had to be the strong one; B.J.'s recovery depended on this. He needed her, and she him, though he might not be fully cognizant of the fact at the moment. She would hold on, and then, eventually, things would get better. With time, they were bound to. Love and affection and mutual sharing and caring would return to their marriage. And then they would live happily ever after, in one another's arms, until death do them part.

God, she needed him, wanted him. They hadn't made love in months. At first, B.J.'s work always seemed to come home with him. And now it was work just to get him to work. B.J.'s dream was starting to become a living nightmare, for both of them.

It was as though everything had come to a complete halt—
the *very* act of living itself—except the worrying, the marvel of the
brain, the mind always on the go, full speed ahead, no matter what,
or where it went.

She hesitated, but then the words were out. "Try not to make
such a big thing out of it."

"But that's just it. Don't you see? It *is* something big.
Nothing ever changes. It's as if someone is trying to tell me
something. It's like I'm really there. In Munich. With the...with the
girl. She's so real. It's as though I know her, from somewhere. And
she's trying to warn me—some such thing.

Gina's eyes looked tired, very tired, but she was a fighter.
She wasn't about to be betrayed by the weakness of her own human
condition. She breathed deeply, softly, and finally caught herself.
"No, B.J., you've got to stop making it into something that it's not.
You're letting it get to you for no good reason. Just look at what it's
done to you. To us."

He looked away, wiping again at the pain in his forehead.

"Whatever it is—" she started, breaking the barrier of silence
between them.

He turned towards her, but too abruptly. He realized it at
once. He paused, to ensure he got the tone just right. "Whatever it is,
it's got some kind of weird power over me. I can't explain it, Gina.
But when I'm dreaming, I'm not really dreaming."

She watched him. She wanted to reach out, to touch him, to
lose herself in his embrace. But she did not know how to do so.
Something crazy was happening, and it just wasn't fair.

#

She found him in the living room, standing on his head, his
feet propped up high against the wall, lending him the support he
needed to keep his balance. "The nightmare, again?"

Her words broke into his concentration and so he began to
totter a bit but then quickly brought himself back into control,
preventing his sudden collapse onto the thickly shagged carpet.

His body was still now, his head facing her, his eyes staring
into her ankles, which were still surprisingly slender after all these
years.

"Two weeks now," he said.

"What's that?" She sat down in front of him, on the carpet, her knees within inches of his nose.

"It's been two weeks now. The dream. Exactly the same. Nothing changed from one night to the next."

Gina waited, then extended her hand towards him. She began rubbing his cheeks, ever so gently, the way he liked it. It reminded her of gentler times, of the day they had stood together on the San Clemente Pier and he had told her of his childhood. The pain he had suffered had been unbearable, and yet his words—the act of confiding in her—seemed to lift him to a great height. It had been a catharsis of some kind. It was as if he had been reborn that day, removed for good from the untold misery of his youth, set above it. That magic moment, in the midst of sea and sky, had provided him with a new lease on life. And it had served him well, until recently.

"I don't like seeing you like this, B.J."

"You think I'm enjoying it?"

"So why not work yourself out of it? It's gone on much too long as it is. You can do it. I've got faith in you, kid." Her recollection of what had transpired on the San Clemente Pier that day, so many years ago, was still vividly etched in her brain.

"What do you think I'm doing? Practicing for the next Olympics?" He knew immediately that his tone had been harsher than he had intended. "I'm sorry, Gina. It's just the strain the dream's been putting me under. Where's it taking me? Where's it gonna end?"

She avoided his eyes. She couldn't bear to have him see what she knew must be obvious in them. What could she do? She and B.J. meant too much to one another. Since the first day they had met, they always had and always would. *Something* had to be done, and soon. She couldn't just sit idly by and watch her world go to pieces.

B.J. broke the terrible silence that had come between them. "The expression in the girl's eyes, Gina. I wish you could see it. It's unbelievable."

"But B.J...."

It was as if he hadn't heard his wife's voice. "Her eyes are so real. She knows. She's trying to tell me something."

Gina studied his upside down face for several seconds. "Can't you see what you're doing to yourself?"

"Don't get so worked up, Gina. This thing—whatever it is—is powerful, like a vice around my neck, but I'm not about to throw in the towel. That's why I'm here now doing this."

"I was afraid to ask."

"I need to clear my head. I know that, Gina. I'm letting the blood into my brain. I think it's starting to work."

"God, B.J...."

"I'm giving it my best, Gina. I never was a quitter—you know that—and I have no intentions of becoming one now." He caught his breath. "But something that's not normal is happening to my head at night. And I've got to find out what. I've got to put a stop to it, once and for all." He waited, but she said nothing. "It's as simple as that."

"Nothing's simple. Not anymore. Things change. People change." Her voice prodded, pushed, challenged. She waited.

"That's what life is all about, Gina."

"No, B.J., this is crazy. With a capital C."

"Look, Gina, I've got to find out what's going on."

"Even *if*–" She was too scared to complete the thought.

"Even if," he said.

She was afraid to respond, so she merely stared back at him, unmoving, trying not to flinch. Something was crazy, frightening, terrifying. It was as if they were living through an episode of *The Twilight Zone*.

Or was B.J. simply losing his mind? That too was a possibility.

No, as she had told him just a few seconds ago, nothing anymore was simple. Life was complicated. Their very relationship was complex. Just surviving in the everyday world was difficult. That's just the way life is.

But there was nothing commonplace about any of this. *Was* the reoccurring dream really the beginning of the end? She winced at the thought.

Man and woman, husband and wife, person to person—they looked into each other's eyes, too scared to verbalize their thoughts. Onwards they plunged, right into the dark unknown, oblivious to the fact that their lives at that very moment were intertwined with other lives half a world away, in both Munich, Germany, and in Riyadh, Saudi Arabia.

Time, gradually becoming their enemy, did a flip-flop, and the now became the then, dying, giving birth to what lay ahead, way beyond the present, biding its own good time, in total control, much like a German panzer unit moving across The Netherlands. Just like the power of Allah under the hot Saudi Arabian sun.

Made in the USA
Lexington, KY
06 February 2015